HONOUR THY FATHER

HONOUR THY FATHER

A Novel

By

NANCY CARSON

Website: www.nancy-carson.com

ISBN: 978-1-9163987-4-0

DEDICATION

This book is dedicated with thanks to all my readers.

ACKNOWLEDGEMENTS

My thanks to the following people who have gone out of their way to provide information for my research.

Ruth Wilson, Administrator, St David's Cathedral, Hobart, Tasmania.

Mark Hosking, Operations Manager, Maritime Museum of Tasmania Inc., Hobart, Tasmania

Mollie Bowen, Collections Officer, SS Great Britain Trust, Bristol, UK

Chapter 1

1853, Hobart Town, Van Diemen's Land

Never could it be said that Isabel Saxby was an ordinary woman, or that she was shackled by the monotony of an ordinary existence. Her life was a catalogue of intriguing events, some immensely good, some unbelievably wretched. She was born and bred in a Worcestershire village in England, but became a citizen of Hobart Town – home to some twenty thousand souls – in Van Diemen's Land. At 31 years of age, and despite abundant offers from suitors, some worthy, some not, she remained contentedly unmarried. Yet she never considered herself on the shelf; such concerns did not plague Isabel Saxby. Some wondered whether she lived without love, and if so, how? Yet she liked men, could take her pick of them and she knew it, especially since men significantly outnumbered women in that remote, far-off island.

Isabel was elegant and slender; a beautiful creature – and she valued her looks. She was one of those whom the gods had favoured with a beautiful face and enthralling bodily curves, and every inch a woman, the epitome of femininity. Men found her bewitching.

For five years she had been the sole owner of a flourishing enterprise on a corner of Hobart Town's Murray Street and Liverpool Street. Her shop occupied two floors, and its large windows gazed on to both streets. To aid the good and aspiring folk of Hobart Town, a black sign with gold lettering heralded 'Saxby's Mantles and Haberdashery'. The store had become the most sought-after and most frequented in and around Hobart Town for discerning women in need of bonnets, hose, ladies' undergarments, crinolines, reticules, gloves and muffs, as well as the finest textiles for day and evening dresses.

Because Isabel recommended the best available dressmakers to her customers, those seamstresses were happy to reciprocate by running up some wonderful creations just for her, at very reasonable cost. Thus, she was always beautifully and fashionably dressed; the lady she had always aspired to be and could afford to be.

An appropriate place to begin Isabel's story is in the late afternoon of a particular day in July in 1853. July is midwinter in Van Diemen's Land, that heart-shaped island off the south-eastern tip of Australia. Isabel was standing at one of the counters in her shop tallying the money that was in the cashbox – the day's takings – so she could deposit them at the bank. As she smoothed out bank notes, and stacked various coins in neat denominational piles on the counter, her two assistants had their noses pressed against the small Georgian panes of one of the windows, inquisitively peering up the length of bustling Liverpool Street.

'Look, there she goes,' one said to the other, with a nudge and a giggle.

Isabel glanced at them with detached amusement.

One of the assistants was Maisie Bennett, unmarried, the daughter of a free settler. Maisie was twenty years old, pretty, fair-haired, blue-eyed and prim. She'd enjoyed a decent education, and while she was in many ways naïve to the ways of the world, in fashion she was instinctively astute, thus an asset to Isabel's business.

The other was Rhoda Dixon, twenty-six, snub-nosed, handsome and presentable, also befitting an emporium that dressed the fine ladies of Hobart Town and its environs. Rhoda was a former female convict from Essex who, ten years earlier, had been transported for a minor misdemeanour and had since been granted her freedom. She was practically illiterate, but she could count money, was artful, and startlingly worldly. Isabel trusted Rhoda despite her criminal record, for the woman was wed to another ex-convict – a carpenter by trade – and enjoying the stability and respectability of a normal married life in Hobart Town.

'Who have you two got your eyes on now?' Isabel enquired, becoming more interested in their girlish curiosity, for even though their cultural worlds were vastly distant, the two assistants rubbed along well.

'That girl from Nathan Moses's across the way, ma'am,' Maisie replied, turning to Isabel. 'We reckon she's off to meet some beau. She's all done up like a prize mare bound for a horse fair.'

'She's off three or four times a week,' Rhoda added, relishing the telling of this valued snippet of insignificant gossip. 'But the way she's all done up, we reckon it must be a chap she's meeting.'

'Lucky girl,' Isabel commented, 'but she does have some claim to good looks. If her beau decides to marry her, whoever he is, maybe she'll come here for her wedding dress.'

'Well, for her sake, let's hope he ain't already married,' Rhoda remarked.

'She's not properly dressed without gloves, though, is she?' commented Maisie, with all the aplomb of a fashion expert. 'I've never seen her wearing gloves, or even a muff. You'd think she would.'

Isabel glanced outside and caught sight of the girl. 'I imagine she's the daughter of a free settler,' she remarked. 'She looks too young to be an emancipist.'

'She bought one of those new hooped crinolines from us a few weeks ago,' Maisie said. 'We should have asked her.'

Isabel donned her own bonnet and checked herself in the long mirror that customers used for admiring themselves when trying on new attire. She put the money – counted, sorted and wrapped – into a soft leather bag and pulled its drawstring tight. Carrying it looped around her wrist, she approached the window to join the two other girls and peered out. People were to-ing and fro-ing over the length and breadth of Liverpool Street as they went about their business. Horses clip-clopped over the uneven road surface, hauling delivery carts, and occasionally the shiny carriage belonging to one of Hobart Town's better-off citizens.

'Mind she doesn't turn around and catch you watching her,' Isabel warned.

'What if she does?' Rhoda replied. 'We could be watching anybody.'

Isabel privately acknowledged Rhoda's logic and smiled to herself. The pale blue dress, which the object of their observations was wearing, spread to a vast circumference at the hem, due to the crinoline. Bonnet and dress were floating along, under the rigid scrutiny of Maisie and Rhoda. They knew nothing about the girl, save what they perceived, but they were content in their perceptions that she was apparently, enviably involved in a romance.

'I wonder if I'll ever get wed?' Maisie remarked.

'You'll have to be asked first,' answered Rhoda. 'Have you been asked?'

'Once or twice,' the girl answered nonchalantly. 'But why should I accept the first fellow that comes along?'

'Well, there's plenty out there, eh? So who are you waiting for? Anybody in particular?'

'Somebody with money,' Maisie replied pragmatically. 'Better than marrying a pauper.'

'Then let's hope you find somebody who fits the bill.'

'I'm not sure I want to get wed, though, Rhoda. I only have to look at my own mother and father. He causes her so much work cleaning up after him, what with his muddy boots tramping all through the house and all that. It's enough to put you off marriage.'

'But married life ain't just about your husband tramping mud through the house, Maisie. There's more to being wed than that. Much nicer things.'

'Oh, I know what married couples get up to in bed if that's what you mean,' Maisie replied. 'But it doesn't sound very lady-like to me.'

Rhoda laughed. 'What's being lady-like got to do with it? You wouldn't be doing it in front of a congregation. That sort o' thing happens in private. The rest o' the world don't know what you're up to, so being lady-like goes out o' the window. Anyway, it's lovely.'

At that precise moment Maisie was distracted, and before either Rhoda or Isabel could reply, she exclaimed: 'Oh, look, Miss Saxby. Your Mister Micklejohn's heading this way.'

'*My* Mr Micklejohn?' Isabel queried, raising an eyebrow.

Rhoda at once turned around to note Isabel's reaction. 'Well, he ain't coming to see me, that's for certain.'

'Why should he be coming here?' Isabel's indifference was feigned. 'He could be going anywhere.'

'Oh, he's coming to see you again, ma'am. He ain't hunting a place, he's hunting a person – you. We reckon he's taken a shine to you, don't we, Maisie?'

Maisie nodded with a smug smile.

'Can't you tell, ma'am?' Rhoda urged with a cheeky grin. '*We* can.'

Isabel sighed. 'It seems I've been the subject of your fanciful imaginations as well as poor Miss Blue Dress, have I?'

'Well, he's a fine-looking fellow, ma'am. Mind you, he's looking very sombre right now.'

Isabel moved towards the door, smiling self-consciously, determined to avoid any further speculation. 'Girls, I must go to the bank. I doubt I'll be more than ten minutes.'

'Very well, ma'am,' Rhoda answered with a knowing glance at Maisie. But when Isabel was outside and out of earshot they both giggled.

'She's taken a shine to that Mr Micklejohn all right, Maisie, and no two ways,' Rhoda remarked triumphantly. 'Did you see how she blushed?'

Outside, Isabel was glad to feel the mild winter air caressing and cooling her burning cheeks as Barnaby Micklejohn approached. He looked striking in his black jacket, and high hat cocked at a jaunty angle. He was in his mid-thirties, a widower, and a government officer with a secure position; in short, a good catch, and Isabel had been secretly carrying a torch for him for some time, having first met him at a house party given by friends some months earlier. They had met up a few times since – just the two of them.

'Good afternoon, Isabel.' He greeted raising his hat, but a little exaggeratedly, as if disparaging the custom, and it hovered above his head for a moment like some courteous raven. His expression was solemn, as Maisie had noted.

With a broad smile Isabel tilted her head appealingly. 'Fancy seeing you, Barnaby. I take it you are well?'

'All the better for seeing you,' he replied sincerely.

'Where are you going this beautiful afternoon? I was on my way to see you. I particularly wish to speak to you.'

'Oh dear,' she remarked with a sigh, faking surprise and smothering her delight at seeing him. 'By the expression on your face, Barnaby, you look as if you might be about to say something disagreeable, so do think twice before you speak.'

'On the matter in hand I have thought twice – ten thousand times over.'

'That sounds a lot,' she teased, deciding flippancy might coax him out of his solemnity.

'Indeed, it's a great many,' he responded. 'Too many.'

'I'll take your word for it. Twice, ten thousand times over is quite a difficult sum to work out myself, and I am not the world's cleverest adder . . . Or perhaps I should say *addist* – adder sounds quite poisonous and serpent-ish, don't you think?'

'Isabel, why are you making frivolous remarks? I want to speak to you seriously. I am not joking.'

'Goodness! I never for a moment thought you were joking, given that your expression is glum enough to grace a funeral. Yet you take the trouble to tell me you're in a serious mood. You might as well have told me you are not at your desk, or not sailing, or not eating a pie.'

'It's not very charitable of you to go on like this, Isabel.'

'Very well, I apologise, so please don't sulk. Sulking puts such a miserable look on your face, which is tolerably handsome when you put a smile on it.'

His expression brightened. 'Then will you listen to what I've got to say?'

'Of course, I will, but I'm on my way to the bank in Macquarie Street.' She raised the leather moneybag and, with a cheery smile, held it before her as evidence. 'I'll be back in a few minutes if you'd care to wait. I daresay Maisie and Rhoda would be happy to entertain you with the local gossip meanwhile. They're always full of it.'

He raised an eyebrow sardonically. 'I would rather forego the imposition of listening to the trivial chatter and local gossip of your shop girls, and walk with you if you have no objection. Besides, my presence alongside you might even deter any young vagabond bent on robbing you of your gains.'

'That's mighty chivalrous of you, dear Barnaby, but any young vagabond intent on robbing me would come off worst, I can assure you. I'm not beyond throwing a hefty punch or two if need be, nor would I stick to London Prize Ring rules,' she remarked, flashing another disarming smile as she resumed her journey towards Macquarie Street and the Commercial Bank while he tagged along beside her. 'Anyway, as you say, it's a lovely afternoon, so do cheer up,' she added brightly.

'It's lovely, yes,' he mumbled. '. . . or it could be . . .'

'So why don't you smile? It's hardly appealing to talk to a man with a face as long as the River Severn. You are normally quite a pleasant fellow.'

'When you are quite finished, Isabel, I would like to have my innings. If you won't listen to me I might as well go.'

Isabel looked to see if he was in earnest, and feared that he might be.

'Have I done something wrong?' she asked, suddenly serious herself. 'Have I offended you in any way?'

'Not at all. Just the opposite, in fact. Look . . . I'm a poor hand at this sort of thing, Isabel, but the truth is . . . I am rather keen to see more of you.'

His directness took her aback, for this she was not expecting. It was news she had not anticipated, but it excited her. And she had been so girlishly trite with him. For a moment she was stumped for an adequate reply.

'How do you mean, Barnaby?' she asked, once she had recovered from the initial surprise.

'I mean I would like to see you more often. Much more often.'

'Well . . . that sounds very agreeable. Anyway, you're seeing me now.'

'Entirely by design.'

'So that's a start.'

'Isabel . . . I want you to know how I have hungered for you – for a kind word from you, and how I have starved when you have withheld yourself.'

'Perhaps I have at times,' she admitted.

'And yet I don't think you have consciously withheld anything, or else I wouldn't be speaking like this today. I didn't wish to speak to you just yet, but I can't go on any longer without revealing what I feel. Thoughts of you constantly come between me and everything else – my work, my home, my daughter . . .'

'And what about your little daughter?' she added with an enchanting smile that signalled her desire for him to press her the more. 'She occupies you as well.'

'But not all the time . . . Oh, Isabel, sometimes, I get the impression that you do care a little for me, and that lifts my spirits, but sometimes you seem to become aloof, and I tell myself that you are only playing with me, which depresses me.'

'You poor boy,' she replied gently. 'You know, when I first met you, I thought you rather stiff and difficult to talk to. Holding a conversation with you was like walking up-hill or rowing up-stream. But now I find you much more agreeable and much easier to talk to.'

'Well,' he replied, 'I certainly take more trouble to be nicer to you than to anybody else.'

'And you succeed beyond your wildest dreams.'

'Now you are patronising me, Isabel. Please don't patronise me. I want your love or nothing at all. If you can't give me that, then I fear I must cast you from my life altogether.'

'But even what we already have – our friendship – is very pleasant.'

'So it is, Isabel. For me, though, very pleasant is not enough. I want your love, and if you don't believe you can love me, please tell me so, then I will go as far away from you as possible and live my life as best I can without you. If you feel you might be able to love me please do tell me so, and I'll be the happiest man in the Antipodes. But please don't toy with me.'

'Forgive, me, Barnaby,' she said remorsefully. 'I'm sorry. It was horrid of me to be so flippant when you're so serious. I didn't mean to disdain your feelings. I had no idea what you wanted to say.'

'Now listen to me, Isabel . . . I have a meeting of the Royal Society in Harrington Street this evening, which I'm obliged to attend. Provided we aren't detained by some old windbag it'll finish about half past nine. Would you meet me afterwards?'

Well, the world was full of lovely surprises. She was unable to offer a plausible excuse why she should not meet him. Despite her partiality to Barnaby Micklejohn, she had been under the impression that he was not particularly interested in her, since he seemed so reserved much of the time, never pushing himself. It was either shyness or formality, she assumed.

'All right,' she agreed.

'Excellent, thank you. You see, I'd dearly like to get something settled.' Barnaby sighed and glanced around him, taking in the citizens within earshot. 'I'm not convinced that Macquarie Street in the afternoon is either the most fitting time or place for an intimate discussion, Isabel, when there's a lot at stake . . .' He paused a moment, theatrically she thought. 'I think moonlight would be much more romantic, don't you? Macquarie Street doesn't provide the ambience or privacy I would have preferred.'

'Well,' she replied. 'Let's hope we can count on moonlight,' she replied flirtatiously.

'Indeed,' he said with a self-conscious little laugh, then added, 'Maybe I'm presuming more than I should, but I'm very fond of you, Isabel. Maybe too fond of you for my own good, and you have tended to keep me at arms' length.'

'*Have* I?' she queried with some surprise, for she had never thought of herself as being aloof, especially where an interesting man was concerned. 'And I always thought it was you keeping *me* at arms' length.'

'Is that what you think? Dear me, no.' He laughed at the absurdity, encouraged. 'Not I, dear Isabel, and I apologise if I've given you that impression.'

'So you'd like us to start courting?'

He rolled his eyes. 'I do hate that word – and yet I love the concept. But, yes, that's what it boils down to – initially.'

She stopped walking and looked up at him with an earnest expression that matched his. 'You *are* serious, aren't you?'

He smiled appealingly. 'Never more so.'

'Good God,' she breathed, her astonishment increasing as the enormity of his intentions began to dawn on her.

'Oh, Isabel . . . I would consider it a signal honour if you would agree to be my acknowledged companion in this town. Who knows? At some future time . . .'

He did not finish his sentence, deliberately leaving the rest to her imagination, and she gulped, unable to keep the delight, and yet also the apprehension, out of her voice at what he was surely implying.

'Barnaby, are you sure you're not thinking merely of providing a replacement mother for your daughter?'

He rolled his eyes but with better humour now. 'Certainly not, Isabel. My daughter has a nanny – governess – call it what you will, whom she adores . . . and who fulfils the post rather well.'

'But not the post of wife?'

'Dear me.' He pretended to be scandalised which made her laugh, but an indulgent sparkle remained in his eyes. 'Well of course she doesn't fulfil the post of a wife, Isabel. Good Lord, what *are* you inferring?'

'Nothing, Barnaby. Don't be silly.' She turned and looked at him, unable to hide her amusement at his reaction. 'I was only teasing.'

'Well . . . the very idea . . .' He rolled his eyes skywards again, before they met hers. 'But I suppose . . . if all went well, we could . . . at some point . . . consider . . . you know . . . marriage? Or doesn't the prospect enthral you?'

'Oh, Barnaby,' she replied, flustered. 'I wouldn't necessarily be averse to marriage . . . It's just that the suggestion – this taking you say you have for me – coming out of the blue like that . . . Well, it's all a bit of a shock – a lovely shock, I admit – but please let me get used to the idea first.'

'So let's forget any notions of marriage – for now, at any rate. Perhaps I'm being too hasty.'

She did not want to forbid him ever mentioning marriage again, but nodded all the same. 'For now, I think that would be sensible . . . let's just allow things to take their natural course.'

They continued walking, at an unaccountably faster pace. Isabel, although welcoming this declaration of his ardour, was also a little uneasy as to how to deal with it now confronted with it.

'You do flatter me greatly, Barnaby,' she admitted, recovering a little.

'You would flatter me too with a mere hint that you approve,' he answered.

They arrived at the bank. Barnaby opened the wrought iron gate set in the iron railings that surrounded the Georgian building. He walked with her along the short path, then, at the foot of the steps, Isabel turned to face him, and sighed.

'I'll only be a minute.' She looked at him with an expression of solemnity that matched his, yet wanted to demonstrate some enthusiasm in her demeanour, so, with undeniable warmth in her eyes, she stood on tiptoe and kissed him fully on the lips. It lasted barely a second. 'There,' she whispered. 'Does that tell you something?' She then turned and went inside.

By the time Barnaby realised what was happening, it was over and done.

Isabel's vivacity enchanted Barnaby. She was adorable, and had such a kissable mouth too. And the lingering impression of that brief, unexpected kiss she had unexpectedly bestowed upon him was a delight. It created a sensation he would hold in his memory and cherish, not least because the spontaneity with which she delivered it was incongruous to the seriousness of her expression. He pondered her while he waited. He pondered the way she held her head with such elegance. He pondered her skin that looked so invitingly smooth, her complexion so clear like the petals of a lily, the soft fullness in her cheeks. He thought about her thick dark hair with its fine lustre, enhanced by the occasional strands of red that glistened as they caught the light, like random threads of burnished copper. Always, her long, dark lashes and the clarity of her sapphire blue eyes, entranced him. This woman was irresistible. She was a prize worth winning, and if he didn't win her, somebody else would.

Once inside the bank, the manager spotted Isabel and intercepted her.

'Miss Saxby,' he greeted gushingly. 'How opportune that you have called at my bank on this very day.'

'Good afternoon, Mr Bradley.' She held up her bag of money. 'A couple of days' takings to deposit.'

'Business is good?'

'I can't complain.'

'Excellent. Would you please accompany me to my office, Miss Saxby?'

He led the way smartly. Following Nicholas Bradley into his office was not a unique occurrence, and it normally meant just one thing. He held the door and allowed her to enter first, then closed it behind them. The sinking winter sunlight was streaming obliquely through the grid of windowpanes, casting a yellow-ish glow on him and highlighting the motes of dust that hovered over the papers placed in an orderly fashion on his impressively vast desk.

'Do sit down, Miss Saxby.'

With a straight back and a silken rustle of skirts Miss Saxby duly sat in the chair that faced Mr Bradley and his commanding desk. He picked up his spectacles and donned them ceremoniously, then fingered through the sheets of paper that rustled softly as he handled them.

'Just today we have received the regular deposit from England, by way of a London Bank,' he began, smiling as he peered over the rims of his spectacles. 'Your account has now been duly credited. I must say, your benefactor is diligent in the regularity of his payments, Miss Saxby . . . and, I am bound to add, not ungenerous.'

Isabel sighed. 'For which I am eternally grateful and consider myself truly blessed. I just wish you would tell me who my generous benefactor is.'

'Ah, if only I could. But even if I knew myself, protocol forbids. Your benefactor wishes to remain strictly anonymous, you see.'

'Yes, I know,' she smiled, 'but it's so frustrating all the same. I do appreciate this anonymous person's reckless willingness to keep me so handsomely in funds, but I would dearly like to choose whether to proffer my thanks or return the money, should I wish. Yet I don't know to whom I should do either.'

'I suspect that since these annual deposits are anonymous, Miss Saxby, your benefactor has no expectation of receiving any note of thanks, or indeed refunds. That's logical. So, if I were you, I would pay the matter no more heed and enjoy it for as long as it lasts. Is there anything else that I may help you with today?'

'Thank you, Mr Bradley, but I simply came to pay in my takings.'

'Then allow me the honour.'

'Thank you.' She handed over the bag, and Mr Bradley left the office to hand it to a teller, while she awaited the stamped receipt.

Isabel eventually returned to Barnaby Micklejohn who was waiting outside, impassively watching the citizens of Hobart Town go about their business while steeped in his own thoughts. They resumed walking slowly in the late afternoon sunshine, back towards the shop.

'Well?' He prompted.

'Well, what?' Isabel queried, her head still full of the conversation with Mr Bradley and speculations about her mysterious benefactor.

'What we've just been talking about. You and me.'

'Oh, of course . . . Pardon me, Barnaby, I was pondering my conversation with Mr Bradley, the bank manager . . . So, back to you and me . . . I'm very flattered, Barnaby, as I said before. And I confess that I have grown fond of you . . .'

'Is there a but?'

'The only but is that it's all a bit sudden, that's all. Will you give me time to think things over – to get used to the idea?'

'Of course. But what's the impediment?'

'Oh, it's not you . . .' She linked her arm through his as a gesture of her affection and sincerity. 'You're not the impediment, believe me. I am . . . Because . . .' She hesitated, trying to find the right words. 'It's just that I'm rather fond of my life the way it is – do you see? I've grown used to it. I want for nothing. I do as I please at my own leisure. I'm independent, beholden to nobody, and it suits me very well. I've been free to see other gentlemen from time to time, and I have, as I'm sure you are aware.'

'I could never stand to share you with another, Isabel.'

'Well, I must first ask myself whether it's going to be worth my while changing all that? I've never seriously expected to marry, or even thought about marriage. You do see, don't you?'

'Yes, I understand all that, my dear, but—'

'So could we not just be good friends who meet regularly, but with no presumptions of more – for the time being at any rate?'

Life in Van Diemen's Land had been exceedingly good to Isabel; beyond her wildest expectations. She was financially secure, and she really did enjoy the company of other suitable men from time to time, as she had openly confessed. There were so many men. Should she now forsake all that freedom? Should she now choose to change all that, and assume the role of stepmother to Barnaby's daughter, whom she had not yet met and might even dislike when she did? It was a daunting step for her.

'But being my fiancée would afford you greater respect,' he suggested.

Fiancée? His referring to her as his *fiancée* made her smile; he was taking a lot for granted already. 'Am I not respected already in this town?' she answered.

'Indeed, it seems that you are, my dear, as an established trader. But not to the same extent that the fiancée or wife of an established government officer would be respected.'

'I didn't realise you still clung to the class distinctions of England,' Isabel remarked lightly. 'Which most people here abhor, by the way – as do I. Anyway, I'm comfortable with the respect I already get. I'm not sure I need or even expect more.'

She turned to look at him and saw the disappointment in his expression. 'Oh, Barnaby, you are a lovely, decent and clever man – even though you are so social status-ish – and I really am very fond of you, but I must think seriously about what you are asking me to give up.'

'Isabel, let me be frank with you,' he replied. 'I am in love with you. And you claim that you are fond of me too – you said so not a minute ago. And just being *fond* is not so bad. You evidently like me, and I think it's sometimes better to simply *like* somebody than to be in love with them, because being in love seldom lasts forever. But, after the headiness of being in love has passed, you are truly blessed if you find you still *like* the person you used to be in love with. Can I take it that you have been in love before?'

'Barnaby, I am one-and-thirty years of age. Wouldn't it be more than a little surprising if I'd never fallen in love with somebody along the way?'

'But you are not getting any younger.'

'Who *is*?' she replied.

He smiled wistfully. 'Well, I suppose if you had never fallen in love by this time in your life, then it might be pertinent to presume you are incapable of it.'

'Well, I'm certainly not incapable of it. I assure you.'

'Then I envy the man – or men – who have won your heart, whoever they were, even though they have patently since lost it.' He looked at her with a mixture of admiration, frustration and disquiet. 'Am I playing with fire, Isabel? Tell me. Because I suspect that in the past you've been a proper heartbreaker with your big blue eyes, your bright smile, and being the lovely creature that you are. Despite your claim that you are fond of me, you are still so frustratingly distant. Beneath that calm and elegant beauty, are you concealing some scandalous affair in your distant past?'

She burst out laughing. 'You don't imagine I'd tell you, do you, even if I were? After all,' she added kittenishly, 'I have my respectability in this town to consider, even if I am only a trader.'

'Oh, such secrets would be safe with me, Isabel. You can be sure of that . . . Nor would it make a scrap of difference to how I feel about you.'

They arrived back at the shop, and stood facing each other at the steps. Maisie and Rhoda were no longer standing in the window, but doubtless still casting glances outside as they went about their tasks, melding into the comparative indistinctness of the interior.

'Isabel . . . I still want to see you later, to discuss this further. I am not discouraged by your first response. Will you still meet me after my Royal Society meeting?'

She looked into his eyes, touched by his earnest expression. 'I said I would. So yes, of course I'll meet you,' she replied gently, 'and in the meantime I'll think on what you've said.'

'Well, I hope to persuade you eventually. I am set on it.'

'Oh, Barnaby,' she sighed. 'It's all well and good these things you've said to me, and yet you don't really know me, do you? All you know of me is what you see. There's much more to me. You know so little about me.'

'So give me the opportunity to know you better.'

She smiled at him wistfully.

'Are you hiding something, Isabel? You are not already married, are you? To somebody back in England?'

She smiled as she looked directly into his eyes. 'No, of course not.'

- - -

It was a beautiful winter's evening when Isabel eventually left the shop and walked down Murray Street alone, towards the harbour on her way home. Her mind was awhirl with Barnaby Micklejohn's surprise revelation. He was not especially spectacular to look at, but the wistful look in his eyes always appealed, as did his honest, open smile and the charm of his gestures. He was always well-dressed, but never grandly so. He was diffident and often seemed unsure of himself, especially where she was concerned. He was forever polite, and his mild manner was part of his appeal, unlike some of those rough blustering men, such as high-ranking army officers, ships' captains and the more cavalier free settlers, as well as some who had never had to pay for their passage out.

Maybe it was time to seriously consider her future; she was getting no younger.

As she left the street behind her the glorious vista of Sullivan's Cove opened out in the twilight. The sun had dipped behind the layers of rolling hills that receded spectacularly to the west, leaving just a glimmer of orange and magenta in the sky behind them. Seagulls, late to roost, wheeled and squealed around a cutter as it majestically approached the far jetty, its masts soon to be lost in the forest of rigging from the multiplicity of ships already at berth or at anchor.

Isabel strolled to the edge of the wharf breathing in the ambience. The smell of the sea was tinged with seaweed and salt and fish, and the tide, nearly full, was lapping close against the jagged stone blocks of the quay. Wagons and handcarts littered the area, as did rope ends, broken spas, tarpaulins, shreds of sailcloth and other paraphernalia that was relevant to sailing ships. A dappled horse nearby tossed its head in its nosebag coaxing closer the last remnants of its meal. She scanned the harbour, taking in the extravaganza of tall ships, the calls and shouts of stevedores, seamen, whalers, and the bustle of activity that still attended them.

How she loved all this. How she adored this spectacular town and its magnificent setting, which lately had been compared favourably to some of the finer coastal towns of Devon and Sussex back in England. How content she was here, how generous Hobart Town had been to her from the moment she had succumbed to its mild embrace.

Isabel turned and continued walking homeward, giving wide berth to a tavern on the quayside known as Salamanca where a clutch of rowdy whalers, already the worse for drink, were posturing outside as they celebrated being ashore, each bent on having a woman if an amenable one could be found. They whistled and hooted after her, while she responded by thrusting her nose in the air and quickening her step. As she turned away from the sea into Kelly Street, the sky's glow had all but disappeared behind the distant hills. By the light of a flickering oil lamp hanging on a wall she climbed the steep flight of stone steps to the Old Battery, a former barracks, with a cursory greeting to an older woman passing in the opposite direction.

Home for Isabel was a fine house built of stone, hewn from local quarries by convicts. It stood high on a thoroughfare called Napoleon Street, which overlooked

Sandy Bay and the Derwent River estuary. From here she could watch the tall ships come and go, bringing mail, and new stock for her shop. It was always a joy to receive the latest bonnets from London and Paris, cloth from Manchester, shawls from Norwich, shoes from Northampton. She awaited them all eagerly.

She arrived at the recently painted front door, its colour now dimmed by the dusk, and opened it. Sarah, her Irish maid, a convict who had earned her Ticket of Leave so she could work in society, greeted her. Her face was in shadow as she stepped into the hall, her fair hair haloed by the glow of a crystal chandelier behind her.

'It's a beautiful evening, Sarah,' Isabel greeted. 'Not too chilly for the time of year.' She smiled, put down her reticule and took off her shawl and bonnet, which she handed to the maid. 'I shall be going out later this evening after I've eaten. There'll be no need to wait up for me.'

- - -

Chapter 2

On her way to meet Barnaby Micklejohn that evening, Isabel naturally pondered his proposition more. Whilst the sea lapped the quay as she walked past, she asked herself whether he would perceive her as stubborn, even selfish, if she persisted in holding on to her seemingly precious independence. She was becoming even more certain that she would be a fool to herself by spurning the amorous ambitions of a man whom any other self-respecting woman would be delighted to accept. He was a worthy contender. If he was hankering for marriage, then why should she not agree to it, and accept his offer? Marriage normally meant children and . . . well, she was getting no younger, as she had already admitted to herself. Maybe she ought not to leave it too long. Who else would look after her in old age if not her own offspring?

Besides, Barnaby was a fine man. He could sound a little pompous at times; perhaps his government work bred pomposity in him, so he could be forgiven. Yet often, his layer of pomposity got peeled away to revealed another, more likable, sometimes humorous, sometimes humbler aspect to his personality; that of being a little unsure of himself. And anyway, his heart was in the right place, and he was honourable.

As she turned into Murray Street, the question of his former marriage was beginning to take on some relevance.

Did it matter that he had been married before? Did it matter that he had already fathered a young daughter? Isabel decided that it mattered not; he was a widower now and free to marry. The daughter by that first marriage, though, might be an impediment. What if she disliked the child? What if she could not take to her? Conversely, what if her own presence made the child unhappy? She could never countenance being the cause of a child's unhappiness, if such a situation arose. On the other hand, did she really want to take on another woman's child? Could she love another woman's child in the same way she would love her own? She did not know.

These thoughts and more swirled through Isabel's mind until she reached the Royal Society building in Harrington Street. Barnaby was already there waiting, and he saw her arrive. His meeting had already finished. Although her face was in darkness, her bonnet silhouetted against the silvery moonlight, he could identify her from her bearing and her figure, and he stepped out to greet her.

'Isabel!'

'Hello, Barnaby! Have you been waiting long?'

'Five minutes. No windbags tonight, thank goodness, so the meeting wound up earlier than I thought. I'm so happy you're here.' He sounded inordinately sincere.

She caught his smile in the dimness. 'Well, I'm not here against my wishes,' she replied truthfully. 'So where are you taking me?'

'I thought a walk in the Government Gardens. I ordered moonlight, so it and the stars will illuminate our way. It's not too chilly for you, is it?'

'I'm wrapped up warmly enough.'

'Well, it being such a lovely evening . . . I thought perhaps we could sit on a bench and watch the estuary glittering in the moonlight.'

'As long as it can stand our combined weight – the bench, I mean.'

He laughed at that. 'Well, you're no weight at all, and I'm not gross myself, so we should be safe. Afterwards, if you're feeling too chilly, we could call at an inn on the way back to your house and sup something warming. Do you agree?'

'Very well,' she answered without enthusiasm, recalling the uncouth mariners on Salamanca, imbibing the cheap rum that was abundant and a curse on the island.

'Then take my arm, eh? Let us look as if we mean to be together.'

She smiled, warmed by his demeanour. During the walk to the Government Gardens Isabel asked, 'What was the meeting about at the Royal Society?'

'Normally, we're treated to a lecture by some visiting personage,' he explained, pleased at her interest, 'but tonight the meeting was about the new Chapter in Launceston.'

'Does that mean you'll have to travel often to Launceston for meetings?'

'No, not at all. Oh, occasionally, perhaps. It's just that some members were concerned that a Chapter there isn't necessary. The meeting was set aside to discuss it. Some of the Launceston members made the journey here specially.'

'And the outcome?'

'The dissenters didn't win the day, I'm happy to say. Why shouldn't they have a Chapter in Launceston? Anyway, let's not discuss the Royal Society, Isabel. Let's talk about you. As we parted earlier you were adamant that I know nothing about you, except for what I see, and the truth of it struck me. So what should I know that I don't, other than the fact that you are evidently no stranger to falling in love?'

The cool winter breeze seemed to whisper secrets through the tops of the trees, moonlight was casting crisp shadows across the cropped grass and the curving gravel path that crunched beneath their feet.

'Everybody falls in love some time, Barnaby,' she replied dismissively. 'Even you.'

'That I cannot deny. I was in love with my wife. Now I have fallen in love with you.'

'Oh, Barnaby,' she said quietly and gave his arm a squeeze. 'And before today I had no idea.'

He was leading her in the gloaming towards a wooden bench that looked out onto the estuary, shimmering in the pale glow of moonlight. All they could hear was the soft swish of her skirts as they walked across the grass towards the bench. They sat down, Isabel's back erect, her gloved hands clasped primly in front of her.

'What brought you to Van Diemen's Land in the first place, Isabel?' he asked with all seriousness. 'It's safe to assume you were not transported here on a convict ship.'

'Do I look the sort?' she replied.

He looked into her eyes, and was moved by the look of softness, femininity and hesitation that exuded from them by the light of the moon.

'I would venture to say that you're not entirely typical of the female convict. So I presume you must have come out here as a free settler. But on your own? Or do you have family here? You've never said.'

'No,' she answered economically. 'I have nobody.'

He moved closer to her and she was aware of his arm behind her, resting on the back of the bench. 'You wanted to get away from England, is that it? Away from a lover, perhaps?'

'A lover would have been a valid reason to stay in England, I would have thought,' she answered softly, and paused. 'No, not a lover, Barnaby,' she continued after a few moments. 'Nor a husband, just to set your mind at rest. Nor any one person in particular. In England I was employed as a governess at the home of a wealthy family . . . but in the end I was not treated well . . . The opportunity arose for pastures new.'

'So, your family . . . whereabouts in England are they?'

'A village in Worcestershire that you've never heard of.'

'Do you want to tell me about them?'

'There's nothing much to tell. My father was a schoolmaster – he educated me – taught me to read and write, arithmetic, languages, history – everything.'

'Useful if you were intent on becoming a governess.'

'I wasn't particularly intent on becoming a governess, it just happened that way. Anyway, I shall be eternally thankful to my father, and I still think the world of him. I adore him. I still miss him.'

'And your mother?'

'I adore and miss my mother too. I remember her when I was just a little girl – she was so beautiful . . . *So* beautiful . . . and when I look back I realise how spirited she was too. I think she had lots of admirers when she was young. And she's quite a few years younger than my father. Perhaps she grew to prefer more mature men. As a wife she was quite conventional, though.'

'So you follow your mother – in looks and ways,' Barnaby suggested.

'I'm more than happy to be compared to her . . .'

'So how long since you've seen them?'

'Oh, a long, long time,' she sighed. 'But I hear from them regularly. We write – oh, exceedingly long letters . . . Pages and pages. I'm the island's biggest user of writing paper, didn't you know?'

'Have you no thoughts of visiting them again?'

'I think about them a great deal, but that's not quite the same as being with them, is it?' She shrugged, and felt his arm around her shoulders, warming and gentle. He gave her a reassuring squeeze. 'Yes, I would dearly love to visit them,' she went on, 'but the voyage is so long, isn't it? Three months is so long to be at sea. But some day . . . Who knows?'

'Like most of us, I suppose you are too wrapped up in your work, in your business,' Barnaby suggested.

'It's my living, and others depend on me . . . Anyway, enough of me, Barnaby. Tell me about your wife and your daughter.'

'My wife was Tabitha. She passed away three years ago from a tumour on the brain. It was heart-breaking to see her suffer, to watch life being sucked from her and not able to do a thing about it. In the end it was a blessed relief . . .'

Isabel saw his eyes well up, tears glistening by the light of the full moon, and saw that he was a moved by the reminiscence. 'I'm so sorry, Barnaby.'

'Thank you . . . it was a wretched time.'

'And your daughter? How did it affect her?'

'She was only three years old at the time.' He stretched out his legs. 'Of course, she didn't fully understand what was happening. Oh, she cried when she realized she was not going to see her mother again, but children at that age are very resilient. In no time, she had forgotten about her mother, and was all wrapped up with her nanny.'

'I think I should meet her, don't you? Your daughter I mean, not the nanny – well, the nanny too if you wish.'

'The sooner the better,' Barnaby replied, at once encouraged by her suggestion.

'So tell me about your daughter.'

'What can I say that's not going to sound absurdly biased? She's a sweet child. Always bubbling over with enthusiasm about something. She's really not a moment's trouble, either to me or her nanny. I love her dearly. I'm rather proud of her to tell you the truth.'

'And so you should be. You've never told me her name.'

'Miranda. Have I not mentioned it? Dear me.'

'Miranda . . . Such a pretty name.'

'Tabitha's choice.'

'So, if Miranda was three when Tabitha passed away, she must be six now.'

'Yes, she's six.'

'Don't you think I'm clever, Barnaby, working that out?'

'Oh, beyond measure,' he replied, and smiled. 'Especially as you are not the cleverest addist in the world, as you alleged yourself this very afternoon.'

They both laughed at that, but remained silent for a few profound seconds, not sure how to proceed, both aware that the child could be a sticking point in their relationship. It was Isabel who broke the silence.

'What if I can't take to her, Barnaby?' she suggested in her usual forthright manner, determined to raise the possibility. 'Or what if she can't take to me?'

He uttered a little laugh. 'Let's not consider that possibility until you've met her. I'm sure you'll like her enormously, and I'm equally sure she'll adore you.'

Well, at least, she had raised the topic, and it gave her a reason to exit this promising relationship if she felt she and the child would not get on.

'Do you want to tell me about your previous affair – or affairs – of the heart, Isabel?' Barnaby probed.

'Not especially,' she responded. 'There was only one. A long, long time ago.'

'Is it to remain a mystery to me?'

'It's all water under the bridge, Barnaby. It's doesn't matter anymore. It's irrelevant.'

'So who was this wealthy family that failed to treat you well?' he asked, harking back to an earlier comment, and indignant that anybody could be so callous to a girl so lovely.

'The Wilsons. George Wilson, of Patchfield House . . . near Tibberton in Worcestershire,' she added. 'A horrid man.'

'Later to become *Sir* George Wilson?' Barnaby suggested.

'He was knighted?' she queried with disdain, startled at hearing the name from Barnaby's lips. 'Pity he wasn't blighted – if it's the same George Wilson.'

'He was the Member of Parliament for Worcestershire North, I think – became a cabinet minister.'

'Then it's the same man. The George Wilson I knew was a Member of Parliament.'

He could not help but notice her scorn for George Wilson. 'He was very influential,' Barnaby remarked. 'Extremely wealthy too by all accounts. Made all his money in the Canadian fur trade.'

'You seem to know more about him than I do.'

'Maybe so. But what went wrong that made him, or the Wilsons in general, treat you badly?'

Isabel gazed out onto the glinting waters of the Derwent estuary. 'It's in the past, Barnaby,' she said decisively. 'I would much rather not talk about it.'

'Very well,' he assented, but with obvious reluctance. 'You shall remain a woman of mystery.'

'Well, I can't have all my skeletons tumbling out of the cupboard yet awhile.' They remained unspeaking for some time and Isabel felt uncomfortable with the pause, thinking he might even be drifting away from her because of her unwillingness to talk about her past, so she decided to switch the attention back to him. 'So tell me, Barnaby Micklejohn – how did you become a government officer in Van Diemen's Land?'

'You really want to know?'

'Naturally. Unless there's a skeleton in your cupboard not ready to tumble out.'

'I began my career as an articled clerk to a law firm at Lincoln's Inn in London, until I was eventually offered an opening in the Civil Service. That's when I discovered the Civil Service was – and still is – a complete shambles. Completely inept. Staffed by nincompoops for the most part. They would employ idiot sons of the aristocracy and the wealthy, who were neither use nor ornament, whether they had a brain or not. I recall one such fellow who could neither read nor write. You can imagine how much use he was. So, when the opportunity arose for secondment to Van Diemen's Land, I jumped at the chance. I was glad to get away from Westminster and its gross ineptitude.'

'Was that before or after Tabitha passed away?' Isabel asked.

'Oh, before. The move to Van Diemen's Land prompted us to get married sooner than we otherwise would have done. We were already engaged, and she wanted to come with me. Marriage was the answer. I've been here eight years now.'

'So you don't regret coming here?'

'Well, you just have to look around you, don't you, Isabel? This whole island is so beautiful. Like England in so many ways. And I feel privileged to be at the heart of making it a wonderful place to live. And now that they've finally stopped sending convicts here, it's important we build a stable society. I want to be a part of that. No, I don't regret coming here. How could I?'

'But there's still much to be done to build that stable society,' she suggested.

'Well, we have plenty of time to do it. This is still a young colony, even though our history has been fairly chequered since the first convicts arrived with the soldiers and sailors. Already there are vast improvements – freed convicts are settling into society, either because of marriage or gainful employment, and are settling well. We are actually becoming quite civic-minded already.'

She shivered and he looked at her. 'You're feeling cold?'

'A little bit.'

'Then let's take a steady walk back.'

'But not to any tavern,' she suggested. 'There are too many whalers and matelots about, the worse for drink.'

'Then I shall walk you home.'

In the moonlight their pace was slow, stretching the time they would remain together that evening, as if each footstep were a measure of time itself. She took his arm, and he began talking about generalities, about his friends, his family back in England, relieving the emphasis from herself.

Eventually, they reached the front gate of her house.

'Thank you for coming to meet me tonight, Isabel,' Barnaby said softly as they stood facing each other.

'There's no need to thank me,' she replied in a whisper, smiling up at him. 'I've enjoyed it.'

'Good. Even though we passed several inns.'

'Not places for women,' she suggested, 'stuffed as they are with drunkards.'

'So, can we meet again soon?' he asked.

'I'd love to.' She was still smiling, and her eyes reflected the moon.

He reached down for her hand and squeezed it. 'Tomorrow? I'd love to take you home to meet Miranda.'

'But by the time I met you tomorrow evening won't it be past Miranda's bedtime?'

He sighed at the realisation. 'Oh . . . of course.'

'Sunday would be better,' she suggested. 'Come to me for

tea, both of you.'

'Excellent,' he said brightly, and gave her a peck on the lips. 'But what about tomorrow anyway?'

'Yes, all right,' she agreed. 'Shall I meet you where I met you tonight?'

'The Quay would be more convenient for both of us – at the Customs House. Shall we say eight o' clock?'

'Eight o' clock,' she said, and turned to open the gate.

'Before you go inside . . .' he breathed, gently taking her arm.

She turned to him.

'A kiss – please?'

Her arms reached out to him, he held her, and they kissed – long, lingering kisses. Her lips were beautifully soft, her cheek fragrant. Between kisses he sensed her trembling, but barely perceptibly – it might have been nervousness or the cool night air. Her response was positive, because she did not shy away or show any inclination to break off. It could even have been desire, but maybe that was too much to hope for.

'Thank you,' he whispered. 'I've been dying to kiss you like that for ages.'

'Well, you seem to have a flair for it,' she replied with a smile of genuine approval. As she turned to go she glanced back at him. 'Goodnight, Barnaby.'

- - -

The whole of the next day Isabel's head was full of Barnaby Micklejohn, their meeting of the previous evening, and the delicious way he kissed her. She was looking forward to seeing him again that night. Of course, she did not mention him to Maisie or Rhoda – it was early days, and nothing might come of the liaison; best to keep quiet until such time as anything definite developed. But by now she was certainly inclined towards a more intimate relationship.

However, when Isabel returned home she was greeted by Sarah, who seemed anguished and on edge.

'Oh, ma'am, I'm so glad you're back.'

'Why, Sarah? Whatever's the matter?.'

'You had a visitor, ma'am. About an hour ago.'

'A visitor? Who?'

'Catherine Wragg's daughter, ma'am.' Sarah took her mistress's mantle and placed it over her arm, her expression grave.

'You mean little Polly? And she was alone?'

Sarah nodded.

'Goodness! What brought her out by herself on this dark night?'

'She came to tell you that her mother is sick, ma'am. The mite was greatly upset and very anxious to see you. The poor little soul was beside herself with worry.'

'Bless her.'

'I told her I'd let you know as soon as you came home, ma'am. She asked if you would be so kind as to visit her momma as soon as you could. It was only an hour ago, ma'am.'

'Then I'd better go and see Catherine right away,' Isabel said with concern. 'My mantle and bonnet . . .'

Sarah returned the mantle to Isabel's shoulders. 'Will you not have something to eat before you go, ma'am? You must be hungry.'

'I'm not hungry,' Isabel said, putting on her bonnet again. 'It's much more important that I go to Catherine. I can eat later.'

'Would you like me to come with you, ma'am?'

'No, Sarah. I hope I shall not be too long away, but don't wait up for me.'

- - -

Catherine Wragg, with chestnut brown hair and hazel eyes, was originally from Sheffield, but had migrated to Manchester where she had been employed as plain cook and housemaid. In September 1841 at the tender age of nineteen she was tried at Lancaster Manchester Quarter Sessions and sentenced to seven years transportation for stealing six shillings and sixpence from her master. She departed aboard her majesty's female convict ship the Royal Admiral on 5th May 1842 along with a further 203 female convicts and 17 children, and arrived at Hobart Town on 24th September 1842, her birthday. Because of good behaviour on the voyage she was assigned directly to domestic service. Early on, she realised that exhibiting good behaviour, if she were conscientious and conforming, would make life much easier, and people would trust her. Thus she progressed and served the rest of her sentence as a housemaid. She was awarded her Certificate of Freedom in January 1849 and released from her duties. But by then she was already carrying a child, unbeknownst to either the government or the father.

In need of a maid, Isabel went one January day to the Brickfield Hiring Depot, which was formerly a prison but at that time used as a staging point for those women prisoners who were allowed to work in society. There she saw Catherine. From the outset they felt a rapport, and when she entered Isabel's service they became close friends. But Catherine, anxious to earn as much as she could in what little time was available, failed to tell Isabel from the outset that she was with child. When her condition became apparent the whole domestic arrangement necessarily changed. Believing that Isabel would neither countenance nor support a pregnant maid, Catherine decided to leave of her own free will. She gave birth to a daughter, whom she called Polly, on 14th June 1849 – mid-winter in Van Diemen's Land. Realizing that the child would be the one to suffer most, Isabel decided that a decent measure of charity would be expedient. So she bought a tiny single-storey cottage for the young mother and her baby daughter and furnished it with essentials. It stood on De Witt Street, near the Old Battery.

Isabel empathised with those women, former maids and shop girls mostly, who had been unfortunate enough to be transported from the countries of their birth, torn away from family and loved ones. The misdemeanours of so many had been petty, hardly worth a reprimand, but still they were thrust into the jaws of a penal system that she considered was unjustly and often brutally severe. Isabel gladly employed female convicts in her shop and in her home; Rhoda was one such, and always without exception, these women responded positively to her kindness and consideration. When they had served their time they were at liberty to settle down as ordinary citizens, marry, and become law-abiding members of society. Isabel liked to think that she might have been an example to some of those women and inspired them to better themselves.

When Isabel arrived at the little thatched cottage in De Witt Street she lifted the latch and entered. It was dark, inside and out, but she heard at once the patter of bare feet on the cold stone flags preceded by light dancing on the walls from a flickering candle that Polly was holding.

'Aunt Isabel!' the child exclaimed eagerly in her small voice, and Isabel welcomed her into her arms.

Polly was four years old, and looked angelic with her long but tousled fair hair flowing in the candlelight.

'Sweetheart, I came as soon as Sarah told me. Where's your mommy? What's the matter with her?'

'She's very, very sick,' Polly said with wide-eyed, trusting solemnity and charming emphasis on the second '*very*'.

'Take me to her, Polly.'

She followed as the child lit the way to the bedroom where her mother lay. When she saw Catherine, Isabel was visibly shaken. The young woman had always looked so comely, so zestful, so spirited. Her comeliness, her zest and her spiritedness appealed to men and, of course, these qualities had been the cause of her ultimate downfall. Now, lying pale and sickly and helpless in that meagre bed, she looked like death. Her face bore the pallor and lines of serious illness, exaggerated by the ghostly light of the candle, and she looked twenty years older than she had a week earlier. When Catherine opened her eyes Isabel witnessed their dullness, ominously lacking their usual sparkle.

'Catherine,' she gasped.

'Hello, Isabel . . . Ta for taking the trouble.' Her voice was thin and her breathing was laboured.

Isabel sat on the bed beside her and took her hand. 'How long have you been like this? Why didn't you send for me sooner?'

'Oh, I got no great wish to be more of a burden on you than I have been already,' Catherine croaked.

'But you're sick,' Isabel protested. 'Just look at you. And Polly's not old enough to look after you.'

'Polly's been a brick, ain't you, my angel?'

The little girl nodded, her eyes big and wide in the candlelight, but full of earnest anxiety over her mother.

'But you're me only true friend, Isabel, and I need your help . . . again.'

'You need the doctor,' Isabel proclaimed.

'The doctor's already been. Polly fetched him.'

'All by yourself, Polly?' Isabel queried, with astonishment and admiration in her voice, and Polly nodded again, with a faint glimmer of pride. 'And what did the doctor say, Catherine?'

'He says I've got pneumonia.'

'Pneumonia? But pneumonia's serious, last I heard.'

'Aye. So it is, Isabel . . .'

Isabel turned and looked at Polly. 'Polly, my angel, do you have some lemonade or something? I'm sure Mommy would love a drink.'

'We got some ginger beer, Aunt Isabel.'

'Then will you fetch it please? And bring another candle if you have one. Light it from the one you've got, but mind you don't burn yourself.'

Polly left the room, taking the solitary candle with her, leaving the bedroom in darkness.

'I don't know what I'd have done without her,' Catherine said feebly. 'Honest, I don't.'

'I do wish you'd sent for me sooner, Catherine,' Isabel reprimanded gently. 'Sarah and I could have looked after you. You can hardly expect the child to.'

'Oh, but she's been wonderful, Isabel. I couldn't begin to tell you . . . And it's Polly I'm worried about . . . I know all about my illness . . . I know the chances are I won't get over it . . . that in a day or two I could be gone—'

'Don't say that, Catherine,' Isabel urged gently, and squeezed her friend's hand tighter in the darkness. 'Of course you'll get over it. I'm going to help you.'

'Did you not hear, Isabel? It's pneumonia I've got, not toothache . . . I might be dead and gone tomorrow. And if I am, I need to know that Polly's going to be all right. I have to know she's going to be cared for.'

Isabel sighed deeply. 'What do you want for her, Catherine? Tell me, and if the worst does happen I'll do my best. Of course I will.'

'Well, I don't want her turning out like me for a start,'

Catherine wheezed. 'I'm no shining example. I want her to be like you. So I'd love for you to take her in. I know you'd care for her . . . raise her proper, like.'

Isabel sighed again, not only at the prospect of such a monumental commitment, but that her friend should place so much trust in her. 'You're putting a lot of faith in me, Catherine.' It was a far greater commitment than Barnaby Micklejohn's proposition, but she could hardly refuse this one and sacrifice the poor child's future, even if it turned out to be at the expense of the other.

'Because I know you'll see it through . . . because I know I can trust you. I know you'll guide her through life . . . And the kid idolises you.'

'I idolise *her* . . .' Isabel paused a moment. 'Don't worry, Catherine, I'd be glad to take her in if needs be. I'd see to her schooling and . . . Polly could be the daughter I never had. But wouldn't you rather she be sent to live in England and be looked after by your family?'

'Never. Arseholes, the lot of 'em. I know where she'd be best off – and that's with you.'

The child appeared, hesitantly carrying two candles in holders; they cast two unsteady blending shadows of her on the wall behind. She placed one candle on the small table beside the bed.

'I've poured mommy a drink,' she declared in her small voice. 'I'll have to go back and fetch it.'

'Thank you, my angel.' Catherine turned to her friend again. 'Under my pillow, Isabel, there's a letter . . . Canst reach it for me?'

Isabel leaned forward and felt under the pillow where Catherine indicated. She withdrew a sheet of folded paper.

'It's for you, Isabel, and proof for anybody who might question what we've talked about. Please read it.'

Isabel opened the letter and by the light of the candle

read the sophisticated swirls that could never have been Catherine's handwriting. It read:

> *I, Catherine Wragg, being of sound mind, hereby will that in the event of my death my only daughter Polly Wragg shall be reared and cared for by my true friend Isabel Saxby. Dated this 19th day of July 1853.*

It was signed with Catherine's asymmetrical cross, and witnessed by Dr James MacArthur.

'The doctor wrote it for me.'

'You were so sure I'd accept?'

'I was sure you could never refuse the last request of a dying friend,' Catherine wheezed. 'Especially as it's Polly's future that's at stake.'

Isabel shook her head. 'Nor could I.'

'So you give your word?'

'I give my word, Catherine. Don't fret yourself, I'll take care of her.'

The patient breathed a sigh and smiled. 'Now I can rest easy . . . Now I can die in peace.'

'Oh, Catherine, you're not going to die when you have everything to live for. Anyway, I'm going to stay with you and look after you and make you better.' Then she thought of Barnaby vainly awaiting her outside the Customs House that evening. But there was no way she could let him know she was not going to be there. It was infinitely more important to nurse her friend for as long as was necessary. Barnaby Micklejohn, unfortunately, must wait.

Catherine forced a smile through her feverishness. 'Thank you, Isabel. But you don't have to stay, you know.'

'Yes, I do, if only to give poor Polly a rest. Come here, Polly . . .' The child had just returned carrying a mug of ginger beer for her mother. 'I'll give the drink to your mommy, then we'll make you a bed in the parlour and you can get some sleep. I'm looking after the two of you.'

- - -

It was a long night, during which the weather turned. The wind began gusting and howling and rain lashed the seaward facing windows. Isabel laid old cloths along the sills to stop the rain seeping in, but the cold and damp persisted. She laid some more wood on the fire that burned in the tiny parlour, resolutely ignoring the smoke that blew back down the chimney at the whim of the wind. Catherine was hot in her fever, but at least Isabel could leave her for a few moments and stand by the fire to warm herself from time to time.

She made up a bed in the parlour for herself and Polly, away from Catherine, to afford them both some rest. It troubled Isabel greatly to acknowledge that the child might also have contracted the infection, that she might yet contract it herself. At one point she heard Polly crying, and was filled with apprehension. She took her in her arms as if she were her own, soothed her with soft words and gentle stroking and, when the child's confusion and distress subsided, she tucked her up again in the makeshift bed with more cuddles. Isabel tarried, watching Polly drift back into sleep, then left her to watch over Catherine, to witness the patient's gasping struggle for life. Catherine was as pale as the whitewashed walls that seemed to be entombing her, but her skin bore a sheen of perspiration as her body was doing its utmost to defy that awful affliction.

As she sat in the flickering candlelight, Isabel's thoughts drifted inevitably to Barnaby Micklejohn. She was eager to be with him again, and that eagerness was sharpened by the knowledge that now she would not be able to. What would he think of her not turning up? She hoped that once he knew the reason he would understand, and felt sure he would. But what a pity it would be if he took umbrage, failed to understand and she lost him; he was a good, reliable man after all.

Her thoughts ran on, all apprehension magnified and distorted by the tyranny of night; if they ever were to marry what if he insisted she give up her shop, which now afforded her some financial and social independence? Having a ready-made family in the shape of Polly – not his own child – would introduce a whole new factor to the notion of marriage. Would he still be sufficiently interested if Polly were a part of the equation?

If so, life might not be so bad; it could be mighty interesting, convivial. Whatever the outcome, life would change radically with Polly in her charge. In those circumstances there could clearly be advantages in being Barnaby's wife. The agreeable social life she already enjoyed would shift focus and expand to the people he worked with. Indeed, her social station might well become elevated, hobnobbing with important men in government, maybe even Governor Denison himself and his spotless wife. She would have to become more domesticated, a capable hostess in the marital home. But it might not be so bad. She had always been able to throw herself whole-heartedly into whatever she set her mind to.

In the grimness of that cold, dark room, with Catherine struggling feverish and unconscious against the odds, Isabel tried to imagine Barnaby and herself in the marriage bed. Long ago, she had indeed learned how it felt to be profoundly in love. Love and desire had once consumed her, and she had given herself whole-heartedly. She had not forgotten it, despite what she had told Barnaby. She could never forget it. And because that love affair would always be so vividly imprinted in her memory, she had reservations as to whether the intense emotions she felt as that young girl could ever be equalled. It was time, perhaps, to allow herself the opportunity to see.

While these thoughts were swirling through Isabel's mind the storm was abating. She sensed Catherine stir. The poorly patient opened her eyes and the moisture in them reflected the yellow glow of the candle as she looked vacantly around her.

'Look at t't frost on t't window,' Catherine remarked with perfect clarity.

Isabel looked at the curtained window and of course there was no frost. Her friend was delirious. She took the cool flannel she had already dampened and pressed it against Catherine's forehead with soothing words.

'T't well will be froze over and we'll have no water. Ask momma if there's already water in t't pail, eh, our Lottie?'

'Course I will,' responded Isabel, answering for the imagined Lottie.

Come daylight she must send for the doctor again. There had to be something he could do.

\- - -

Dr MacArthur, a Scot by birth and known to Isabel, arrived at midday. It had been raining heavily again and he doffed his wet cloak and hung it on a nail hammered into the back of the front door.

'How has she been, Miss Saxby?'

'Hot – bothered – delirious,' Isabel replied. 'Her breathing has been laboured. She seems so weak, Doctor.'

The doctor held Catherine's wrist, counted the beats of her pulse as he checked it against his fob watch, and shook his head ominously.

'She seemed to get worse through the night,' Isabel remarked. '*Is* she worse?'

He nodded. 'She's certainly no better.'

'Is she going to get better?' Their eyes met.

'That, I cannot say,' he answered quietly. 'Giving her something to drink regularly will help. Boiled milk is always good – it's nourishing. But boiled water as well. Keep her still and keep her cool.'

'Do you think she has reached her crisis, doctor?'

'Maybe tomorrow, Miss Saxby. I'll call again tomorrow morning. Meanwhile, be patient and tend to her as you already have. It's fortunate indeed that you are here to look after her, for the wee lassie could never have coped.'

'What about the wee lassie, doctor?' Isabel said, deliberately repeating his words. 'Do you think she might have caught the infection?'

'How does she seem?'

'So far, so good.'

Doctor MacArthur flashed Isabel a professional smile that conveyed a fund of sympathy. 'I'll take a look at her now, and again when I come tomorrow. At least the odds are with her, not against her.'

'Let us hope so.' Isabel sighed, glad of his opinion. 'Oh, and, Doctor . . . Please don't worry about your bill for all this. Send it to me. I'll pay for everything in full, just as soon as you remit it. Whatever treatment you think either of them needs, please don't hesitate to give it.'

'Thank you for your reassurance, Miss Saxby.'

\- - -

Thursday 21st July 1853

Dear Barnaby,

As I have not heard from you or seen you since I failed to meet you the other Evening, as we had arranged, I suppose I am no longer in your good Books. You must think it very unmannerly of me to appear to have scorned you, and I offer my sincere Apologies especially if you waited a long time for me. The Truth is I did not scorn you. You see, Events prevented me from meeting you. Please rest assured I have not been trying to avoid you.

I must explain. That same evening we met, I was called to the House of my close Friend Catherine Wragg. She was taken ill with Pneumonia and was being looked after by her little Daughter Polly who is but a child, even younger than your own daughter Miranda. Once I was there I found it impossible to leave them, because Catherine was so ill and the Child so helpless and frightened, and far too young to cope. I have not even been to my shop since, which is why neither Maisie nor Rhoda would have any notion of where I was, even if you went there looking for me.

Poor Catherine passed away Yesterday and because she has nobody else it has been left to me to organise her Funeral and to take in little Polly as my Ward, which I have sworn to do. The Funeral is to be at half past eleven o'clock next Tuesday the 26th with Interment at the Burial Ground.

In the circumstances I am deeply sorry, but I think it proper to cancel our arrangement for Sunday afternoon anyway, and hope we can arrange it for another time, if you still feel inclined. So you see, Barnaby, I have not been quite as unmannerly as you might have thought, and I hope you can find it in your Heart not to think ill of me. I know this puts a different light on what we talked about, but I would love to hear from you, and I hope to remain your friend whatever you decide,

Isabel Saxby

\- - -

Chapter 3

On the day of Catherine's funeral, the morning began sunny yet seasonally cool; the weather in Van Diemen's Land, although generally calm and temperate, could be notoriously fickle. When the ceremony inside the church was over the two solitary mourners and David Galer – Chaplain of the Cascades House of Female Correction, who was officiating – picked their way to the main gate of Hobart Town's only graveyard, between simple burial mounds and the elaborate monuments of the better-off.

Polly clutched Isabel's hand anxiously. The blue sky had become laden with dark clouds and a vigorous wind was blowing cold from Antarctica across the Southern Ocean. As the chaplain's vestments flapped in the gusts, the dark clouds unleashed their burden of winter rain. The trees swayed and flowers that had been lovingly arranged on surrounding graves shook their heads as if in sympathy. Isabel stood with her hands resting consolingly on little Polly's trembling shoulders as they both peered tearfully into the rectangular hole in the ground, precisely dug out by two convicts now working some distance away with an overseer. She felt the grief of losing her friend so suddenly and so unexpectedly, but realized it was nothing compared to the confusion and uncertainty the child must be feeling – and her heart went out to her.

'*Man that is born of woman hath but a short time to live,*

and is full of misery . . .' intoned David Galer, the words almost lost from their hearing, snatched from his lips by the raucous wind. '*In the midst of life we are in death: of whom may we seek for succour but of thee? . . .*'

Wearing new clothes suitable for mourning that Isabel had provided, Polly looked up at her with watery, questioning eyes. She did not understand this rigmarole with its arcane language, nor had she entirely grasped the reason for it. Isabel shivered at the awful loss of this life, so vital to the child, and pondered the effect it would ultimately have, not only on Polly, but on herself as well. Taking on Catherine's little daughter was an enormous commitment, a lofty mountain that rose up from the level plain of the life she had grown used to. It also made a mockery of the promise of a settled life with Barnaby Micklejohn. But Isabel was determined to see through her responsibility.

Four other convicts working in the same gang as the others lowered the coffin, suspended by two ropes, into the grave, and Isabel heard it scuff against the sides on its measured descent. The convicts then pulled the ropes free, looping them around their elbows and forearms before shifting quietly away towards their overseer.

'*Forasmuch as it hath pleased Almighty God of his great mercy to take unto himself the souls of our dear sister here departed, we therefore commit her body to the ground. Earth to earth, ashes to ashes, dust to dust . . .*'

The wet earth clumped onto the lid of the coffin and, as Isabel felt Polly's slight weight press against her, she steadied her. It had not been her wish for the child to attend the funeral, but Isabel had come up against the immoveable will of a small but tormented creature, suddenly bereft of its mother without comprehending why. It seemed to Isabel that while the child believed there was a chance of her being reunited with her mother she should attend this event. She obviously understood that her mother was at the centre of all these strange arrangements, and the even stranger ritual.

In her gloved hand Isabel was already holding a small lace handkerchief. She lifted her veil and dabbed at the tears that were rimming her eyes, and gave another squeeze of sympathy and affection to Polly. The wind and rain squalled, she held on to her black bonnet and looked out across the graveyard, through the gum trees and the wooden picket fence painted white that surrounded it. People in Davey Street beyond were privately going about their business, unaware of this personal tragedy and all its implications.

When it was all over the chaplain kindly offered his condolences and made his way back to the vestry in haste to escape the weather. Isabel took Polly's hand and they lingered tearfully at the graveside, peering deep down at the smatterings of rain-soaked earth that lay upon the drenched lid of the coffin as if it were leeching blood.

'When will my mommy be coming back, Aunt Isabel?' Polly asked, so poignantly.

Aunt Isabel, on whom the child depended so much now, looked into the unfathomable depths of Polly's large eyes, round and moist and heartbreakingly defenceless, and tried to imagine what she was thinking, what she was feeling. It was then she realised Polly was too young to comprehend the concept of death, that she would not see her mother again. Disregarding the mud that would soak into the hem of her dress, Isabel stooped down before her, taking both hands in hers, wondering how best to answer the child.

'Sweetheart . . . Mommy won't be coming back,' she answered, as kindly as she knew how. 'She was very poorly, remember. So poorly, that Jesus had to take her to heaven.'

'Will she get better in heaven?'

'Oh, yes, it's a certain fact.'

'So can I go to heaven as well, to see her, when she *is* better?'

'Well . . .' A brief pause for a feasible explanation. 'Not for a long time, I imagine, Polly,' she uttered at last. 'You see, Jesus has to decide when it's time for us to go to heaven. But that's when we'll see her again.'

'Jesus has to decide?' Polly queried, wide eyed.

'Yes. Going to heaven is something that's decided for us,' Isabel suggested carefully. 'We can't decide it for ourselves. We are not allowed.'

Polly pondered the notion a moment and seemed to accept it. 'How will she get to heaven, Aunt Isabel?'

'Jesus will come and fetch her – but not till after we've left here.'

The child nodded thoughtfully. 'Do you have a mommy, Aunt Isabel?' she asked, a little more brightly.

'Yes, I do.'

'Has she gone to heaven with Jesus?'

Isabel shook her head and smiled. 'No, she hasn't, sweetheart. At least she hadn't last time I heard from her. But she lives in England, you see, a long way away on the other side of the world, and it takes three months for a letter from her to reach me here in Van Diemen's Land. So who knows what might have happened in the meantime?'

'My mommy told me she used to live in Ingaland before she came to Van Diemen's Land.'

'She told me, too.' Isabel smiled again at Polly and with the tip of her gloved fingers wiped an errant tear from the little girl's cheek. 'In a town called Sheffield. But that was a long time ago.' Isabel stood up again. 'I think it's time to go home now, Polly, out of the rain. Don't you think so?'

Polly nodded.

'But let's just say goodbye first to your mommy.'

'Yes . . .' The child turned around and waved her tiny hands at the coffin in the grave. 'Goodbye, Mommy . . . Goodbye and God bless. See you in heaven.'

The poignancy of the moment brought another haze of tears to Isabel's eyes, dissolving into the rain that lashed her face even through her veil.

'Isabel!' a man's voice hailed from behind.

She swivelled round. 'Barnaby! Good gracious!' She immediately felt her colour rise. 'How long have you been here? I didn't see you.'

'Forgive my tardiness, Isabel,' he said with suitable gravity. 'It was my intention to be here early and offer you some support, but I was detained by government business.'

'That was thoughtful of you,' she replied sincerely, appreciative of his intention.

'I've been here only a few minutes, watching. I presume this little lady is your late friend's daughter?'

Isabel nodded. 'Yes, this is Polly. So you received my letter.'

'I did, and thank you. I was sorry to learn of your friend's death.'

Isabel glanced at Polly trying to discern whether the dreaded word held any meaning for her. It seemed not, for half-hidden in the folds of Isabel's skirts she was gazing intently, but expressionlessly, up into Barnaby's face.

'Barnaby, Polly is my ward from now on, as I explained in my letter. Polly, say hello to Mr Micklejohn.'

Barnaby stooped to the child's level and smiled. 'Well, Miss Polly, how pleased I am to meet you,' he said kindly as he reached for the little girl's hand. 'And how fortunate you are to have Miss Saxby as your ward.'

'Are you Aunt Isabel's daddy?'

Barnaby laughed. 'Indeed, Miss Polly, I am not. I'm just

a friend.' He glanced up at Isabel as if for reassurance.

'I'm gratified to know it, after I let you down that night and the Sunday after,' Isabel considered it fitting to mention it first as last. 'I hope you do not think ill of me.'

He let go of Polly's hand and stood up. 'Isabel, in the circumstances I can hardly think ill of you. There is nothing to forgive. What you have done for this little girl is admirable. Noble, in fact. It tells me a great deal about your integrity. But look, why don't we all go to the coffee house in Liverpool Street, out of the wind and rain. You must be soaked through, both of you.'

'Thank you for the offer, Barnaby, it's kind of you,' Isabel replied sincerely, lowering her eyes. 'But in the circumstances I don't think it would be proper. After all, we're in mourning. Besides, I have a hansom waiting to take us home.'

'Can we not arrange to meet some other time, then? A more suitable time?'

She smiled, pleased at his apparent wish to see her again. 'Barnaby, why don't you come to my house for tea *next* Sunday, as we had arranged to do last week,' she suggested brightly. 'Bring your daughter, of course. I think it would be good for Polly to meet her, too. They would enjoy playing together, I'm sure.'

Barnaby grinned contentedly. He noted that the responsibility Isabel felt in having charge of this child seemed to soften her.

'I was hoping you would suggest it,' he said. 'Miranda will be beside herself, bubbling with anticipation when I tell her. So . . . good day to you, Isabel. Good day to you, too, Miss Polly.' He touched his hat and went on his way.

- - -

In the meantime, Polly settled into Isabel's comparatively spacious and comfortable house on Napoleon Street. She enjoyed having her own cosy bedroom, which Isabel had quickly arranged to have swathed with girlish drapes, and adorned with girlish toys and girlish knick-knacks that she bought in Elizabeth Street.

Already Isabel was considering that Polly would benefit eventually from an education. The ability to read not only bestowed social advantage, as she knew well enough, but offered a priceless permit as well to learn about the world and all its wonders. Her own father, a long time ago, had told her that reading was the key to all knowledge, and she recognised it as fact. So she decided she would begin to teach her ward to read and do simple arithmetic almost at once.

The child, indulged too by Sarah the maid, was only too eager to help in the kitchen, to help with the dusting, the sweeping and the cleaning. These tasks had been taught her by her mother, who had envisaged for her the regulated life of a housemaid. While Isabel was working at the shop, Polly and Sarah became inevitable companions and spent hours together, accompanying each other to the market for provisions, and other excursions.

That Sunday morning, Polly helped Sarah in the kitchen making cakes and dainty sandwiches in readiness for the visit of Barnaby Micklejohn and his daughter. They speculated intensely on little Miranda, wondering whether she would turn out to be a sweet little girl or a horror, thin or fat, fair or dark, blue eyes or brown.

At last father and daughter arrived and all their questions were answered. Barnaby introduced Miranda, who turned out to be a likeable, talkative, confident and polite child. After only a few minutes of tentativeness, the children decided by a mutual but unspoken accord, that they would prefer each other's company to that of their elders, and Polly asked permission to venture out into the garden, which was bathed in winter sunshine.

'Since you are going outside wearing nice clean clothes, please make sure that they are just as clean when you come back inside,' Isabel exhorted with maternal caution, directing a wink at Barnaby. The pair nominally agreed, then flew through doors, oblivious to her concerns, to run around in the garden.

Barnaby laughed. 'I see you have fallen quite easily into the role of a mother. It quite becomes you.'

'I don't find it half as difficult as you might imagine.'

'Is that so?' he grinned.

'It is,' she answered earnestly. 'Polly is a sweet child, she's unspoilt and very bright.' Isabel led him into the sitting room that overlooked the garden and Sullivan's Cove. 'She's a quick learner . . . and look, she seems to like Miranda.'

'Miranda evidently likes Polly, too. It seems to me that little girls easily make friends with others of their age.'

'Oh, they do.'

'School is a fine place for children to make lasting, or at least memorable friendships,' he commented.

'I hope so. I am arranging for Polly to go to a small private infants' school when she's old enough. I'm certain she'll be happy.'

He signalled his approval with a singular nod of the head, and sauntered over to the window. 'You have a spectacular view from here, Isabel.'

'Don't I just?' she answered, smiling because of his approval. 'I love to watch the ships come in and imagine the relief of all those people on board at the sight of dry land, when they might have been seasick for so long.' She stepped towards him and stood at his side, yet was more inclined to watch the novelty of the children playing at that moment, than admire the view so familiar to her.

'Tell me about your late friend Catherine.'

'Catherine? . . . Well, I found Catherine when I went to the Hiring Depot looking for a maid . . . Please, do sit down, Barnaby.' She gestured which chair he should occupy.

He did as she bid, crossed his legs, his elbows on the arms of the chair, and made a steeple of his fingers before him. 'You mean the Brickfield hiring depot?'

'Yes.' Isabel thought she detected a hint of disapproval.

'Isn't that where people hire convicts for service?' he asked, and she thought she detected contempt in his voice.

'Yes,' she said again, and heard defiance in her own voice.

'Do I presume then that Catherine was a convict?'

'Yes, Barnaby, she was *once* a convict.' Isabel looked at him squarely. 'Leastwise, she didn't pay her own fare to this island. That's why it was fitting for the Reverend Galer to conduct her funeral service.'

'But don't you think St David's was a little grand for the despatch of a mere convict, Isabel?'

'No, I don't – because she was not a convict when she died,' she corrected. 'In any case, since it's near the only burial ground in Hobart it was more convenient than holding the service at St George's, then having to cart the coffin over to the cemetery for the committal.'

'I suppose so,' he agreed. 'But what crime did she commit that warranted transportation?'

'She was found guilty of stealing six shillings from her master, a crime she swore she did not commit.'

'And you believed that? You believe she was innocent?'

'Yes, I do. She had no reason to lie to me since I already knew she had been a convict?'

'But British justice does not sentence innocent people to transportation to far-off lands, Isabel.'

'Are you quite sure of that?' she said, deliberately effecting some scepticism in her tone. 'Especially since the Civil Service in England is so riddled with incompetence and class distinction, as you yourself have admitted.'

'That does not necessarily apply to the judiciary, Isabel.'

'Does it not?' she scoffed. 'Unless, of course, the judiciary – magistrate or judge – is in the thrall of somebody of higher authority or greater influence . . . a friend or benefactor, or somebody in a position to affect their career for better or worse,' she countered spiritedly.

'Do you think that's possible?'

'In certain circumstances, Barnaby, yes I do. There's no question of it. Oh, I know that some women are bad, some even worse than men with their drinking and swearing and promiscuity, but not all are.'

'So what about the child?' he asked, changing direction. 'One presumes your friend Catherine must have been married at some point. Where's the father?'

Isabel could not help but smile. 'Barnaby, she never married,' she replied matter-of-factly. 'She was carrying Polly when I hired her, but she saw fit not to inform me of that particular detail – because she was desperate to work and earn money for as long as she could. I could hardly hold that against her. Of course, I couldn't keep her on as a maid for long, but by this time we'd become firm friends and I liked her . . . Besides, she was in trouble, thousands of miles from home, without a soul in the world she could turn to. I wanted to do something to help her and the unborn child. She had nobody else. I felt it my duty.'

'But, Isabel, you were under no obligation.' He uncrossed his legs and leaned forward, clearly agitated.

'She was my *friend*, Barnaby,' Isabel reasoned earnestly. 'Of course I had to do something.'

'So what did you do?'

'First of all, I offered to pay for her passage back to England, but she didn't want that. She wanted to remain here in Van Diemen's Land, so I bought a small cottage for her and the baby to live in. And I continued to pay her.'

'Good God,' he said and stood up, astonished at this revelation of what he perceived as irrationality. But his concern was a manifestation of his desire to protect Isabel from exploitation rather than to denigrate Catherine for her social and sexual misdemeanours. 'You are even more noble than I thought. Didn't the father of the child offer some support, though? Who was the father of the child?'

Isabel shrugged. 'How should I know?' she answered, looking up at him. 'Some matelot she met, she told me. I imagine she succumbed to a bit of flattery and the promise of a few moments of tenderness and pleasure. But him being a sailor he's long since gone.'

'Ships in the night, eh? Well, I must say, Isabel, you were taking a distinct risk befriending such a woman – a convicted felon, because in my opinion such people never change.'

Isabel could understand his viewpoint, for it was a conventional notion. It was clear he had never been close to a female convict who had been snatched from family and friends to be transported for a minor misdemeanour, and she saw this as an opportunity to set him straight.

'Barnaby,' she said patiently, 'too many of those women – many of them just young girls – who were transported had done nothing *seriously* wrong, and some nothing at all. Yet they were dragged away from their loved ones to travel in those awful convict ships, usually in squalor. Many were treated so badly, so brutally. Some were used as concubines by the sailors in charge of them on the voyage out, treated like scum or prostitutes. It's a crime against humanity to treat women so.'

'If that happens, then I agree, of course. And you evidently feel very strongly about it.'

'I do. Believe me, Barnaby, you'll never know just how strongly I feel. I know these women, I have worked with them, I know how some have suffered. There's no wonder some of them succumbed to drink and became wayward. I think it's perfectly excusable for them to want a little love and tenderness in their lives after all the brutality and roughness they've endured. One of the women in my shop – Rhoda Dixon – was a convict. You did not know that, did you?'

'Rhoda?' he queried, incredulous.

'Yes, Rhoda. Yet I trust her with my business and with my money. She's not dishonest. There's not a dishonest thought in her head. She's hardly a criminal, merely misjudged by some bigoted judge or magistrate, who might well have been the best friend of the shop owner who brought the prosecution. Nowadays, she's a respectable married woman, a model citizen.'

'Yet she must have done something amiss.'

'In somebody's opinion, obviously,' Isabel protested. 'But I'm convinced she did nothing wrong. She was just another poor soul – in the wrong place at the wrong time, blamed for stealing a yard of ribbon from the shop where she worked . . . Imagine – a yard of ribbon! It's a petty enough offence over which to sentence some poor soul to transportation. And besides,' she went on, 'being blamed does not necessarily mean she was guilty, which she swears she was not. I have every sympathy with her. I have every sympathy with so many of them . . .' She paused, then added more calmly. 'You might as well know this, too . . . my maid Sarah is on her Ticket of Leave.'

'But she's not wearing government clothes.'

'Because in my house I won't allow her to. Why should

she wear those dowdy things when she's in my employment? It's so demeaning.'

'And you trust her in your house, not to steal, not to misbehave or make your life difficult?'

'She's a decent human being, Barnaby, and I treat as an equal. She's kind and thoughtful. I hope she'll meet a decent man, marry and have children. It's what she needs, it's what she deserves. It's what Van Diemen's Land needs too. She'd make a good wife and mother. And she adores Polly.'

'So . . . I have some sympathy with your feelings about those who have committed petty offences, but what about murder, Isabel? What of those women who have murdered, or done away with their unwanted children, for instance?'

'Murderers deserve all the punishment the law can mete out, provided it can be proved beyond doubt that they're guilty . . .' She turned her head to see through the window, mindful of the children. 'Look, don't they play well together?' She smiled, delighted at their antics. 'See how they chase each other around in their pretty dresses . . . And you know what? Till this very moment I hadn't realised what they have in common.'

'What on earth can they possibly have in common?' Barnaby asked with some disdain.

'Each has lost her mother . . . And that's a dreadful thing to happen to a child.'

'Indeed, yes,' he said with humility at the sudden realization. 'You are quite right, Isabel – I hadn't considered it.'

'Polly idolised her mother, Barnaby. Losing her has been very painful for her.'

'And even though she is illegitimate that is not her fault, poor child,' he conceded. 'Well, I must say, it's a monumental responsibility you have taken on for yourself, adopting her.'

'I'm well aware of it,' she agreed.

'I've learned more about you in this last five minutes than in all the time I've known you hitherto.'

'Well,' she said, 'I hope I haven't gone down in your estimation.'

'Indeed not, Isabel,' he said with a broad smile. 'On the contrary, I'm in awe of you.'

'Well, thank you,' she answered, realizing that here was her opportunity to find out how he felt about them now as a couple. 'But because of Polly, I suppose you look upon our relationship quite differently now?'

He smiled again, which made Isabel aware how much thought he must have given to the situation already. 'As a matter of fact—'

At that moment the two little girls came bouncing in with the boisterous energy of their years, giggling, glowing and panting from their exertions.

'You two look hot,' Isabel remarked kindly, prepared to postpone the moment of knowing his thoughts. 'We're about to have tea. Come and sit down at the table and cool down a little. You can sit together.' She glanced at Barnaby.

'Ooh, yes,' Miranda said enthusiastically. 'I'll sit in that chair and you sit beside me, Polly.'

Polly grinned contentedly and bounced onto the chair Miranda had suggested. Already it was obvious that the two little girls were friends. Already there was a bond of affection, of sorority.

Isabel rang for Sarah to bring in the sandwiches, cakes and tea.

While the two little girls chatted and giggled between themselves, Isabel prompted Barnaby. 'You were about to say . . . how my changed situation must throw a different light on us – on what we talked about the other day.' She smiled and tilted her head appealingly.

'Of course, I've given the matter a great deal of thought,' he said pleasantly. 'And I've come to the conclusion that it should not make any difference at all.' There was a gleam in his eye. 'I reckoned that your new situation might have reinforced the logic of my proposal.'

Inside she was bursting with pleasure at his revelation, but it was not in her nature to shriek with girlish delight. There was much more she wanted to get straight in her mind anyway, so she remarked calmly, but with a demure smile, 'It's something we must talk about more.'

'Aunt Isabel,' Polly interjected, in her small, appealing voice, 'can Miranda come and play with me again another day?'

'Of course she can, but it is up to her father.'

'Ooh, yes please, Papa!' Miranda exclaimed with girlish enthusiasm.

Papa forced a smile and looked into Isabel's eyes. 'Of course you can, my dear—'

'Oh, Papa, can we make it very soon, please?' Miranda's eyes lit up. 'Polly can come to my house.' She turned to Polly. 'I have a garden, too. Just as big as yours.'

'We'll have to warn Candida, your nanny, that she'll have two little treasures to contend with on that occasion – shall we not?'

Isabel looked at Barnaby and they both laughed. It was a delicious moment.

\- - -

Chapter 4

'How long have you been blessed with a boat?' Isabel asked.

She and Barnaby were walking arm-in-arm through the Government Gardens towards the small sailing boat moored alongside others that belonged to various government officials. He was carrying a picnic basket filled with a selection of sandwiches, savoury pies and cakes which Isabel had provided – more than enough for just the two of them. Under his other arm was a plaid travel rug for them to sit on when they arrived at the destination he had in mind, which was a mystery to Isabel. The day was clear and bright with a comfortable winter temperature of about 55 degrees on the Fahrenheit scale, with a mild breeze – perfect for sailing up the Derwent estuary.

'I bought it soon after I came to Van Diemen's Land,' he replied. 'There it is, look – *Lilting Jenny* . . .'

'Why *Lilting Jenny*?' she asked.

'I've no idea. She already bore the name when I bought her. She was second-hand, you see, and it's said to be bad luck to change the name of a boat.'

They reached the vessel and Barnaby suggested that Isabel sit on a rock close by while he hoisted the sail and prepared the seat at the stern which they would share.

'Are you sure there's nothing I can do to help?'

'Nothing at all, my dear. Rest meanwhile. It'll only take a minute or two to rig her up. But you're likely to get your feet wet as you clamber aboard, so I would recommend that you take off those dainty boots while I see to the boat – and may I dare suggest perhaps even your stockings. I promise not to peep.' He smiled and his eyes creased with a mixture of humour and warm reassurance.

She laughed, turning away from him to protect her modesty as she did as he suggested. Meanwhile, he placed the picnic basket and travel rug aboard, then went to a small lock-up and returned bearing seat squabs and oars.

'It would be rather hard on your poor, delightful rump without the squabs,' he said, as he placed them inside the boat. 'They should protect such precious hind quarters.'

'I'm a woman, not a horse,' she replied with a chuckle.

'And more precious than any prize mare I've ever encountered.'

He set about preparing the craft, and Isabel looked on. After a short while he announced that all was ready, and removed his own shoes and hose.

'Come on, Isabel – clamber aboard.'

Self-consciously carrying her boots and stockings in one hand she lifted her skirt to save wetting the hem.

'Ooh, the water's so cold,' she exclaimed as she paddled out in her bare feet. She dumped her boots and stockings on the floor of the boat, and raised her skirt higher to prevent it snagging on any unkind protrusions. 'This is not the most elegant entrance I've ever made,' she remarked apologetically, hoisting herself up.

'Perfectly forgivable,' he replied with a smile. 'Under the circumstances.'

'Trousers would be just the thing, you know, Barnaby. I'm sure there must be a market for ladies' trousers.'

'Perish the thought,' he remarked.

'Well, you might think so, but I shall get some made up and show my customers. Why should trousers remain only a male entitlement?'

As he coaxed the little boat into the water the main sail was already fluttering in the breeze. He pushed off, then climbed aboard himself. Under his shifting weight it rocked unsteadily as it was taken up by the waters of the estuary. He sat beside Isabel at the stern, took the tiller and began to trim the sail. At once, she felt the gentle power of the breeze as it caught the little boat, moving it forward, with a slight list.

'Should I put my shoes and stockings on again?' she asked. 'What's your recommendation?'

'It's up to you,' he said brightly. 'But if you do, I suspect you might have to take them off again when we disembark. Anyway, don't you fancy dangling your feet in the water?'

'Ooh, don't be silly, it's much too cold,' she protested, and thrust her feet, still cold and wet from paddling, from beneath her skirt and peered at them.

He peered at them too, quite involuntarily. They were exquisitely formed, her toes slim with neat pink nails, and even this glimpse made him deeply conscious that this excursion was providing another level of intimacy; a few days ago he could not have envisaged being in the sublime situation when he would actually see her bare feet, let alone her ankles, yet here she was freely displaying them. It seemed to confirm her growing closeness, her feeling more at ease with him, and he saw it as a significant step forward in the evolution of their relationship. She had still not yet affirmed that she considered them actually 'courting', but he sensed they were consciously drifting into that happy state.

'You look very lovely,' he remarked, shifting his focus to her face and enjoying the leisurely scrutiny.

'Thank you,' she replied, turning to him with a smile of pleasure at his compliment. 'It's nice of you to say so.'

It was not just the gentle curves of her face that made

her so lovely to look at, it was her blue eyes so clear and wide, her nose, slightly upturned and nostrils so delicately formed. Her lips too, which were exquisitely curved and delightful to kiss, bestowed such enchanting smiles and revealed a beautiful set of teeth. She was elegant, even wearing the plain, unadorned day dress and bonnet she'd chosen to wear for this Sunday outing, instead of the beautifully finished creations she wore for evenings out.

Yet for Barnaby that day, he perceived another Isabel – that of foster mother to the orphaned child of her erstwhile friend. He wondered which of these two versions was the true Isabel Saxby. Was this version beside him, now trailing her fingers languidly in the cold Derwent, closer to the natural Isabel, or further away? He could not make up his mind. However, he did resolve that it was not in the least important when she filled all roles so well. And aside from all this, to have her exclusive companionship in any situation still filled him with incredulity that he should be so fortunate.

She had agreed – enthusiastically – to accompany him on this picnic, using his own sailing boat which was now bearing them upstream to a suitably remote spot with easy access for a landing place. It was a voyage of discovery for both, and the sun beaming down on them with spring-like eagerness enhanced their moods. The little boat sailed on along the broad and winding estuary, flanked on either side by picturesque hills clad with forests. The foothills lay gently sloping, lawn-like, green almost to the water's edge, with Mount Wellington dominating the landscape.

For just a short time they were deserting their routine worlds, whose joys and anxieties they knew well enough, to inhabit a private domain which, for a few precious hours, they would make their own. The occasion was therefore special, with Barnaby all too aware that he was with a beautiful woman, still casually trailing her fingers in the cool wate. She seemed content not to speak, happy with her own thoughts and the companionable silence, which was broken only by the creak of the mast and the sounds of the Derwent as it babbled under their prow. As he tacked and steered the craft contentedly he told himself that if she was happy, he was happy,.

Presently, he broke the silence.

'D'you remember that old prison hulk, *The Anson*, which used to be moored in the Estuary near Risdon?'

'Yes,' she replied, looking at him quizzically. 'Why do you ask?'

'Well . . . your late friend . . .'

'You mean Catherine Wragg?'

'Yes . . . Catherine. She must have spent her first six months aboard it when she arrived in Van Diemen's Land.'

'No, she didn't . . . Catherine arrived here before the Anson. But Sarah, my Irish maid did – and so too did Rhoda, my shop girl.'

'Presumably, they regaled you with stories about life aboard that hulk?'

'Yes, and under the guardianship of Mrs Bowden, the woman who managed it, it was a worthy institution, contrary to the report which I hear was sent to the Home Office by the Governor at that time. It was a place of reform, not punishment like the Cascades female factory.'

'You mentioned that some female convicts were taken as concubines.'

'On the voyage out here some were. But not on the Anson, at least they weren't when it was moored on the Derwent. But on those convict ships that were transporting only women, the crewmen were often worse than animals. Oh, I know some women were artful and hardened, but so many were vulnerable too. The younger they were – and the prettier they were – the more vulnerable they would be. It was usual for a matelot to pick out a pretty girl for a bed partner, often for the duration of the voyage. If she refused she would be vilified and victimised, so she would most likely go along with it, because it would provide an element of protection, and maybe even some privileges. It's not surprising, is it, that so many girls arrived here carrying a child?'

'I've heard of such goings-on, Isabel. But I can't believe that any honourable ship's captain would allow such shenanigans.'

She looked at him with astonishment that he could be so naïve. 'Oh, Barnaby! Some captains set the very example. It was one of the unofficial perquisites of manning those ships. Such a captain would always have first pick, for the choicest girl.'

'It's appalling . . . To think . . .'

Isabel looked at him. He was looking straight ahead, privately pondering how any man could be so callous towards susceptible women.

'I suppose you've never given much thought to such things before, have you, Barnaby?'

'I confess I haven't. I'm simply appalled. And I'm beginning to understand your opinion on the matter of female convicts. However, dear Isabel . . . it leads me on to another observation that you need to explain to me . . . something about certain of your values has been making me curious . . .'

She turned to look at him, drawing her hand from the water which fell in glistening drips onto her skirt.

'What values in particular?' she asked hesitantly.

'Your late friend Catherine . . .'

'What about her?'

'The fact that she had a child out of wedlock. Did you

feel any disdain that she must have been a woman of easy virtue? Were you contemptuous? Did you disapprove?'

'Not in the least,' she admitted flatly, and with some defiance. 'Why should I?'

'But why shouldn't you?'

'Just because she was unmarried, you mean?'

He nodded.

'Barnaby, human nature is just the same whether a person is married or not. It's nature's way, surely? Women feel sexual desire no less than men do, I assure you. It starts in the early teen years and can be very intense. Marriage is just a formal arrangement to make sleeping together, conceiving children and giving birth to them, socially acceptable.'

'Yes,' he conceded, 'I suppose it is. I'd never considered that notion before. Hmm.'

'Well, marriage is man's invention after all, isn't it? I mean, animals couple and conceive, but they don't have marriages. Besides, lots of couples don't go through formal marriages – they often just live together. The woman takes the man's name and that's that. It's been that way since time immemorial, and I see no harm in it.'

'Dear me, how broad-minded you are,' he exclaimed, but with a smile of admiration. 'I never realised just how broad-minded until this moment. But you are not against marriage, are you, Isabel?'

'Of course not. I just believe it's not necessary for some people.'

'But to live together as man and wife, and not be married, would be regarded as scandalous in a civilised society like ours. You must see that.'

'But not in *all* societies,' she replied, and smiled deliciously. 'In ours it pays to conform and not live in so-called sin if you don't want to be ostracised.'

'Would it bother you greatly if you were ostracised for living in sin, Isabel?'

'Not greatly,' she answered honestly. 'For some in the lower classes it's normal. If you consider yourself as belonging to a higher class, then living together unmarried is not acceptable. It's a class thing.'

Barnaby was not at all sure how he felt about that response, but it was significant enough in itself to stall conversation for a little while.

So they sailed on, the estuary widening the further inland they travelled, and with the winter sun caressing the hills and adding transient sparkles to the water, Isabel marvelled at just how lovely the aspect was in whichever direction she looked.

'Where are we mooring up?' she asked. 'Is it far?'

'There's an inlet – a small bay – just beyond that headland,' he answered, pointing.

She guessed that he had visited the spot before with his late wife, but considered it unnecessary and tactless to mention it.

Presently, they arrived at the place Barnaby had chosen, and the little boat grounded on the sandy beach. As he lowered the sail, Isabel clambered forward and onto the side of the boat, then jumped down onto the sand clutching her skirt to her. Mount Wellington loomed, snow-capped and all-pervading, dwarfing the bay. Grassland rose steadily beyond the beach, melding into woodland that clad the steepening hills. Behind them was the calm stretch of the Derwent, deserted but for another small boat bearing a fisherman casting a line far, far away towards the opposite shore. She looked around at the secret spot they had reached; they and the boat seemed insignificant within the vastness and emptiness of their surroundings. The sun felt warm on their faces, the air sweet and enchanting. When

Barnaby spoke his voice seemed to be an intrusion on the profound silence.

'Perhaps I should have helped you out of the boat and carried you to the dry sand,' he suggested experimentally, wondering whether she might view such an action premature, and inappropriate to the supposed innocence of the excursion.

She laughed and said, 'That would have been very gallant, but quite unnecessary, Barnaby. I am quite capable of doing it myself, without putting you to any trouble.'

When he had secured the sail, he took the travel rug and spread it out on the dry sand, then lifted out the picnic basket which he also set down. They sat side by side on the rug, both conscious of their physical proximity to one another and the remoteness of the place.

They chatted randomly for a while, about generalities, about her business, about his work, about the children in their respective charge. But Isabel had a differing perception of the situation to Barnaby; as far as she was concerned the conversation was going nowhere, due to his reserve; they were not talking about what she knew in her heart Barnaby wished to talk about.

'Why are we here, Barnaby?' she asked, changing tack, 'in this lovely little bay, miles from anybody and anything?'

He was not prepared for such a direct inquiry, presented so candidly and so soon. But he did not know Isabel well enough yet to have anticipated it.

'Why? Can't you guess?' he said, stalling for time while he formulated a viable response.

'I believe I can, but I'd dearly like to hear your version.' She had still not donned her shoes and stockings, and, as she sat with her arms around her knees, gazing at him from around the edges of her bonnet, her bare feet and ankles were visible beneath the hem of her dress.

'I invited you here because I wanted to be with you in complete isolation, Isabel, with no children to intrude upon us, no maids, no shop staff – nobody. I hope – and fondly imagined – you wanted that too.'

'Why wouldn't I?' she answered softly. 'So why are we being so shy of each other? We're adults, aren't we?' She undid her bonnet, took it off and laid it on the rug beside her. 'It's not as if we are in our teen years.'

He was not prepared for that either. Yet he had already realized that honesty and directness always seemed to elicit favourable responses from Isabel; so his response to this would be based on the same principle.

'For my part, Isabel, because I'm not sure of you yet . . .' he said, and paused, looking directly into her eyes for a hint as to her reaction. 'Since I first confessed my feelings for you we have met some six or seven times, have we not? And each time we both seem to enjoy each other's company the more.'

'I can't disagree,' she remarked.

'Yet I've not felt any further romantic inclination from you.' He looked at her candidly. 'For me, though, each time has been an episode of discovery.'

'Yes, it's all been lovely, Barnaby – us getting to know each other a little better every time.' She released her knees and leant back a little, propping herself up on her arms, her face tilted towards the sun, which had the effect of thrusting her breasts forward, although that was not her intention.

However, his eyes caressed her as he scanned the pale skin of her neck and at the hollow of her throat, so smooth, so girlish, which fed his desire. What he was feeling was more than just sexual though; he wanted her in so many other ways, ways associated with normal everyday life. He wanted to come home to her every evening . . . As a man, he naturally wanted to explore her body, savour her soft skin, feel her breasts yield to his touch, and go beyond – much further beyond. But that ultimate state of bliss still seemed so far from being pledged or attained – or even possible.

'The thing is,' he went on, 'we're still only progressing, aren't we? But, you know, Isabel . . . if you will suffer me to be candid – you're so lovely – you're so desirable . . . and I am just a man, with a man's yearnings.'

The yeast was stirring . . . She lowered her lids and felt herself blushing. Of course, she knew exactly what he meant.

'Yes, Barnaby,' she said quietly, 'I know only too well that you are a man. I am as aware of it just as intensely as you are aware of me being a woman, if you grasp my meaning. But I'm not sure we've progressed far enough yet for *that*. Can we not delay such things a while longer?'

'But *such things* might help sway you.'

'*Such things* might – I would not disagree.'

She stood up and walked away from him so that he should not see her reddening cheeks. This, she sensed, was to be an epic moment.

'You do understand that I love you, Isabel, with all my heart and soul?'

His confession made her tremble a little, but she tried not to show it. 'Yes, I understand it very well . . .'

'Well . . . as you say, it's Nature's way. And in the light of that, what about you, my love?'

'I'm not so far away as you imagine, Barnaby,' she admitted, and turned her head so that their eyes met briefly.

Then she walked towards the water and raised her hem, allowing the wavelets to lap around her bare feet. His eyes followed her, and he perceived that she was smiling.

She was smiling because souls were being bared and already the day seemed more beautiful, the mood less troubling because of what had been said. The forbidden topic of sexual liaison had been reached, and was a massive barrier smashed down. From here on they could talk about everything freely. In consequence, they both knew what was in store if the progression that Barnaby had mentioned was maintained – perhaps even before any marriage. Isabel, totally unfettered by conventionality, had no problem accepting it.

She remained paddling in the water, thoughtful, quiet, unspeaking for some time. Barnaby watched, not sure what she was thinking, but painfully aware of his own desires, and his fears as to whether he had overstepped the mark too soon.

When she spoke again, it was with a lighter, more confident voice, and she was still smiling, which put him more at ease.

'I'm almost there, Barnaby,' she said again, returning to him. 'But not quite.' She knelt by his side. 'There are so many considerations to take into account. Oh, I know you want us to marry, and when I'm certain that I am entirely in love with you – and satisfied that our different situations can be merged – you'll know it. We get along very well, my love, and I *am* drawn to you in every way, without question. I always have been, and I know now that you've felt the same as me all along. It's been a beautiful journey . . . And here we are now – alone – just the two of us in the solitude of this pretty sandy bay – and I'm loving it, Barnaby. You say you love me and want me, and I understand exactly what you will expect of me . . . We could consummate our relationship now, commit to each other right here on this very rug, on this remote beach, and nobody but the two of us would be any the wiser . . . But, I . . .' She paused, knowing what she wanted to say, but wondering momentarily how best to say it. Then it came to her, and she went on.

'I've been proposed to before, Barnaby. Over time, several men have asked me to marry them, or to sleep with them. Nor is it so surprising, I suppose, because women are in the minority in Van Diemen's Land. I get invited to lots of things . . . and there are lots of unmarried men around, let's face it, either seeking a wife or just a bed partner. One or two proposals I have half considered, but then something has happened that's made me think twice.' She shrugged, an earnest expression on her face. 'I've caught him in a lie or detected insincerity – something has always caused me to turn and walk away. I suppose I have become quite an accomplished proposal-refuser . . .'

She put her hand on his and looked into his eyes that were full of love, and yet so anxiously hanging on her every word. Her tender touch was comforting, and cancelled out all odious thoughts of those other men who also desired her, who wanted to make love to her, whom she had thankfully denied.

'But now there's you,' she breathed, 'and never have I thought of walking away. There has never been an insincerity, a lie, or anything that has made me reconsider where I might be heading with you.' She paused a moment. 'Oh, I know you can be reserved and a bit old-fashioned, but I trust you implicitly, and this *progression* you talk about has been at a steady rate that I've been content with. I've enjoyed every moment.'

He put his free hand over hers. 'Isabel, you have no idea how happy I am to hear you say as much.'

'I truly am on the very brink, Barnaby,' she went on. 'There are so many things I adore about you, so many things about you that I truly love already.'

'Isabel, my sweetheart, you are breaking my heart . . .

You are so near me and yet still so far away.'

'I'm not so far away, Barnaby.' Her eyes misted with tears of emotion and she wiped them away with the back of her hand. 'Thank you for being so patient with me. But you are asking me to take a monumental leap.' She leaned forward and gave him a reassuring kiss on the lips, instantly banishing all awkwardness, all reserve and timidity.

At that moment he clearly perceived the inferiority of other women, finally realized that every woman he had known hitherto, his mother, aunts, sisters, cousins – even his late wife – were not women as nature intended, even though he had admired them all. None were like Isabel – not a single one of them. All were afraid to be joyous, loath to be considered pretty in case they were frowned on for flaunting themselves. In the way they dressed they baulked from elegance and from stylishness. Playfulness or kittenishness was shunned as being akin to wantonness. Even a smile might be construed as a sign of idiocy. Those women held themselves back instead of letting themselves go, assuming every pleasure was a crime until it was universally declared acceptable.

Isabel was free of all that, openly rejoicing in her charms, aware of her fine looks and allure and certainly not inclined to repress them. She was confident in her opinions and beliefs and had the courage to declare them. Nor did she attempt to disguise her wish to please. Her entire demeanour shouted, 'I am a woman and you are a man, and I was born to be what you want me to be – except that it must be on my terms.' Well, good for her. She was not blind to the carnal considerations of life, or in denial about them. The relevance of such considerations to both Isabel and Barnaby was out in the open, due to their brief yet intimate sojourn on the banks of the Derwent River.

Barnaby threw his arms around her and they held a

delicious, lingering kiss. He eased her around, backwards, and she submitted, allowing him to lower her gently down, so that she ended up lying on the rug beside him.

'This is new,' she remarked flippantly when they broke off.

'Kissing you makes me want you the more. In every way possible. I want to wake up lying next to you like this every morning of my life – beginning as soon as possible. I make no apology for saying so.'

'No apology necessary,' she said in a whisper. 'The notion of you lying beside me troubles me not at all. In fact, I find the prospect rather agreeable.'

'Yet for all that, you are still only on the brink of love?'

'But, Barnaby, I'm so close to toppling over the edge. In your scale of progression one more kiss, might just see me fall, enchanted.'

'Do you really think so.'

'Try it.'

He kissed her again, lingering, savouring her lips.

'Well?' he said, raising his head and looking into her eyes. 'Have you toppled over the edge yet, or are you still on the brink?'

She laughed, but at herself, not at him. 'But the brink is such a lovely place to be, Barnaby.' She kissed him again, briefly, but meaningfully, lingering just a little more than a second. 'Give me just a few more days – please?'

He sat up, and looked into her eyes again, but more earnestly. 'Listen,' he said, looking profoundly serious. 'I have volunteered to go to Launceston for a meeting next Tuesday. That chapter of the Royal Society I told you about . . . Why don't you take a couple of days off from your business and come with me? I understand there'd be no problem finding a good hotel that could accommodate us for a night or two.'

'Launceston?' she queried. 'But how would we get there. By ship? I mean, it takes a couple of days to get to Launceston overland. Then there's the journey back.'

'You're behind the times, my love. It's being done overland in only twelve hours these days.'

'Twelve hours?' she queried. 'But even twelve hours, stuck inside a smelly, crowded coach would be unbearable – and hardly romantic. Besides, I have Polly to think of now, as well as my business.'

'But are you opposed to the excursion in principle?'

'No, not in principle . . . Not at all. But I cannot go to Launceston with you.'

'I see . . .' His disappointment was manifest.

'I have a better idea.'

He grinned, wondering what swipe at convention she would come out with this time. 'I'd love to hear it.'

'I own a cottage in Bellerive—'

'You own a cottage in Bellerive?' he queried with wide-eyed incredulity. 'As well as the one your friend Catherine occupied – not to mention your own house?'

She smiled and nodded.

'I never realised you were a woman of so many properties. So was this cottage acquired to house another of your compromised female convict friends?'

'No, it wasn't,' she answered, laughing. 'I heard about it from one of my clients, and it sounded too good to miss. So I went out to see it. It stands at the end of Bidassoa Street overlooking the estuary and Hobart Town. I loved it as soon as I saw it. So I bought it.' She shrugged, self-effacingly, as if it were of little consequence. 'It's so pretty. I use it as a hideaway in summer.'

'It sounds delightful.'

'Well . . . I was about to suggest that I could arrange to be there and, when you return from Launceston, you could come to me there instead of going home, if you can arrange it – if you want to – if you don't consider me too forward.'

'Oh, Isabel,' he beamed, stuck for a more appropriate answer. 'I trust you mean with no maids, and no little girls dancing attendance?'

'No maids, and no little girls. 'Course, we must be discreet. Sarah will look after Polly, and I presume your maid and Miriam's nanny are capable of taking care of her and each other for one extra night.'

'I see no reason why they shouldn't.'

'Then that's settled,' she said, beaming. 'I shall merely say that I have some business to attend to that entails my being away from Hobart Town for the night—'

'Two nights . . . perhaps?' he interrupted.

She laughed non-committedly. 'So you'd better let me know when you expect to arrive, and I shall be there, with fires lit and food aplenty.'

'Isabel, you truly are an amazing woman. Are you quite sure you want to do this?'

'I'm sure. Just as long as on the grand scale of your *progression* you don't consider me a hussy.'

'Oh, but the very sweetest kind.'

'Well, Barnaby,' she answered candidly, 'In for a penny, in for a pound, that's my opinion. As you once told me, I'm getting no younger, and I'm too unconventional to bother about saving myself for any wedding night, if that's where we're eventually headed.'

- - -

Chapter 5

On the Thursday morning Isabel told Sarah that due to her important business trip, she should not be expected back home until sometime on Sunday. Polly, though, was feeling left out and was anxious to accompany Isabel, and pouted with disappointment when she was refused. Rather, Isabel insisted kindly, she must be a good and helpful little girl for Sarah, who would be looking after her. The promise of a present when Isabel returned put a smile back on Polly's face.

So, having said her farewells, Isabel left her house on Napoleon Street carrying a leather holdall. Apart from the clothes she stood up in, she took with her just one more day dress, clean undergarments, stockings and another pair of shoes. Especially for the tryst she had procured the most diaphanous nightdress she could find.

The day was fair but chilly and, as she stepped onto the ferry she smiled and nodded to several familiar faces. She was loath however to engage anybody in conversation lest they became too curious, and she inadvertently gave too much away.

During the ferry crossing she gazed meditatively at the little town of Bellerive approaching on the opposite shore. She understood that this next couple of days would most likely change her life forever. There was no doubt in her mind now that she was completely in love with Barnaby. She was finally reconciled to the notion of marriage, and to giving up her precious independence, although she saw no reason for giving up her shop.

There was, however, still one aspect of this relationship that was unknown to her, and it was of some significance; because years ago she had given herself completely to the young man with whom she had been besotted, not out of wantonness but driven by her ardent love for him. Since that time there had been nobody else she had felt the slightest inclination to give herself to, until Barnaby entered her life. Now the same primitive urge was taking control. She had been familiar with the exotic, irresistible sensations two people in love can bestow on each other, and she was not a woman who believed in half measures. If she committed herself, she did so whole-heartedly. The depth of love she was now feeling, the sense of devotion, had been steadily increasing and she wished to allow it to take its natural course without further hindrance.

The ferryboat moored up and, on the dry land of Kangaroo Bay Isabel walked the entire length of Bidassoa Street, towards the other side of the small peninsular that accommodated Bellerive, passing shops and taverns of this burgeoning and pleasant little community. Soon she reached her cottage, unlocked the door and went inside.

It seemed cold and damp for want of occupation, hardly the place right then for a romantic interlude with Barnaby. So when she had put down her bag, she ventured back outside to the wood store, and returned with armfuls of kindling and logs. She laid a fire in the parlour, in the bigger of the two bedrooms and in the cast iron range in the scullery, then located the box of Bryant and May matches left behind on her previous visit. When the fires were drawing well she fuelled them with the heftier logs, and put fresh bed linen to air before she made up the bed.

By then, it was then time to go out again to buy meat,

vegetables, bread, butter, fruit, milk, tea for her and Barnaby, soap to cleanse them and oil for the lamps to light their evening. On her return she cleaned the cottage from one end to the other, thinking the whole time of their intensifying romance, how the evening's promised intimacy might affect Barnaby. She felt no shame for suggesting this tryst and all that it implied. And why should she, a woman barely heedful of conventional attitudes?

If it ever became common knowledge, however, it would be the biggest scandal since the exposure of the affair between Mary Ann Maconochie (the daughter of the Norfolk Island penal colony's governor) with a convict tutor. Her sharing a bed out of wedlock with a trusted, respected government officer would be perceived no differently. Knowledge of such intimacy simply had to remain hidden and must never reflect on Barnaby's situation. Such were the imported dictates of convention which she felt forced to uphold.

Isabel returned, checked the fires and, happy that everything was in order, decided to stroll along the beach. The weather remained fair, and she reckoned that as long as she was wrapped up warm against the sea breeze, the fresh air and exercise would do her no harm. She would be able to ponder things while she walked; and the more time she had to think, the easier it was to reconcile her shamelessness and candour with Barnaby's innate reserve, and excuse herself. So she walked for an hour, barefoot across the sand, carrying her shoes, frequently wondering where Barnaby might be at any given moment as he returned from Launceston in the far north. Doubtless he would be tired and hungry when he arrived.

Afterwards, leaving the beach, she put her shoes back on, her legs aching from the exertion of walking on sand. In Bidassoa Street again she ambled towards the shops in search of a vintner. Although rum was plentiful and cheap she wanted to buy a bottle of Scotch whisky. She was tired by now, but her appetite was huge, and back at the house she ate heartily. Alone with her thoughts she sat curled up on the settle and drifted off to sleep.

Outside, meanwhile, the late afternoon sun was lending a deepening yellow and orange glow to a sky smeared with wispy cyan and magenta clouds as it started its spectacular descent behind the distant hills across the estuary. Eventually, Isabel awoke, and she looked through the window and saw how utterly beautiful the sunset was. If only she had the skill to capture its fleeting beauty with paper and watercolours while she waited for Barnaby. So she lingered, watching the sun go down.

Then, in the dusk, she saw him approaching and smiled to herself. To her, he appeared self-conscious – almost furtive – as he carried his overnight bag, peering around him to make certain he was heading for the right cottage. She smiled to herself as she hurried to the door, opened it and waved to him. He waved back, quickened his step, opened the garden gate and at once she was in his arms.

'So this is your secret hideaway?' he said.

'Such as it is,' she answered with eyes sparkling. 'It was cold when I got here this morning, but it's lovely and cosy now. Come inside. Better not stand at the front door. You never know who might be watching.'

He stepped inside. She closed the door, he put his travel bag down and followed her into the parlour.

'What time did you start out from Launceston this morning?'

'Six o' clock. I managed to sleep on the coach a little, though. Anyway, we made good time.'

'You must be worn out,' she suggested. 'Sit down and I'll get you something to drink? D'you fancy tea?'

He sighed. 'Tea would be wonderful, thank you.'

'Are you hungry?'

'I can always eat. We stopped at Jericho and ate while they changed the horses. But that was ages ago.'

'I'll cook us our meal, Barnaby. Why don't you rest meanwhile?'

Barnaby fell asleep sitting up on the settle. Isabel, understanding how tired he must be after the long, tedious journey, smiled lovingly and prepared their food in the scullery. While she cooked and he rested, her small hideaway merged gradually into the landscape as night descended, holding the two lovers hidden, private and invisible.

- - -

Presently, when the meal was almost ready, she woke him. While they ate they talked by the light of two oil lamps and the flickering fire. The cottage was warm and embracing, enhancing the sense of intimacy.

For Barnaby this was a new experience in the persevering progression of his wooing, and he felt moved just being alone with Isabel in this private little world, which had occupied his imagination, fuelling his hopes and dreams over the past few days. He had never in his wildest dreams anticipated such an occasion as this. Yet she had offered it, and his heart was beating much faster than usual. Isabel looked so lovely, her hair loosely bound, her eyes large and sparkling as the firelight danced enchantingly within them. She wore a simple, plain blouse and skirt and little else, as far as he could judge merely by looking, and the ensemble seemed to accentuate her slenderness.

However, for all that this intimate situation implied, the familiar sense of nervousness between them seemed to have resurfaced. It was the uncertainty of not knowing how to proceed without giving the impression that all was being taken for granted. They were two adults, neither a stranger to sensuality, but for his part it arose from an uncertainty as to whether they were to be fulfilled lovers after all; whether they were to actually get as far as lying together yet; even whether it was something she really wanted. His own characteristic sense of conventionality was giving him doubts; was this situation right and proper, and even honourable, since they were still miles away from being a married couple?

At the same time, he sensed that she was expecting him to take the lead. Yet he was fearful of spoiling everything by simply presuming too much, too soon, or too adamantly – or even doing nothing. He was unsure of the limits of her expectations and acquiescence. For all she had implied the last time they met, maybe she had not intended that they be as intimate yet as man and wife would be, and rightly so, but that they should spend this time together merely amicably. Did she perceive it as a gentle precursor to marriage, to see if she could discern any quirks before deciding whether or not she could live with his quirks. Or indeed, had she made up beds in two separate rooms?

But Isabel rescued these moments of uncertainty with her usual candidness. He was helping her to wash dishes and saucepans in the scullery, and in what seemed like one deft movement she dried her hands, slid her arms around his waist and offered her lips. With grateful astonishment, he kissed her then hugged her, nuzzling her hair as he relished the warmth and softness of her body through the thin layers of material that made up her clothes. She looked up into his eyes and he was moved beyond recovery.

'Is my rate of progression outpacing yours now?' she asked kittenishly, sensing his nervousness.

'Oh, Isabel, my love . . . if *you* believe it is, I could not be happier.'

They both laughed, kissed ardently, and suddenly everything was all right.

- - -

Barnaby's admiration for Isabel had lived with him for many months, had grown from mere physical attraction, through desire and into love. He had wooed her unhurriedly, with kindness, intelligence, patience, humour, never overstepping the mark. As those short weeks passed by, he had sensed her increasing regard for him in turn, how she responded to him with greater warmth and ease each time they met, how she returned his kisses lately with apparent pleasure and even enthusiasm. Often, she was the one to instigate them.

Before dawn broke, Barnaby awoke from a deep sleep and his mind was at once awhirl with the tenderness and passion that had consumed them earlier. Here he was, lying beside her in a bed that was strange, but a bed he would always remember. It was also a night he would always remember. For more than three years – ever since his wife died – he had remained celibate. He was not sure for how long Isabel had, but it mattered not at that moment. The abandoning of this celibacy had been overwhelming, astounding in its delicious purity and wholesomeness. Both had become drenched in sensual ardour.

He felt Isabel stir at his side, and her arm went around him.

'So you're awake?' he whispered. 'Still?'

'Not still,' she answered dreamily. 'I've been sleeping like a log. And you?'

'Like a log . . .' He sighed as he stretched. 'Do you mind if I light the lamp?'

'Why d'you want to light the lamp?' she asked.

'So I can see you.'

She gave a little chuckle. 'I don't think it will be that

pleasant a sight,' she remarked self-deprecatingly.

'Nonsense.' He sat up, reaching for the box of matches that he was aware was on the bedside table beside him. He found it, struck one and by its flare he lifted the glass of the lamp, lit the wick and blew the match out. 'There . . . I can see you now.'

'Don't you think you should try and get back to sleep, Barnaby?'

He smiled. 'If it's all the same to you, my love, I don't regard this as a time for sleeping.'

The sight of her moved him as much as it had done earlier. She looked tenderly relaxed, her lovely face framed by her dark hair, waywardly spread across the pillow. She looked up at him admiringly, as if he had done something immensely good. By the light of the single oil lamp, her eyes somehow looked even more beautiful, softened by a warm serenity which seemed to embrace him.

She reached out to him with both arms, with the result that her breast was bared. They seemed to be looking into each other's eyes for an age, and he perceived a change in her expression from one of admiration to one of welcome and acquiescence. Thus encouraged, his mouth skimmed her breasts delectably, his tongue teasing her nipples.

He pushed the sheets and blankets away with his feet. The contours of her body, highlighted by the yellow flame of the oil lamp, were enhanced and seemed to shimmer with smoothness. He strained his eyes to better appreciate the sight. The sweet smell of her skin aroused him further and, as his hand ventured again over her belly to the warm soft place between her legs, she turned her face to him and kissed him. He could just discern the smile in her serene look. He breathed her name and, hungry for her lips, pressed his open mouth on hers. He wanted her again so much that he thought she must be able to hear the pounding of his heart. His hands wandered all over her body, savouring the silkiness of her skin and the firmness of her flesh, exciting her too, but stimulating him further. In their heightening passion she took the initiative, and rolled onto him. As he lay beneath her, her easy weight was a joy, her smooth skin pressed against his was exhilarating. Then she guided herself gently onto him like a butterfly settling on a blossom, and with a profound sigh she felt him enter her.

Neither slept afterwards. It seemed that this their second lovemaking, prolonged and delicious, established the astonishing reality of the first time. It cancelled the desire to sleep, and freed them of any further awkwardness. They were now true lovers, free to enjoy everything else they could give each other without constraint. She was content, and happily committed.

They chatted randomly until the light of the southern sky seeped into the room. As he looked beyond Isabel to the light that permeated the curtained window announcing the day, it was apparent to Barnaby that he had won her at last.

'I think we should stay here at least one more day and night,' he suggested.

'I second that,' she said softly, and smiled as he turned his head to witness the compliance to his suggestion in her facial expression, which enraptured him.

'After all, what do I pay a nanny for if not to look after my daughter, and a maid to clean and cook?'

'I couldn't agree more.'

\- - -

So they stayed two days and two nights. Never had two lovers felt closer as they sat at the table in the small scullery, enjoying breakfast before leaving the cottage and returning to the normality of life in Hobart Town. Barnaby was to leave first, so that they should not be seen disembarking together from the ferryboat at the wharf, which might naturally invite dangerous speculation.

'What if a baby starts, Barnaby?' Isabel asked while they were having breakfast. 'What if I'm with child after this?'

'My angel, if a baby starts we should marry as soon as we are aware of it,' he replied pragmatically. 'But we should marry anyway, with no undue delay. You know my feelings on the matter, and you've given me every indication now that you're not averse to the notion.'

'Propose to me then,' she said girlishly, her eyes alight with playfulness as she peered over the rim of her cup that contained the tea she was drinking. 'So far you haven't. So far, it's only been an intimation.'

He smiled at her teasing. 'Do I have to go down on one knee?'

'No, that won't be necessary.'

'I shall anyway . . .' He left the table and knelt. 'Isabel Saxby, will you marry me?'

She returned her cup to its saucer, and leaning towards him, looked into his eyes directly. ''Course I will,' she replied simply. 'When?'

He grinned with happiness. At last, he had drawn from her the promise to marry. 'Well, first let's announce our engagement. You shall have a fine ring to confirm the fact . . . And why don't we make Christmas Day or Christmas Eve our wedding day? Christmas would be a wonderful time to begin our married life. It's a decent enough period anyway after announcing our engagement.'

'Unless a baby is already on its way,' she said.

'In which case we shall bring the wedding forward. I concede it's possible you might be having a child, Isabel, after these last two glorious nights.'

'Well, it would be no great surprise, would it? We didn't

exactly restrain ourselves.'

'Would you mind, though? If you were with child?'

'No,' she answered simply. 'But for the sake of your reputation and career, it would be better if I'm not.'

'So, assuming we're blessed with the preferred course of having no events to provoke a scandal, is Christmas agreeable to you?'

'No, Barnaby,' she said frankly. 'We should be married early in December. By Christmas we would have had a few weeks together, in which to prepare for a jolly time. We have two little girls to consider in that respect.'

'And, by the way, they must be bridesmaids, no doubt?'

'Of course,' she replied happily.

'Then I'll make all the arrangements. The ceremony must be at St David's, and the wedding breakfast in the banqueting hall at Government House, pending the consent of the governor, of course.'

'You've already thought about all that, haven't you?' she remarked with a smile of approval.

'I unashamedly confess it, dear Isabel. Yes, I have.'

'Are you sure you haven't already arranged everything?'

'No. I thought it better to get your consent first. However, now that I have it, I shall be the proudest man in Van Diemen's Land when I present you as my fiancée at the ball at Government House on the 10th of August.'

'What ball?'

'Oh . . . to mark the end of transportation. Did you not know of it?'

'Well, yes I did, Barnaby. But I hadn't harboured any expectation of going to it.'

'Well, you will naturally accompany me there!'

She laughed contentedly.

- - -

Chapter 6

The engagement of Barnaby Micklejohn, Esq, government officer, to Miss Isabel Saxby, was announced in both The Courier and The Hobarton Guardian, prompting messages of congratulations and best wishes from everybody who knew them. The two little girls, Miriam and Polly, were enchanted to learn that come the day, they would not only be sisters, blissfully living and playing together, but bridesmaids too. At the shop, Maisie and Rhoda were full of self-congratulatory told-you-sos and were delighted for Isabel, more especially when she confirmed that she would continue to run the business even after she was wed, not least because it would be safeguarding their employment.

The wedding was arranged for the fourth of December, which fell on a Sunday, at St David's Cathedral the Governor, Lord Denison, agreed that the banqueting room at Government House could be used afterwards for the wedding breakfast. In the meantime, the couple would draw up a list of people with whom they wished to share their happy day.

- - -

Meanwhile, prior to the celebratory ball on the evening of the tenth of August there was the daytime Jubilee Festival, organised to observe the cessation of convict transportation to Van Diemen's Land. As a government official, Barnaby was invited to the evening event being held at Government House; the perfect opportunity to introduce Isabel as his fiancée to the upper echelons of Hobart Town society.

Isabel and Barnaby had arranged to take Miriam and Polly to the daytime festivities. The streets were thronged with folk from surrounding farms and villages, arriving by horse, wagon and on foot. Union Jacks, as well as bunting and flags of the Australasian Anti-Transportation League, fluttered in abundance. Macquarie Street became the gathering place for a great horde of people, many spilling out from the numerous churches where services of thanksgiving had been held. The military band, splendid in red coats, marched through the town, drums beating, trumpets blaring and colours flying. Every rejoicing child that day received a slice of a monstrous cake that measured fourteen feet in diameter and was six inches thick. At its centre it bore a representation of the Union Jack. They also enjoyed endless sandwiches and tarts, ginger beer and lemonade. All this ample jollity was overseen by the chairman of the Hobart Town branch of the Australasian Anti-Transportation League. Polly and Miriam were enthralled with it all, but thought their day was too short when they were forced to part at sundown to return to their respective homes.

In the evening, a carriage with Barnaby already on board, called to convey Isabel to the ball at Government House. He stepped down to greet her and kissed her, then she climbed into the carriage as elegantly as she could. It was a cold night, and the half-moon was bright in the cloudless sky, promising frost. Her excitement was palpable, and she bubbled with animated chatter on the drive to Government House, wondering whom they might befriend, and at the prospect of meeting Barnaby's colleagues. The dancing, too; she loved dancing, but occasions for such revelry in Hobart Town were limited.

Government House was a curious two storey brick building, stuccoed and painted, with a long wooden veranda extending across the broad frontage. As successive occupiers had required additional rooms the house had been extended, so it had ended up a mass of wings and annexes, randomly arranged and with little regard for aesthetics.

When they reached their destination, the carriage drew to a halt in the driveway, which was illuminated with burning oil lamps. Barnaby alighted, then took Isabel's hand as she stepped down, careful of her wide skirts. A servant was on hand to direct them up the portico steps into the reception hall, where a another hired help relieved them of their topcoats and hats. Lieutenant–Governor Sir William Denison, a balding, hefty man in middle–age, and decked out in official regalia, greeted them amiably, his wife Lady Caroline at his side. Lady Caroline, wearing a dark green satin evening dress with short, laced sleeves, said how much she admired Miss Saxby's delightful off-the-shoulder creation with its flounces. She was even more interested to learn that Miss Saxby was the owner of the emporium on the corner of Murray Street and Liverpool Street that supplied similarly fashionable concoctions to many of the town's ladies.

Indeed, Miss Saxby knew for certain that several such ladies would, that very night, be gracing Government House wearing dresses conjured from materials originating from Saxby's Mantles and Haberdashery. She believed that the governor's wife might be tempted to do so as well on some future occasion.

'Lady Caroline loves my dress,' Isabel chimed when they had moved on.

'So do I,' Barnaby replied. 'You look ravishing.'

She wore a sky-blue silk evening gown delicately

trimmed with matching ribbon and *broderie anglaise*. Her shining dark hair, fashionably parted at the middle, was adorned with matching blue-ribbon knots. The stunning effect was enhanced by a simple gold chain at her neck, tasselled earrings, and bracelets on each wrist. Barnaby was less modishly attired, but appropriately wearing dark tailcoat and trousers and a white cravat,

Outside, the sounds of horses' hoofs, carriage wheels crunching the gravel of the drive, and joyous laughter heralded the arrival of more guests, who subsequently appeared in the hall to be likewise greeted by the hosts.

Isabel admired the chandeliers, bright with hundreds of candles, mirrors, fine chairs and couches, and other expensive furnishings placed strategically. As the room filled up with beautifully clad women, the occasion could have been fairly described as a pageant of bare shoulders. Officers in beribboned military uniform, other men in formal wear, seemed openly animated at being among so many lovely, well-dressed women. In any case it was a wonderful show of fashion for such an out-of-the way island, manifesting the progress made in the evolution of a civilised society in so short a time span.

Those who knew Barnaby, or worked with him, were quick to congratulated him on his choice of fiancée when they were introduced to Isabel; Isabel, by this time sipping French white wine from a crystal goblet, was the epitome of charm, sophistication and wit.

As the room filled, the guests at first drifted into uneasy groups that soon became more animated and responsive. Eventually, everybody was hushed and the Governor addressed them, commending the historic day. After he had spoken, the scraping of bows across the strings of fiddles and cellos told that dancing had begun. The first dance was a quadrille, which those familiar with the routine danced. Others stood and watched, or gossiped as they occupied the various chairs and couches. Save for the dancers, wherever you chose to be in that room you could overhear discussions, both serious and informed, or flippant and speculative. Generally, the topic was the ending at last of the exporting of so many felons to Van Diemen's Land. A popular side issue was how to introduce more culture, and how a fair, just, prosperous and law-abiding society was everybody's dream, and within grasp.

Between dances, Isabel and Barnaby chatted with other guests, including the harbourmaster, clergymen, millers, army officers, ship owners, shipbuilders, wood merchants, a seed merchant, together with their respective wives, making new acquaintances to add to the people they already knew. Many swapped stories of how they came to be in the colony in the first place. Before they knew it, it was time for food. So Barnaby duly led Isabel towards the grandiose buffet laid out on elaborately covered trestles.

Isabel and Barnaby joined an animated line as they waited to be served by an array of female servants. One of them caught Isabel's eye. As their eyes met briefly across the room she was suddenly filled with apprehension, and anxious not to encounter the woman, so she made her excuses to Barnaby.

'Barnaby, I'm feeling so hot,' she said, and drew the back of her hand across her brow as if to confirm it. 'I'm going to find a cooler spot. Would you mind bringing me a sandwich or something?'

'I'll come with you if you're not feeling well,' he offered with concern.

'No, I'll be all right, really. It's the dancing. Just be sure to get some food for yourself.'

He smiled attentively. 'Are you quite sure?'

She nodded.

'Very well, my dear. If you're quite sure.'

As he passed along the tables, accepting various titbits served from the buffet onto the two plates he was holding, he eventually found himself in front of the servant who had recognised Isabel. She was offering *vol-au-vents*.

'Your lady-friend looks very grand, sir,' she remarked, placing a *vol-au-vent* on each plate.

'Indeed she does,' Barnaby replied with a tentative smile, but taken aback by such unwarranted familiarity from a servant. 'She happens to be my fiancée.'

'Fiancée, eh? She's to be congratulated then, sir,' the woman went on to declare. 'Done well for herself, so she has, since Gilbert Henderson. Gone up in the world, and no two ways. Give her me compliments, eh, sir? She always was a cut above.'

'Thank you,' Barnaby replied with a nod. 'I'll be sure to tell her.'

Barnaby found Isabel sitting on a chair in the lobby that they had first entered where it was cool. Other people were milling about. He offered her the plate of food he'd obtained, and she thanked him.

'Feeling cooler now?' he asked.

'Yes, thank you, Barnaby.' She gave a great sigh. 'I don't know what came over me.'

'You look a little pale, child. You're hungry, perhaps. Eat up and you'll feel better. Shall I get you more wine?'

'Oh, no thank you. I've had enough wine.'

'One of those women serving food said she remembered you.'

'Oh?' Isabel felt any colour that Barnaby considered she had lost returning to her cheeks at her concern over what the woman might have said.

'She said how lovely you look, and asked me to pass on her compliments.'

'That was nice of her.'

'She mentioned something about a Gilbert Henderson.'

'Gilbert Henderson?' Isabel presented him with a frown of puzzlement.

'Yes. Who's Gilbert Henderson?'

'I have no idea, Barnaby. I don't know any Gilbert Henderson. Nor the woman who mentioned it, whoever she is. There was nobody there that I know.'

'Not even from the Brickfield Hiring Depot? She might have been a former convict.'

Isabel shook her head.

'Well she certainly seemed to know you. She commented on how you'd come up in the world since Gilbert Henderson.'

'Then she must be confusing me with somebody else.'

'Yes, I suppose so,' he agreed.

\- - -

Months passed and Van Diemen's Land was blessed with a fine early summer. Isabel considered herself also blessed inasmuch as she had not conceived. They had been privy to opportunities enabling them to do the delectable things that made conception possible, though only occasionally. Their work, social undertakings, living apart and the responsibilities wrought by children and servants dictated largely what little time they might have to themselves as a couple. In that respect, both looked forward to their marriage and no restriction.

It was decided that once they were wed they would live at first in Isabel's house on Napoleon Street, since Barnaby's was a government-owned property. Later, they would either build their own new house in a more desirable location, or extend Isabel's with its delightful view over Sullivan's Cove and the harbour. They would retain Sarah as a maid until such time as she was in a position to marry, if marriage were ever in the offing.

As the big day drew closer, everybody connected with the couple grew more excited and Isabel herself was becoming nervous, consumed by bridal concerns that all would go smoothly. Her wedding dress was finished and fitted her to a stitch, and both Rhoda and Maisie drooled over its loveliness.

Then, just one week before the wedding, on the Saturday, a letter arrived.

My dear Isabel,

I hope you are keeping well and that your Affairs still prosper. It has been some time since we had a Letter from you, but I suppose you are busy. As for Myself I am well, as are your Sisters but your Father has been Ailing for some Time and fares Worse as time goes on. Doctor Stirling says he has a malignant growth in his Bowels and that his Days on God's Earth are numbered. The poor man is always asking for you, and asking where you are and when you are going to come Home. I beg you therefore to consider returning Home to see him at once to bring him some peace and comfort in his last Days. He always was so devoted to you. Through thick and thin he stood by you and only ever had your best Interests at Heart. He loves you dearly.

Please come home, my dear eldest daughter. I beg you to honour this last request from a man you owe so much to.

Your loving mother
Susan Saxby
PS. Your sisters send their love.

- - -

If her mother meant that leaving Van Diemen's Land for good was a possibility for Isabel, it could never be. Her future was in Hobart Town and she had no intention of returning to live in England. In any case she was about to be married to a wonderful man, a respected government officer of Van Diemen's Land. Between them they already had the makings of a close-knit family, and hoped to have children of their own, who would be raised and educated on the island. A visit to England, mooted so unexpectedly and inconveniently, seemed to be obligatory. The journey would take an age; three months at sea to get there, three months to sail back, plus a reasonable lengthy stay to make the journey to the other side of the world worthwhile.

Only yesterday evening Isabel had watched the arrival of the mail boat and wondered at the hundreds of Hobart Town's citizens that would receive letters, many from England, Scotland, Wales, and Ireland, never imagining for one minute that this time she would be a recipient.

Isabel fretted undecidedly over her letter. What an awkward and thoroughly inconvenient time for it to arrive, just one week before she was to be wed. Sarah had presented it to her when she returned home early with the intention of getting up to date with her accounts. Bills and statements had to be sorted, her bank account reconciled.

As she sat at her bureau, little Polly appeared at the door. Isabel was aware the child had been in the garden playing, enacting the role of a mother with a rag doll, her make-believe baby.

'See what I've got, mama.' By this time Polly had grown used to Isabel's mothering and had slipped into calling her 'mama' of her own accord, and Isabel was not about to correct her, for she loved it.

She looked up from her work with a smile that quickly turned to a frown. The rag doll was no longer in her arms. What the child was embracing looked like a sheaf of prickles. 'Oh, Polly, please get that thing out of here.'

'But he's mine,' Polly pouted with acute disappointment at being denied the pleasure of showing off her new prize. 'I found him in the garden and I want to keep him. He's so sweet.'

'Sweet or not, we don't want the thing inside the house. Please take it outside and put it back where you found it.'

The strange object of Polly's instant affection was an echidna, reminiscent of a hedgehog, but seemingly flattened, thus wider, as well as being larger. The species possesses spines like a hedgehog, but a tubular snout, is docile, waddles ungainly, and is afflicted with thoroughly poor eyesight. Hence Polly had easily caught it.

Isabel realized that to encourage the child to give it up she would have to go outside with her. She rose from her bureau.

'Where did you find the poor thing?' she asked as they stepped into the warm sunshine of the garden.

'Over there.' The child nodded in the appropriate direction as she clung with both arms to her prickly companion.

'It's not because I don't like echidnas,' Isabel claimed as they ambled towards the spot. 'They're sweet creatures, I grant you, but it could have picked up fleas or midges, or anything like that that bites you, and we don't want that sort of thing in the house, do we?'

The dreaded word *fleas*, and what fleas implied, was already instilled into Polly's psyche and, on hearing it, she felt she had no choice but to agree. She duly placed the echidna on the ground and watched it waddle off. Isabel saw the sadness in the little girl's eyes, the delicate, pouting mouth at having to give up the animal, flea-ridden or not.

'Now you must go inside and change your frock, and ask Sarah to give it a scrub to wash away any flees you might have picked up. So off you go, Polly. And when we've had dinner we'll take a walk to the Government Gardens and listen to the band playing. It's such a lovely day. How about that?'

Accordingly, they set off on the trip hand in hand, Polly skipping happily alongside Isabel in a clean frock, the episode with the echidna a distant memory. The Government Gardens were laid out like an English park, with flower beds, lawns, winding pathways and cultivated shrubs, and would have enhanced any of the finest English towns. Well before they came within sight of the circular bandstand they could hear the regimental band playing, the brassy sounds moderated by distance and transit through the still, warm air. Polly looked up at Isabel as she held her hand, and grinned contentedly. A group of regimental officers, dashing in their uniforms, admired Isabel to a man, and she could hardly fail to notice with some satisfaction their handsome moustachioed countenances and smiling eyes fancifully following her. It pleased her that men so obviously appreciated her looks. Following the officers at a virtuous distance, yet conspicuous by their gaiety and colourful clothes, was a group of giggling girls in their late teen years, the daughters of free settlers, patently out to attract the attention of the officers.

Young children yelled as they tumbled about on the springy turf, and Polly watched their antics enviously. Couples promenaded languidly arm in arm as they listened to the band, while respectable married settlers sat on the grass picnicking, their children allowed the freedom to run unrestricted, and making the most of it. Neighbours stopped to chat, while soldiers, waifs, and even male and female convicts in their government clothing who had earned permission to roam, had come along to savour the conviviality and excitement that permeated the Saturday afternoon concert. Inevitably, there were a few people of both sexes who were the worse for drink, for the allure and effects of the blight that was cheap rum had not been entirely eradicated.

'So many people, Polly,' Isabel remarked.

Beyond the Gardens, through the trees, the River Derwent was glistening in the sun's heat as it wound its way majestically through the green wooded valley to Sullivan's Cove and the sea. Isabel and Polly sauntered on hand in hand, relishing it all, and wondered why on earth she would want to leave all this, even though her mother evidently wished it.

It was then that she espied Barnaby with Miranda some distance in front. Polly too, alert as ever, had spotted them and slipped Isabel's guardian hand to race towards them, frantically calling Miranda's name. Barnaby turned around and saw Isabel looking radiant. His eyes lit up as he saw them approach.

'Fancy seeing you here,' Isabel greeted pleasantly.

Barnaby rubbed his nose. 'Well, it being such a beautiful day, we decided we ought to come and listen to the band. I would've suggested us meeting here this afternoon, Isabel, but I imagined you'd be at the shop.'

'I left at midday. As you say, it's such a beautiful afternoon, and Polly needed the distraction to divert her from a poor echidna she'd found in the garden and fallen in love with.'

Isabel turned around, looking for Polly with maternal vigilance. She and Miranda were chasing each other around a tall gum tree and giggling.

'Those two are in their element, look.' She paused a

moment, her thoughts inevitably turning to the problem of her mother's letter, and that she must alert Barnaby to it without delay. 'It's quite convenient happening upon you like this, Barnaby . . . I need talk to you. I need to know what you think. Something's cropped up.' Her expression had changed, and he saw how serious she had become.

'What's the matter? Is there something amiss?'

'I've received a letter from England today . . . From my mother . . .'

'Oh?'

'She wants me to return home at once.'

'Oh,' he said again, this time sounding concerned, and manifesting a frown. 'Why?'

'My father is very ill and his days are numbered, she says. Of course, I had no notion of it. He's suffering from a malignant growth in his bowel according to his doctor. He's asking for me.'

'Oh, dear. The poor man.'

'It's been a while since I heard from them, and I haven't seen them for such a long time – years, in fact . . . I do feel obliged to go, Barnaby. I feel so guilty. I owe my father so much, and they must think I've neglected them both for so long. I really ought to make the trip back to see them, my father especially . . . before it's too late. But what about our wedding?'

'Well . . .' he answered, then pondered the implications for a few seconds. 'Have you written to them telling them you are engaged to be married on the fourth of December?'

'Ages ago, but I reckon my letter and hers must have crossed – somewhere in the Atlantic Ocean, I daresay.'

He looked at Isabel with a mixture of veneration and looming disaster. 'I sense your nobleness coming to the fore.'

'Believe me, Barnaby,' she replied. 'I feel that I really

ought to go. I really owe it to my father. We were awfully close. He educated me. I have that – and more – to thank him for, and I've always adored him. Yet, I realise how awkward it is for you and me . . . just as we are about to be married.'

'I'm inclined to think you should fulfil your obligation as a daughter, Isabel my love,' he answered. 'But not until after we are married . . .'

'So, after we are married, could you not accompany me to England? After all, wouldn't you like to see your own family again?'

'I would dearly love to, Isabel, but it's unlikely I could get leave of absence from my duties here for the months I would be away. It would mean resigning my position, and that I'm not willing to do. It would be sheer folly.'

'Oh, Barnaby . . . Are you quite sure? Now I'm having second thoughts about going at all if you can't come with me. We'll have been just married.'

'Yes, I realise it only too well, my sweet. I'll be in the depths of despair if I have to let you go for biggest part of a year.'

She sighed profoundly, faced with the impossible decision she must make, then said, 'In any case, Barnaby, how would I know what ship to take, where to sail from and when? Do ships sail directly to England from Hobart these days, now that there are no convict ships returning?'

'Believe me, you would not want to travel in a convict ship,' he asserted. 'Even an empty one.' He pinched his nose to illustrate his distaste. 'You would have to sail from the mainland – either Melbourne or Sydney, I suppose. Why don't you let me do some investigating on Monday when I'm at my desk? We'll have information to hand about shipping.'

'Yes,' she said, feeling some relief that she had shared the burden with the man she loved, and he was not without some understanding and sympathy. 'Let's see what arrangements might be on offer and then decide.'

'We'll talk more about it tomorrow, my darling. In the meantime let's enjoy today.'

- - -

Chapter 7

On Monday afternoon, Isabel was in her shop when Maisie Bennett, the younger assistant, crept up to her.

'Mr Micklejohn is heading this way, ma'am,' she said with a whispered smile and a nod in the direction of Liverpool Street. 'I've just spotted him.'

'Oh, good,' Isabel replied blandly. 'He might have some news for me.'

'News, ma'am?'

Isabel smiled at the girl's natural curiosity. 'You'll find out soon enough, Maisie.'

Barnaby Micklejohn entered the shop breezily. He greeted the assistants with a nod and an affable smile as he doffed his hat. Isabel rose to greet him, and ushered him into the tiny back room into which Maisie and Rhoda generally retired for refreshment, and where minor repairs and alterations were effected to articles purchased from the shop.

'So?' Isabel queried expectantly, turning towards him.

'So this is the inner sanctum . . .' He glanced around, taking in the old chairs, the wood stove with its crooked chimney that exited through a back wall to the yard outside; the shelves loaded with the paraphernalia of business, from which hung wire files bearing bills and hand-written advice notes. He noticed the old oak cupboard with its crooked door and its crazed and peeling varnish – a relic from England that had mysteriously found its way into the backroom of this shop in Van Diemen's Land. There was a cast-iron fireplace, a kettle, an earthenware teapot, drinking mugs, a tea-caddy, a tray . . .

'A ship, Barnaby. D'you have any news about a ship?'

'Ah, yes, a ship.' He heaved a sigh. 'As a matter of fact, I do – unfortunately for me. The *SS Great Britain* is indeed anchored presently in Hobson's Bay, Melbourne, and is due to sail for Liverpool on the fourth.'

'The fourth?' she gasped. 'But that's our wedding day?'

'Oh, I know it only too well,' he replied glumly.

'That's no good, Barnaby. Unless we could bring the wedding forward a day or two,' she suggested.

'We might,' he said, but Isabel perceived that he was humouring her, and a significant 'but' was coming. It did. 'But I doubt we could fit it in today, even if we could find a free parson. In any case, you would need to be aboard the *Tasmania* tomorrow when she sails for Melbourne, to be sure of reaching the *SS Great Britain* in good time.'

'So there'd be no chance of us getting wed at all if I decide to leave on this *Great Britain* ship?'

'That's so, I'm afraid, my love.' He sighed again. 'We would have to postpone our wedding till you return – though it breaks my heart to say it.'

'Oh, Barnaby . . . Everything is arranged, down to the last detail. What are we to do?'

'It's your decision, my love.'

'But if I don't go to see my father now it might be too late, and I shall regret it for the rest of my life. Yet if I don't marry you on Sunday as planned I shall regret that as well.'

'But not necessarily for the rest of your life, my love, don't you see? It would mean postponing our wedding, of course, but it would be something for us both to look forward to whilst you are away.'

'But I'll be away for months.'

Barnaby mused privately that this woman's loyalty to her father was indisputable, profound, and heart-breaking too as far as he was concerned, but it was commendable, so he could not denounce it. Nor could he make the decision for her, it was a decision only she could make. Emotionally, it was crippling him to realize that his ardent wish to marry Isabel was being thwarted by her sense of duty towards her parents, despite all the firm wedding arrangements they had made, and despite her own admitted love for him.

'But I can't possibly be ready to leave by tomorrow,' she said.

He smiled, hope renewed that she would not go after all, but he should not discourage her from doing what deep down she believed to be the right thing.

'Well, Isabel, that depends on whether you are set on making the journey or not . . . Think of your father, whom you say is literally dying to see you. And there's not another passenger ship worth mentioning that's sailing for England for some time, according to the schedules we've got.'

'By which time . . .' Isabel whispered, unable to finish the sentence. She clenched her fists in anxiety and frustration. 'What d'you know about this ship, Barnaby, the *SS Great Britain*. I do believe I've heard of it.'

'You might well have heard of it – it's rather famous, in fact – a vast iron ship, steam-powered, fast and quite luxurious by all accounts. It plies the seas between Liverpool and Australia – rather more quickly and more reliably than a mere sailing ship.'

'So how can I book a passage?'

'You can't – until you get to Melbourne. I imagine there would be cabins available. But you can buy a ticket for the *Tasmania* from its master for the voyage to Melbourne.'

'That's a new ship, isn't it – the *Tasmania*?' she queried. 'It's quite big.'

'Yes,' he replied. 'It's also powered by steam as well as sail.'

Isabel sighed profoundly. 'Oh, Barnaby, what should I do?' Tears were misting her eyes. 'I so want to be married to you, to be your wife. It's all I've dreamed of ever since . . . but it seems fate is against us . . . Oh, please *tell* me what to do.'

'Have you thought about Polly and your duty to her?'

'Of course I have . . . One minute I think I ought to take her with me, the next I think it would be a rather selfish thing to do, and that she would loathe being cooped up in a ship for weeks and months. She's very bright and inquisitive, and needs the challenge of learning to occupy herself. Besides, she and Sarah, my maid, get on very well. Sarah will gladly look after her while I'm away.'

'No doubt Polly would miss you, though.'

'I'm sure she would,' Isabel agreed. 'I would miss Polly, too.'

'You have taken to motherhood easily, Isabel,' he commented. 'Caring must be in your nature.'

'I believe I understand children, Barnaby,' she replied, 'and Polly is easy to love and to care for. My life is all the richer because of her. It would hurt me to leave her for so long.'

'Allow me to make a suggestion,' he said.

'Oh, please do, Barnaby,' she implored earnestly.

'Make this trip to see your father, and let us agree to marry as soon as you return.' He held up his hand to stall her from making any comment yet. 'As to Polly, she can live with us. Miranda will be thrilled to have her permanently at her side, and her nanny will not be overwhelmed in the least by the addition of another little girl. That way, Polly wouldn't miss you too greatly, she'll be too absorbed with Miranda.'

'And you would do that for me? And for Polly?'

'I just suggested it,' he replied, smiling his reassurance. 'She's going to be an important part of our family anyway. As to Sarah, your maid, she can either return to the Brickfield hiring depot, or I'll see if I can get her transferred into my charge. She can't accompany you to England anyway, as her status wouldn't allow her to travel with you beyond these shores. Which would you prefer?'

'That she's transferred to your charge, for that's what she'd like best,' Isabel said without hesitation. 'And I think you would have the influence to arrange it. She's a fine servant, Barnaby, and a good cook. I don't think you would regret employing her. I'd much rather she come to you, than risk her being assigned to some uncaring master or mistress elsewhere.'

'Then that's settled.' He took a deep breath; it had been agonising to reach this decision. 'So, Isabel, my love . . . *Honour thy father . . . and thy mother—*'

'That thy days may be long in the land which the Lord thy God giveth thee,' she quoted, interrupting him. 'The fifth Commandment, as I recall. And if it be true then I have no choice – I must go.'

'Then I'll accompany you to the Master of the *Tasmania* and book your passage to Melbourne.'

- - -

Thus, together, they made the agonising decision for Isabel to make the long journey. She was reassured by Barnaby's support, but there was so much to arrange in so short a time. A new trunk she bought was delivered to her house that very afternoon, she called at the bank and withdrew a substantial sum of money to pay for her passage on *SS Great Britain* and all eventualities that might crop up during the trip, including her return fare. She arranged for Rhoda and Maisie to have joint authority to make payments to suppliers out of her trading account, at the ultimate discretion of the bank manager. They were to look after the shop to the best of their ability and put each day's takings into the bank religiously. If all was to her satisfaction when she returned she promised them a handsome bonus. Meanwhile, Barnaby would also look in on them regularly to check that all was in order. Rhoda especially knew the routine, knew what wages to pay themselves, what to order to restock and from whom to obtain it. Isabel had no qualms about entrusting the running of the business to them.

Finally, she ordered a cab to take her and her baggage to the harbour.

- - -

On the day of her departure, Hunter Street Jetty where the *Tasmania* was berthed, was busy with hawkers selling trinkets, while others loaded baskets of food and provisions onto the ship for the voyage.

Barnaby was already at the harbour, waiting to say goodbye.

'So, Isabel, this will be the last time I see you for some time,' he said, turning to walk alongside her towards the *Tasmania*. 'I just want to say . . . before we part . . . that you will be on my mind constantly. But I think you know that already.'

'Please, Barnaby . . .' She felt her eyes flooding with tears and looked down at her feet as she walked, her dainty shoes blurred, appearing and disappearing in turn under her skirts. She felt strangely humble because of this man's devotion. 'It's breaking my heart to leave you for so long, and especially so because we were to be wed in a few days.' She smiled through her tears and looked directly into his eyes. 'So let's take heart that in just a few short months we shall be together again, shall we not? Then, we shall be man and wife before you know what's hit you, and all this will have been forgotten.'

'Well, it can't come quickly enough, Isabel. You're very precious to me, so all I have to look forward to meanwhile is endless waiting.'

'I know, my darling, and it's going to be just the same for me,' she answered softly.

He nodded solemnly. 'Anyway, I've cancelled our wedding arrangements – or rather – I've postponed them. Sarah and Polly are delivering themselves to my house afterwards, as you have instructed them. I'll check your house from time to time as well as the shop. So, you see, my darling, everything is under control. You won't have to worry about a thing.'

'Barnaby . . .' Isabel stopped, and turned to face him, looking into his earnest eyes. She smiled, a smile of sympathy, for she understood just how kind, considerate, noble and self-sacrificing this man was on her behalf. How fortunate she was to have gained his love. 'You'll be in my thoughts too, my darling – always – even though I shall have so much else to contend with besides.' She put her hand on his arm and gently squeezed it. 'I love you so much, Barnaby.'

'And our love will sustain us, my lovely one.' He wrapped her in his arms emotionally. 'Now I wish you *bon voyage*. Enjoy this adventure. I look forward to your return, so please make it as early as you can.'

'Oh, I will, I will.' She placed a kiss succulently on his lips. Then with a gleam in her eyes, said, 'I might even write to you.'

'I sincerely hope you will, Isabel.' He laughed at her flippancy at such a time. 'But you haven't given me the address in England where I can write to you.'

'But of course . . .' She sighed at her oversight. 'I know –

when I get to Melbourne I'll write, and so you shall have it.'

'So till then . . .' They let go each other reluctantly, and with a profound sigh of longing he watched her walk away, his lips tingling from the sensation of her delicious kiss. But for all that kiss, she was now a million miles away from him once more. Despite the finality and success of his *progression* she was still as elusive as ever, for the time being at any rate.

Would she always be so?

A crew member took her baggage and led her to her cabin. She left it untouched, wishing to go back on deck for a last sight of Hobart Town and Barnaby.

It would be a couple of days before she caught sight of Hobson's Bay and the vaunted *SS Great Britain,* which would convey her to Liverpool and the old country, to her poor, sick father, her mother and her sisters. What memories might the return invoke? What traumas? An adventure of some sort it might well turn out to be.

Seagulls wheeled over the *Tasmania* as the three-masted ship sat at its moorings. Like *SS Great Britain* it could use steam power to drive a propeller, or the winds if they were favourable. Men on the quayside eventually slipped the moorings free, and hurled the ropes back onto the deck. The captain must have been anticipating using sail once the ship had reached the open sea, for although smoke was coiling out of the ship's funnel, sailors were already swarming up the masts, as nimble as monkeys. As the ship nosed out from its moorings under steam, the sailors aloft began unfurling the sails. To yells and banter they tightened the ropes as the sails flapped and billowed in the breeze. Isabel watched as the wall of the harbour slid away, and with tears in her eyes looked up to catch a last glimpse of Barnaby waving farewell. More watchers had gathered on the quayside and were waving goodbyes also to the other passengers, but all were becoming gradually smaller as the ship glided away into the vastness of Sullivan's Cove.

Where the gentle River Derwent met the rolling tide of the Tasman Sea, the sails filled with wind and the ship gathered speed, its bow dipping and rising on the increasing swell. Isabel gripped the rail to support herself in this commotion, and recalled her long sea journey to Van Diemen's Land all those years ago, when she had to keep her eyes fixed on the horizon to avoid feeling seasick. She remained on deck for the best part of an hour, mesmerised yet strangely comforted by the persistent rush and roar of the waves against the hull of the *Tasmania*. Had she made the right decision in foregoing her wedding for the sake of her dying father? Heavy-hearted, she was still not sure. Only time would tell. Eventually, chilled by the wind, she decided it was time to go below to her small cabin, and steadied herself against the rolling of the ship as she made her way.

Once in her cabin she sat on the lower of the two bunks and wept.

~ - -

Melbourne, in the recently established Colony of Victoria, was a new town, founded only eighteen years earlier at the mouth of the River Yarra on Port Philip Bay. Because of the gold rush, which began two years or so earlier in 1851, it was rapidly evolving into a thriving, bustling hub for finance and trade.

In the late afternoon of December 2nd, the *Tasmania,* nudged by a gentle breeze, ploughed its way towards the mouth of the Yarra River. Isabel slid out of her bunk, washed and dressed and went on deck, where she watched the mooring up, looking forward to disembarkation.

'You'll need some help with your trunk, ma'am,' a crew member suggested considerately as he approached.

'Thank you, yes. That would be much appreciated,' she replied brightly.

She looked around. There were many other ships berthed, some being loaded, others off-loaded. Cranes swung round, raising and dipping their long arms. Horses stood patiently while the carts to which they were harnessed were being filled or emptied of freight.

The crewman re-emerged with Isabel's baggage, loaded onto a sack truck. She followed him off the ship.

In Hobson's Bay to the east of the river, the *SS Great Britain* was lying majestically at anchor, too big and yet seemingly too distinguished to venture into the confines of the river itself. Its black iron hulk, trimmed with a broad band of white, punctuated at regular intervals by deadlights, was surmounted by two funnels sitting side-by-side, four masts and webs of rigging that looked inordinately complicated.

'Come Sunday, that's the ship I'll be sailing on, bound for Liverpool,' Isabel commented brightly to a woman standing close by.

The woman looked at her and smiled. 'I don't envy you *that* journey, ma'am, even in such a big ship. You're going home to England?'

'Just for a visit. Not for ever. I'll be back.'

'But it's such a long way, just for a visit, my dear. I see you wear no ring. Are you going back home to get wed?'

Isabel laughed at the irony. 'Indeed not. My father is ailing badly, and I feel the need to see him again before it's too late.'

'Then I wish you God speed, my dear.'

'Thank you.'

Isabel dined and slept that night in an hotel at Port Philip Bay. Next morning, the 3rd, she awoke after a fitful night's sleep, and breakfasted before heading to the port in warm sunshine. She had gleaned that the office of Bright Bros & Company, who owned the *SS Great Britain*, was the place to enquire about securing a berth for the voyage. The company's representative told her that cabins were readily available, since only one hundred and ninety-nine passengers had paid for berths so far.

'I would wish to travel first class,' she said. 'Is there a cabin I may have?'

'We call it Saloon Class, ma'am,' was the polite reply. 'And yes, there are Saloon Class cabins available.'

'At what cost?'

'Seventy guineas, ma'am.'

'And is Saloon Class very much better than second class?'

'Are you traveling alone, ma'am?'

'I am.'

'Then for a lady of your obvious breeding and status, ma'am, I would most certainly recommend Saloon Class. It is much more suitable.'

Isabel smiled at the compliment.

'Already in Saloon Class,' the representative went on, 'you will join two doctors and their wives, two parsons and their wives, a Roman Catholic priest, an Anglican priest, various officers from the army, most with their wives, and a baronet. There are other ladies traveling unaccompanied, like yourself, and some with their maids.'

'Very well. Seventy guineas it is.' She opened her reticule and counted out the money.

'The *SS Great Britain* is a fine iron ship, ma'am,' the representative remarked as he counted her money. 'A giant of a vessel. The most comfortable ship ever built.'

'I'm pleased to hear it,' she replied. 'The ship I came out here on was not so comfortable.'

'The *SS Great Britain* has set new standards.'

'What time do we sail tomorrow?' she enquired once she had hold of her ticket.

'That depends on the captain, but I believe eight o' clock in the morning is the intention,' the man replied. 'That being high tide.'

'So shall I be allowed to spend tonight on board before we sail, or must I stay at my hotel?'

'It's preferable to spend the night on board, ma'am. You may embark right now if you wish and settle yourself in.'

'Oh, that's wonderful,' she replied with another disarming smile. 'Then I'll arrange for my things to be ferried out to the ship.'

Having thus secured her passage, Isabel returned to her hotel to retrieve her belongings. Before she left she wrote a loving note to Barnaby, giving him the address of her mother and father in England, and urging him to write frequently. After seeing it safely posted, she left for the port by hansom cab along with her baggage.

The owner of a small ferry boat rowed her and her baggage to the SS Great Britain. She sat at the prow, and the little boat pushed off to the gentle creaking of the rowlocks and the splashing of oars. The ferryman made small talk about her long voyage ahead, but Isabel kept him amiably engaged with questions about the gold rush.

When the ferry got closer to the ship, Isabel was astounded. How anything so big and made of iron – and therefore extremely heavy – could remain afloat seemed astonishing. Soon they were alongside, and their little ferry boat vied for position among others at the platform at the base of the iron staircase, which ascended to the main deck. Besides her fare, she tipped the ferryman a shilling, and this seemed to persuade him to help load her trunk onto the platform. It was taken by a member of the ship's crew, labelled and stacked with others.

On board, the main deck was bustling with crew and visitors, many of whom were on board just to say goodbye to friends and relatives. It was not easy to perceive who was available to help and who was there to hinder. Soon enough Isabel was able to garner the attention of a crew member and show her ticket, whereupon another member of the crew was tasked to escort her to her cabin on the Promenade Deck.

'Shall we travel all the way to England under steam?' Isabel enquired of the man.

'Unlikely, ma'am,' he replied. 'Only if we are otherwise becalmed. With good winds, such as we get across the Southern Ocean, we shall be entirely under sail. We cannot carry sufficient coal to see us all the way to England in any case, without stopping somewhere to take on more, which would be awfully expensive.'

'I see,' she answered. 'And I suppose coal is not so plentiful in other places as it is in England.'

''There are coaling stations on the way if we need them,' he answered. After a pause he said, 'Here is your cabin, ma'am.' He opened the door for her. 'I hope you will be comfortable. Captain Matthews sends his compliments.'

As on the *Tasmania*, the cabin housed two bunk beds, one above the other, but also the luxury of an upholstered sofa, and even a washstand. There was a shelf to accommodate her more frequently used personal items, as well as a mirror, a candle lamp, and a deadlight to allow some natural illumination during daytime. But space was confined. However, she had it to herself, so it was private.

As she set about organising her clothes and everything else she had brought with her, she resigned herself to the depressing monotony of a seriously long voyage. Once settled into the cabin she decided to pass the time by making a brief exploration of the ship. On the weather deck, the crew were loading and penning livestock – sheep, cows, pigs, chickens – which would be slaughtered for fresh meat during the voyage to feed the passengers as the need arose. It sounded and smelt like a farmyard even though the deck was wet, having just been swabbed. On the other side of an iron barrier, groups of third-class passengers stood talking and peering over the side of the ship. It had not struck Isabel till that moment that saloon class passengers would not have exclusive occupancy of the entire deck.

At twelve noon she ventured down to the Saloon Class dining room for lunch, which consisted of hot soup with bread, cold meat and cheese. The dining-room comprised of two rows of tables separated by a broad carpeted aisle interspersed with iron support pillars. All the tables were flanked on either side by upholstered benches. The backrests of the benches could be swung from front to back and *vice versa*, so that when the meal was over, sitters could still sit comfortably facing the centre of the room, to enjoy whatever activity or entertainment had been arranged. Feeling yet strange in this unfamiliar environment, Isabel made no effort to socialise with other passengers, only to assess those passengers also taking lunch.

Dinner was at four o'clock – rather early, Isabel thought – and she found herself sitting opposite an attractive young woman who introduced herself as Ann Carter. Isabel had noticed Ann earlier, and as she also appeared to be travelling alone, struck up a conversation. They talked generalities, while the stewards passed bowls of Scotch broth, plates of roast beef with fresh potatoes and green vegetables to the diners. Isabel merely mentioned she was returning to England to see her family, with no mention of her deferred wedding. Ann, fair haired and pretty and in her mid-twenties, offered no personal history except to say she hailed from Guildford, a town in Surrey.

After dinner, Isabel returned to her cabin and slept a while. When she awoke she saw how the light coming in through her porthole had dimmed, and realised dusk was falling. She roused herself, re-did her hair and wondered if it was suppertime yet. But she did not feel like eating again. Her thoughts inevitably veered towards Barnaby and to Polly. She so ardently hoped that Polly would be happy staying with him and Miranda.

She decided to go up on top to the weather deck once again. But the climate in Melbourne could be mercurial, changing drastically from one hour to another. She breathed in the sharp freshness of the sea. Even though it was summer it had turned chilly, and a stiff breeze was blowing from the south. She shivered as she walked towards the stern, yet that cool December evening was no colder than the chill she felt deep inside.

She looked up at the sky. A crescent moon, hanging low over Hobson's Bay, seemed jaunty and bright compared to her heavy heart. It began its inevitable climb, and a few stars were already shining like pinpricks of light piercing a dark blue and purple backdrop. *Oh, Barnaby,* she said to herself, *what have I done, leaving you so I can visit my father when I should rightly be with you tomorrow for our wedding?* Leaning on the cold handrail she looked out across the bay towards the port. The flickering lights of Melbourne, no brighter than the emerging stars, failed to cheer her. *Barnaby, Barnaby, just what have I done?*

Tears stung her eyes. She must be two or three hundred miles away from him by now, and in two months it would be twelve thousand. He might as well be on that quarter moon that looked all hazy now through her tears. How on earth would she endure the separation? It would be months before she even received a letter from him. Already, she was wishing she had not been so easily influenced by Barnaby's self-sacrificial suggestion, that she embark on the voyage for a final reunion with her father.

She walked slowly over to the other side of the ship. Below, she could discern from the chatter and laughter that people were still embarking. She peered over the side and could make out a ferryboat swaying as two more passengers and their baggage were transferred to the ship, with another boat waiting to off-load. If only Barnaby would take it upon himself to book a passage and join her. Maybe they could be married aboard the ship. Her heart leapt at the thought. If only she had thought of it before . . . But of course he would not come; he could not come because of the children; he had already said it would be folly to give up his career just to make the trip.

Another tear formed and quivered for a moment on her eyelashes before running unchecked down the curve of her cheek. Then, she felt an arm around her and was startled.

'Miss Saxby, are you all right?' Ann Carter said gently. 'I wondered why you hadn't been in for supper, so I took it upon myself to look for you.'

'That's very thoughtful of you, Miss Carter,' Isabel replied. 'Thank you.'

'My goodness, you are weeping, unless I'm very much mistaken. Are you quite sure you are all right?'

Isabel nodded, and another flood of tears trickled down her cheeks.

'You are upset . . . If you want to talk I am perfectly content to listen,' Ann said kindly. 'I believe it helps to talk – that is if you feel like talking.'

'You're very kind,' said Isabel with a great shuddering sigh. 'You see, it was all arranged that I would be married tomorrow to the most wonderful man . . . But just a few days ago I received a letter from my mother in England telling me that my father was dying, and begging me to return home to see him. It was such a difficult choice . . . but I could not refuse her.'

'Oh, you poor dear . . . I understand and I sympathise. And you must be freezing cold . . .' Ann wrapped her new friend in her arms consolingly. 'Miss Saxby . . . Do try not to upset yourself more. I am sure that your fiancé must be feeling equally sad at your leaving him. So I expect everything will work out well.'

'I've only been away from him a couple of days and already I'm missing him,' Isabel blurted. 'What will I be like when I'm on the other side of the world?'

'Don't think about it, Miss Saxby. He'll still be waiting for you when you return, and I'll wager he is as anxious and distressed as you are.' Ann turned Isabel around to guide her back down the stairs to the warmth of the lower decks.

'Please call me Isabel,' Isabel exhorted. 'And trusting you have no objection I'll call you Ann.'

'Thank you – Isabel. As I was saying, don't you think he's missing you just as much as you're missing him?'

'I imagine so. Goodness, I know so. Pardon me, Ann, for being all weepy and pathetic . . . Perhaps I should get off this ship after all and go back to him.'

'And miss this last opportunity to see your poor suffering father?'

'Perhaps not,' she sighed. 'Oh, bother! What should I do?'

'Well, you'll have to decide soon, Isabel. We sail first thing tomorrow.'

- - -

It was after nine when Isabel finally awoke, although she had no notion of the hour. Her bunk was warm and it was comfortable. For a few seconds she was disoriented, waking up in that strange, small cabin. She soon realised where she was, and could hear and feel the throb of the enormous steam engine that was propelling the ship towards the Port Philip Heads. She recalled that she had been in two minds about leaving the ship and returning to Hobart Town by the first available packet. But already they were on the open sea. If she wanted to disembark now, it was too late. She stretched and yawned, then sat up in her bunk before clambering out of it. As her feet found the floor, she tottered due to the gentle rolling of the ship. She stood on tiptoe in her nightdress and peered out of the high deadlight. The south coast of Australia was gently slipping away. There was no turning back now, nothing for it but to resign herself to the anticipated two months at sea and whatever fate had in store.

She was on her way to England.

At once reconciled to her situation, she washed, cleaned her teeth, did her hair, dressed and made her way to the lavatory, of which there were two on that deck in Saloon Class. On her way back she met Ann Carter.

'Good morning, Isabel,' Ann greeted with a concerned smile. 'How do you feel today? You have not been to breakfast yet.'

'Would you believe I overslept?' she remarked, returning the smile. 'Anyway, oversleeping has sealed my fate. Even if I had decided to leave the ship, I woke up too late. We were already at sea.'

'So do you feel a little less sad today?'

'Not in the least. Today was to have been my wedding day.' She sighed profoundly. 'I have to accept that I'm here instead, stuck in this ship somewhere at sea, and the man I love and should be marrying is getting further and further away.'

'Why don't we meet later, Isabel,' Ann suggested kindly. 'We could sit at the stern on the Promenade Deck. It's rather pleasant there. We could get to know each other a little better – if you wish . . .'

Isabel smiled. 'Yes, why don't we? In an hour, say?'

'Yes, in an hour. Meanwhile, are you not going to have breakfast?'

'I don't want breakfast, Ann. I just want to go home.'

Ann patted Isabel's hand sympathetically. 'I'll see you later,' she said and went on her way.

Isabel returned to her cabin, still feeling deeply sorry for herself. Although her chance to leave the ship had passed, she could not cry. Her thoughts were mainly about Barnaby, about Polly, and how much she regretted she was not with them now.

As she sat in her cabin it struck her that feeling morose and melancholy was not going to get her anywhere. She was on board the biggest and most luxurious passenger ship ever built, whether she wanted to be or not. She might as well pull herself together and make the most of it; the two months at sea she had heard quoted as the voyage's anticipated timescale would pass infinitely faster if she did. Better to involve herself with life on board and take advantage of everything it offered. Better to put a smile back on her face. She was Isabel Saxby, a respected woman of some substance, just embarked on a voyage she would doubtless remember for the rest of her life. What was the point in hiding away and feeling sorry for herself? Why not simply enjoy it, exploit it to the full, meet new people? As Ann had said, Barnaby would still be waiting with open arms when she returned home. What was wrong with enjoying herself, even though she was missing him? She simply had to make an effort to push him to the back of her mind. Doing so did not mean she was not in love with him.

So Isabel looked at herself in the mirror, tossed her head proudly, as if to shake off the dejection, and smiled back at herself. Forcing that smile induced a real smile, because she at once appreciated the paradox. Having put on her bonnet, and looking infinitely more presentable, she ventured upstairs and outside to the Weather Deck.

But the Weather Deck was teeming with people who wanted to catch a glimpse of the diminishing Australian coastline as they sailed eastwards across the turbulent waters of Bass Strait. As she held onto the rail on the port bow she stood watching the bays and inlets of the shoreline slowly slip by. The cattle were lowing, the pigs snorting and the fowl clucking, while crew members were busy high among the rigging, unfurling the sails so that they unravelled like great white clouds as they immediately caught the breeze. If the same strong wind persisted it would speed them on their way and preclude any need to use their steam power.

She had no notion of how long she had been standing at the rail, enjoying the morning sunshine and the fresh breeze, which was ruffling the flounces of her skirts and the ribbons of her bonnet, when she was aware of a man at her side. She glanced at him, caught his curious gaze, and her heart lurched.

- - -

Chapter 8

'It *is* Isabel Saxby, is it not?' the man asked, raising his hat.

Isabel Saxby's heart pounded with a jolt at seeing a man whom she had never expected to see, ever again. Scarcely able to believe he was so incomprehensibly at her side, she felt hot, and her legs began to tremble under her skirts. It was simply impossible that he, of all people, should be on the same ship as she, that he was even present in the southern hemisphere; last time they saw each other they were both on the other side of the world.

'Robert . . .' She spoke his name in a husky whisper, almost breathless with surprise, shaken with emotion. Her throat was suddenly dry. Her heart had started thumping remorselessly.

'Isabel . . . I cannot believe it's you,' he said, 'and judging by the look on your lovely face, nor can you believe it's me standing beside you.'

'Oh, my goodness! This is such a shock.' She was shaking and felt bewilderingly self-conscious, and tongue-tied. 'I . . . I really don't know what to say to you,' she managed to utter honestly, shaking her head and instinctively inching away from him along the deck's handrail. 'You are the very last person . . .'

'For me also . . . But how *wonderful* to see you, Isabel.'

'Is it?' she replied contemptuously, still trying to recover. 'It's certainly a surprise to see you.'

'I know, but who would have thought it?' There was an

earnest look in his eyes. 'It's been so long . . . so ridiculously long . . . But you look simply capital, so beautiful – and so well.'

'It's good of you to say so,' she answered, for want of something less shallow to say in her perplexity and disdain.

'But it's true . . . You are far more beautiful than ever you were. I only remember you as a girl in your teen years, but now you are a woman. Oh, Isabel, it's been so long . . . and so much has happened in the meantime. You cannot imagine how often I have wondered about you. Ye gads . . . All those years . . . All those years I've wondered where you were, how you were, what you were doing . . . And all the time you've been flourishing. Oh, this cannot be real, Isabel . . . you, standing before me – out of the blue – like an ethereal visitation – yet in the most unlikely of circumstances. I am pinching myself – look – I am – to make sure that this is really happening and not just a dream.'

'I can scarcely believe for a minute, Robert, that you have ever wondered about me,' she said, her scorn becoming evident in her tone, fuelled by a re-awakened pain.

'I cannot blame you for thinking as much, but nevertheless it's true. You are the last person in the world I expected to see – ever again.'

'And *you* are the last person in the world *I* expected to see – ever again,' she responded.

'Yet we are sailing on the same ship as each other back to England. How strange is that? Could this be the most fortuitous coincidence in the history of man, or pre-ordained by some higher authority? Please tell me you are finally returning home . . .'

'My father is dying,' she stated economically. 'I am on a visit to see him before it's too late.'

'I'm sorry to hear it. I recall your father well. A fine man.'

'As you say, a fine man.'

'Pardon me for saying so, Isabel, but it's as obvious as the pretty nose on your face that you are as surprised to see me as I am you. I get the distinct impression that you are not amicably disposed towards me, which is upsetting.'

Isabel rolled her eyes. 'How perceptive of you, Robert. But why should that surprise you? If you want the truth, long years of considering my past has convinced me that I should only ever feel indifference towards you.' There, she'd said it. But her indifference was ebbing even as she spoke; he was so much more manly now, so much more mature than the youth she had known, and so much more desirable.

'Oh, dear God, how I hate indifference,' he sighed. 'If you will permit me to say this, Isabel, we have, I suggest, a great deal to talk about, quite some ground to cover, maybe some things to explain, certainly some things to apologise for.'

'I have nothing to apologise for, Robert. Absolutely nothing.'

'I agree, you have not. Yet perhaps *I* have. If not only for myself then perhaps for my family. This could be an opportunity for me to make amends.'

'You . . . your family . . . Who else? Perhaps you would like to make a list.'

'But so much has happened since last we saw each other, Isabel. Not just for me, but for you as well. Would you deign to join me at dinner? I would relish the opportunity to speak at length with you. We do, after all, have a lot to talk about, a lot to reminisce about.'

'Don't you think there's a lot best forgotten too,' she countered pointedly. 'But, yes, Robert, I will sit with you at dinner, if only to give vent to the frustration, the distress and regret I have suppressed all these years, and so lay a few ghosts. I cannot promise that I shall be particularly scintillating company.'

He smiled, a smile that sent her heart beating fast, as it always used to. 'Thank you, Isabel. That's a start at least. If I can only raise a smile from you. You always did have the most enchanting smile.'

'Well, I can't promise you a smile either.' And yet she unwittingly smiled all the same.

'There . . . you see what I mean?' he said. 'Thank you . . . But I still cannot believe you are on board the same ship as me.'

'Nor can I,' she answered. 'Regrettably, I am. And so we shall both be for the next couple of months. I suppose I shall have to come to terms with it.'

'It might be difficult trying to avoid each other, so I hope you will not go out of your way to avoid me.'

\- - -

At the appointed time, Isabel met Ann Carter who was wearing a fashionable green dress with broad flounces edged with white lace, buttoned to the waist and with ruched sleeves, as well as the warm smile Isabel had already come to associate with her. She had not yet, however, decided whether this was the sincere smile of a well-wisher or that of a potential antagonist. Yet that might have had more to do with her own mood, and the after-effects of meeting Robert.

'Let us sit down, Isabel, before we keel over,' Ann suggested as the ship rolled gently.

Isabel laughed. 'Goodness, that would be a sight – us keeling over in our crinolines.'

'Aren't you hungry since you've had no breakfast?'

'Not in the least. I seem to have lost my appetite.'

'Oh dear. Still languishing for your lovely Barnaby?'

'I daresay I'll be languishing a while yet. I shall look to you to cheer me up.'

'Well, I'll do my best.'

'I've just had rather a shock, Ann – quite some shock to tell you the truth – so I apologise if I seem a little preoccupied.'

'What sort of a shock?'

'A man I used to know. I knew him very well . . .' Tears welled up in her eyes, and she tried to stem them, for she had no wish to weep over Robert Wilson. 'He's on this ship. We encountered each other half an hour ago.'

'By the look of you, he's obviously had quite some impact on your life.'

'Yes, quite some.' Isabel wiped away her tears.

'Do you feel like unburdening yourself?'

'Yes, Ann, I think perhaps I do, if you care to listen.'

'I assume he's an erstwhile lover?'

Isabel nodded sombrely. 'I've agreed to sit with him at dinner. Against my better judgment.'

'You do know that the table at which you first sit is supposed to be the table at which you will dine for the rest of the voyage?'

'Well, I shall not necessarily oblige the local rules,' Isabel suggested. 'I shall sit wherever I choose, whenever I please.'

'That's the spirit. But dining with your erstwhile lover might be quite fun, had it not?' Ann suggested, her eyes twinkling mischievously.

'Fun?' She sniffed, and dabbed her eyes again with her kerchief. 'I doubt it will be fun. It will bring back too many painful memories.'

'You were in love with this man?'

Isabel nodded. 'Oh, madly. Dangerously. I was also too young . . . Headstrong, too. Oh, and very naïve.'

'And now you're more sagacious?'

'Sagacious? What a lovely word. Yes, I'd like to think I'm more sagacious in my advancing years.'

'You're also at an age when you can turn the tables, Isabel. If he loved you once, chances are that his love can be easily rekindled. Let's face it, you are a lovely-looking woman, and so elegant too. You turn heads, even women's heads I've noticed. I imagine you could lead him a merry dance if you chose to. So enjoy your dinner with him, that's my advice, and don't give in to any inclination to be vindictive.'

'I'm not the vindictive type, Ann. I don't seek revenge. I've already told him I'm simply indifferent now. And with good reason. But seeing him again after all these years . . . he's so much more a man . . .'

'So you are not as indifferent to him as you have claimed, Isabel?'

'The moment I first saw him all memories of the past came flooding back and I did feel indifferent – but also tormented, and resentful. I've always been inclined to believe that people think what they say, and say what they think. Now I don't know . . . What should a woman do or say when she is indifferent to a man, or resentful, or tormented?'

'Tell him that he is a delightful creature, that he is a most excellent person, and you have the greatest respect for him, and let him see that you are delighted he's invited you to dinner.'

'But I showed no enthusiasm for it. I only agreed so I could express my pent-up angst.'

'Then maybe he has seen through you already, Isabel. Because, if a woman feels indifference and angst for a man, it means she cares for him, or has cared for him. Do you want to tell me about him?' Ann's curiosity was increasing relentlessly.

'I'm not sure that I know you well enough.' Isabel smiled to soften the comment. 'That's not to say I won't ever, or that I don't want to know you well . . . Anyway, come dinnertime I might be ready for some food, unless I am seasick in the meantime, which is likely with the movement of the ship.'

'Oh, this is nothing. This is tranquil. I'm told it will get worse the further east we go. The roaring forties and the howling fifties are noted for their rough seas and high winds. The tour around Cape Horn is said to be quite rough.'

'You seem well-versed in nautical affairs.'

'Nautical affairs?' Ann laughed and rolled her eyes as if recalling some event.

'Why are you laughing?'

Ann put a hand on Isabel's arm. 'Well, now, Isabel . . . If you wish to talk of nautical affairs . . . As applied to you, I understand well enough that you are languishing over the separation from your fiancé, and that you are shocked to the core at seeing an erstwhile lover so close at hand. So an affair on board the ship might well be the best thing for you. It's my experience that a shipboard romance is a sure way of taking your mind off pining for your loved one. A nautical affair with this man might be just the medicine for you. A little flirting and a stolen kiss or two don't necessarily have to amount to a commitment or anything permanent, but can be a delightful distraction. And it seems you have met the perfect man already for such a delicious escapade, especially if you have already been lovers and he is still drawn to you.'

'Goodness, Ann! What *are* you suggesting? That I betray my poor Barnaby as soon as his back is turned? I couldn't.' She shook her head. 'I wouldn't be able to live with myself.'

'But what harm is there in it?' Ann suggested. 'Why would we want that mischievous little archer Cupid to be idle aboard this ship? Your Barnaby is not to know anyway . . . And besides, you wouldn't be the first woman to enjoy a little unofficial dalliance – it's not so uncommon, and no wonder. Best of all, it would certainly help take your mind off your Barnaby.'

Isabel remained silent for a few seconds, pondering her new friend's words, while hearing the creaks and groans of the ship. 'Have you, Ann? Ever?' she asked eventually. 'Have you ever had an unofficial dalliance, as you so quaintly put it?'

'Since you ask, yes, I confess I have. On board this very ship. And very pleasant it was too.'

Isabel was wide-eyed with astonishment at this surprising revelation, and Ann chuckled in turn at Isabel's reaction.

'Are you shocked?' she asked.

'No, not shocked, Ann. Nothing shocks me. Not anymore. But I don't know whether to applaud you or disapprove. So do tell me more, now that you've admitted to it, then I can make my mind up.'

'Oh, but I'm not sure I know you well enough, Isabel,' she remarked with a smile.

'*Touché*!' Isabel laughed, appreciating her own comments thrown back at her.

'But I'll tell you anyway. It might cheer you up.'

'Oh, please do, Ann. I love a good story. Then I'll tell you mine.'

'In that case . . .' She shuffled on the seat and drew closer to Isabel so as not to be overheard by other passengers. 'I came out to Melbourne on this very ship with my two brothers when it left Liverpool in August. My husband—'

'You're married?' Isabel exclaimed in amazement.

'Oh, yes, I'm married.'

'Well . . . *Mrs* Carter . . . And do you have children?'

'Not so far.'

'But you're not wearing a wedding ring.'

'Why should I indeed? A wedding ring on a woman's finger tends to put off potential wooers.'

'So, do you intend having another shipboard fling?'

'I am not averse to a little romance, Isabel, if there's somebody worthwhile I could enjoy a little romance with. I don't claim to be a saint, having abandoned all wifely saintliness when I left England. Anyway . . . as I was about to tell you . . . I came home one day after an afternoon with some friends, to find my husband and one of our maids in his bedroom, both in a state of undress, and their arms and legs intimately entangled.'

'Oh, you poor, poor thing. Were you angry? Devastated? Heart-broken?'

'Angry, yes. Devastated, no. Heart-broken – not really. Just disappointed.'

'So, did you leave him?'

'We still live together, but he doesn't visit my bed anymore. I have forbidden him.'

'Have you forgiven him, though?' Isabel asked.

'Yes, somewhat, but he doesn't know that yet. Naturally, he was full of remorse, said what a complete fool he'd been. But unbeknownst, a remedy was looming that would separate us for a while.' Ann paused and sighed. 'You see, I come from a brewing family, and my two enterprising younger brothers decided to start a brewery in Australia. A land of opportunity, they said. There would be so much organization required, what with arranging for all the equipment and ingredients that are necessary for producing beer in commercial quantities, that they thought I could be a great deal of help to them, having worked helping in our father's business. The opportunity was a godsend – because it would allow some breathing space between me and my husband.'

'And your husband was prepared to let you go all the way to Australia, and be away from him for months on end?'

'He really had no choice. He agreed that we needed time away from each other if we were to be eventually reconciled. In the meantime, it's highly likely he has found our replacement maid quite entertaining. She's not unattractive either.'

'And you don't mind if he does?'

Ann shrugged. 'If he does, he does, and that will settle it. But he's still married to me. And what's good for the gander is good for the goose, as I see it.'

'And I thought *I* was open-minded . . .'

'Anyway, I met a man on board this ship on the journey out,' Ann revealed. 'A sweet man, and I think he was quite taken with me. It was quite delectable. He was a young clergyman, of all things, about to take up a living at Sydney Cove.'

'A clergyman?' Isabel repeated incredulously, laughing like a bell. 'Ann, you are the absolute limit . . . Well, I think I applaud you after all. I never heard of anything so mouth-wateringly scandalous. It's lovely.'

'You see, Isabel, it's not always the hero or the genius that wins a woman's attention, it's the man who is there on the spot, and available.'

Isabel laughed. 'I suppose that's true.'

'So bear it in mind. Anyway, I'm glad you approve of my unofficial dalliance. Of course, nothing could come of it, not that either of us wanted it to, but it really was enchanting all the same . . . while it lasted.'

'Was he married?'

'No, he was a bachelor. Had he been wed I'm sure he would have been too virtuous to make me an adulteress or himself an adulterer,' Ann declared with a twinkle in her eye.

'Unlike your husband then.'

'Yes, quite unlike my husband. I'm presuming that.'

'You see? You should have waited and married the clergyman,' Isabel suggested, tongue in cheek.

'And end up in obscurity in some tedious parish in the Australian outback?'

'But he might have become a bishop eventually, had you married him and been behind him,' Isabel suggested.

'Oh, no, Isabel. He would never have been suitable to rule over a See, though he was quite perfect for kissing and all that . . . He had beautiful eyes,' Ann added.

'Did he conduct any services while he was aboard the ship?'

'Apart from services on me, you mean?' Ann asked frivolously.

Isabel laughed at her candour. 'No, I mean did he preach?'

'Yes, he preached,' Ann confirmed. 'But I don't remember his sermons at all. I only remember his delightful kisses – and his beautiful eyes.'

'And did you arrange to see him after you left the ship?'

'Of course not. He and his toe-curling kisses were destined to remain just a fond memory.'

'So how did you hide this affair from your brothers?' Isabel asked, fascinated.

'I didn't.'

'But didn't they disapprove?'

'Not they. They knew of my situation. They know my husband. They turned a blind eye, which I thought was very considerate.'

'Was there any possibility that you might be with child by this clergyman?'

Ann shrugged. 'I'm not carrying a child, nor was I.'

And so they chatted on, warming to each other. In return, Isabel gave an account of her life in Hobart Town. She told Ann about her friend Catherine and how her death required her to become Polly's ward, and how her relationship with Barnaby Micklejohn progressed to the point of arranging their marriage.

'Shall you go in for supper tonight?' Ann enquired. 'Or dally with your rediscovered erstwhile lover?'

'No, I think it might be fitting to feign indifference a little longer and leave my erstwhile lover, as you call him, to his own devices after dinner.'

'Then meet me for supper and we'll talk more.'

Isabel smiled. 'Very well, Ann. Supper. I shall look forward to that.'

\- - -

Isabel entered the dining room for dinner wearing a plain sky-blue dress made of silk that emphasised the colour of her eyes and contrasted with her dark hair. It was unadorned, without frills and fussiness, but it revealed her bare shoulders and a hint of cleavage, where hung a white pearl necklace. Many eyes followed her as she swept through. Ann, already seated in the dining room and conversing with a young couple, saw her appear and understood that she had dressed to impress and perhaps even provoke her escort. Their eyes met, and Ann flashed a smile of approval.

Robert was already seated on the opposite side of the room to Ann, his back towards her, and with a broad smile he stood to greet Isabel.

'You look ravishing, Isabel.'

'Thank you,' she replied, as if they were complete strangers.

He took her hand and handed her onto the bench-like seat facing him.

'Would you like a drink? An aperitif? Wine, perhaps? Sherry? Port? Madeira?'

'Thank you,' she said again. 'Perhaps a dry sherry. I'm sure they will have dry sherry on board.'

He caught the attention of a steward and requested two schooners of dry sherry. Bottles and decanters were stored in a rack attached to the wall behind the tables. The steward retrieved a bottle and poured two glasses, and Robert thanked him.

Isabel scanned the room, filling with diners – an odd assortment of characters she thought – but nobody had yet decided to sit near them.

'When did you board the ship, Robert?' Isabel enquired. 'You weren't at dinner yesterday, leastwise you weren't while I was in here.'

'I boarded late last evening,' he answered.

'So what brought you to Australia in the first place, so far from home?' She was sounding more amenable now. 'The gold rush?'

'Not the gold rush *per se*, but something that's proved relevant to it,' he answered, then took a sip of sherry. 'Over the past few years I've become involved in the world of banking. I've been advising the Union Bank of Australia regarding the interests of investors in the new Geelong and Melbourne Railway Company. I'm an investor myself and I have a rather large interest in it. That's why I've been in this strange, far-off land.'

'And your wife was not without some misgivings at letting you out of her sight for so long?' Isabel suggested, at which Robert seemed that he was about to interrupt her, but did not. 'I presume it was Elizabeth Hulme you married?' she continued. 'At least I always assumed you would marry her.'

'Yes, I married Elizabeth,' he said, lowering his eyes before looking directly into hers again. 'But Elizabeth died two years after we married.'

'Oh, Robert, I am sorry to hear that,' she replied sincerely. 'Of course, I had no idea. How did she die?'

'In childbirth. It would have been our first child. The child was stillborn. Of course, the difficulty encountered in the birth caused her death.'

'That must have been a difficult time for you,' Isabel said sympathetically.

'It was.'

The steward returned, asked what they would prefer to eat from the menu.

When he had left them, Isabel said, 'That must have been some years ago. Have you not remarried?'

'No, Isabel, I have not remarried. I am my own man now. You see, my father also passed away, some seven years ago.'

'I didn't know that either. But your father was awarded a baronetcy, I understand.'

'How on earth did you hear about that, so far away as you are?'

'From a friend in Hobart who worked in the civil service back in London.' She saw no reason to mention Barnaby by name, or give any clue as to who he was at this point.

'Yes, it's true. He became Sir George Wilson, Bart.'

'So . . . since the eldest son of a baronet inherits the title from his father, you must now be *Sir* Robert Wilson?' Isabel deduced.

He smiled. 'For my sins, yes. In polite society I am turned by that handle these days.'

So he's the baronet she was told would be a fellow passenger aboard the ship, she thought. 'The lord of the manor,' she remarked. 'And with time on his hands, by the sound of it.' And more money than he knows what to do with, was her next thought.

Money . . . He was involved in banking . . . She was about to thank him for the money he was sending to her bank account every year. Indeed, for setting up that bank account in the first place which, once she was informed of it, was a complete surprise to her. It had to be his doing. However, it was too soon yet to make any such comment, for she had no wish to feel beholden to him – which she would if she acknowledged it.

'And you,' he said, looking into her eyes intently. 'I see no wedding ring. Have you not married?'

She cast her eyes down so that she was peering into the depths of her sherry schooner. 'No, not yet,' she replied softly.

'Not yet? Is there a suitor? Hang it all, there has to be a suitor – a woman like you.'

Isabel sighed and looked at him squarely. 'I was due to be married today, as a matter of fact.'

'Today?'

'Yes, today.'

'Is the lucky man on board this ship?'

She smiled sadly. 'No, he's still in Hobart Town. We had to postpone our wedding because of my need to return to England to visit my father . . . and the fact that this ship was the only one immediately available for the journey.'

'Well, well,' he mused. 'So today was to have been your wedding day . . . Fancy that!'

'Please don't make it harder for me by dwelling on it, Robert, or making light of it.'

'Isabel . . . I am sorry to learn that you have sacrificed

your wedding day so that you could visit your father in England . . . If I'd had my way things would have turned out quite differently for both of us. It was my intention to marry you. I appreciate that after what happened you must regard me, my family and the entire household with some animosity, some rancour.'

'To put it mildly . . .' She sighed. 'But I got over it – eventually. I was naïve in those days. We were both so young. I accepted long ago that Fate had intervened, that things didn't turn out anything like I wanted them to, but for a good reason.'

'I blame my mother and father,' he stated. 'I blame the gentry that always sticks together to protect itself.'

'Not yourself?'

'Myself as well, yes . . . to some extent. I could not be with you when you needed me most, but in my defence I was not aware of the situation. Since then I've had ample opportunity to reflect on things. I was a callow youth at that time. Life had not hardened me to its grim realities. I suppose I was swept along on a tide of events over which I had no control. But I want you to know, Isabel, that I never stopped loving you. I never have. There have been other women . . . Yet never a day goes by that you are not in my thoughts at some point . . . The passage of time has made me realize that I should have been spending the rest of my life with you, no matter what. Being with you again – here – now – so unexpectedly, has rekindled the flame in my heart. Seeing you again has turned my whole world upside down, breathed new life into it in the space of just a few hours. This entire afternoon I have relived those delectable times we shared. Nor will I ever forget them. They are etched on my memory, and will be till my dying day.'

A pretty speech, she thought, but replied, 'As I said, Robert, events and society – even Fate – dictated a somewhat different destiny for us two. Maybe we should simply heed destiny and accept it. My life has turned out rather beautifully. I have no need whatsoever to try and recapture what might have been. My future is already assured.'

'Then I envy you, Isabel . . . But do you remember the day we met?' he asked.

'Distinctly,' she replied, with a smile that was spontaneous.

- - -

Chapter 9

28 June 1838
Worcestershire, England.

By noon on that auspicious Thursday, the mist that had been shrouding the grounds of Patchfield House had thinned to a blue haze, allowing the cedars in front of the lake to stand out in dark, dignified contrast. By the time the folk from the local villages appeared an hour later the sun had burst through triumphantly. The movement of air, which could scarcely be called a breeze, caused the union flag, hitherto flying proudly from the roof of the house, to droop languidly in defiance of the celebration; for this day proclaimed and celebrated the coronation of Her Majesty Queen Victoria.

George Wilson, Member of Parliament for Worcestershire North, had thrown open his sixty acres to the villagers of Tibberton, Spetchley and Crowle, and was treating them to roast beef, potatoes and cabbage, followed by plum pudding, to be helped down with beer brewed at the hall. Various make-shift tables and chairs had been arranged on one of the lawns for the purpose of dining. This is not meant to imply that George Wilson was by nature a generous person, for he was not. He was, nevertheless, a very wealthy person, whose riches came by way of the Hudson's Bay Company.

George Wilson had fathered four children, ranging from his son, Robert who was nineteen years old, down to the youngest, a daughter Henrietta who was five years old.

George had ably helped to arrange the festivities at Patchfield House, which included games on the lawn, a tug-of-war, skittles, a Punch and Judy show for the children, and even a game called French cricket. A small brass band had also been engaged.

Positioned near the entrance to the house and grounds to greet visitors, Robert's attention was drawn to an exceedingly pretty dark-haired girl aged about fifteen or sixteen. She was accompanied by two younger girls and presumably their mother and father. He raised his hat and smiled at this exceedingly pretty girl, who blushed as she smiled back coyly. To make an impression on the young dark-haired beauty he detained the family in an overly long welcome, informing them of the fun on offer and that a roast beef dinner with mustard, pickles, home-baked bread and salt would be served by house servants at about two o'clock, and fireworks during the evening. When Robert finally let them pass, under pressure to greet the increasing throng of other visitors, the exceedingly pretty girl turned round to confirm her initial opinion that he was an exceedingly good-looking young man, who was so polite and friendly with his bright, sparkling eyes.

So for the first time in her life, this pretty girl entered the grounds of Patchfield House. The house itself was an edifice of Georgian opulence. Its Palladian façade dominated the sweep of a trimmed lawn on which a marquee and a makeshift bandstand stood. She had suddenly been thrust into a new, wide world of placid waters, formal gardens, a walled-kitchen garden, and green parkland populated with magnificent oaks, cedars and beeches, beneath whose shade early arriving villagers were already standing gossiping in groups.

At two o'clock everybody was urged to sit down at the tables, and George Wilson MP, full of his own grandeur, delivered a short speech venerating Her Majesty. Then he called upon the local rector to say grace. Eating began in earnest, and the band played while everybody chewed their roast beef and cabbage and swigged their beer. After the plum pudding, servants delivered pipes and tobacco to the tables for the men, re-filled glasses with ales specially brewed for the occasion, and poured out more ginger beer for the children. Led by the band, everybody rejoiced in singing a few songs. When he had heard enough of the singing George Wilson MP stood up and proposed the Queen's health, which provoked an enthusiastic cheer. The band duly struck up the national anthem and everyone stood to the best of their ability.

It was after the food had been served and consumed, and the singing had finished that the exceedingly pretty dark-haired girl was struggling to teach her younger siblings the rudiments of pall mall, a game the rules of which she herself was not quite certain, when Robert appeared.

'Pardon me, miss, but may I join your game?' he called from the edge of the particular lawn on which they were standing. His handsome face bore a disarming smile that made the girl's insides churn. 'I'm rather fond of pall mall,' he added.

'I'd be glad if you would,' she called back politely, her complexion instantly taking on the hue of a poppy. 'Perhaps you can set us straight on the rules.'

'It's quite simple really.' He walked towards them casually. 'The blue and the black balls play against the red and the yellow ones. The first side to get both of their balls through all of those hoops laid out on the ground – and hit the peg at the end – is the winner.'

'Thank you, I thought it was something like that,' she said with a broad smile that showed her beautifully even teeth. 'But I wasn't sure how the coloured balls were paired.'

'The best way to learn the game is to play it,' he said with unassailable logic, and looking directly into her eyes. 'Would you agree to a suggestion that you play with one of your sisters and I play with the other?'

She smiled radiantly. 'Oh, that would be lovely.'

'Excellent. I am Robert Wilson, by the way. What's your name?'

'Isabel Saxby. These are my sisters Kitty and Daisy.'

Kitty and Daisy looked on, in awe of this Robert Wilson – who was handsome even to their young eyes.

'You two go first,' Robert suggested brightly. 'I am sure you'll do very well.'

They each smiled at him in admiration, took a mallet and, with girlish giggles of self-consciousness, Kitty awkwardly struck a ball. Throughout the proceedings they laughed, feeling exquisitely at ease with Robert Wilson, and thoroughly enjoyed the game. So they agreed on another.

When they had finished, the two younger siblings went haring off to find their mother and father. Robert and Isabel lingered however, wandering what ruse to employ next to detain each other.

'I wonder, Miss Saxby,' he began, unsure of himself, 'whether you might enjoy a stroll with me around the lake, and maybe the gardens?'

'I'd love to,' she replied sincerely. 'But I ought to let my mother and father know where I am first.'

'Of course. Perhaps I should ask their permission.'

So, they sought William and Susan Saxby, and found them in conversation with some neighbours.

'Papa, this is Mr Robert Wilson . . .' Isabel interrupted.

'Ah, Mr Wilson,' William Saxby greeted with a deferential bow. 'We meet again. The day seems to be going well, sir. Everybody is enjoying the party.'

'Thank you, Mr Saxby, yes. It seems to be a huge success. But such an auspicious occasion as the coronation of our queen cannot be marked without some form of celebration.'

'Indeed, it is perfectly fitting, sir.'

'I . . . er . . . have been teaching your daughters how to play pall mall, Mr Saxby, and I have asked Isabel to accompany me for a walk around the lake and the gardens – subject to your approval of course. I would deem it a signal honour, sir, if you were to give me your permission to do so.'

'By all means,' William Saxby agreed, and glanced at his wife to gauge the extent of her approval at the eminent young man's apparent interest in their daughter. It was confirmed with a smile and a nod.

'Be sure not to get cold, our Isabel,' her mother counselled. 'Shall you be warm enough as you are?'

'Yes, mama,' Isabel replied, impatient to be away from parental authority for the first time in her life. 'It's a lovely warm day. I'll see you in a little while.'

So Isabel ambled alongside Robert while her mother and father watched them go, flashing knowing but anxious looks at each other. Perhaps this young Robert Wilson, heir to George Wilson MP, Patchfield House and the rest of his entire estate, might ultimately be well out of reach of their lowly daughter, but if this was typical of her potential to attract a husband of some standing, then her future must be bright.

'I presume you live hereabouts, Miss Saxby?' Robert asked.

'I live in Crowle.'

'Crowle? I've seen you before, you know, when I've been driving our gig. One does not forget a girl as pretty as you in a hurry.'

She flushed again. 'It's truly kind of you to say so, Mr

Wilson,' she replied, 'but I'm sure there must be much prettier girls around.'

'If so, I've not yet had the pleasure of encountering any. I've not encountered your father before today, either.'

'Perhaps because my father is a schoolmaster in Worcester. Although it's possible you could have seen him travelling to and from Worcester at some time.'

As she spoke, Robert was discreetly studying her. This girl was the essence of femininity and grace, youthfully slender and perfectly proportioned in her white muslin frock with its fashionably abundant sleeves. Her complexion, shaded as it was by her straw bonnet, appeared as translucent as porcelain, her wide blue eyes were as clear as crystal and framed by long dark lashes. The skin of her elegant neck looked invitingly smooth, and her lovely mouth was obviously formed to give and receive the most delicious kisses.

'It's possible you might have noticed me before, Mr Wilson,' she remarked, 'but I confess I have never seen you before.'

'Please call me Robert.'

She laughed diffidently. 'Thank you – Robert. Please call me Isabel.'

'Isabel . . . Such a pretty name.' He smiled, as if an amusing thought had just struck him. 'And in the form of a question.'

'A question?' She looked at him perplexed. 'How do you mean?'

'As in, Isabel necessary . . . is a bell necessary? D'you see? Is a bell installed in the tower? You do see, don't you?'

She laughed again and rolled her eyes with embarrassment. 'Yes, I see. I'd never thought of it before. But now you make me self-conscious of my name.'

'Please don't take it so. Isabel is a lovely name and it suits you. A beautiful name in fact, for a beautiful girl.'

She blushed again at the compliment. 'Why don't you tell me about yourself?' she suggested, in an attempt to divert his attention.

They were ambling beneath rustling oaks and cedars alongside the lake. The foliage produced dappled sunlight that fell in shifting highlights onto the grass on which they were walking.

'I suspect I'm rather boring actually,' Robert claimed modestly. 'Nothing much to tell. I went to the Shrewsbury School and now I'm at Cambridge.'

'And what do you do at Cambridge, Robert?'

'I study mathematics – at the university.'

'Oh,' she said brightly. 'That must be interesting.'

'Hardly that. But life is not all boring there, thank God. It can be quite a jolly jape at times, especially with the various pranks we play to keep us entertained. I shan't go back there now till the beginning of the next semester . . .'

'Do you have any brothers and sisters?' Isabel asked, changing tack.

'Yes, I have a younger brother, Alfred, who is still a boarder at the Shrewsbury School, and two little sisters, Charlotte and Henrietta. Charlotte is seven and Henrietta is five.'

'Are your sisters here today?'

'They are. Would you like to meet them?'

She gasped at being honoured with such a surprising invitation. 'Oh, that would be lovely, if it's possible.'

'Then you shall.'

'But where?'

'Inside the house, of course.'

'Inside the house?' Isabel queried with disbelief. Was she really to be allowed inside that great mansion?

'Well, that's where they'll be. Mother considered them

too young to be out of doors with so many strange people about, many of whom she thought might be unruly and uncouth and in their cups. They don't have a governess at present to be with them, you see, so they aren't allowed. But first, let's finish our walk.'

As they ambled, Robert explained that Patchfield House was built at the turn of the century. 'It replaced an old, moated manor house. The cost of building it bankrupted the then owner, and my father bought it in 1820. The moat had been partly filled in, but my father had the part that remained vastly extended, so that it now forms the lake around which we're walking.'

'So this was going on when you were still a child,' Isabel suggested.

'Just so.' He smiled appealingly.

They arrived at the end of the lake where it met the original moat, and walked along a strip of grass alongside it towards a statue raised on a cylindrical plinth. As they got closer, Isabel could see that it was of a man, larger than life-size and supposedly swathed in a cloth that did nothing to uphold his modesty.

'Let me introduce you to Apollo,' Robert said, stopping to admire the artefact. 'The god of Light, of the sun, of music and prophesy.'

'I prophesy he'll freeze to death in winter,' Isabel remarked flippantly, to disguise her reactions that were an instant mixture of embarrassment and admiration.

Robert laughed. 'It would have to be an extremely hard winter to make him freeze, I suspect,' he answered. 'But he is beautiful, don't you think? He has a tremendous physique.'

Together, they walked around the statue, gazing up at it.

'I do get the impression that in ancient times people walked about wearing next to no clothes. Do you think so?'

'I suspect they wore disconcertingly little in such places as ancient Greece, especially in summer when it tends to be rather hot . . . I imagine it could have led to some sublimely interesting encounters with the opposite sex.'

'Goodness me!' she exclaimed, attempting to visualize the sort of encounters he might have been referring to.

'How old are you, Isabel?' he asked.

'Sixteen.'

In an unspoken accord, they turned away from Apollo and continued their walk. Servants had cleared away the trestles and chairs, and on the vast grassy area between the house and the lake a new activity was taking place, involving some kind of mysterious apparatus, with attentive men at the hub of it. A group of curious visiting villagers was gathering around it all.

'What's going on over there?' Isabel enquired.

'My father is going to make an ascent in a balloon.'

'A balloon?' she repeated, wide-eyed. 'I didn't know there was to be a balloon.'

'There certainly is. He wanted it kept quiet though, because it all depended on the suitability of the weather. You can just see the balloon growing.'

'Oh, that striped thing,' she said.

The balloon was being filled with hot air and was already visible through the trees, and other people were flocking towards it to witness the strange phenomenon.

'Your father is really going to ascend into the sky in a balloon?' Isabel asked incredulous.

'That's the plan.'

'He's a brave man, Robert.'

'A touch foolhardy,' Robert suggested. 'We've all told him so, but his mind is made up . . . Come on, let's watch.'

A brazier filled with yellow glowing coke had been placed in a gondola and was sitting beneath what appeared to be a huge bag – the balloon – the base of which was being held open by several men. Being filled with hot air, it was growing, unfurling as it inflated, taking on the form of a massive red and white striped egg, tethered by taut ropes and swaying slightly in concert with the caprice of the breeze. A man fed more fuel onto the brazier and at a signal George Wilson stepped into the gondola to join him. The man gave the order to untie the anchoring ropes and the balloon began to rise gently, hauling George Wilson, the pilot and the brazier skywards, to the delighted cheers and applause from the onlookers.

'I've never seen anything like it in my life,' Isabel said excitedly, 'but I have read something about balloons. Some French brothers called Montgolfier invented it.' And she pronounced *Montgolfier* with a distinct French accent.

'Fancy you knowing that,' Robert remarked with a grin. 'I'm impressed.'

'Thank you,' she responded with a mock curtsy. 'My father, being a schoolmaster, has taught me lots, including about the Montgolfier brothers.'

'And judging by the way you pronounced *Montgolfier*, I suspect you can speak French?'

'Yes. He taught me French, and German . . . And Italian.'

'My goodness. You impress me, Isabel, beyond measure. Now come and meet my sisters.' He turned and looked up at the house, pointing. 'There they are, look, standing at that central window upstairs, watching our daring-do father as he ascends recklessly into the sky.'

Isabel smiled as she saw the faces of two children peering upwards, each with a look of wonderment on her face.

'Give me your hand,' he said.

He took her hand, which made her heart flutter, and jostled his way through the throng of villagers gathered to watch the spectacle, while she tagged along keenly. They made their way to a pillared portico, ascended the broad flight of stone steps and entered the great doorway.

Inside, the light was dim after the bright sunshine of the outdoors, and her eyes took a few seconds to become accustomed. The atmosphere seemed to be permeated by the natural odour of Patchfield House, assumed over decades; of wood fires, blended with age-old stone, and pot-pourri. Their footsteps echoed off the tiled floor. A broad staircase swept upwards, lit from behind by two tall leaded windows of coloured glass that imparted a mellow radiance into the high and broad hallway.

'I'll take you to the library, Isabel, then I'll send for my sisters to join us.'

The library overlooked the garden, and the summer sun shone through the large rectangular window, providing ample light, but highlighting the motes of dust that floated through the air. Robert rang a bell and eventually a servant appeared, to whom he gave the instruction to bring his sisters to him. Within a very few minutes the two little girls had joined them.

'Ah, Charlotte, Henrietta,' he greeted. 'I want you to meet Miss Saxby. Miss Saxby lives in the village of Crowle, and has two younger sisters of her own.'

'Good afternoon, Charlotte and Henrietta,' Isabel greeted with a friendly smile that at once put the two girls at ease.

'Good afternoon, Miss Saxby,' they chorused in unison.

'What did you think when you saw your papa ascending up into the sky in that great big balloon?' Miss Saxby enquired.

They looked at each other for an answer, then in her little girl's voice Charlotte said, 'I wondered if he was scared. I would be.'

'I would be scared as well,' agreed Henrietta, the younger of the two.

'Well, I would be scared too,' Isabel admitted. 'It must take a lot of courage to do something like flying in a balloon – so high in the sky – especially if you're scared. So your father must be a very brave man.'

Charlotte nodded thoughtfully in response.

'Later, why don't you draw a picture of your papa going up in his balloon?' she suggested.

'Oh, let's do it now,' Charlotte said with instant enthusiasm, and ran off to grab paper and chalks. Henrietta followed hard on her heels.

They quickly returned suitably equipped and shuffled excitedly to sit side by side in the same chair at their father's desk where they set about the task with some fervour. Isabel watched them from behind, chatting to them affably as the drawings took on some resemblance of the balloon, and sticklike figures hanging below it in a sort of box. She nodded her approval to Robert.

'I like your drawings very much,' Isabel said when they were finished. 'May I take them with me, to show my own sisters?'

'Oh, but I want to show papa first,' Henrietta said, 'but you can take mine afterwards. It is my present to your sisters.'

'Thank you, Henrietta, that's so kind. Now, what else can you draw?'

'I can draw our house – and our horses,' Charlotte claimed, and set about proving it.

'Why don't you sit down while they draw their pictures for you, Isabel?' Robert suggested.

'Thank you.' She sat down as she was bid. 'Your sisters are delightful, Robert.'

'It's evident to me the sentiment is reciprocated. See how

well, how easily they respond to you.'

'I'm glad you think so.'

'I do. As a matter of fact, Isabel, the girls are desperately in need of a governess. They had a governess until quite recently, but she was getting on in years and rather crotchety.' He hesitated for a few seconds, then said, 'Would you be amenable to the notion that I recommend you to my father as their new governess. I think you have the makings.'

She gasped. 'Do you really?'

'I'm presuming that you would be available for the situation?'

Henrietta looked up and smiled with approval, as she overheard the conversation.

'I've never considered becoming a governess but, yes, I suppose I would be . . . providing my father agrees. Which reminds me – I must go back to my mother and father,' she said regretfully. 'They'll be wondering what has become of me. But first I must look at your sisters' drawings.'

She got up to admire their work while Robert explained that he and Miss Saxby must leave them. Once they had finished their pictures, however, they must return to their nursery, he instructed. So Isabel bid goodbye to the daughters of George Wilson and Robert led her outside into the sunshine again.

'I shall offer my quite insincere apologies for detaining you,' Robert declared, 'and take the opportunity to ask your father if he has any objection to your being proposed as a possible governess here.'

So, content in each other's company, they set off in search of Susan and William Saxby, and saw them once more in convivial conversation with a small group of other people.

'Isabel,' Robert said, and she looked into his eyes at the

way he addressed her. 'Had you and your family planned on staying for the display of fireworks later? I imagine a lot of the villagers will have left by then, since it will not take place before nightfall.'

'No, they are not planning to stay.'

'Well, do you think they would agree to you staying?'

'I'm sure they would not approve of me walking all the way home to Crowle alone, along dark lanes. But thank you for the lovely thought.'

'But I would return you home myself afterwards in our gig.'

She beamed with pleasure at the prospect. 'In that case they might agree.'

'Very well, let's see what your father has to say.'

\- - -

Because Robert Wilson promised to return Isabel safely home after the fireworks display, William Saxby consented for her to stay. Then she related joyously that she had been inside the house and had met the two delightful little girls, the daughters of the eminent George Wilson.

'I trust my daughter has not been an imposition upon you household,' William Saxby remarked.

'On the contrary, sir,' Robert replied. 'Which leads me to request your further consent on a matter about which Isabel and I have already spoken.'

'So let us hear it,' William Saxby urged, fearful of just what they might have already discussed.

'Well, sir, I would like to propose Isabel for the vacant position of governess to my two young sisters. Of course, I shall have to discuss the matter with my father. But before I do, I must know whether you have any objection.'

'My goodness, it would be a golden opportunity for my daughter,' William replied. 'I am delighted that you judge her worthy of consideration.'

'Then I shall seek out my father as soon as he returns from his balloon flight, and arrange for him to meet her.' He turned to William and shook his hand. 'It has been a pleasure, sir, to make your acquaintance. You, too, Mrs Saxby.' He bowed, while Mrs Saxby duly dropped a curtsy.

'Isabel, please look out for my father's return. Footmen have already left with our carriage to pick him up, I believe. When you see him return, wait for me on the steps of the portico and I shall meet your there.'

When Robert was out of earshot, William Saxby said, 'Don't count your chickens just yet, Isabel. You have Mr George Wilson to contend with, and he might have different ideas to his son.'

'Oh, I daresay, papa, but I'll try and give a good account of myself.'

'I have no doubt you will charm him, my dear. But he's a wily devil by all accounts, and hasn't got where he is by following the whims of others, leastwise his eldest son. So my advice to you, child, is to be careful, and keep your eyes wide open. I don't want you to be exploited in any way. Do you get my meaning?'

'I'm not sure, papa.'

William Saxby took his daughter gently by the arm and led her away from the ears of her younger sisters. 'Let me put it this way,' he said almost in a whisper. 'Young Robert Wilson seems very much taken with you – you are a pretty girl after all. But rest assured that there can never be any sort of match between the two of you other than servant and master, because of the wide gap in our social standings. I simply don't want you to be hurt. Now do you see?'

'Yes, I understand, papa, and I am not counting my chickens yet, as you put it. But you never know what might happen. I would not like to squander such an opportunity if it's offered. I would prefer to let life take its course . . .'

'But just be aware . . .'

Isabel, however, was already head over heels in love.

\- \- \-

Chapter 10

'My apologies, Isabel, if I've kept you waiting,' Robert greeted.

'You haven't,' Isabel remarked with a smile of familiarity, as she rose from the steps to the pillared portico of Patchfield House where she had been sitting, mulling over what her father had said. 'I take it your father got back safely from his ballooning.'

"He came down on the other side of Droitwich, where they eventually picked him up, unharmed and in fine fettle,' he explained, walking slowly towards the grassed area in front of the portico.

'I'm glad,' she remarked. 'I was wondering how far they might travel.'

'That man who travelled with him, whose balloon it was got burned by the hot coals. I'm told they had a bumpy landing.'

'Oh dear. Was he badly burned?'

'Not seriously, thank goodness. Anyway, my father is home safe and sound . . . And . . .' he paused for effect. 'I have spoken to him about you . . .'

'So soon?' Her heart started pounding. 'And what did he say?'

'He and my mother have agreed to see you. So I am to present you before dinner.' Their eyes met, and they exchanged smiles; his seeking her admiration, hers expressing approval.

'Oh, goodness!' she sighed. 'But this dress I'm wearing – I've had it on all day – do you think it suitable for such a meeting with your mother and father? I would rather have worn something better.'

'You look ravishing, Isabel, and my father will be enchanted. I know it.'

As they ambled along companionably, Isabel's thoughts ran on about the possibility of becoming the governess at Patchfield House; she would be living in the same house as Robert, see him every day. That prospect alone was sufficient incentive to try and impress George Wilson MP.

'I do hope your mother and father think me suitable,' she said at length. 'I rather have a taking to be governess to your two sisters. They're delightful.'

More people than she had expected were lingering in the gardens. Many of the daytime throng of villagers had left, but among those who remained she could see the rector of the village church, the miller, the baker, the blacksmith, and many more whom she did not recognize, all accompanied by their respective wives.

Robert took his fob watch from his waistcoat pocket and looked at it. 'I am to take you to them in half an hour or so,' he announced. 'Meanwhile, let us go for another stroll.'

The stroll took them towards the summerhouse, a hideaway wooden construction furnished with squabbed seats and plump cushions, a chaise longue, and rugs. They went inside and sat talking. They conversed easily. He seemed so worldly, so interesting, so handsome, charming and attentive. He made her feel as if she were the only girl in the world, and she was acutely aware that she was in love. Nobody had ever shown an interest in her like this, and she was immensely flattered, because it suggested that he was just as taken with her as she was with him. But how far would any liaison be allowed to develop, so drastically far apart as they were on the social scale, as her father had pointed out?

After about half an hour had passed Robert led her once again back towards the house and into the great hallway with its sweeping staircase and tall windows. A footman was hovering. He looked Isabel up and down approvingly and flashed her a smile.

'Badger,' Robert said, addressing him. 'Are my mother and father in the library yet?'

'I believe so, sir,' Badger answered deferentially.

'Excellent. Please wait here, Isabel. I'll make sure they're ready to see you.'

So Isabel waited, realizing she was trembling with anticipation. This was all happening so quickly, but it could be the beginning of a whole new life.

'It's a pleasant evening out there, miss,' Badger the footman offered, aware that Isabel, by dint of what she was wearing, was hardly royalty and therefore approachable.

She turned to face him and smiled amenably. 'Yes, it's lovely,' she replied. 'The whole day has been lovely.'

'We been lucky with the weather for the coronation, eh?'

'We have, it's true.'

'You was here earlier, weren't you? I thought I spotted you watching the malarkey with the balloon.'

'Yes, it was quite a spectacle.'

'I followed it to Droitwich and beyond in the carriage with the coachman, you know, so as to pick up Mr Wilson and bring him home. I'm his valet, you might say – among me other duties.'

'I see,' Isabel responded.

'You live hereabouts, miss?'

'Quite close.'

'You gonna stay for the fireworks?'

'Yes, Mr Wilson has invited me.'

'You mean Mr Robert?'

'Yes, I mean Mr Robert.'

'Well . . . I admire his taste. Pretty girl, ain't ye?'

Isabel shrugged. 'I don't know,' she answered modestly.

'Aw, come on – I reckon you own it right enough.'

'I don't own it particularly,' she answered modestly, 'but thank you all the same for the compliment.'

'Not at all, miss. Credit where it's due. What's your name?'

'Isabel Saxby.'

'Nice to meet you, Miss Saxby. I hope to see you again.'

'You never know,' she smiled ambivalently, just as Robert was reappearing.

'My father will see you now, Isabel.'

She felt her colour rise and her heart pound with nervousness at this extraordinary opportunity.

'I'll take you to him.' She followed him out of the hallway. 'Has Badger been keeping you entertained?'

'Well, he's been talking to me,' she remarked obliquely. 'He told me he's your father's valet.'

'He's got a nerve talking to you. I shall reprimand him. You could've been a duchess for all he knows.'

'Oh, please don't say anything, Robert. I suppose he was just trying to be sociable.'

Robert looked at her and, with a smile, nodded his endorsement as he tapped on the door of the library. To Isabel the room seemed different compared to how it had seemed earlier in the day, when the two little girls were present, and the afternoon sun had shone so brilliantly through its vast window. Now that the sun had moved around the house it was darker, more sombre and smelled more of tallow due to a servant having lit candles already.

'Father, mother, this is Miss Saxby,' Robert announced straight-faced.

Mrs Wilson remained seated beneath a window, but George Wilson stood up behind his huge oak desk and, unsmiling, looked Isabel up and down. He was a big man, tall and well-built, with long side whiskers that meandered almost as far as his chin. To Isabel he seemed full of his own importance and self-belief . . . and overbearing.

'Miss Saxby – my father . . .'

'Good evening, sir.' She curtseyed deferentially with a disarming smile. 'Thank you for agreeing to see me.'

'And my mother . . .'

Isabel stepped forward and shook her hand. 'Good afternoon, Mrs Wilson. I am sure this is a terribly busy day for you.'

'Please be seated, Miss Saxby.' Mr Wilson indicated the chair drawn up facing him. 'Robert, you may leave us now.'

At the door he turned to glance at Isabel.

'So, Miss Saxby . . . I understand that my son has been keeping you company during the celebrations.'

'Yes, sir. He very kindly offered to teach my sisters and me the rules of pall mall because he could see we were struggling. After that, he offered to give me a tour of your lovely grounds before he escorted me to watch your ascent in the balloon.'

'And, having spent some time in your company – and in the company of my two young daughters I believe – he is of the opinion that you might be considered suitably qualified for the vacant position of governess?'

'I am flattered that he thinks so, sir.'

'So what qualities can you offer that would induce me to consider you for such a responsible situation, Miss Saxby?'

In her naivety Isabel was a little taken aback by such a direct line of questioning. But her quick-thinking ensured she formulated a suitable response.

'My father is a schoolmaster in Worcester, sir. He

teaches classics, and he has educated me to the same standards that he would educate the boys at his school. I have learnt history, geography, the scriptures, the classics, Latin. I read and speak French, German, and some Italian. Besides, I have met your two young daughters and I find them enchanting as well as intelligent. I am sure I could be of benefit to them in their learning, as well as being their companion.'

Mrs Wilson spoke. 'Would you consider yourself able, Miss Saxby, to instruct my daughters in the use of the globes, in music, drawing and dancing?'

'We have a large globe at home, ma'am, and I am familiar with all the countries upon it. As to music I play the pianoforte, I draw, and paint in watercolours. I cannot claim dancing to be one of my strong points though, having little opportunity in Crowle to practise the art.'

'I see,' said Mrs Wilson. 'Equanimity of temper and cheerfulness of disposition are also indispensable requisites, would you not agree?'

'Oh, indeed, yes, Mrs Wilson. I consider myself even-tempered, and try to smile pleasantly as often as is compatible with maintaining a reputation for sanity.'

George Wilson smiled to himself at the cleverness of her reply and rubbed his whiskers. 'The situation of governess, Miss Saxby, would involve you living here at Patchfield. Your bedroom would adjoin my daughters' bedroom, and you would be at their beck and call day and night. A nursery maid is already on hand. She would assist you at all times. As such, you must be a shining example in every way possible. Have you any previous experience of being a governess, Miss Saxby?'

'Not formally, sir. But I have two sisters, slightly older than your daughters and I have enjoyed helping them with their learning, even after they began to attend our village school. Therefore, I am familiar with the needs of little girls and how to deal with them.'

'Since you have had no formal position hitherto, Miss Saxby, I presume you have no character reference?' suggested Mrs Wilson.

'That's so, ma'am,' Isabel replied candidly, 'but I am sure my father would offer a glowing one.'

A smile again spread across the face of the otherwise stern George Wilson. 'I concede, Miss Saxby, that you appear to be mistress of all the accomplishments required of a governess,' he remarked. 'So in this matter I have no objection to engaging you, although you are younger than I would have wished. You will receive an annual salary appropriate to the position, of five-and-thirty guineas, payable by the month, with one half day holiday every Sunday, so that you might see your parents and your sisters. Is that acceptable, Miss Saxby?'

'Oh, yes, sir,' she beamed. 'Thank you. I am sure you will not be disappointed with my work, sir.'

'But my dear,' Mrs Wilson remarked, speaking openly to her husband, 'it is not customary to take people into one's service solely on the recommendation of a close relative. Is there no other person connected with Miss Saxby to whom we can refer?'

'Well, Miss Saxby?' George Wilson asked.

'I can give you the names of many people who know of my respectability and upbringing, ma'am, including the rector,' she replied. 'But as I have never been away from my family before, I suppose my abilities will be best judged by trial.'

George Wilson turned to his wife. 'I believe, my dear, that we must trust our own judgement with regard to Miss Saxby's character, references or no. I am quite content with my own assessment of the young lady.' To Isabel, he said:

'The earlier you begin your duties, the better. May we expect you here on Monday, first thing?'

'Oh, indeed, sir. To be sure. And thank you.'

'Whilst you are in my employment,' George Wilson added, 'you must respect your position and conduct yourself accordingly at all times.'

'Oh, I will sir. And thank you again.'

'Before you go, Miss Saxby,' Mrs Wilson interjected, 'As with all servants, I have an objection to my servants receiving relatives and friends while in this house. It is very inconvenient to have such people knocking at the door, perhaps at the same moment that the carriages of my visitors arrive.'

'I understand, ma'am.' Isabel replied. 'That will not happen.'

'Thank *you*, Miss Saxby. Now, on your way out, perhaps you would be good enough to ask my son to come back here to me right away.'

Isabel rose from the chair, dropped a curtsy and left the library. Robert was sitting in the hallway and he stood up when she appeared.

'Well?' he said.

'I am to be the new governess as of Monday,' she beamed, her eyes bright with excitement, her smile wide.

'Well done, Isabel,' he beamed proudly. 'I knew it.'

'Anyway, your father would like to see you right away.'

'Very well. Wait here till I come back. Then we'll take a walk before dinner.'

Robert returned to the library.

'Sit down, Robert,' his father bade. 'I have appointed Miss Saxby as governess for Charlotte and Henrietta. I hope I have made the right decision. She will begin her duties on Monday.'

'I knew you would find her suitable, sir,' Robert

answered proudly, trying to catch his mother's eye to seek her approval.

'She is a very personable young lady, and not at all unpleasant to behold. In that respect I can understand that you might well be attracted to her.'

'Well, I do find her thoroughly engaging, sir, I must admit.'

'Then remember this, my son – even though she evidently comes from a respectable family, she will be nothing more than a servant in this household. So I strongly request that you curb any enthusiasm you have for the girl, and any thoughts that you might harbour about a romantic adventure with her.'

'Your father is correct, Robert,' his mother concurred earnestly. 'The girl is not for you. She is more suited to a footman or a tradesman. We can do better. Much better.'

'In fact,' his father went on, 'I already have in mind a liaison for you that will profit us all immensely, to a delightful young lady – an only child – the daughter of an eminent and wealthy family. I am confident that a suitable arrangement can be achieved since her father and I have already spoken of it. I hope to have it all agreed when the House sits again.'

\- - -

It was all well and good his parents requesting that he refrain from forming a romantic attachment with Isabel Saxby, but how could he help himself, especially if she were of the same mind as him and amenable? She was such a delightful thing, affable, warm, and so deliciously pretty that he just wanted to take her in his arms and feel her pressed against him while kissing her very kissable lips. Why should he be interested in anybody else, especially some nameless, faceless young woman his father might have in mind, just to further his own political ambitions?

Robert saw himself as too much of a rebel to countenance going against his own inclinations, and to hell with the consequences.

When he left the library, he escorted Isabel outside and they began their ramble through the formal gardens, where various other people were admiring the flora. They headed unwittingly towards the summerhouse again, where they sat side by side on the chaise longue.

'Since you are to be the new governess,' Robert said softly. 'I shall see you every day while I am at home. And what better reason for me to escape Cambridge at any opportunity. I am so glad of it.'

'I am glad too,' she replied looking at him with a look of pure adulation. 'For the same reason.'

'Do you really mean that, Isabel?'

'I do,' she answered as solemnly as if she were taking her marriage vows.

'Splendid. Soon it will be time for dinner, Isabel, and I have to get changed. I imagine you are hungry too by this time.'

Her heart flipped at the immediate prospect of being invited to join the Honourable George Wilson MP and his family at the dinner table. How she had suddenly come up in the world.

'I'll show you the servants' quarters,' he added, 'and you can get some dinner there. You must introduce yourself to Mrs Truby, the housekeeper, as the new governess. She will look after you.'

Isabel's heart sank. How naive of her to think she had suddenly become so elevated as to be invited to join his family at their dinner table. Already, her father's words were proving wise; of course, she would be regarded as no more than a servant.

'Afterwards, Isabel, wait for me by the steps of the

portico where we met before, and we shall watch the fireworks together before I take you home.'

\- - -

Chapter 11

SS Great Britain

There was a buzz of multiple conversations and polite laughter as the dining saloon grew busier, and people who had never cast eyes on each other previously engaged in the process of introducing themselves and relating snippets of information about themselves. Wine glasses chinked, and cutlery scraped against porcelain plates, and every table was a hub of flickering amber candlelight, which lit up animated faces and compelled jewellery to sparkle.

'Tell me about your wife,' Isabel invited, as she turned a half-empty wineglass around on the tablecloth. She felt a change of subject was needed from how she and Robert had met and their first hours together. 'I only ever heard her name mentioned.'

'Well, as you may recall,' Robert began, replenishing her glass, 'my father was anxious for a matrimonial arrangement between Elizabeth and me. I suspect the first and most important reason – from his point of view – was that a marriage between our two families would benefit his own parliamentary career. Indeed, once the deed was done, and we were irrevocably wed, he was elevated to the cabinet and a baronetcy was bestowed upon him. Elizabeth's father, Sir Joseph Hulme, had tremendous influence with the Whigs, by virtue of his wealth and his donations to Lord Melbourne's government. Yet I believe there was another, less selfish reason, for which I must give my father his due; he realised that Elizabeth – an only child – was heiress to all Sir Joseph's wealth, which would ultimately fall to me as her husband, as indeed it has done, since Sir Joseph predeceased Elizabeth.'

'So she inherited everything before she died?'

'Indeed, yes.'

'I don't remember ever seeing her,' Isabel mused, privately realizing that Robert must by now be immeasurably wealthy and owner of whatever house and estate Sir Joseph Hulme bequeathed his daughter, besides Patchfield. 'Although I was aware of her presence at Patchfield House on at least one occasion,' she continued. 'I was kept well away.'

'Of course, you were still governess when the Hulmes were invited to stay with us. That first visit was arranged solely that I should meet Elizabeth.'

'I recall it,' Isabel admitted, the memory fuelling her disdain. 'And what did you think of her? For I never saw you again after that day. I was made aware that she was there, and why . . .'

'I had no interest in the girl whatsoever, Isabel. I had no intention of ever marrying her. I was quite prepared to defy my father, because I wished to marry you.'

'And yet you suddenly disappeared from Patchfield House, and you did marry her after all . . .'

'Oh, I heard about the manner in which you were dispatched, Isabel . . . And once you had gone, I was bereft . . . There seemed nothing left for me in life worth living for. Some few months after that I was invited, and thus obliged, to spend a few weeks with the Hulmes at Timberlake, their home, and Elizabeth really took the trouble to get to know me – to understand me. We walked and talked – a great deal, I may say – and I began to realize that whilst she was not outwardly beautiful, she was an extraordinarily kind and thoughtful soul, and delightful company. I began to like her – very much. We quickly became close friends. Just one more push from my father and a reminder to myself that you were gone forever, and I asked for her hand . . . We were engaged in the summer of eighteen-forty . . . We were wed in June of eighteen-forty-one.'

'More than twelve years ago,' Isabel remarked. 'So when did she die?'

'A little more than nine years ago. October 1844. In childbirth . . .' Isabel saw that Robert's eyes misted over as he recalled it. 'I lost the child as well. A boy.'

'I am so sorry to learn this, Robert. You have obviously had your tribulations as well.'

'We both have, Isabel. You, no less than me. Now, pray fill in for me the parts of your story that I have unfortunately not been privy to.'

She smiled and looked into his eyes, which were studying her intensely. 'Oh, some other time, Robert,' she sighed, and looked away, into the reflections and highlights of the now empty glass. 'First, let me get used to the idea that you are aboard this ship.' She looked at him again. 'In such a confined space we shall doubtless see more of each other over the next two months or so. You must understand, Robert, that it was a massive shock to see you again after so long.'

'No less so for me, Isabel.'

She smiled again and answered softly, 'I accept that. However, I have enjoyed your company. Thank you.'

'So would you consent to dine with me again, or even meet me for a spin on the promenade deck? Tomorrow, perhaps. I am entirely free at all times and at your disposal.'

'Now that I have overcome the initial shock, Robert, I

am not averse to dining with you again if you wish.'

'And I hope we can get to know each other once more, a little better.'

'I see no reason why we should not be friends,' she conceded.

'Well . . .' He touched her hand that was still twirling the wine glass. 'At least that's a start. So why don't we take a turn on the promenade deck now and have supper together later?'

'I cannot . . . I have arranged to meet a new friend for supper,' she declared.

'Somebody you have already met aboard this ship?'

'Yes.'

'Oh . . .' He sounded disappointed. 'Man or woman?'

'A woman. Ann Carter. I might even introduce you to her at some point. But not tonight . . . Now, please excuse me, Robert. I'll take my leave of you if you don't mind, so that I can rest before supper.'

'Of course.'

Longingly, he watched her go as she walked away from him, still so elegant, still so statuesque, still so beautiful, and yet so changed, so different to the young girl he remembered.

\- - -

'It crossed my mind that you might not make it to supper, Isabel,' Ann Carter remarked as her friend sat down opposite her at the table in the dining saloon. 'I thought you might prefer to be otherwise engaged with your rediscovered friend.'

'I'm not that easily swayed,' Isabel replied, glancing around to ascertain whether Robert had decided to take supper in that bustling candle-lit saloon, noisy with the sound of so many competing voices.

'So how was dinner?'

'Edible.'

Ann grinned. 'I wasn't enquiring about the food.'

'I know. To tell the truth, Ann, it was much better, and much more pleasant than I imagined it was going to be. We talked – about how we met . . . It brought back so many poignant memories.'

'I am all ears, if you would like to relate the tale.'

Stewards entered the salon and formed a line, passing platters of cold meats, cheese, bread, butter and pickles from one to the other, which they placed in turn on the two rows of tables that lined the room.

'I'm not hungry at all,' Isabel remarked, hoping to side-track Ann. 'I shall not eat anything. Perhaps I'll sleep all the better for it.'

'I must confess,' replied Ann, likewise ignoring the platter that had appeared on their table, 'the constant rolling of the ship makes me feel quite queasy, however gentle it is at present. So eating less food is sensible. Besides, all the ship's creaks and groans make it impossible to sleep soundly.' Ann's face then lit up. 'Oh, but have you heard? There is to be a meeting tomorrow morning after breakfast – here in the saloon – to elect a committee which will organize entertainment. Shall you attend? Might you offer your services? Can you sing, or play a musical instrument?'

Isabel laughed. 'Sing? Goodness, no. Nobody would gain any pleasure from hearing me sing. In fact, it will be a singular kindness to everybody if I don't sing. I used to play pianoforte, though, but I have not played for some time. And you?'

'To tell you the truth, Isabel, I can't play an instrument, but I do enjoy singing.' Her eyes creased into an attractive smile as an idea struck her. 'But why don't we offer our services anyway? I'll volunteer to sing, if you'll accompany me on the pianoforte. As you can see, there's one available here in the saloon.'

'Oh, I'm sure there are better pianoforte players than me among the passengers.'

'Maybe so, but that's not the point, nor indeed the spirit of the thing. I don't believe an audience on this ship would be expecting perfection. Just entertainment to relieve the monotony of sea faring – a bit of fun.'

'I believe you are rather partial to a bit of fun, one way or the other,' Isabel remarked congenially and with a knowing look. 'So, do you have the printed music for any songs you could sing?'

'By a strange quirk of fate I have, my dear. And I am sure we could get permission to rehearse in here when the room is not in use. Practice makes perfect, you know! In any case, half of the passengers will be too drunk to care whether we are good or bad, if that group over there is anything to go by.'

The group in question were at one of the further tables playing cards for money, and becoming more boisterous in their drink.

Ann said, 'They must have been drinking all day, Isabel. I don't think I want to be near them when they start arguing, which they inevitably will if money is concerned. If we are not going to eat now why don't we retire to the ladies' saloon?'

'Yes, let's,' Isabel agreed.

'Then you can tell me more about you and your friend Sir Robert Wilson. I'm intrigued . . .'

\- - -

Chapter 12

28 June 1838
Patchfield House

'A good show of fireworks, Badger,' Robert Wilson declared. 'Well done.'

'Thank you, sir.'

'Now, would you please tack up my gig, light the lamps, and bring it round to the front of the house?' Isabel stood at his side. 'I am returning Miss Saxby to the tender mercies of her family.'

Many of the guests were dispersing after seeing the fireworks display. Badger had been one of the men detailed to set them off, and was ambling back to the house when Robert intercepted him.

He turned to look Isabel up and down. 'I could drive Miss Saxby home meself and save you the bother, sir.'

'That won't be necessary, Badger, but the offer is noted. Off you go.'

As the couple waited at the front of the house for the reappearance of Badger with the gig, they bid goodnight to other departing visitors. A few carriages rumbled up out of the shadows and respective owners and their corresponding wives stepped aboard and hailed farewells to anybody within earshot. Those who had been invited to stay the night and occupy a bed made their way slowly up the broad flight of stone steps to the front door, lit on either side by an elaborate oil lamp, chatting amiably with other house guests.

Eventually, Badger reappeared with the horse and gig. As he approached Isabel and Robert, the gig's lamps lit up her eyes, rendering them beautiful and clear, like enchanting yet dangerous pools that promised Badger a blissful drowning if ever such an opportunity came his way. He stepped down and stood next to Isabel, offering his hand as she stepped up.

'Thank you,' she said, aware of his interest, and shuffled herself comfortable on the seat.

'Thank you, Badger,' Robert called and flicked the reins. 'Are you warm enough, Isabel?'

'Yes, thank you. It's not cold.'

'I do believe Badger has a taking for you,' he commented, and turned his head to look at her for her response as he flicked the reins.

'If he has, I have no taking for him,' she answered.

'I'm glad to hear it. You can do so much better for yourself.'

'I hope to, Robert.'

To the rumble of the wheels and clip-clop of the horse they were soon away from the house and turned into the lane at a steady trot. A crescent moon hung in the sky lighting their way.

'Have you always lived in Crowle?'

'Always,' she affirmed. 'At one time, my father thought we should move to Worcester, due to his school-mastering there, though we never did. My mother used to live in Worcester, though, before she married my father.'

'Well, Crowle is closer to Patchfield House than Worcester is, so it will not be too inconvenient for you to visit your folks on your afternoon off.'

'True,' she agreed.

They remained unspeaking for some minutes, each taken with their own thoughts, happy with the events of the day, and contemplating the implications of this short drive. Isabel was privately hoping that Robert might kiss her before they parted; conversely, Robert was pondering whether she would mind if he did.

At length, he said, 'You must direct me to your home, Isabel.'

'A little further along this lane,' she replied, shaken by the uneven surface.

'I'm just sorry it's such a bumpy ride. All these ruts and holes.'

'All the same, it's kind of you to go to all this trouble.'

'Well, it's what I promised your father, Isabel, and I intended to keep my word . . . Anyway, I have another reason.'

'Oh?' She smiled to herself. 'And that is?'

'Rather selfishly, to keep you to myself for just a little bit longer, and out of sight of prying eyes.'

She made no reply. She could think of no reply that might be suitable, while Robert concentrated wordlessly on driving the gig. The night was silent but for their own presence, the rattles of the gig, the creak of the leather harness, the muffled rumble of the wheels and the rhythm of the horse's hooves on the dried, compacted mud of the lane.

'Here we are,' she said at last, pointing to a thatched cottage with the glow of candlelight visible in a downstairs window.

He drew the gig to a halt at the front gate. 'There. You're home, safe and sound.'

'Thank you so much, Robert – for everything. Because of you, I've been given the chance to be governess to your lovely sisters. I owe you so much.'

'Do you think so?'

'Of course.'

'A kiss would be sufficient payment, if that might be acceptable to you,' he suggested, thankful for the cue.

She turned to him smiling her consent, and he slipped his arms around her, as the waxing moon lent its silvery light to her delightful expression of anticipation.

He held her close, she tilted her face towards him, closed her eyes and their lips met. Their kiss was tentative at first, but quickly became an astonishing pleasure that set her heart pounding, and fuelling their mutual ardour. Isabel had never been kissed in this way before and it was a revelation. Yet, for the sake of propriety, she felt that she should break off.

'All day, Isabel, I've longed for this moment,' Robert whispered. 'From the moment I first set eyes on you I've wanted to kiss you. You have such kissable lips, and they have certainly lived up to their promise.'

'I'm glad,' she replied almost breathlessly with the inadequacy of the inexperienced, and her heart thumping so hard that she imagined he could feel it too.

'I shall never forget this moment, Isabel.'

'Nor will I, Robert . . . And I've had such a lovely day, thanks to you . . . Evening too.'

Conversation stalled once more, neither knowing quite how to proceed, until Isabel took the initiative.

'I ought to go in now,' she said with reluctance. 'My mother and father will wonder what's become of me.'

'Indeed,' Robert grudgingly agreed and took his arm from around her. 'I hope to see you soon, if you are not too busy with my sisters.'

'Yes, I hope so too . . .' As she leaned towards him she smiled serenely and gave him another tantalising peck on the lips, then stepped down. 'Goodnight, Robert.'

By the moonlight, he watched her walk away from him, open the front gate, turn and wave, then disappear from view, hidden by a bush. Before he turned the horse and the gig around he heard the sound of the front door latch, confirming she had entered the house.

Isabel could barely get to sleep that night for thinking about Robert Wilson. She relived every moment in her mind, turning over and over in her head every word, every admiring look they had exchanged. When she eventually fell asleep, fatigued, he was foremost in her dreams, as he was the moment she awoke.

- - -

The sun shone bright and joyously that morning of the first Monday in July. It was the day Isabel was to leave her family, and the house that had been home all her life. She rose from her bed, opened the window, looked out onto the flower beds, fresh and vividly coloured. A cuckoo called out from a neighbouring copse, amid the twittering songs of other birds. She washed, dressed in clothes that she and her mother thought suitable for the arrival of a new governess, and went downstairs, sad that she would be leaving all this behind her, yet thrilled at the challenge of what lay before her.

She bid a tearful goodbye to her father as he left for his school, and he wished her well. 'But always remember your place, my dear,' was his parting shot.

When he had closed the door behind him she sat down to her breakfast.

'I shall walk with you to Patchfield House,' Susan Saxby, her mother declared.

'Please, mother, no.' Isabel replied, as she tucked into bread, cheese and apple. 'There's no need.'

'But I want to see you there safely, and introduce myself to Mrs Wilson as the mother of her new governess. I'm sure she'll consider it only natural. Besides, you'll need help with your belongings.'

'No, mother. I can manage my baggage. It's not as if I need to take a lot with me. I can always pick up other things I might need when I visit you on Sunday. In any case, Mrs Wilson has already told me that she doesn't want relatives appearing at her front door.'

'Why indeed would she take such an attitude?' Susan queried indignantly.

'She's the mistress of the house, mother. I suppose she feels she can do as she pleases. She seems a funny woman, though. A bit of a stickler. I think the best way to describe her is pompous.'

'Pompous? Well, pompous or not, I hope she's never unkind to you, Isabel. You don't have to stay there under tyranny. I would hate it if you were unhappy there.'

'Oh, don't worry, mother,' Isabel answered as she chewed her apple. 'I don't expect I'll see very much of her.'

Outside, the sound of a horse blowing its lips prompted Susan to peer through the curtains onto the lane.

'My goodness, Isabel. It looks as if that young Mr Wilson has called. Maybe he's come to collect you. Were you expecting him to?'

'Indeed not,' Isabel replied, all at once feeling hot at what his appearance might imply. 'I'm as surprised as you are.'

'Then you had better go out to him.'

'I can't yet, mother,' she protested. 'I haven't finished my breakfast. Let's wait until he knocks the door.'

'But you cannot keep him waiting, Isabel,' Susan asserted.

'If I must, I must. After all, I'm not expecting him.'

Hurriedly she finished her breakfast and stood up. They heard the anticipated tap-tap at the door.

'Do I look all right, mother?'

'Yes, you do, so answer the door.'

She went to the door and opened it. Robert's beaming face greeted her.

'Good morning, Isabel. It occurred to me that you might have a trunk of your belongings or some such to bring with you on your first day of governessing,' he said, to explain his presence. 'Thus requiring some assistance in the form of transportation.'

'That's very thoughtful, Robert. Thank you. As it happens, I don't have much, but I'm almost ready. Please come in.' She stepped aside and he entered. 'Please excuse me a moment while I go upstairs to don my shawl and bonnet.'

Isabel's two younger sisters soon appeared at the bottom of the staircase and shyly entered the room. They smiled up at Robert as he greeted them affably using their names.

'I believe I passed Mr Saxby going the other way in the lane as I drove here,' Robert remarked to Mrs Saxby.

'I daresay, yes, Mr Wilson,' Susan replied. 'He left some quarter hour since. He enjoys the walk to Worcester, especially when the weather's fine. Reckons it's good for his constitution. And besides, he dearly likes to arrive early at his school.'

Isabel appeared at the foot of the stairs wearing her bonnet and shawl. 'I'm ready,' she said softly to Robert.

'Capital.' He turned to Mrs Saxby. 'Then we shall take our leave of you, ma'am. I shall see to it that your daughter is safely delivered to Patchfield.'

'I shall see you all on Sunday,' Isabel declared. She hugged and kissed her sisters and her mother in turn. 'I'm sure I'll have lots to tell you about my new position.'

Once installed in the gig with her baggage, Robert flicked the reins and said, 'I've been thinking about you a great deal these last few days, Isabel. I couldn't wait to see you again, so I decided to fetch you today first thing. I hope I did the right thing.'

'It was very thoughtful of you, Robert.'

- - -

As the gig drew up at the front steps of Patchfield House, Abel Badger appeared at the portico and approached. As Isabel stepped down he looked her up and down as usual.

'Morning, Miss Saxby,' he greeted with a grin. 'May I take your bag?'

'Thank you, Badger,' Robert replied on her behalf. 'If you would kindly take it to the bedroom attached to the nursery it would be most helpful.' He turned to Isabel. 'Miss Saxby, would you please follow Badger.'

She thanked him again for having the kind consideration to collect her, then followed Badger as she was bidden.

Isabel was confused when they passed beyond the sweeping staircase which she imagined would be the route to her bedroom. Instead, Badger led her along dismal, narrow corridors towards the back of the house, where they encountered a narrow staircase.

'This is the servant's staircase,' he told her. 'This is the one you'll use, except when you have to bring the children downstairs, or take 'em back up again.'

His boots clumped noisily on the bare wooden stairs as he ascended in front of her to the second storey. Along another corridor, through another door and they were walking on carpeted floor again.

'This is the nursery,' Badger announced as he stopped at another closed door. 'Your room is next to it. You'll be sharing it with Rosie.'

'Oh?' Isabel responded, taken aback. 'Who is Rosie?'

'Didn't nobody tell you? Rosie's the nursery maid. Mind you, she ain't half as pretty as you.' He opened the door and stood aside to let her pass. 'In you go then, and meet your charges.'

The two little girls, Charlotte and Henrietta, were evidently eating breakfast as they sat at two of the four straight-backed chairs placed round a large table covered with a green cloth. At sight of Isabel they each beamed and politely wished her good morning.

Another smaller table, placed against the wall, was piled with books, slates, chalks, drawing-paper, pencils, and a colouring box. A blackboard and easel stood forlornly to one side. Close by stood a Robert Wornum upright pianoforte. One wall was adorned with maps, all of them scribbled over with ink and pencil marks. Over the mantelpiece was a mirror and on one side of the chimney breast stood a chest of drawers, on which lay a workbasket and more books. At the other side of the fireplace stood a tall cupboard filled with crockery and glass. A well-worn carpet showed some stains, and the curtains seemed to have lost their hue. In Isabel's view the nursery was not as cheerful or as tidy as she had imagined it would be and, facing due north, was deprived of sunshine.

Charlotte and Henrietta were being overseen by a young woman whose age Isabel guessed to be about one-and-twenty. She was seated but evidently slender with a thin face and thin lips and eyes that were large and brown that lit up with admiration at sight of Abel Badger.

'This is Rosie,' Badger declared. 'Rosie, this is Miss Saxby, the new governess. Handsome, ain't she?'

'Handsome is as handsome does,' Rosie riposted, but with a narrow grin intended to soften the remark. 'But since you are a man, Abel, I suppose you'd notice such things.'

'Aye, I'm a man right enough, Rosie.' He looked at her knowingly, then at Isabel to ascertain whether his remark had impressed her. 'Well, here's Miss Saxby's bag. Why don't ye show her her bed?'

Rosie got up from her chair reluctantly. 'This way, Miss Saxby.' She turned to Badger. 'I'll see you later, eh, Abel?'

At hearing this comment, Isabel wondered whether there might be something going on between Rosie and Badger.

'That you will, Rosie. I'll see *thee* later as well, Miss Saxby.'

The room was sparsely furnished with two beds, each with a small bedside table on opposite sides. Between the beds stood a chest of drawers bearing an oil lamp. On one wall was a small cast-iron fireplace, devoid of kindling material, and crowned with a mantelshelf which bore a clock, and from which hung a pincushion full of pins and needles of various sizes. Against another wall stood a chest of drawers. The window of that small bedroom commanded a view over the grounds at the rear.

'This is my bed,' Rosie declared proprietorially, indicating that nearest the window. 'So the other one is yourn, Miss Saxby.'

'I'd like it better if you call me Isabel,' Isabel entreated. 'After all, as we shall be working together, it would be lovely if we could be friends as well.'

'To my mind you seem a bit too young to be a governess,' Rosie stated bluntly. 'I was expecting somebody older, older than me at any rate, like the last governess we had.'

'I don't know how you expect me to answer that, Rosie. Mr Robert Wilson recommended me to his father, Mr George Wilson. He and Mrs Wilson considered me suitable despite my age, although they did have some reservations about it, I confess.'

'Fancy him, do you? Young Mr Robert?'

'I only met him last Thursday, Rosie,' Isabel answered

with a shrug. 'On coronation day. So I can't say I know him that well, but he's been truly kind and considerate to me.'

'And well he might. Abel told me as how you spent all day with him. Nor did he take ye home till after the fireworks, so I reckon he must fancy you anyroad, eh?'

'As I said, he's been kind to me,' Isabel replied, surprised at Rosie's forthrightness.

'Whether or not, just remember as you're only a governess and he's Quality, and ne'er the twain shall meet, as they say.'

'Everybody keeps telling me so . . .'

'And if you can't have Mr Robert, keep your big blue eyes off Abel Badger, eh?'

'Abel Badger?' Isabel replied, trying to hide her indignation, but taken aback by Rosie's sudden and unwarranted insinuation. 'You've got nothing to fear from me where Abel Badger is concerned.'

'No? Well I have seen how he looks at you . . .'

'Even if that's true, I can't help how he looks at me, can I?' she responded defensively. 'But I assure you, I have no interest in him.'

'Ah, well, perhaps you don't have no interest in him if ye got your eye on Mr Robert.'

'As you say, Rosie, I'm here just as a governess. He's of the Quality, as you just reminded me. I have no great expectations. But that doesn't stop me liking him, any more than it might stop you.'

Rosie shrugged in response. 'Well I got no notions of ever having the likes of young Mr Robert to meself. I know me place. Abel Badger'll do nicely for me, thank you very much . . . Now then,' she said, changing tack, 'We'd better count the crockery together.'

Rosie led Isabel back into the nursery and advanced to the tall cupboard, which she opened.

'Why do we need to count the crockery?' Isabel enquired, puzzled.

''Cause Mrs Wilson said we must. Mrs Wilson said as I ain't gonna be responsible no more for the nursery crockery now as you've come. So if you don't count 'em, and see 'ow many is already cracked or missin' afore ye came here, you'll have to pay for 'em.'

'I'm not paying for crockery,' Isabel protested. 'Nor do I believe I should be expected to. I shall ask Mrs Wilson about it.'

'Suit yourself. But her won't be pleased if you're going to question what her said.'

'That's up to her.'

'All the same, Miss, you'd better count it and make a list – for your own good.'

'Will you help me then, Rosie?'

Rosie agreed and together they made a list of all the crockery there was in the nursery, counting and noting any items that were cracked or chipped, including the breakfast things the little girls had been using.

'I shall hand this list to Mrs Wilson,' Isabel said when they had finished. 'Now I must spend some time with the children. That's what I'm here for.' She turned to Charlotte and Henrietta. 'Tell me, girls, have you learned your letters?'

'Not yet, Miss Saxby,' Charlotte replied. 'Are you going to teach them us?'

'Would you like that?'

The two little girls said they would.

'Good. They're easy.' She turned to the maid. 'Rosie, would you be so kind as to clear away the breakfast things, so that the girls have room on the table for their slates?'

Wordlessly, Rosie did as she was asked but with a disgruntled sigh.

'I really think, Rosie, that the entire nursery could do with tidying up, don't you? Would you be good enough to put away all the clutter that's lying about, so that everywhere is neat and tidy? Please, Rosie?'

Isabel turned the blackboard and easel towards the children and took a piece of chalk. She noticed Rosie's grudging expression.

Rosie deeply resented this new situation which had been thrust upon her, rendering her subordinate to a mere sixteen-year-old girl, just because the girl was the new governess since the master's son fancied her. Somehow, she would bring the girl down a peg or two at every available opportunity.

Likewise, Isabel astutely perceived that she should expect to fight some battles of will with the nursery maid in the future.

'I shall write the letters of the alphabet one by one on the blackboard,' Isabel said to the children, with a smile, 'and I'll teach you what each letter is called and the sound of speech it represents. Then, I'd like you to copy them onto your slates. Are you ready?' To the squeak of chalk against the blackboard's painted surface she began writing and pronouncing the name of each letter of the alphabet.

After a while Henrietta said, 'May I have a drink?'

'You mean, "may I have a drink, *please*",' Isabel corrected. 'It's important and always polite to say please when you are asking for something.'

'Very well,' Henrietta conceded, but with a hurt look. 'May I have a glass of water, please, Miss Saxby?'

Isabel turned to Rosie. 'Rosie, would you be so kind as to fetch us all some fresh, purified water please?'

'But there's some beer left in that jug over there,' Rosie replied sullenly, pointing, suggesting the alternative in an attempt to save her a trip to the kitchen.

Isabel stepped over to it, looked into the jug and sniffed its contents. 'It's stale by now, so let's get rid of it, shall we? Besides, I don't hold with giving beer to children so young, when there must be purified water in a house like this.'

'So there is, Miss, but I'm afeard I won't be able to get none,' Rosie answered grudgingly, ''cause the butler has got the key to the cistern where it's kept, and I don't want to be on the end of a telling-off for troubling him.'

'Then why not ask the butler politely if he would be so obliging as to lend you the key so you can get the water yourself, and so save him being troubled? If he still refuses, tell him the new governess requests it for the master's children, because they are sick with thirst.'

'You don't know the butler.'

'I don't yet, Rosie, but I'm sure I'll make his acquaintance soon . . . Anyway, I imagine that mentioning the master's name will rouse him into action if all else fails. Don't forget to take this stale beer with you. You never know,' Isabel added brightly, 'you might see Mr Badger on your way.'

'Are ye suggesting we drink stale beer together?'

'Not at all, Rosie. I simply meant that the possibility of you seeing him might put a smile on your face.'

'As long as he don't put a smile on yourn, miss.'

\- - -

Chapter 13

SS Great Britain

Isabel and Ann found that for a while they had the Ladies' Saloon to themselves after dinner, so they settled themselves down on the upholstered seats.

'So, Isabel,' Ann began, turning towards her new friend. 'I want to know all about this Robert Wilson.'

'You mean *Sir* Robert Wilson,' Isabel corrected with an expression of sham smugness.

'*Sir* Robert Wilson.' Ann Queried, wide eyed. 'He's a knight of the realm now?'

'Oh, not because of his dashing chivalry. He inherited his father's baronetcy. His father was a cabinet minister in the government, but he passed away some years ago.'

'And presumably he's inherited his father's wealth also?'

'Not just his father's. His wife's father was a very wealthy man and he died not long after they were married, so she inherited everything, being an only child. Then she died.'

'So your Sir Robert is a widower . . . and a wealthy one at that . . .'

'Extremely wealthy. Not only did he inherit his father's estate, but also the wealth and estate of his later father-in-law.'

'Goodness, Isabel . . . He gets more interesting by the minute. Just think – if you were to marry him instead of your Barnaby you would be a titled lady, with two houses to live in.'

Isabel laughed. 'You and your romantic notions are running away with you, Ann. I am already engaged to Barnaby, remember. I certainly would not marry for money, anyway – two grand houses or not.'

'But what if you were to fall in love with *Sir* Robert all over again?' Ann suggested. 'It's not beyond the realms of possibility.'

'Yes it is. Way beyond. I'm older and wiser now.'

'But he's a handsome fellow, Isabel. You cannot deny it. In your position, *I* would be tempted. Then there's all that wealth to boot.'

'But the wealth would be his, not mine.'

'But it would benefit you, don't you see? It would be a most advantageous settling for you. Just think of the beautiful dresses you could amass, the bonnets, the shoes, the jewellery. And you'd look deuced well wearing a diamond tiara, my dear, and make an exceptionally beautiful mistress of whichever of his country seats you might be residing in.'

'I have some horrible memories of Patchfield House,' Isabel remarked. 'I have no wish whatsoever to return there – ever – especially as Robert's wife.'

'Then his other house and estate that his late wife inherited.'

'It's of no interest to me, Ann. Anyway, he's not asked me to marry him. Nor would I accept if he did.'

'You cannot possibly know that, Isabel. Anyway, I suspect he might ask. I've seen the way he looks at you. There is love, admiration in his eyes.'

'Any sign of lust?' Isabel quipped with disdain.

'Lust? Oh, lust too, I suspect. But that's always a healthy sign. What's wrong with a bit of vigorous lust in a man? I've been thankful for it a few times in my life.'

'Oh, I am not averse to lust in a man, vigorous or no, as

long as it's the right man and you are both driven by love,' Isabel replied, reminded of those deliciously intimate times she had very recently shared with Barnaby Micklejohn.

'Now who is being romantic?' Ann suggested.

'Perhaps I am, but the likelihood of Robert and me ever marrying is remote. It was never meant to be.'

'So you say now . . . But tell me . . . what horrible experiences did you suffer at his family home?'

'I cannot say,' Isabel answered firmly. 'I would rather not talk about it.'

'Was it the master himself who was so horrible to you,' Ann persisted. 'Or maybe his wife, the children, or perhaps the servants?'

'The children were delightful, and I became very fond of them. As for Mrs Wilson – I didn't like her much and I believe she didn't like me . . . for one reason or another. Maybe she suspected that Robert and I were fond of each other, and they considered me totally unsuitable.'

'And the servants?'

Isabel sighed. 'There was a nursery maid – Rosie Duckworth. I inherited her from the previous governess. She was already there when I arrived – to assist me I was told. She was older than me by 4 or 5 years, and she hated that I was of higher status in the house's hierarchy. She was lazy, cantankerous and insubordinate. She had a lover – one of the footmen – Abel Badger – and she was convinced that I was trying to steal him away from her. I wasn't, of course. But I was all too aware that Abel was interested in me, because he asked me several times to meet him, as well as making passes at me if ever we happened to meet in a corridor or on the stairs . . . at other times too . . .'

'You mean he stopped you and took you in his arms?'

'Nothing quite as romantic. Grabbing me, trying to kiss me, yes . . . Trying to feel my breasts, yes. But I always struggled free, although he was very strong. I couldn't bear him to touch me. After all, I was hopelessly in love with Robert. *He* was all I wanted. Unfortunately—'

At that moment, two other ladies entered the saloon and bid them good evening.

'Do you mind if we join you, ladies?' one of them asked.

'If you wish,' Isabel declared, feeling reluctant to admit them to their company, but relieved that their appearance had prevented Ann from probing for more information.

They introduced each other and there followed a period of small talk, questions and answers about why each was aboard the ship on its voyage to England. One woman was the wife of a Church of England priest, the other a doctor's wife.

'So when we disembark at Liverpool, where are you bound for?' the vicar's wife enquired.

'Guildford,' Ann said.

'Worcester,' Isabel replied.

'So how long since you were in England, both?'

'About fourteen years,' said Isabel.

'Then you will perhaps not be aware of the massive spread of the railways in recent years,' the woman said. 'Trains galore, everywhere, you know.' She rolled her eyes. 'From Lime Street Station in Liverpool, where we disembark, it's possible to get to almost any town and city in the country by steam train.'

'So I believe,' Isabel replied. 'We are not so cut off from civilisation in Van Diemen's Land that we have not heard of the wonderful railways.'

'Oh, but we hear that Van Diemen's Land is lawless with so many vagabonds and charlatans on the loose,' the doctor's wife remarked.

'Then I would say such stories are exaggerated,' Isabel replied with an affable smile. 'There are vagabonds and charlatans in every society, and perhaps we have our fair share, but life in Hobart Town is really very civilised.'

'I am greatly encouraged to hear it.'

And so the conversation went on . . . until Ann and Isabel declared their intention to take the air on the weather deck. So they left the company of the two ladies.

But the ship was listing slightly in the breeze and sea spray threatened to drench them from time to time, so they returned to the promenade deck below to continue their private conversation.

'So how did your romance with your Sir Robert develop?' Ann enquired, determined to press for more information.

'In faltering steps at first,' Isabel replied, 'and then in leaps and bounds. You see, after we first met I couldn't get him off my mind. I was so sure that he felt what I was feeling, but in that first week I was at Patchfield House I didn't see him at all, so I began to wonder. I had all but given up any idea of my first romantic adventure ever developing. But a week later – it was on the Monday – I decided that because the weather was so fair and the sun so warm and bright, I should take my two little charges into the parkland. It was my intention to instruct them on nature – the trees, identifying their leaves, the flowers, the different birds and so on. After a few minutes Robert arrived. It seems he had seen us leave the house and venture into the parkland, and he chose that time to approach me.'

\- - -

Chapter 14

Patchfield House

In the grounds of Patchfield House, the beech trees, the oaks, the elms, and the sycamores were celebrating their full greenery, their leaves rustling gently in the warm breeze. It seemed that every bird in Worcestershire was busy flitting between the branches, joyously singing their contentment at being alive in the glorious summer.

Isabel shepherded her two charges across green velvet lawns towards the lake, the sun beaming down on them. She chose a suitably shaded area beneath an oak tree and all three sat on the grass. She found an acorn lying close to her and began talking about it. Within a few minutes, she heard a man's voice call her name, and turned to see Robert Wilson approaching. Immediately her colour rose, and her heart started beating fast.

'Isabel, this is well met.'

'Robert,' she beamed, and stood up to greet him and walked towards him, smoothing the folds of her skirt. 'This is a pleasant surprise.'

'I hope you are well and settling into your new situation,' he answered, squinting against the blue brightness of the summer sky.

'Indeed I am, thank you,' she said.

'I hope my intrusion will not interfere with my sisters' tuition, Isabel.'

'Of course not, Robert, it's lovely to see you. I was just telling the girls about acorns and oak trees.'

'It all sounds very educational,' he said.

'I thought that it being such a lovely morning I would bring them out into the sunshine,' she remarked by way of explanation for their presence outside, at the same time wondering about his presence and whether he had deliberately sought her, or whether finding her was accidental. 'The fresh air will do them good. Would you like to join our little lesson?' she enquired with a bright smile, her colour diminishing. 'Perhaps there is some aspect of the nature around us that you would like to instruct us on yourself. If so, Robert, feel free.'

'You are the governess, Isabel. Far be it from me to try and emulate your patient disposition and ability as a tutor. I fear all three of you would succumb to wool-gathering if I were ever to try.'

'I can't speak for your sisters,' she responded. 'But I'd have no difficulty keeping awake, whatever subject you were enlightening me on.'

He perceived some ambiguity in that response. 'Is that so?' he remarked, raising his eyebrows and with a broad smile that showed his even teeth. 'But perhaps that depends on the subject being discussed.'

'Well, perhaps so,' she conceded artlessly. 'I suppose some subjects are more interesting than others.'

Robert turned to his young sisters and addressed them. 'Girls, would you like to see how many fishes you can see in the lake while I speak to Miss Saxby?'

They both looked up at Miss Saxby seeking her consent, and when she nodded, they scampered off to the water's edge.

'My sisters seem very much at ease with you,' he said when they were out of earshot.

'I'm at ease with them as well, Robert. We have fun together.'

'It's gratifying to hear . . .'

After an awkward pause, Isabel said, 'So how are you, Robert?'

'Well, thank you, but I've been thinking about you a great deal, Isabel,' he replied, and her heart jumped as if she had suddenly stumbled over a stone. 'I, er . . . I haven't tried to see you since you arrived here last week. I wanted to allow you time to find your feet, so to speak. You are seldom out of my thoughts and I would like to see more of you. Perhaps we could meet if you are amenable?'

She could not help her eyes glazing with tears of emotion and strove to push them back. Her hands began shaking and she held them behind her back, hidden by the folds of her skirt, so he should not see them trembling. But her blushes were blatantly evident through his eyes that were warm upon her. She hazarded a fleeting glance at his handsome face and in that brief moment perceived that he seemed as unsure of himself as she herself felt. Tongue-tied, she lowered her misty eyes decorously.

'Well?' he pressed.

'Yes, I would like to,' she answered softly, raising her gaze to meet his. 'I would like to very much, Robert. But how can it be arranged?'

'I think I have the answer, Isabel . . .' In a swift but gentle movement he took her hand and there was no doubt in her mind as to his earnest desire to love her and be loved. 'After the girls have had their supper and been put to bed,' he continued, 'leave the house by the servants' entrance at the rear and go to the summer-house. If I'm not already there, wait for me, and I shall come to you when dinner is over.'

'I'll try,' she said. 'But wouldn't Sunday afternoon be better, since it's my holiday?'

'Sunday afternoon is not an ideal time for us to meet. We would be easily seen, and people would certainly connect us. So I have been racking my brains to think of some way for us to be together, and this way is ideal, I think. Nobody comes to the summerhouse in the evening . . . And I really have been aching to see you.'

'But what if I am seen leaving the house when I am supposed to be with the girls all the time?'

'You are allowed some time to yourself, Isabel, especially when they are asleep, I would suggest. You cannot be with my sisters all the time. Besides, there's Rosie your nursery maid.'

'But what about Rosie? She would know when I am absent and wonder where I was.'

'Then allow her to be absent too from time to time,' he suggested.

'For what reason?'

'Well, rumour hath it that she and Abel Badger are fond of each other. I will leave you to make the arrangement with her.'

'So when should we meet?'

'Tonight,' he said decisively, his confidence returned. 'In the summerhouse.'

She smiled, her heart still pounding like a drum. 'Tonight, then. I think I'll take the girls there now and teach them more about their letters.'

- - -

Back in the nursery, Isabel said, 'Rosie, if you would like to dine in the servant's hall when the children have eaten their supper, I'll put them to bed. But be sure not to be late back.'

'How come?' Rosie asked, surprised at the unexpected suggestion.

'Because it will give you an opportunity to see Abel Badger.'

'I'm not sure what you mean, Miss Saxby,' Rosie queried suspiciously. 'Why are you suddenly so anxious that me and Abel should see one another?'

'Because it will give you and Mr Badger the chance to spend more time together.'

'Fancy,' Rosie declared. 'I don't know what's come over you. It's a bit of a surprise you offering that. So what's in it for *you*?'

'Nothing. But tonight I would like to get away from the nursery for an hour or so. When the children are abed would be a good time.'

'Ah . . .' she said. 'So's ye can meet Mr Robert, eh?'

'Who says I'm meeting Mr Robert?'

- - -

The sun was low in the sky and radiating slanting beams from behind clouds taking on the many vibrant colours of sunset. Having already worked out her route to the summerhouse, which was made more circuitous by dint of needing to remain unseen or confuse any witnesses, Isabel arrived and was content that nobody was any the wiser.

The sun's slow descent was bathing the earth in a deepening golden glow and lengthening the shadows of the trees, which would soon meld with the darkness of night. Isabel sat on one of the cushioned chairs and waited. trembling with nervousness and anticipation, and attentive to any sound that suggested Robert might be approaching.

At last he arrived, and she stood to greet him.

'You came,' he breathed, and his smile was as warm as the summer's day.

'So did you,' she said, stating the obvious, but at a loss to find other meaningful words.

'Were you seen?'

'I don't think so. But I am uneasy about staying too long – because of Rosie.'

'But you must stay till the sun has gone down at least.'

She smiled, looking into his eyes, and she nodded her assent.

'Oh, Isabel,' he breathed. He reached out and placed his hands on her shoulders before sliding them down to her waist by way of her arms. He pulled her close and kissed her on the lips. 'Isabel, my love, I have thought of nothing but you since the moment I first cast eyes on you,' he declared softly. 'If I thought for just a fleeting moment that it has been the same for you I would be the happiest man alive.'

She smiled in response but gave no answer.

'Well?' he probed.

'Yes, of course I've thought about you, Robert, but I've had other things to think about too.' She smiled sweetly. 'Being a conscientious governess to your sisters, for example.'

'I believe you are a most conscientious governess,' he conceded, 'so I accept that, so long as you confess you have thought of me sometimes.'

She laughed, delighted at his persistence. 'I just told you I have.'

'But I want to hear you say it again.'

'I have thought about you night and day, Robert. There – I've said it again.'

'Isabel . . . dearest. Now . . . I have a question for you.'

'What?'

'Will you be my sweetheart?'

The look in his eyes made her feel that she ought to run away at once, yet at the same time told her that she could never run away from him as long as she lived. However, quickly weighing up her two incompatible viewpoints, she stayed.

'Do you really want me to be your sweetheart?' she

queried, as if there could be some doubt in his mind, just as there was in hers.

'More than anything else in the world.'

'I would love to be your sweetheart, Robert,' she answered earnestly, looking into his eyes, 'but the difference between us must be an obstacle. I am only a servant, remember, while you are gentry . . .'

'I see,' he said, letting go of her and turning away. 'So tell me – do you consider your own father gentry?'

'Hardly. He is but a schoolmaster.'

'Do you think that matters?'

'I think it's important, Robert.'

'So do you consider yourself inferior to me?'

'I believe I'm as good as anybody else.'

'And so you are. But this difference in our classes that you feel, Isabel – this obstacle as you describe it – it exists only in your imagination. I don't feel it, so please don't let it hold you back. You're right for believing you're as good as any princess or duchess living, and I will treasure you, no matter what. As far as I'm concerned there is no gulf between us, no obstacle. So will you be my sweetheart?'

'Yes,' she sighed, and he took her in his arms again. In a torrent of emotion she nestled her head on his chest, and he stroked her hair, planting little kisses in it.

'Come,' he whispered. 'Sit on my lap and let me hold you. Let me satisfy myself at last that you are real, that you are warm flesh and blood, and not just my imagination playing tricks.'

And so they sat together, Isabel cradled in his arms, her head on his shoulder as she snuggled up to him. She was aware of the bats flitting silently under the trees outside, but was wrapped up in the fact that Robert had revealed his feelings, and she was relishing the moment. Not yet was she thinking of how this liaison might eventually develop.

He gently lifted her chin and planted a kiss on her lips, like a butterfly landing on a blossom. It quickly evolved into a deliciously long, lingering kiss that seemed to go on till Isabel was swoony with the pleasure of it, and the swollen red sun had sunk below the horizon.

'Will you meet me here again tomorrow after dinner?' he asked when they broke off.

'Yes, if I can,' she responded, breathless from the prolonged kiss. 'Of course I will. But if I don't come you must not imagine it's because I don't want to. I just don't know whether it will be possible all the time. If one of your sisters is unsettled or poorly when it's their bedtime, then I would have to stay with them.'

- - -

And so those first deliciously innocent meetings in the summerhouse set a pattern of countless secret trysts that inevitably grew in pleasure and intensified their love. As the summer progressed, they decided that their meetings should occur later when darkness had fallen, and so eliminate the possibility of being seen. So Isabel began making the deception of going to bed earlier, and waiting for Rosie to fall asleep before making her exit from the bedroom they shared. To avoid the possibility of waking Rosie, Isabel collected her clothes together and took them into the nursery where she could dress herself without disturbing her.

On the first evening of these later assignations she was sitting in his lap, and Robert was anxious to reveal his innermost secret thoughts that he hoped would change the nature of their relationship.

'Are you quite sure you love me, my sweetheart?' he began.

'Of course I'm sure,' Isabel replied. 'Else I wouldn't be here.'

'But I want to know how much you love me.'

'Well . . .' She hesitated thinking of a suitable response. 'I would take an oath to that effect in a magistrate's court, without running the slightest risk of perjury.'

He laughed and kissed her. 'What delicious nonsense you talk.'

'So how much do you love me?' she asked in turn.

'As much as is possible, and that's a great deal.'

'But how much is that?' she persisted. 'It's only fair you tell me exactly how much you love me.'

'More than you love me, I suspect,' he answered.

'So how much do you think I love you, Robert, if you are so certain you love me more?'

'You cannot expect me to give an accurate assessment, my darling. But I should have thought that a girl as clever as you could answer a simple question like that.'

'Oh, I don't set myself up as being that clever, Robert, whereas you go to Cambridge and study mathematics.'

'Well, I do pride myself on being able to put two and two together,' he riposted.

'In which case,' Isabel said gleefully, 'a mathematician of your ability should be able to measure such a simple thing as the degree of his love for his sweetheart, even without a protractor.'

'Ah, but even the very cleverest mathematicians cannot measure infinity,' he said triumphantly and kissed her again. After they had broken off their kiss he said, 'You know, I lie awake in my bed at night, just thinking of you.'

'Tell me what your thoughts are,' she probed, curious to hear, and snuggled up to his warm embrace.

'Oh, Isabel, I dare not. They are a mite racy. I fear you would not approve.'

Her laughter was like a bell tinkling. 'How shall I know, Robert, until I've heard it? Anyway, I thought we agreed we would have no secrets. Only ever the truth, so tell me.'

'Well . . . If you really want to hear it—'

'Of course I do.'

'I try and imagine you lying beside me.'

'You mean in your bed?'

'Of course in my bed.'

Her heart started beating like a drum, but she was not sure how she should respond.

'But not merely lying beside me . . . I imagine you lying *naked* beside me . . .' He paused, awaiting her reaction.

'Oh,' she said, but she laughed again, showing no sign of disapproval.

'I lie with my eyes closed and imagine your lips on mine and remember the taste of you. Then I smother your entire naked body with soft kisses.'

'Oh,' she said again, her heart by this time pounding. 'You're making me feel quite hot.'

'I kiss every mound and hollow of your body – your bellybutton and beyond – and I hear you sigh with pleasure . . .' He turned his head to look at her in the dimness. 'Do I shock you, my angel?'

'Such kisses might be a shock to my bellybutton – and beyond – but I'm sure my love for you would welcome them.' Her voice was taut, her throat suddenly dry and her mind was awhirl as she tried to imagine herself in that situation.

'Do you ever have such thoughts about me?' he asked.

'I dare not,' she responded. 'But sometimes, when I lie awake, I think what it might be like wedded to you.'

'Being wedded to me would entail all those things and more, my angel. Hence the term *wedded and bedded*,' he quipped.

'Yes, I know that's all part of being wed. So I suppose such thoughts cross my mind.'

'And how do your thoughts run on?'

'Well, because you are not there with me, I put my arms around myself, and imagine they are your arms . . .'

'And?' he prompted, a lump in his throat. 'Is there more?'

'Some . . .' She giggled girlishly. 'But I'm not about to tell you.'

'But we have no secrets, Isabel. The truth, remember?'

'You'll only think me a hussy.'

'Not so,' he said with tenderness. 'I can only love you the more. You must tell me.'

'Well . . . Then, I . . .' She hesitated, not sure whether to proceed. 'I cannot say it, Robert. Please don't make me.'

'No secrets . . . Remember?'

She sighed, wishing to confide her secret, but uneasy as to what he might think of her.

'Go on, Isabel . . .'

'No, I cannot bring myself to say such things,' she said virtuously. 'But my thoughts are not so different to yours . . .' Her voice was low, barely audible, and she realised she was blushing, glad the dusk concealed the fact.

'Why are we just imagining these things?' he breathed. 'Why should we deny ourselves any longer what we both dream about and long for?'

'But we cannot, Robert,' she sighed. 'We are not wed.'

'How conventional you are, Isabel. Not being wed does not confound our physical ability. It simply means we would be flouting the stupidly rigid conventions of society. In any case, we love each other, do we not? We would do it for love of each other, to make each other happy as opposed to being frustrated. Society has no knowledge of what we do anyway, so society could hardly condemn us.'

'So in your opinion it doesn't matter that we're not wed?' she asked, seeking reassurance.

'We are but flesh and blood, my darling girl. Why should the lack of a marriage certificate dictate that we should not enjoy each other and make the most of our love? Are we not in love?'

'We declare it often enough, Robert, but where could we do such things?'

'Here, of course. Nobody can see us, nobody ever comes here at night, nobody will be any the wiser. Tell me you are not loath, my sweetheart.'

'I am not loath,' she whispered, and gave him a hug to emphasise the fact.

The air was sweet and cooler now, permeated by the heady scent of flowers in bloom. Last night she had hardly slept for thinking about Robert. All day she'd been on tenterhooks waiting for their tryst.

Enchanted by the warmth of her affection, which she gave so unstintingly, he held her close. He suggested that they remove the cushions from the chairs and lay them on the wooden floorboards of the summerhouse to create a bed. She helped him arrange them, then lay down as if it were a bed fit for a bride. As he lay beside her she turned her face to him and smiled, but with apprehension, all her love and her trust exuding from her clear blue eyes that looked so heartbreakingly beautiful in the fading twilight. His lips caressed her smooth eyelids, with the lightness of a butterfly's wings. He found her mouth and she tasted him with pleasure as she ran her fingers through his hair in an ecstasy of bliss at her absolute love for him.

He was inexpertly fumbling with the buttons at the back of her dress, so she raised her shoulders to make it easier.

'Wait,' she whispered, realising the potential for absurdity that could mar those precious moments. 'Let me take it off.'

He watched in wonderment and reverence as she stood

up and undressed, apparently unabashed. Soon, she was standing before him entirely naked, her youthful slender body still discernible and exquisitely beautiful and enticing in the gloaming. She sat beside him, her knees drawn up and her arms around them girlishly while he pulled off his boots. He stood to remove his jacket, then his shirt, then his breeches, until he was as naked as she was. She watched him in turn, apprehension and desire co-existing within her, for this episode was as thrilling as it was unanticipated. She was about to give herself, willingly, unambiguously, because of her fervent love, and her trust in him.

They lay together on the cushions again and he rolled onto her and kissed her on the mouth once more, his hand gently kneading one firm young breast.

Before long, he broke off. 'I want to kiss your breasts,' he breathed, as if seeking permission, and his mouth skimmed her breasts delectably, his tongue teasing her nipples till she thought they would burst. He kissed her warm belly, then between her legs. She lay sprawled, astounded with pleasure, hardly able to believe that this was happening at all, that it felt so wonderful and so right. 'Oh, Robert,' she sighed, fondling the soft curls of his head between her fingers.

He found her warm, soft and deliciously wet, and they were both panting like hounds. After a while he slithered up to her till they were face to face again. He kissed her lips and, as she felt the lithe weight of his warm naked body, his chest against her breasts, she could hear her own whimpers of desire. Instinctively, she parted her legs a little to make herself more accessible.

He entered her slowly, gently. It stung a little and she winced. 'Oh, Robert,' she murmured.

He sensed her recoil and drew back at once. 'I'm so sorry, my love if I hurt you.'

'It's all right,' she breathed. 'Don't stop.'

He had no intention of hurting her, so was as tender as the situation allowed, which he realized was strange to her. But every little twinge that accompanied every tender push was a joy, and she raised her legs to accommodate him the more as he gently probed deeper into her. The pleasure increased with each tempered, careful movement, and they soon found themselves locked into a rhythm of sighs and gentle rocking that grew more compelling. Her breathing came in short gasps as she rubbed herself more firmly against him, for she found that it intensified the pleasure. Before long, all knowledge, all sense of who or where she was, had faded.

She held onto him fervently, her hands gripping his shoulders, then around his waist, then his buttocks in a hug of passion and pleasure as he thrust into her unstoppably. Some hitherto unimaginable, magnificent, tingling sensation developed in the pit of her groin that seemed to spread through her entire being, right down to her toes. She did not want this sensation to stop and was staggered by its absolute beauty and intensity. Then he groaned . . . and sighed . . . and eventually ceased to move . . . Aware of tears running down her cheek and around her ears, she cleaved to him. There seemed no doubt that this was the extraordinary and beautiful way things would be from now on. Everything had been building up to this moment and she welcomed it with all her being. If only she could make time stand still, for this was where she wished she could always be. If only this moment would last till eternity.

They lay silent, each aware of the enormous significance of what they had shared, aware of the sheer intimacy, the forbidden heights of unmarried ecstasy they had scaled and shared, but not regretting it, nor ashamed of it. There was no turning back. She was utterly content. All she wanted was to go to sleep in his arms, to awaken with him at dawn and smile into his soft eyes . . . and make love like that again.

But they must leave the summerhouse, and when they had both dressed, they stood holding each other.

'When shall I see you?' he asked.

'Tomorrow?' she replied.

\- - -

The nights were drawing in, and in the dark there was barely any chance of somebody seeing her as she made her way to the summerhouse. For that reason, Isabel no longer dressed on leaving her bed to meet Robert. She went there wearing only her nightshift and a dressing-gown. Logic decreed why get dressed, only to undress in the summerhouse, then dress again to return to the house, and undress yet again to get into bed on her return, all the time risking waking Rosie?

As summer thus progressed through September and into autumn, their skill at pleasing each other progressed with it. Any refinement of pleasure they could imagine they tried with tenderness, excitement and often with laughter, lying naked for as long as they dare, touching and teasing each other. Never did they lose their youthful enthusiasm for, or tire of, these wondrous exchanges of love and the pleasure they gave each other. Just being together under the thatched roof of the summerhouse was always magical. Being so deeply in love was simply magical.

But then there was the inevitable occasion when their delectable affair came to light.

\- - -

Chapter 15

Patchfield House

Discovery occurred on the day that the Wilsons were entertaining important guests for a few days.

For one, Mr Justice Oliver Russell, the well-known and handsome circuit judge, notorious for his womanising, was due to arrive. He was an associate of George Wilson in parliament, and a regular guest at Patchfield House at the time of the Worcester assizes, having enjoyed for many years a standing invitation. Consequently, he had become a close friend and confidant.

Robert, however, had been kept in the dark about the other guests expected that day; Sir Joseph and Lady Hulme with their daughter Elizabeth. The main purpose of their visit was to introduce Robert to Elizabeth, the intention being that they should eventually wed. Sir Joseph, a member of parliament and a Cabinet Minister in Lord Melbourne's government, was a prolific donor to the Whigs and wielded vast influence. It had been implied that if George Wilson could pull off the marriage of his worthy son to his equally worthy but undeniably plain daughter, the sky would be the limit politically and socially for George. This was sufficient encouragement for him to exert maximum pressure on Robert if necessary.

And so, after breakfast, George, his greying hair and whiskers bristling, summoned his elder son to the library where they could converse in private.

'So what do you wish to talk to me about, father?' Robert enquired. He sat facing his father whose face was rendered shadowy against the sunlight streaming in from the window behind him. Outside, Robert could see the gardeners at work sprucing up the flowerbeds. One of the men was pushing a new-fangled Edwin Budding lawnmower, recently acquired, across the extensive areas, leaving the grass impressively manicured.

'Sir Joseph Hulme and his good lady are due to arrive today at around mid-day,' George Wilson announced. 'Their daughter Elizabeth will be accompanying them, and you will be expected to spend some time with the girl.'

'Is this the same girl you once mentioned that you have set your sights on as an ideal match for me?' Robert asked astutely.

'She is a fine girl,' his father replied. 'The same age as yourself, and sole heiress to the Timberlake estate near Oxford and thus her father's entire wealth. I am reliably informed by those who enjoy her acquaintance that she is charming, personable and educated.'

'I take it then that you yourself have not met this girl, sir?'

'Indeed, I have not yet had the pleasure.'

'It follows then that you do not know what she looks like.'

George smiled. He had already deduced that the girl was no looker, but reckoned such a failing was irrelevant, especially where vast wealth and influence were concerned. Therefore, he replied, 'I strongly suggest to you, Robert, that whatever she looks like is of no consequence. She might be the most beautiful creature on God's earth. On the other hand she might not be. Either way it's of no consequence, as I say. Women are all alike once you get past the colour of their hair and the structure of their faces. And believe me, even those attributes are of no matter once you've got used to them . . . And looks certainly don't matter in the dark, you know,' he added with a knowing look. 'Now – with your best interests at heart – I have agreed a most admirable and advantageous match for you that will serve you propitiously for the rest of your life.'

'I see, sir.' Robert said, trying to hide his resentment at this unwarranted interference. 'I take it, then, that you do not trust me to choose my own bride.'

'My son, you are young and headstrong, and you have some hard lessons to learn about the world we live in and how it works. I repeat – I have arranged a most admirable and advantageous match for you that will serve you propitiously for the rest of your life. Barring a Hanoverian princess falling in love with you, you could do no better for yourself if you scoured the earth. You must grasp this extraordinary opportunity with both hands and be thankful for it.'

'But what if I were to tell you, sir, that I am already in love with somebody already – a worthy young lady – a princess in my eyes – so therefore have no interest whatsoever in this Hulme girl, however well-endowed she might turn out to be?'

'And who might that particular princess be?' George asked disdainfully. 'Not your sisters' governess, I trust, with whom you were so obviously infatuated recently.'

'I am not prepared to reveal who the girl is at this point, sir. But because I am in love with one girl, how can I offer another any sincere affection?'

George Wilson sighed profoundly. 'Sentiment is an expensive luxury,' he declared. 'Are you really prepared to overlook a handsome fortune for the sake of a pretty face? I prefer a pretty woman myself, but the Timberlake estate and all that goes with it is an extremely large sum to pay for the difference of a tenth part of one inch between the length of two sets of eyelashes. Anyway, does this mystery girl you are so attached to come from the aristocracy? Does she bring with her a handsome dowry, an ample inheritance? Or is it our recently installed governess after all, with the long eyelashes and big blue eyes?'

'I am not prepared to reveal who she is.'

'I must remind you, Robert, that you are not yet one-and-twenty years old, and that my consent to any marriage that is against *my* better judgment will not be forthcoming, whether to a governess or anybody else.'

'That is no more than I would have expected, sir,' Robert answered with a shrug of frustration. 'But such a threat does not deter me. I am sorry to offend you, sir,' he added, 'but I shall not marry this Elizabeth Hulme girl.'

'Don't apologize to me, Robert. Of course, I am bitterly disappointed in your attitude, as well as your abject refusal to see common sense by shunning a vast fortune. However, it will trouble me not to alter my will, and so leave my entire estate to your brother. You will not receive a penny.'

'Sir, the possibility of poverty does deter me. I have made up my mind to marry this girl. She is penniless, and with no dowry, but she is straightforward and honest, and the only girl in the world for me. Nothing will alter my decision.'

'Noble sentiments,' George remarked with a mixture of sarcasm and scorn. 'If it were not so frustrating to encounter such naivety it might be refreshing. If you go on like this you might even restore my childhood belief in fairies and pixies. But I would like to know whether this young lady would be as inclined towards you if she knew you were not about to inherit my estate. I would like to know whether poverty is as attractive to this young lady, whom you say you have set your heart on, as it appears to be to you. Anyway, I wish you to understand that the apparently genuine admiration you have for this girl will in no way alter the disposition of my estate. So pray be in no doubt on that point.

'Do you not understand,' George continued, 'that I – and others – have it within our power to ensure that you are excluded from every lucrative prospect of making a handsome living, either in government or in private enterprise? Even from university.' This was an exaggerated claim, but George felt it a threat worth citing. 'Go against my wishes and who do you think will pay the fees to your college, and everything else thereafter while you struggle to find your feet? Certainly not I.'

'But what's in this for you, father?' Robert asked shrewdly. 'You seem overly adamant that I should comply with your wishes.'

'Because it's for your own good,' George replied emphatically. 'You must understand, Robert, that Sir Joseph is highly influential, and a man not to be trifled with. This is not an arrangement to be glibly spurned, and I shall not allow you to spurn it, since any spurning might involve repercussions not merely for you, but for our entire family. Do I make myself clear? Such a liaison as we both propose is a signal honour for you – for me, for all of us. Naturally, it is also intended for the benefit of his daughter. You—' he wagged his finger at Robert to stress his frustration '—you blind jackass, are perceived as an ideal match for her, because of who you are. Be glad of it.'

Robert realized he was going to get nowhere with his father's fixation on the proposed match, so decided some show of co-operation would be appropriate meanwhile, not simply to gain some time, but to relieve himself of the tedium of being preached to. After all, circumstances might change; this Elizabeth Hulme, yet unseen, might herself register no interest in marrying him anyway.

He sighed, and said, 'Very well, father. I shall be the perfect gentleman and make my acquaintance pleasantly and with good humour with this Elizabeth Hulme, but my heart will not be in it.'

'Thank you,' George said solemnly. 'Someday, Robert, I conceit you will thank me for this. Nobody expects you to ask for the girl's hand immediately – that would be too unseemly – but get to know her a little on this first occasion. You might yet be enchanted, you might at least like her. And meanwhile, seriously rethink your unwise and ridiculously unprofitable attachment to this other young woman.'

- - -

A little later, Robert ventured outside into the garden hoping to find Isabel with his sisters, to let her know that he would not be able to meet her in the summerhouse that night, as his presence was required with guests.

But the earlier sunshine had disappeared, the sky had clouded over, and there was no sign of Isabel or her two charges. So, dismally, he made his way back to the house, wondering how he could let her know without making their liaison obvious.

As he approached, he saw a fine black carriage, drawn by a pair of well-groomed black horses, halt in front of the portico. Within seconds his mother and father were on the portico steps to greet the visitors, with broad smiles, outstretched hands and a troop of servants. Two footmen, one of whom was Abel Badger, attended to the visitors' trunks and in turn engaged in conversation with the carriage's driver and footman.

Robert held back and stood behind a tall elm waiting for Sir Joseph, his wife and daughter to enter the house. Once they had gone inside he made his way unseen to the library and wrote a note to Isabel, telling her not to venture to the summerhouse that evening as his presence was requested to help in the entertaining of the visiting family.

Having written his note he made his way back to the hall, where Abel Badger was conveniently descending the sweeping staircase, having taken the visiting family's baggage to their rooms.

'Ah, Badger!' he said. 'This is well met.'

'Can I help you, sir,?' Badger enquired.

'A word in private, if you will . . .' he led Badger outside onto the steps of the portico, now devoid of visitors and servants. 'This note . . .' He spoke in hushed tones as he proffered it to Badger. 'I wish it to be handed to Miss Saxby, the governess. If you are to encounter Rosie, your friend the nursery maid, as I understand you might—' he gave a knowing wink – 'perhaps you would be good enough to hand it to her to pass on to Miss Saxby.'

'Of course, sir,' replied Badger. 'I daresay as I shall see Rosie when 'er comes down for your sisters' dinners at mid-day, sir. I'll see as her gets it.'

Robert smiled. 'Thank you, Badger. But keep this to yourself.'

'Of course, sir.'

Robert went in search of the guests, while Badger slipped the note into his pocket and went about his business. In a quiet corner of a service corridor he withdrew the note from his pocket and opened it. When he had read its message he pondered it, then tore it up and disposed of it. A little later, when the servants were assembling in the servants' hall for their mid-day meal he saw Rosie and pulled her to one side. What he had learned was too intriguing to keep to himself, and he felt he must share it with her.

'Did ye know as Miss Saxby and Mr Robert are enjoying each other's company on the quiet?' he asked.

'I can't say as I'm surprised,' commented Rosie. 'But how d'you know as much?'

''Cause he's as good as told me.'

'Why would he tell you?'

'Never mind why. But there's been some shenanigans going' on in the summerhouse after dinner of a night.'

'The summerhouse? So that's where she's been a-going.'

'Aye, the summerhouse. But whatever you do, don't let on to her as you know, else there'll be trouble.'

\- - -

So, after dinner, with the family entertaining the guests, and a time for relaxation from his duties, Abel Badger made his way slowly and unobtrusively to the summerhouse. The September sun was already sinking below the horizon as he approached. As he crept towards the double door stealthily, he discerned in the dimness that Isabel was not there. So he waited.

He waited what seemed like an eternity. Then, at last, in the silence he heard the faint scuff of footsteps on the gravel path, and retired to the dark depths of a corner, his pulse racing. When the door opened he saw her, a silhouette against the dark grey of the night. She looked as if she was ready for bed, wearing what looked like a dressing gown, which she doffed. He could see in the dimness that she was wearing only a nightshift as she settled herself on the chaise longue, her legs outstretched along its length.

He watched her for a while, his lustful imagination running riot, then made his presence known. His suddenly appearing from behind her in the darkness startled her, for it was patently not Robert.

'Is that you, Mr Badger?' she exclaimed.

'Good evening, Miss Saxby.'

'What are you doing here?' she asked, indignant at his unwanted presence.

'I might ask you the same question,' he replied. 'But happen I know. You're here to meet Mr Robert, ain't you?'

'Am I?' she said.

'I know it just as well as you do, miss. And I can tell you as he ain't gonna show.'

'Has he sent you to see me?'

'Aye. I got a message for you. He can't come tonight 'cause there's house guests and he's entertaining 'em.'

'I knew some guests arrived earlier today. So who are they?'

'Well, first of all, we got Mr Justice Oliver Russell, the famous circuit judge. He comes and stays regular for the assizes. But then we got Sir Joseph and Lady Hulme staying and all, with their nineteen-year-old daughter Elizabeth. As Mr George's valet, I'm privy to a lot more information than anybody else in this house, and I get the feeling as marriage is being planned for her and Mr Robert, with an almighty dowry chucked in for good measure. A wealthy man is Sir Joseph. Very wealthy.'

Suddenly the bottom fell out of Isabel's world, and she felt sick at the thought of everything this information implied. 'How can you be certain about this?' she asked, a tremor in her voice. 'I don't believe you.'

'I'm as certain as anybody can be.'

'So what has Mr George told you that he wouldn't tell anybody else?' she asked.

'It ain't so much as what he said to me directly, like, but I overhear talk. And every snippet o' conversation that don't mean much on its own, can mean a lot when strung alongside other snippets. It's like putting a puzzle together.'

'So, Mr Robert asked you to let me know that he would not be able to meet me tonight?'

'Ay. Like I said. To my mind it's an unkind way of lettin' you down, so 'tis, a comely educated young madame like yeself.'

Audaciously, he sat beside her on the *chaise longue* and lifted his legs up, to rest alongside hers.

'Hodge over a bit. I ain't got much room here.'

She made to get up at once, but he grabbed her, thwarting her escape. 'There's no rush to go,' he said smoothly. 'You should be glad as there's somebody as'd be happy to take you on. Me, for instance, 'specially now you know as *he* ain't interested no more.'

'I don't believe you, Badger,' she said icily. 'I don't believe a word.'

'Then go to the house and take a gander for yourself. You'll find our Mr Robert intimately engaged in a cosy chat with that Elizabeth. Good-looking madame she is, and all. You might even see 'em taking the air out here together, if you wait long enough.'

To Isabel's surprise and outrage he leaned over and kissed her on the lips, and his hand went straight to her breast.

'What do you think you are doing?' she protested, pulling away.

'Oh, come on, Isabel,' he said impatiently. 'It's all right if I call you Isabel, ain't it? After all, we're both servants in the same house.'

In that instant, he pushed her down so that she was lying on the *chaise longue*. He spread himself on top of her, still trying to kiss her, his free hand clawing at her shift. She turned her face from him, protesting vehemently, trying to push his hand away from her thighs, which he was now groping having pulled her shift up. But he was bigger and stronger than she was. He forced his knee between her legs, hurting her as she resisted, and she yelled in exasperation as he thrust his hand between her legs and fingered her.

'*Badger*!' she shrieked again, to no avail, and began thumping his back with clenched fists. But it made no difference. Pressing his whole weight upon her, pinning her down, he unfastened his breeches and she sensed him release himself.

She was about to be raped.

She screamed, so he clasped his hand over her mouth to silence her. 'You should understand, Isabel,' he rasped as he put all his strength into tearing away her shift, 'that right now I'm the master in this here summerhouse, and so long as you're in here with me you'll do as I want ye to do. The sooner you accept this, the easier it'll be for you.'

Isabel made one last gasping attempt to free herself, to shove him away. She managed to get one arm free, and she brought her hand up to his face, and tore her fingernails down it, feeling the resistance of the flesh from his temple, across his cheek, and down to his chin as she dug them in deep.

He yelled with pain, loosed her, but slapped her hard across the face in retaliation.

'You little minx!' he roared. 'You'll not get away with that.'

Because he had let go of her, she quickly got up from the *chaise longue* and made her escape. He ran after her, but she ran faster than him back to the house, and managed to reach the safety of the nursery before he could. She locked the door, just in case.

Thankfully, the children were asleep in their bedroom, and Rosie was evidently still asleep. Feeling drained of all strength and dignity, Isabel sat on one of the nursery chairs in the darkness and wept, her head in her hands. Never had she expected to be so humiliated and used, treated so abominably. Abel Badger was a brute, but whether he was a lying brute she was not sure. Because Robert had not come to meet her, she accepted that he must have been expected to keep company with guests. But was there really a plan afoot to marry him off to some wealthy aristocrat's daughter?

In the two seconds it had taken Badger to say that a marriage was being planned between Elizabeth Hulme and Robert, she had spiralled into a deep chasm of heartbreak and gloom, where desolation prevailed. In those two seconds she had become the only person in the world cared for by nobody. Was Robert really promised to another? Never had she known such abject despair. And to be so ruthlessly abused by that rat Abel Badger was the final humiliation. She felt empty and abandoned. Her dreams were lying in tatters, her hopes in terminal jeopardy.

But she had been forewarned. As a servant in the Wilson household she counted for nothing, and she recalled her father implying as much when he recognized her infatuation with Robert. So had she brought this shadow of disillusionment on herself, for allowing herself to become rapt in a romantic affair that must inevitably end nowhere, except in tears?

She stood up and gazed out of the window into the darkness of the night. The trees were barely discernible shapes against the cloudy sky. Her normally sparkling eyes were puffy and red and streaming with tears.

There was always the possibility, of course, that Abel Badger had drawn the wrong conclusion from conversations he had overheard. Or, he could have been lying, just to curry favour for himself. As soon as she could, she must see Robert and discover the truth. On the other hand, all this might be a horrible dream, from which she would wake up, and everything would be as it should be.

But this was no dream.

What she had learned in the summerhouse and the abuse she had suffered told her this was no dream. Nor even a nightmare. There must be repercussions.

Yet how could she possibly report Badger's abominable behaviour to Mrs Wilson without implicating herself and Robert in their conspiracy of hearts?

She could not.

It was impossible.

- - -

Later that night, George Wilson rang for his valet. It was time for bed and Badger must aid George's usual bedtime rituals of undressing, washing, hanging up discarded clothes or consigning them to the laundry.

'I hope you had an enjoyable evening, sir,' Abel said as he removed George's coat and draped it over a hanger to be put away.

'Thank you, Badger. It was very pleasant.'

'I trust the good judge Mr Russell was in good form, sir, and ready to dole out just deserts tomorrow at the assizes.'

'You needn't worry your head about the good judge, Badger. He's a fair man and can normally see any chink in a defendant's story – or a plaintiff's for that matter.'

Badger took George's cufflinks and returned them to their usual abode. 'What little I saw of 'em, sir, Mr Robert and the visitin' young lady seemed to have their heads together. Is there something in the wind, sir?'

George turned and smiled at Badger's usual mischievous inquisitiveness. 'Do you wish me to say, yes, there is, Badger, so that you can spread rumours below stairs?'

'Not at all, sir. Especially if 'tis only a rumour.'

'What's the matter with your face, Badger?' George asked, avoiding the question. 'You have scratches all down one side, and they're bleeding.'

'I know, sir.' He sighed. 'I was fondling one o' the cats, as I like to do, and held it up to me face to feel its soft fur against me cheek, when it scratched me.'

'That's bad luck, Badger.'

George sat on the bed and offered his right leg to his valet so he could pull off his boot.

'I, er . . . I learnt one thing today, sir . . .' He eased off his master's boot, stood it on the floor and readied himself to pull off the other.

'Oh? What's that, Badger?'

'Young Mr Robert has been secretly meeting Miss Saxby, the governess,' he declared. 'Of an evening in the summerhouse . . . It's been a-going on for some time, I believe.'

'That is most interesting, Badger. Thank you for reporting it to me.'

'But might I respectfully ask, sir, that you don't tell nobody as it's me what told ye?'

'How so, Badger?'

''Cause Mr Robert hisself told me to let Miss Saxby know as he wouldn't be able to see her tonight, sir. If you say anything sir, he'll know as it was me what told you. Also, sir, if you give Miss Saxby her marching orders, she'll likewise know as it was me as told you.'

'Very well, Badger. I shall not implicate you.'

'There's more, sir . . . I was charged with letting Miss Saxby know, so I waited for her in the summerhouse where she was to wait for Mr Robert.'

'I see,' George mused, obviously disturbed by the information. 'Are you quite sure you acquired those scratches on your face by fondling a cat?' He flashed him a knowing look.

Badger nodded his head vigorously. 'Oh, aye, sir. Like I said, sir it was one o' the blessed cats.'

'Well, something must be done, Badger,' George said. 'We have to put a stop to their shenanigans. The governess is hardly a suitable match for my son.'

'I agree, sir. But what, sir?'

'Robert is due to return to Cambridge soon. I can arrange to have him despatched thence without delay, without implicating you. Then I think it would be appropriate and well received that he should enjoy an extended visit to the home of Sir Joseph Hulme where he can enjoy their hospitality over the Christmas season. I'll fix it today. Furthermore, any letters from my son that might arrive here for Miss Saxby we shall destroy.'

'Buy what about the governess, sir?'

'She's crossed the line, Badger.'

'Let her stay, sir. I would if I was you. I'd keep it quiet, otherwise there'll be tittle-tattle, and folk'll blow it all up into a scandal.'

'Thank you for your advice, Badger,' George said, tongue in cheek. 'You are right, of course. The last thing we want at this time is a scandal.'

'Quite right, sir. I can ask Rosie the nursery nurse to keep an eye on her and report to me everything. Besides, sir, as a governess, she seems very good, and I'm told your daughters are very fond of her.'

'It strikes me you have a *penchant* for the wench yourself, Badger.' Another knowing look, for George was a wily old bird. 'It would be a more suitable match, I grant you. Think you can divert her?'

Badger grinned. 'I'd like to try, sir.'

'We don't want any undue scandal attaching to my family, or to anybody in this household. Not with so much at stake regarding Robert and the Hulme girl.

Badger grinned triumphantly. 'I thought so, sir.'

'Very well, Badger. You can take your chances with the

governess as your reward for bringing this unsavoury liaison to my attention. But let's keep this conversation entirely to ourselves. Is that clearly understood?'

'Yes, sir. You have me word. Thank you, sir.'

- - -

Next morning, Rosie awoke to the sound of children's voices. Charlotte and Harriette were evidently up and scuffling about in the nursery. Rosie duly rolled out of bed, pulled down her nightshift to cover her legs and rubbed her eyes. She stood up, stretched, and went into the nursery.

'You're up early and no two ways,' she said, addressing the two little girls collectively. 'What's up?'

'We're thirsty,' Harriette declared, 'and we got nothing to drink.'

'Well, if Miss Saxby had been where she should have been last night, she might've made sure you had some water by your beds.'

'Can you get us some water, please, Rosie?' Harriette asked. 'I can't reach the jug 'cause I ain't big enough yet.'

'I'll get it for ye.' She opened the tall cupboard and lifted out the jug and poured each of the girls a mugful. 'Here, and don't let Miss Saxby hear you say "ain't", else she'll be correctin' you all day long.'

'Thank you, Rosie,' they said in unison.

'Now go back to bed till it's time to get up proper,' Rosie said, and ushered them back into their bedroom.

When she returned to the bedroom she shared with Isabel, Isabel was stirring. She stretched her bare arms out and ran her fingers through her loose hair. At once she recalled the harrowing events of last evening and recoiled back under the sheets and blanket.

'Your arms is all bruised, miss,' Rosie remarked. 'Been in a fight, have you?'

At once anxious, Isabel thrust her arms out of bed and

inspected them. Indeed, both her upper arms were bruised and so was one wrist.

'I fell,' Isabel answered, pulling out of thin air the only excuse she thought plausible.

'Where?' Rosie asked astutely.

'I fell up the back stairs last evening when I came up.'

'Is that why you didn't come to bed right away? I heard you come back but ye seemed ages in the nursery afore you came to bed.'

'Yes, I was nursing myself.'

'You need to be more careful, miss. You need to look where you're a-going.'

'I was careless, Rosie.'

'Let's have a look at your knees.'

To satisfy her own curiosity Isabel pushed away the bedclothes, and her nightshift that had ridden up in her sleep revealed her legs. Her thighs were bruised also.

'You must've took a proper tumble accordin' to that,' Rosie said. 'All that wandering about in the dark. If you don't mind me saying so, miss, 'tis my opinion that you've been spending too much time away from the nursery of a night. It's all well and good thinking all's well and good, 'cause Rosie'll be there to fend for Charlotte and Harriette if they happen to wake up, but what if I told Mrs Wilson how often you ain't here?'

'Oh, don't do that Rosie.'

'Then tell me what you been up to and I won't say nothing.'

'I haven't been *up to* anything, as you put it, Rosie. Just minding my own business, that's all, which I suggest you do also.'

'Oh, getting uppity now, are we, miss? And look how your shift is all ripped . . . Well I reckon as I know what you been up to. Is that how you got your bruises?'

'Oh, Rosie, I don't know what you're talking about,' Isabel replied indignantly and buried her legs, her arms, her torn shift and her head under the bed clothes. There she remained, reliving the horrors of last night, until Rosie had got dressed and had gone to fetch their breakfasts from the kitchen.

But what Isabel did not witness was the conversation between Rosie and Abel Badger when they met in the servants' hall at breakfast time.

'God, Abel, what've you done to your face?'

'I was mollycoddling one o' the cats last night afore I turned in, and when I nuzzled me face into its fur it scratched me with its sharp claws.'

'Then ye should drown it, as soon as you get the chance. You're not the only—' She was about to say he was not the only person that morning to be nursing wounds, but she stopped herself as her alert brain made a logical connection. 'Are you sure it was a cat as done it. Abel?'

'What makes you say that?'

''Cause it looks to me like it's somebody's fingernails what's done it. Them scratches are too far apart to have been done by a cat's paw, unless it was the size of wench.'

'No, it was a cat, Rosie, you dimwit. Course it was a cat.'

'Sure it wasn't a wench? Looks suspiciously like a wench's work to me.'

'Don't be stupid, Rosie. What wench?'

'Oh, I think I know what wench. I presume you got your wicked way with her. Was she worth it? Was she better than me? If so, your scratched face is your just deserts?'

Badger looked her squarely in the eye. 'Rosie, you got a vivid imagination. It was no wench.'

'So how come as Miss Know-All up there in the nursery has got bruises and marks all over her arms and thighs this mornin'? And a torn shift. Only *you* knew where her was due to be last night. Remember? I reckon you went to her, eh? Did you?'

'Like I say, Rosie, you've got a vivid imagination. Just simmer down and don't be so blooming daft.'

- - -

Chapter 16

SS Great Britain

From Captain Matthew's viewpoint the voyage had so far progressed satisfactorily, experiencing only light winds and relatively calm seas. On most days the sun shone, so that spending time walking and sitting on the weather deck was pleasant. Due to the light winds, the *Great Britain* was forced to burn coal, using its steam power much of the time to augment sail. When the winds were strong enough for sail only, the crew would raise the propeller to reduce drag, by means of a cleverly engineered system.

Three weeks into the voyage, and it was Christmas Eve. The ship had reached Cape Horn, and passengers gathered on deck to witness the numerous icebergs, and marvel at their vivid blue and white shimmering as the sun reflected off them. Yet everybody was apprehensive about the potential for havoc. On Christmas day, a Sunday, a Divine Service was held in the main salon, attended by passengers and crew, preceding a hearty Christmas luncheon. The evening was a time for parties, glees, poetry readings and singing. Dancing had become possible since those passengers with musical ability and instruments to play had been identified and persuaded to form a band. Some of the more conservative passengers frowned on such merriment on the Sabbath, but the festivities went ahead anyway. In steerage, fights broke out, blamed on the drinking of excessive amounts of alcohol by those involved. Some of the culprits were clapped in irons till they sobered up and calmed down.

By this time, Isabel and Ann had become more involved with the ship's entertainments. Isabel's out of practice pianoforte playing improved along with the increasing frequency with which she was requested to accompany the various passengers who were cajoled into singing, although she often willingly gave way to more competent pianists. It transpired that Ann Carter had a delightful soprano voice and her talent was frequently in demand. One passenger magically produced some copies of Much Ado About Nothing and suggested that Shakespeare's comedic play should be rehearsed and performed. Some complained that it was too challenging a project, arguing it would be impossible to do it justice unless appropriate properties and scenery could be contrived. However, they agreed to rise to the challenge. The project leader, one Jeremiah Entwistle, suggested that Robert Wilson play the part of Benedick, and Isabel the role of Beatrice. Ann was delighted when asked to play Hero, but indifferent to an army officer, Captain James Cuthbertson who had volunteered to play the part of Claudio, because he believed it would bring him close to Ann Carter, whose good looks and bearing he admired.

At the first rehearsal, Isabel and Robert both privately perceived that the interaction between Benedick and Beatrice was to some extent a reflection of their own personal positions. By this time they had become friends again. Robert was still intent on wooing Isabel, but more passively, by taking his time and showing that he still cared for her, rather than pressing her. As a result, she had become more relaxed in their renewed but undemanding platonic friendship, although she was still careful to keep him at arm's length. They had avoided further reminiscences and reminders about their past liaison, because one aspect in particular of their relationship was too sensitive to mention, so it had not been broached; it remained an issue, looming and unaddressed – the elephant in the room. For now though they could be friends and laugh with each other again at appropriate moments. Sometimes they dined together, sometimes they were invited to sit at the captain's table with other passengers, including Ann Carter. Because Ann and Isabel were known to be traveling unaccompanied, and had become friends, and were both good-looking, their joint invitations to the captain's table were frequent.

After luncheon on the afternoon of 30th December, rehearsals for Much Ado About Nothing were well in progress. The ship had rounded Cape Horn and its enigmatic icebergs. But very soon after that, it began rolling and dipping violently; it was increasingly evident that a storm was brewing. The group had reached the point in the play when the stage directions indicated that Beatrice and Benedick must kiss, and this time it was decided they must go through the motions.

So kiss they did . . .

It was a strange and exhilarating moment for both. The kiss took place in full view of the rest of the cast, and to some frivolous banter. It set both their hearts beating fast, but for different reasons. Robert ensured the kiss lasted meaningfully longer than it need have done, and eked pleasure out of it since it aroused poignant memories of their ardent youthful embraces. He hoped it might reawaken Isabel's appetite for him likewise. As their lips parted they exchanged a fleeting but telling glance before the next scene was enacted.

However, the rehearsal was suspended soon after, when the violence of the storm increased noticeably. The cast decided that their preferred places to ride it out would be their cabins, so each departed thence, leaving Isabel, Ann, Robert and Captain Cuthbertson in a lingering, indecisive foursome.

Meanwhile, the crew had leapt into action, appearing everywhere, from nowhere. From the open top deck, sailors clambered the masts to reef the sails, battling the ferocious wind and the heavy spray. The dipping and rolling of the ship was magnified alarmingly the higher up in the rigging they had to climb. Inside, others began lashing down any furniture that could move, including the piano which seemed to have a mind of its own as to which direction it wanted to dangerously lurch.

'I'm scared,' Isabel unashamedly admitted as she tottered unsteadily, reaching for something rigid to cling to.

'So am I,' Ann declared. 'God knows how long we shall have to suffer this. What if we were to sink?'

'I agree, it's not the most comfortable of conditions,' Robert commented, his voice raised so he could be heard over the racket.

'Perhaps we should make our way to the stern where there are some comfortable fixed seats,' Ann suggested.

'The stern is the last place you want to be,' Captain Cuthbertson proclaimed. 'The rise and fall of the ship will be exaggerated at the stern. It will be akin to being on a giant see-saw. The middle of the ship – the beam – is the best place to be.'

'I think I'm going to my cabin anyway,' Isabel announced. 'Would you like to come with me, Ann? We might bring some comfort to each other.'

'I don't believe I could offer you much comfort, Isabel,' Ann answered, reluctantly clinging to James Cuthbertson as if her life depended on it. 'I'm scared too. I would be of no comfort whatsoever.'

'Hold tightly onto me, Isabel,' Robert suggested earnestly. 'And I shall see you safely to your cabin.' He offered his arm and she grabbed it, lurching forward as she did.

'Thank you, Robert.'

Unsteadily, they made their way to Isabel's cabin, leaving Ann and Captain Cuthbertson to their own devices. On the way they encountered a crew member who exhorted them to return to their cabins immediately.

At her door, Robert said, 'Shall you be all right, my dear?'

'Once I've retched,' she answered pragmatically, anxious for him to go before she did so in front of him.

'Then I'll leave you. You've lost colour, you know. You look very pale.'

'I'll perk up once I've retched.'

He smiled sympathetically. 'Yes, I trust you will. But try not to be too frightened by the storm. I have every confidence in this ship's ability to survive it.'

'I do hope your confidence is justified. Sorry, Robert, I must go.'

'I'll call later to see how you are.'

'Thank you. That's very thoughtful.'

She opened the door, closed it behind her and immediately vomited into the basin on the washstand. At once she felt better, but the anxiety of what might happen to the ship in such a violent storm persisted. What if it were to sink? She lay down on her bunk, trying to settle, but soon felt nauseous again, so she sat up. This was an ordeal she had not counted on and she loathed it.

A gigantic sea was running at the ship from the stern. The Great Britain would rise up on the swell, balance herself on the crest and then plunge into the trough of the wave with a malicious sideways roll. The next towering wave would then swamp the ship while it lolled still trapped in the depression of the last one, when tons of water would engulf it with thunderous crashes onto the top deck and the hull. Every heart-stopping rise and fall produced pandemonium that wrought private terror among the passengers, and even anxiety among the crew, let alone the animals penned in on the Weather Deck.

Sometimes the sea thrashed and thudded against the hull, all at the whim of the gale, which howled through the wet greyness of the day as if its sole intention was to terrify. The Great Britain was adrift in a pitilessly raging ocean, its grey fury whipping it up into a torrential ice-cold spray. In that wind-driven, spiteful deluge icebergs still lurked, unseen in the limited visibility. The ferocity of the storm was enough to scare even the uniformed hierarchy of the bridge.

After about an hour, Isabel, still terrified, and sitting on her bunk, heard a knock at the cabin door. She stirred and answered it. Robert Wilson stood unsteadily, facing her.

'I've called to see how you are.'

'Still terrified,' she replied economically.

'Do you still feel seasick?'

'A little, but not as bad as before. You'd better come in and sit down before you fall over.'

'I will, thank you.'

'I suppose there's a convention that suggests I should offer you a dish of tea,' she quipped, trying to make light of the situation. 'But, as you can see . . .'

He laughed. 'No matter.' He sat on her bunk and caught her as she listed over in the opposite direction to the roll of the ship. 'You'd better sit down before you fall, Miss Saxby,' he said, guiding her onto the bunk beside him.

'I dread to think how long this storm will last,' she remarked.

'Who knows? I sought out Captain Matthews after I left you and spoke with him and Mr Grey, the First Mate. Both said that a storm like this could last for days here in the South Atlantic, so for the comfort of the passengers and the animals, the captain has set a course for the Falkland Islands where we can shelter, but also take on more coal. So it should soon be over – for us at any rate.'

'How long before we get there?' she asked.

'During the night, he believes.'

'It can't come soon enough.'

'Try not to fret, Isabel my dear,' he urged. 'We shall survive the onslaught. This ship is British built and sturdy, and will withstand any storm. Furthermore, I have faith in the intrepid Captain Matthews and his doughty crew to see us through. Try and rest.' He put his arm around her and drew her to him.

Compliantly, she nestled into his embrace, glad of his tender care, glad of his reassurance, and glad of his company.

'Try and sleep a while,' he said softly into her ear. 'I am not going anywhere. I shall stay here with you.'

She was shaking with fear, she was cold, so cold, and the warmth and affection she felt emanating from him was like a cosseting blanket. He stroked her hair, his lips caressed it and it soothed her. She closed her eyes, aware that she was in the arms of Robert Wilson again, the man she had loved in her teen years with all her heart and soul. Never in her life had she envisaged she might see him again, let alone be in his arms. Yet here she was, admitting to herself that she was glad of it.

Eventually she fell asleep and dreamed a strange dream that she was back at Patchfield House and had just seen

Robert for the last time. In her dream she was weeping, heart-broken, feeling utterly desolate, yet being mocked by the repulsive servant Abel Badger and sworn at by an angry and jealous nursery maid.

Eventually, she awoke, feeling nauseous again. Still in Robert's arms she rubbed her eyes and looked up at him.

'How long have I been asleep?'

'Hard to say. An hour, maybe two. I don't know because I drifted off myself.'

'The storm is still raging,' she remarked.

'And yet we're still afloat. Once we get into the lea of land it should become calmer.'

'Thank you for being so kind to me, Robert,' she said. 'I might have died of fright had you not been so.'

'Well, you seem to have got your colour back at any rate.'

'Have I? I don't see why, because I feel so queasy again. I think it would be best if you leave me now. I can't imagine that you would wish to witness my retching. It's not a pretty sight. But I trust I shall see you once we've made the Falkland Islands.'

'I hope so, Isabel.' He unhanded her and stood up unsteadily. 'If you're quite sure that you are going to be all right, I will leave you for now.'

'Do you not feel seasick?' she asked.

'No, strange to admit, I've never been afflicted by the phenomenon. At any rate, I am hoping that the galley will have been able to cook up some food. Will you join me later?'

'Oh, Robert! Food is the last thing I want. No, I shall stay here, suffer the storm and try to sleep.'

\- - -

Isabel awoke during the night and noticed with relief that the cacophony of crashing waves, bangs, creaks, the howling wind and the lashings of rain and sea spray had abated. She swung her feet to the floor, rose from her bunk, and discovered that she could stand without teetering over. The ships' rolling had all but ceased. She felt around in the darkness and found the bottle of pure water the ship supplied daily, and drank from it. Then she rubbed her eyes and returned to her bunk. Her thoughts drifted between Robert Wilson and his consideration towards her during the storm, how he had comforted her. Then she remembered they had kissed earlier, as Beatrice and Benedick, and how that kiss reminded her so vividly of their youthful kisses and delectable lovemaking in the summerhouse at Patchfield. Did she still feel something for him, she asked herself? Could his kisses and his kindness reignite her long-extinguished passion for him? He was still as kind and considerate as she remembered him, still the gentleman, even more handsome, certainly still desirable, and infinitely wealthier. To her, though, his wealth was irrelevant, though she admitted to herself that her young girl's passion for him had left its indelible mark. Yes, she was still moved by him, which surprised her.

Were it not for Barnaby . . .

Then she considered Barnaby, at home in Hobart Town with those two delightful little girls, her ward Polly and his daughter Miriam. And she felt guilty that she had enjoyed being kissed by Robert as part of the rehearsals for the play, that she had been held in his comforting embrace for hours and had welcomed it. If only she could be with Barnaby and tell him how much she loved him. By rights she should be his wife by now, not troubled by the presence of the man she fell hopelessly in love with as a naïve girl of sixteen. If only she was tucked up in bed with Barnaby right now, as they had been on those few precious times when they had been able to slip away to her hideaway in Bellerive. Never had she felt so happy and so fulfilled as she did on those occasions, lying contentedly and dearly loved in his arms.

As she lay, these thoughts meandering through her mind, she began to realize that not only was it quiet and the motions of the ship had ceased, but that dawn had broken. She got out of her bunk and stood on tiptoe to peer out through the deadlight. It was early morning and she could see hills. They had reached land. Between the hills and the shore were a few scattered buildings, a jetty. The ship had anchored and between the jetty and the *Great Britain* were other sailing ships, all at anchor. So this was the Falkland Islands. This must be Port Stanley.

It was also New Year's Eve.

Then Isabel realized she was hungry.

- - -

Isabel and Ann arrived in the saloon for breakfast at the same time, so sat together. Conversation at first was about the storm and how miserably long they had endured it.

'Did you sleep?' Ann asked.

'Eventually,' Isabel replied. 'Did you?'

'Eventually . . . After James had left me . . .' She glanced at Isabel for her reaction.

'Oh, I wondered whether . . . And when did James leave you?'

'Well, dawn had broken,' Ann replied frankly.

'Ann, you are the limit. I hope nobody saw him leave your cabin, else your reputation will be ruined.'

'I don't give a fig about my reputation on this ship, Isabel. Nobody knows me but you—'

'And Captain Cuthbertson,' Isabel interrupted.

'Nobody else. Anyway, my reputation on this ship won't follow me from the railway station in Liverpool when we arrive there. I know I told you that I wouldn't be averse to a little unofficial dalliance aboard this ship,' she added defensively, 'but it was not like that with Captain Cuthbertson. We were not intimate. I'm not that keen on him.'

'Unlike your previous dalliance with the clergyman.'

'I see you don't believe me, Isabel. I would happily have exchanged Captain Cuthbertson for your Robert.'

'And you'd be welcome to him, Ann. So is that why you are so touchy this morning? Because Captain Cuthbertson made no attempt on your chastity?'

'Well it does make one wonder if one is losing one's appeal.'

Isabel laughed at her friend's pique. 'Robert came to *my* cabin yesterday. Mind you, he didn't stay long. He left in the early evening.'

'And did you?'

'Did I what?'

'Oh, you know . . .'

'Certainly not,' Isabel protested amiably. 'I felt terrible, and I must have looked it. But I did fall asleep in his arms for a while.'

'What was it like to kiss him again after all those years?'

'I only kissed him as Beatrice,' she was eager to explain. 'It was . . . not like our kissing of 16 years ago. It was too contrived to be spontaneous or romantic. And we had an audience.'

'But did you like it?' Ann asked.

'I suppose I liked it well enough,' Isabel answered with a frisky smile. 'Who doesn't like kissing a handsome man who kisses nicely?'

'So, has he set your pulse racing again? Has he turned your head at last, and diverted you from your Barnaby?'

'No, Ann,' Isabel sighed. 'Nothing will divert me from my Barnaby. Besides, I have good reason for not wishing to be romantically involved again with Robert Wilson.'

'It's strange, Isabel – I think over the past month I have got to know you rather well, and it has become more obvious to me that there is something more about what happened between you and Robert Wilson that you haven't mentioned.' She looked at Isabel enquiringly.

Isabel gave a hint of a shrug and raised her eyebrows.

'Am I right?'

Isabel sighed. 'Yes, you're right, Ann. I have not discussed it with Robert either. It's too . . .' She hesitated, trying to find the right word. 'It's simply taboo.'

'Do you want to tell *me* about it?'

Isabel pondered the suggestion for a moment. 'I don't know, Ann. Perhaps I should. Like you, over the past month I think I have got to know you quite well too. You have become my *confidante,* my mentor, and I trust you to keep things to yourself, as I do for whatever you tell me in confidence. So yes, perhaps I should unburden myself. It's time I did. It's something that's lived inside me like a canker all these years. But I shall not tell you here in the saloon with stewards and other passengers bustling about, all within earshot. Let's meet later. If there's a ferry that will take us and bring us back, I rather fancy going ashore to Port Stanley for a long walk. I fancy feeling my feet on dry land again. Then I'll tell you more, where only you and the wind will hear my words and scatter them out to sea.'

'So a long walk and a long talk,' Ann remarked. 'I hope you enjoy walking.'

'I'm as fond of walking as I am of talking, Ann, which is saying a great deal. You could say I'm as walkative as I am talkative.'

'Isabel, that's rather good – *walkative*.'

Isabel smiled impishly. 'I know. I just made it up. Meanwhile, though, I'm going to sit and write a letter to my Barnaby. I shall be able to post it to him in Port Stanley, and it will be delivered to him long before I reach England. At least he will know that I'm surviving and missing him terribly.'

'And what shall you say to him?'

'That I love him more than ever, and hope that he and our two little girls are well.'

- - -

Port Stanley was growing in importance for seafarers, especially since it was becoming a restocking depot for essentials such as coal, ship repairs and the exporting of wool. Whaling vessels were commonplace, and there was a small garrison of soldiers. At whatever port the *Great Britain* appeared, crowds would turn up to catch a glimpse of the legendary ship. Port Stanley was sparsely populated, but the Governor of the islands, George Rennie, saw fit to come aboard, which he did to a warm welcome, watched by what few citizens of Port Stanley were not at work.

Captain Matthews let it be known that the ship would be taking on coal and other supplies, which he hoped might suffice for the remainder of the voyage, and that they would be anchored at Port Stanley for a few days. Anybody who wished to go ashore during that time would be ferried across. Different rowing boats carried Saloon Class passengers, second class and steerage to the port.

Isabel and Ann took advantage of the service and set foot on the Falkland Islands, happy to feel solid ground under their feet. The sky however was overcast, rain threatened, and the air was cool, rendered cooler by a stiff breeze. Isabel posted her love letter to Barnaby and they set off on their walk.

'Isn't it strange,' Ann remarked, 'how you still feel as if you are on board ship even when you are on dry land? I keep trying to compensate for the ship's movements with every step I take.'

'I know,' Isabel replied. 'It's peculiar. I noticed it the first time I disembarked from a ship.'

'I trust you've spoken to Robert this morning?'

'I have. When we left the saloon after breakfast he tapped on the door of my cabin, to see how I was. I told him I was much better, and that perhaps I would see him when you and I returned to the ship. He said he would like to join us on the island, so I daresay he'll come ashore, if only to feel the earth beneath his feet also.'

'But fancy living here,' Ann said, the corners of her mouth turning down in aversion. 'It's so bleak. There's nothing, is there? Just a few houses and other buildings.'

'I bet there's a tavern somewhere, though,' Isabel suggested. 'There are whaling ships here, and you know what whalers are like.'

'No, I cannot say I do. I can only imagine. So tell me.'

'Well, let's say they're partial to drink, as well as being a lecherous, uncouth lot. We see plenty of them in Hobart and they're best avoided . . . They're too fond of rum . . . Now that's reminded me of home,' she sighed.

'Now, Isabel, don't get all sentimental on me for Hobart Town and your Barnaby,' Ann chided gently as they strolled along a narrow coastal path, 'because I can see exactly where you are heading. Instead, tell me the taboo bits about Robert and your stimulating love affair when you were just sixteen years old. You got as far as telling me that you'd given up hope of it at one point, but then he found you with his sisters in the grounds of the house.'

Isabel recounted how she and Robert came to establish their romance. 'Oh, it was delightful . . . We arranged to meet in the summerhouse as often as we could. It was all very secret and grew all the more intense because of it. And, as the summer rolled on, our trysts evolved into more than just kissing and cuddling.'

'You mean losing your virginity?'

'Oh, yes . . .' For a moment Isabel was misty-eyed. 'I loved losing my virginity. I loved doing what we were doing. It was addictive, I was in love, and I just couldn't get enough. I ached for him every hour of the day. We would meet late at night – every night – when my nursery maid Rosie had gone to bed and was asleep.'

'So how long did this go on, this unashamed, obsessive coupling?'

'Oh, Ann, you make it sound so unromantic, but it was delicious – and very romantic. We were passionately in love – and I mean passionately. Anyway, it went on like this until halfway through September. Then all hell broke loose. His father had arranged for a wealthy family to stay with them. They had a daughter the same age as Robert, and their fathers had arranged for them to marry. Little did I know then that it would be the last time I would see him as my sweetheart. But then, a couple of weeks or so after he had gone, I realized I was carrying his child . . .'

'Oh, my God!' Ann exclaimed. 'So what did you do?'

'Well, I felt I could not go to Robert's father and confess my plight, although looking back now I realize that perhaps I should have done. I don't suppose he would have allowed us to marry, but at least I might have received something in acknowledgement, some recompense perhaps, if only to keep my mouth shut and avoid a scandal. I was also too proud and too ashamed to throw myself on the mercy of my father, although again, looking back, I know that's exactly what I should have done. Instead, I kept it all to myself. I told nobody. I was just sixteen, naïve, and I didn't know what else to do. As my belly grew, I grew plump with it, but I hid my lump with the clothes I wore. I don't think anybody guessed I was with child, they just saw me grow thick around the middle.'

'But at some time, Isabel, you must have given birth. So where is your child?'

- - -

Chapter 17

Sunday 12 May 1839
Worcestershire

For Isabel's seventeenth birthday the Saxby family held a small celebration at the family home. It was a bright, sunny Sunday, the only day during the week that she was allowed free time in which to visit them.

As they sat at the scullery table, conversation was random, peppered with giggles and playfulness from the two younger sisters. Apart from Isabel they all looked rather Sunday-ish, still dressed as they were for the morning service at church earlier. Susan Saxby meanwhile was trying to speak seriously to Isabel about fellow churchgoers, which led to questions about people and events at Patchfield House.

'There's nothing much happening there that's any different,' Isabel declared unenthusiastically.

'You sound quite down in the dumps, my dear,' her father commented. 'Is everything all right?'

'Why shouldn't it be?' Isabel answered defensively.

'I don't know,' he replied. 'But your demeanour leads me to wonder whether you are altogether happy there.'

'Sometimes I ask myself whether I am cut out to be a governess,' Isabel admitted.

Susan flashed a concerned glance at her husband. She too felt that something was troubling her daughter, and was anxious to know what.

'But the children who are in your charge . . .' William Saxby said. 'I trust that you correct their childish sins, and comfort their childish sorrows?'

'I do my best, father.'

'I'm sure you do,' William concurred, 'but has there been any criticism of your work?'

'I'm not aware of any. If there has been, nobody's said anything to me.'

'Is Mrs Wilson treating you fairly?' Susan asked. 'As I've said before, you don't have to stay there if she's not, or if anybody else there is making you unhappy. You can always come home.'

'I'm not unhappy in that respect, Mother,' she replied evasively. 'I rarely see Mrs Wilson, and if I ever do she looks straight through me as if I were invisible.'

'And what about the rest of the household? The servants?'

Isabel shrugged. 'Most are pleasant enough.'

'And the nursery nurse who assists you?' Susan persisted. 'Is she any easier to work with lately?'

'She's the same as ever, Mother – lazy, uncooperative, brusque, and coarse.' She shrugged again. 'It doesn't bother me. I just get on with what I have to do – being governess to the children.'

'Have you seen much of young Robert Wilson?' Susan asked hoping she was getting to the heart of the matter.

'I haven't seen Robert Wilson since he returned to Cambridge last September,' Isabel answered, feigning it was of no consequence. 'He's not been home since.'

'So is that why you are down in the mouth?' There was an abundance of sympathy in Susan's smile. 'I know you seemed quite taken with him – and he with you, unless I'm very much mistaken.'

'Yes, I liked him very much, mother.' Isabel said frankly,

'but he's gentry and I'm only a servant . . . remember?'

'You're getting plump, our Isabel,' Susan remarked. 'Too much rich food they're feeding you, I suppose. No wonder the gentry all seem to get so fat, if they indulge in heaps of rich and fancy foods all the time.' Such was their faith in their daughter's virtue, neither parent would ever consider that her increasing roundness was due to being pregnant – she was not that sort of girl. There could be no doubt whatsoever that she was a virgin, and would remain a virgin till the day she married.

'I don't go out of my way to indulge in rich and fancy foods, mother. I eat the same as the other servants – often the same as what's been provided for the family and any guests. I admit, though, I am getting plump, as you claim, but I intend to lose it.'

It was a pivotal moment. Isabel saw that she was faced with an opportunity to confess there and then that the cause of her apparent increasing plumpness was because she was carrying Robert's child, and close to the end of her term. It would shake them out of their wits. But the prospect of any contempt, hostility and her absolute dread of their ultimate rejection, prevented her from owning up to the fact. Isabel regarded her mother and father as strictly conventional, pious and virtuous, befitting the family of a respected schoolmaster. To fall foul of their elevated standards would be unthinkable. Time would be the arbiter. Time alone would decide whether things would work out satisfactorily, or otherwise.

When it was time to leave home and return to Patchfield House, the weather had changed and a belated April shower was falling heavily. Despite the rain she bid them her goodbyes with waves as she went down the garden path onto the lane, with promises to visit as usual next Sunday. She tightened her shawl around her and thought of Robert.

She was always thinking of Robert. But Robert was gone, spirited away. The promise of eternal happiness, marriage and an ever-present father for her child was gone with him.

How futile their delicious romance had all been, but for the fact that it was now a cherished memory. However, the fact that she was about to have Robert's child she welcomed with all her heart. The child would be a part of him, a constant reminder of the joy and pleasure they shared, and she would cherish it. She had no idea what life had in store once it had been born. Yet one thing was certain; she could not remain as governess at Patchfield House with her own child.

On the other hand, since she had already proved to herself that she lacked the heart and the courage to confess her plight to her parents, her only option would be to have the child without anybody's knowledge, a goal she artlessly believed she could achieve. Then she would leave Patchfield House at once, to make her own way in the world. She would not return home with a bastard child in her arms, and throw herself on the mercy of her mother and father. After Robert, she could endure no further rejection.

Her child would restrict what she might be capable of achieving, of finding work or lodgings, but somehow she would cope; she loved the child already – it was Robert's child – and spending all her time with it would be her main purpose in life, and a joy. She had no thoughts, no notions of meeting another man when the passage of time had finally healed her broken heart. She could love no other man like she loved Robert. But she would at least have his child, and his child would be her saviour, her amulet.

The rain became a downpour, drumming on the spring foliage of the trees that lined the rutted lane, but she walked on. If only she had thought to bring her umbrella – a cherished Christmas gift from her father, and made from whalebone covered with alpaca. The rain and the wind could not hurt her. She would survive it, like she was surviving the heartache. The relentless rain, however, began to seep into her shawl; her bonnet was becoming limp and bedraggled, and the drops of rain trickled down her face like an excess of tears. What would Robert think of her if he could see her now, with her nine-month belly and soaked to her very skin, looking rotund, bedraggled and ungainly? She hardly resembled the vibrant, slender, pretty young thing she was when they first met. But she would emerge from this all the wiser, all the more worldly, and all the more compassionately.

And then she felt it; the first pang that suggested her baby was on its way. She winced, stopped and gripped her belly. When it passed she quickened her step. She must get to Patchfield House as quickly as she could. With no practical experience of giving birth, having never attended a birth, her only understanding of it was from overhearing conversations of other servants, and it all sounded distinctly unsavoury.

- - -

Wet and dishevelled, Isabel climbed the back stairs unseen, and reached the nursery. Thankfully, nobody was there; the children were with the family as they normally were on a Sunday; Rosie had not yet returned, doubtless out courting with Abel Badger. Isabel took off her wet things, draped them over the fireguard to dry in front of the fire. Undressed, she donned her nightshift and slipped into bed. Another contraction. She winced and groaned. Rosie would return soon. What would she tell her when she did?

Soon after, Rosie appeared, entering their bedroom, also soaked from the rain.

'You're in bed early, Isabel. What's up with yer?' she

enquired, taking off her wet shawl and bonnet.

'I'm not well, Rosie. Ever since I left my father's house I've been getting pains in my stomach.'

'Pains in your stomach, eh?'

Isabel nodded, looking sorry for herself.

'Something you ate?'

'No, I don't think so.'

'I wonder what it could be then . . .' Her eyes met Isabel's challengingly, knowingly.

'Just leave me be, Rosie, and I'll be all right. Will you see to the children when they come up?'

'Aye, I reckon I'll have to.'

'Thank you.' Isabel turned over to lie on her side.

'Isabel, d'ye think I'm stupid or somethin'?'

Isabel peered over the bedclothes warily. 'What do you mean?'

'Can I be frank with you?'

'Go on,' she answered impatiently.

'Well . . . I have to say this . . . I share a bedroom with you, and have done for nigh on a year now. I see you undressed. You ain't the slender little thing you was when you first came here, are you? Your belly's got big, and d'you think I ain't noticed as you've used no clouts for your monthlies for the past seven or eight months? That tells me you've had no monthly bleedin'. Come on, wench, you're with child and I reckon you're about to drop it, or I'm a monkey's uncle.'

Isabel's eyes grew misty with tears. 'Has it been that obvious, Rosie?'

'It has to me.'

'Has anybody else mentioned it?'

'Not in my hearing. That don't mean to say as nobody else has noticed though.'

'Well, you're right,' Isabel admitted. She sat up and

wiped her tears with the back of her hand. 'I'm having a baby, and I think it's on its way.'

'I knew it. So whose is it? Abel Badger's or Robert Wilson's?'

'Oh, whose do you think, Rosie, for goodness' sake?' she asked impatiently.

'If I thought it was Abel's I'd stifle the little bastard first chance I got, be sure o' that, 'cause I know as how he might've had you that night you came back all bruised and in a state, and him with scratches all down his face. Not that he would ever admit to it.'

'Well, it's not Abel Badger's child I'm carrying, Rosie. He never *had* me as you so eloquently put it, you can be sure.'

'Says you. And I'm supposed to believe that, am I? You ain't such a goodie-goodie after all, are you? On the other hand, if it's Robert Wilson's bastard, that's tough on you anyroad, and I feel sorry for you, 'cause he ain't never gonna marry ye or even admit to it. But I did warn you – the gentry don't wed their servants, they only bed 'em – then they stick together, the gentry. I reckon you've been too blinded by love to see all that, an' too obsessed with that tingling you get between your legs when he's having his way with you.'

Isabel winced and whined with pain again as another contraction assailed her.

'You're gonna need some help, missie, and no two ways, if you want to have the child.'

'Of course I want it. So will you help me, Rosie? Please?' she pleaded. 'But don't let anybody else know I'm having a baby. When it's come I'll just leave this place. I don't want anybody to know.'

'Oh, and what am I supposed to do with all the mess? Has your water broke yet?'

Isabel shook her head, not sure what Rosie meant.

'There'll be wet everything – sheets with blood all over 'em most likely. D'you think the laundrymaid won't notice? Then there'll be the afterbirth to be got shut of. How? And what about when somebody hears the little bastard a-crying, eh? The children will hear it for certain. They'll want to know why there's a baby a-crying in the bedroom next to theirs. Once they know, everybody else will know, and I'll be blamed for not reporting it.'

'Let me have my baby first,' Isabel pleaded. 'You can report it when I'm gone. I'll be gone as soon as I can.'

'Listen, I'll help you to the best o' me ability. But I ain't no midwife, I'm just a nursery maid, so don't blame me if it all goes wrong. When it's over, I'll have to let Mrs Wilson know what's happened, else I could lose me position here. You see that don't you?'

'Yes, Rosie, I do . . . Thank you.'

- - -

As the night wore on, Isabel tried her utmost to stifle her cries of anguish so that the children, by this time sleeping in the next bedroom, should not be woken up and become alarmed. By daybreak Rosie had delivered her of a perfect baby girl, and handed the child, smeared and slippery, to Isabel who held her with a look of wonder and instant devotion. Immeasurable joy filled her heart, and she was confident the future would take care of them both. The world was infinitely benign, awash with human kindness, and would regard Isabel Saxby and her beautiful baby girl with a benevolence befitting her own humanity. This was the start of a new phase in her life. If she had the blessing and support of her parents after all, all well and good, for it would relieve her of some of the responsibility of raising the child; if not, she would embrace the challenge, and the obligation she had to her child, to ensure its well-being.

All hope of an idyllic future as the wife of Robert Wilson

was in the past; it was certain he had never even been aware that she had been carrying his child. He had not written; he had not been home for Christmas. According to what she had gleaned, he had been despatched to the home of the Hulme family, then to Rome, no doubt to marvel at the remains of the Forum and the Appian Way. Nor had he been home at Easter because he had been invited to stay with the Hulmes again.

'You done well, Isabel' Rosie remarked but grudgingly, interrupting Isabel's contemplation. 'Let me have the bab and I'll clean her up.'

Isabel handed the baby back to Rosie, whereupon Rosie duly cleaned the child, scrutinizing her to ascertain if she could discern any likeness to Abel Badger, for her suspicions had not been entirely allayed.

'You need to rest now, miss. But hold the bab first while I clear out the top drawer o' the chest over there. I'm going to line it with something soft for the poor little thing to lie on.'

'That's a good idea,' Isabel answered, taking the child back into her arms. 'Thank you. And I expect she'll need feeding soon.'

'I expect she'll let ye know when she's ready. But in the meantime you need to rest.' Rosie emptied the drawer and lined it with a pillow, then took the child and laid her in it. 'What you gonna call her, eh?'

'I don't know yet, Rosie. I'll think of something.'

'Well, try and get some sleep now.'

'I think I ought to get up. I shall leave as soon as I can with my baby.'

'Listen, missie, you'll be in no fit state to leave here till tomorrow at the earliest. You've just given birth, not had a shit.'

Isabel winced at Rosie's coarse comparison.

'Get some rest,' Rosie repeated. 'You need it. Then be on your way tomorrow if you feel well enough.'

'I'll try . . . Thank you for being so kind, Rosie. I don't know what I would have done without you.'

'No, nor do I.'

Soon, Isabel drifted off into a deep sleep. When Rosie was satisfied that the girl was sleeping soundly she made her way to the servants' quarters. Most of the servants were already up and about their business, including Abel Badger whom she drew to one side.

'I got something to tell ye that might just interest you,' she began.

'What?'

'I been up all night with the governess.' She looked into his eyes challengingly.

'So?'

'Did you know as she was carrying a child, Abel?'

'No, but how should *I* know? She don't confide in *me*. I could see as she was getting a bit thick round the middle, though. Jesus! I should've twigged it.'

'Aye, well, her being thick round the middle was a child.'

'What d'you mean, *was*?'

'She dropped it this morning at daybreak. A girl.'

'Jesus! Are they both all right?'

'Both hale and hearty, Abel. Why? Are you worried?'

He shrugged. 'Why should I be worried? But as long as they're all right.'

'I asked her if you was the child's father. I know well enough as you'd set your cap at her, and you might've had her.'

'Me? I never had her. I told you. Nay, it ain't my child, Rosie. You can be sure o' that.'

'That's what *she* said.'

'Then why not believe her? It'll be young Mr Robert's

bastard, and no doubt about that, what with all their goings on in the summerhouse.'

'Well Mr Robert ain't here to gainsay it or confirm it, is he, Abel? So if the child ain't yourn, what if I asked you to do away with it?'

'You mean kill it?' He laughed at the absurdity of the suggestion.

'But that'd prove to me as the little bastard ain't yourn – cause nobody would ever kill their own child, would they? And it'd prove your love for me once and for all.'

'Nay, Rosie, you're asking too much, you expect too much o' me. I ain't going to gaol for nobody, 'specially for some daft whim like that.'

'But we could say as she killed the child herself, 'cause she didn't want it. After all, she couldn't stay here as governess and keep the little bastard, could she? She's sleepin' now – fast as a rock after pushing all night long. Now's the perfect time. You could do it, Abel, and nobody would be any the wiser.'

'Listen, Rosie, don't say a word to anybody about any o' this,' Badger warned, harking back to George Wilson's demand for the utmost discretion. 'The master won't want any tittle-tattle from servants that reeks of a scandal. I'd best go tell him what you just told me. The child is Robert Wilson's without a doubt, so the master must be told, and I shall tell him straight. I can talk to him, man to man. Then it's up to him to decide how to deal with it. I'll tell him when I go up to him.'

\- - -

George Wilson, Member of Parliament for Worcester North was still in his nightshirt when Abel Badger, his trusted Patchfield valet, made his appearance. It was six o' clock and the spring sun was already casting its first slanting yellowy rays through the large window into the bedroom.

'Good morning, sir,' Badger greeted.

'Good morning, Badger,' George reciprocated. 'Lovely morning.'

The niceties over, George decided what he was going to wear and Badger duly laid the garments out.

'Would you like me to shave you, sir?' Badger asked.

'Indeed, Badger.' The master replied. 'Shaving's one chore I despise doing for myself. When I'm in London there's a capital barber shop I frequent, you know, owned by an aging Italian. I insist on him shaving me and not his Cockney – and cocky – assistant.'

'Wise choice, sir. Excuse me, sir while I fetch some hot water.'

Badger duly sped to the kitchen to get the water and towels necessary to shave Mr Wilson. On his return he set everything before him on the washstand and George Wilson sat down next to it. Badger wrapped a towel around his master's chest and shoulders, then lathered his face using a soft shaving brush, before proceeding to scrape away the whiskers with an open razor.

'Anythin' interesting going on in the House o' Commons, sir?' Badger enquired conversationally.

'Nothing that might interest you, Badger, unless you're interested in the Imprisonment for Debt Act, or the suspension of the Jamaican Constitution. All dry stuff, Badger. Very dry. It would bore you to kingdom come. What's been going on here while I've been away? Something a trifle more interesting, I hope.'

Badger gently straightened the flesh of George's cheek while he slid the razor deftly across it, then wiped the blade on the towel.

'Well, sir . . .' The perfect opportunity to repeat what he

had just heard. 'There just happens to be something as you should know about, what was brought to me attention only this morning, sir.'

'Oh? What's that, Badger?'

'The young governess was delivered of a baby girl at daybreak, I'm told, sir.'

'The governess?' A look of alarm was evident in his eyes.

'Aye, the governess, sir. The nursery maid, Rosie Duckworth – my sweetheart – was in attendance. It was she who told me.'

'I see . . . and what do you make of it, Badger? Who is said to be the father of the child?'

'Well, sir . . .' he hesitated. 'You won't like this, sir, but it's a certain fact as the father of the child is your son, Robert.'

George let out an explosive gasp. 'Damn and blast his hide, the young fool,' he chafed. 'Are you sure? This is not just hearsay, is it?'

'Definitely not hearsay, sir. Nobody else knows about it.'

'I thought he had given up the waif.'

'Oh, I believe he did, sir. You saw to that yourself as I recall. But not before he'd put her in the family way, sir.'

George pulled the towel from around himself angrily, and with one half of his face covered in white lather and the other side clean-shaven, he got up from his chair, clearly agitated.

'And you are quite sure of this, Badger?'

'Dead certain, sir. As we discussed last summer, they'd been a-meeting up in secret of a night in the summerhouse. I daresay you can imagine what they was up to.'

'Then this is a calamity of epic proportions, Badger. My son stupidly fathers a child by the governess, when we are shortly hoping to announce his engagement to Sir Joseph Hulme's daughter. Nothing must be allowed to interfere with that. There is too much at stake. There must be absolutely no scandal attached to this household which could jeopardize that arrangement.'

'Of course, sir. Exactly me own thoughts, sir.'

'Have you any notion of how we might avoid a scandal, Badger?'

'No, sir.'

'No, Badger, I wouldn't expect you to. Well . . . Let's simply say that the child is yours, shall we?'

'Mine, sir? Nay, sir,' Badger replied defiantly. 'That puts shame on me, sir. My sweetheart is already afeared it might be my child, but it ain't, sir. Not at all.'

'On the other hand, you could wed the governess and claim the child as your own. That would resolve the issue to everybody's satisfaction. You liked her well enough a while ago as I recall. You admitted as much.'

'No thank you, sir. I ain't about to be a father to another man's child.'

'Well, I suppose that's understandable, Badger. Let me think about this . . .' George Wilson sat down again, head in hands, deep in thought. 'If we pack the girl off, back to her mother and father, there could still be gossip about Robert being the child's father, and therefore trouble from her parents,' he surmised after a pause. 'We could pay her off, ask her never to name the father, but that would only add fuel to the fire. We cannot risk that under any circumstances . . . The only way forward I see is to get rid of the evidence – the child. If she's told nobody that she was with child, then there need be no child.'

'But how, sir? How do we get rid of the child?' The master, it seemed to Badger, was echoing Rosie's notion.

'Strangle it, suffocate it. Just kill it.'

'Well if you're ordering me to arrange it, sir, I reckon now is as good a time as any while the governess is fast sleep. But who can you get to do it, sir?'

'You, Badger. You are a loyal and trusted servant, and I have always thought very highly of you. If you would do us all the greatest of favours by killing the child . . . Yes, kill the child and let it be known that the governess killed it herself. I shall back you up entirely.'

'I don't know as that's such a good idea, sir. What if it comes to light as it's me what done it? I would swing for it on the nearest gibbet.'

'Well, Badger, I understand your reluctance, but I shall vouch for you, you may depend on it. Also, our renowned circuit judge, Mr Justice Oliver Russell, is an associate of mine in parliament, as well as being a close friend, and is currently indebted to me over an incident – which we shall not discuss here. The High Sheriff of the county, Enoch Bailiss is also a good friend. They will be cooperative when the matter of an infant's untimely death inevitably comes before the court, the young mother herself accused of doing away with her child. So you may count on everybody's cooperation and discretion.'

'I see, sir,' Badger said, still uncertain as to whether he was prepared to go along with such a dastardly scheme.

'Furthermore, Badger – just in case you need any further incentive – you may depend upon my generosity. I shall see to it that you are handsomely rewarded.'

Badger smiled; curiosity and greed were getting the better of him. 'What do you have in mind sir?'

'A hundred pounds will go a long way, don't you think?'

'A hundred pounds?' Badger's eyes lit up and he beamed. 'I believe it's worth more than that, sir,' he replied astutely. 'There's a lot at stake here. My freedom for one thing.'

'Very well. A hundred and twenty.'

Badger grinned. 'A hundred and twenty. Thank you, sir. I shall attend to it now while the girl's still asleep.'

'Let me know when it's done.'

Badger picked up the open razor that still lay on the washstand.

'Not that, Badger,' George Wilson gasped. 'That would be too incriminating. Think, man. What access does a governess have to a gentleman's razor?'

'Aye, you're right sir. None.'

'Pick up something suitable from the kitchen. Oh, and just make sure my two young daughters are not privy to what you are doing.'

'You can trust me, sir.'

- - -

Abel Badger first made his way to the kitchen. A kitchen maid was bending down at the range taking something from the oven. While she was thus occupied he chose a sharp knife, hid it up the sleeve of his tunic, then duly made his way to the nursery. When he entered, all was quiet. He silently checked that George Wilson's two young daughters were still asleep in their room, then opened the door to the governess's and maid's bedroom. Rosie was sitting on her bed feeling ill at ease. Abel put his forefinger to his lips to signal that she should not speak, and with his thumb indicated that she should leave the bedroom quietly. With just a faint rustle of skirt, she tip-toed out of the room and silently closed the door behind her.

He peered at the governess. Her youthful look of peace, innocence and contentment while she slept made his heart lurch, for to him, Isabel Saxby had been the essence of perfect youthfulness and he had coveted her above all others.

He tip-toed over to the child lying asleep in the drawer. With her tiny fist she rubbed her nose. He baulked at the terrible thing he was expected to do. He was at heart a rough country lad, but it was not in his nature to kill a defenceless new-born child. Tears filled his eyes. What if the child had been his after all? What if this were Rosie's child and he was the father. Would he still be prepared to kill it, even for a hundred and twenty pounds?

Jesus! A hundred and twenty pounds . . .

A hundred and twenty pounds was a great deal of money. He could do so much with it, even bunk off to America if things were to get hot after this exploit. He could set up his own business in America with a hundred and twenty pounds.

Without further hesitation he withdrew the knife from his sleeve and sank it deep into the child's throat. Then he left the blood-stained knife on the small table at the side of the bed where Isabel Saxby lay still sleeping, and swilled his own bloodstained hands in the hand basin on the washstand.

\- - -

Chapter 18

Monday 13 May 1839
Patchfield House

Abel Badger left the nursery, his temples throbbing, his mind awhirl in a commotion of guilt and remorse at the heinous crime he had just committed at the behest of his venerated employer, George Wilson, the honourable Member of Parliament for Worcester North. But it was done, and could not be undone however remorseful he felt. It was a despicable deed that would haunt him forever, but he had done it out of a combination of loyalty for his employer and personal greed for the huge amount of money he would receive. For now, though, his first task was to find Rosie and warn her that the governess's new-born child was dead.

He found her loitering on the back staircase. She seemed anxious and fretful.

'Well?' she asked, apprehension manifest in her eyes.

'It's done,' he said in a whisper. 'I ain't proud of it neither, but it's done, as the master ordered.' He beckoned her with a tilt of his head to follow him outside where they could talk and not be overheard. When safely out of earshot of anybody he said: 'There's a bloodstained knife on that little table at the side of her bed. I left it there so's it looks like she done it herself.'

'Jesus!' Rosie exclaimed and rolled her eyes. She was suddenly terrified that she would be accused of complicity in a murder, if the truth ever became known.

'Get back to your bedroom right away, afore the children wake up,' he instructed.

'Why?' she asked fearfully.

'You have to witness the scene, that's why. Then you must report it to the master.'

'What if I'm seen and somebody thinks it's me what's done it?'

'Just witness the scene, Rosie. As soon as you've witnessed it I'll take you to see the master so's you can tell him what you've found, and that it looks like the governess has killed her own new-born child. See?'

'I see.'

'Meet me back here once you've been up there.'

Rosie nodded her understanding and, her mind in turmoil, made her way nervously to the bedroom she shared with Isabel. She opened the door silently and saw thankfully that the governess was still sleeping. But what she saw in the top drawer of the chest made her heave. 'Jesus God,' she uttered to herself.

She ran out of the room at once, skipped down the back stairs, to Abel waiting alone outside.

'Well?' he said.

'Jesus God,' she repeated to him. Her only words.

'I take it she's still asleep?'

'Yes, but her'll have a shock when her wakes up. Jesus God,' she said again.

'I'll take you to the master,' he whispered.

'Can't you tell 'im yourself?' she asked.

'No, it has to come from you. You're just reporting what you saw when you went back to your bedroom. You're innocent. See? You mustn't let on as you know as I did it.

Let him think as you know nothin' about the bab's death, other than you just went back to your room to see to his daughters, and you saw what you saw. Tell him you found the knife she used at the side of her bed, and that it looks like the governess done it herself. He'll know what to do.'

'Won't you come with me, Abel?' she asked.

'No. That might incriminate you, and I'm trying to protect you. I'll take you to his room, then I'll leave ye. But remember, he mustn't think as you know it was me what done it. You're not supposed to know as I did it, see?'

Rosie nodded her understanding and followed him. Another servant passed her by going in another direction and they exchanged smiles. In the corridor close to George's bedroom he left Rosie. She knocked on the door and heard him bid her enter. George was sitting on his bed reading a letter.

'I'm sorry to trouble you, sir,' she began hesitantly, 'but I just been back to the nursery to see to the children, sir, and in the bedroom I share with the governess—' Her voice cracked with emotion and she broke down weeping.

'Come, girl,' George urged. 'Pull yourself together. What is it you are trying to tell me?'

Rosie lifted her apron and wiped her eyes. 'Oh, sir . . . In the night the governess went into labour, sir. Nobody knew as she was with child, sir, least of all me. But I was the only one to help her, and at daybreak she gave birth to a little daughter, sir. She didn't want anybody to know about the child, and she said she would leave this house next day. But when I went back up there after me breakfast to take the milk to the children, sir, I saw that the baby was dead . . . She's killed it, sir . . .' Rosie sniffed and wiped her eyes again with her apron. 'The poor little mite's throat has been cut, sir, and the bloodstained knife as she did it with is still lying at the side of her bed on her little table.'

'My God, girl. What sort of a calamity have you wrought upon us with this dreadful news? You are telling me that we have a governess who was with child, about which nobody knew, and she's murdered the infant as soon as it was born?'

'She told nobody she was with child, sir. Kept it all to herself, she did, sir. Told nobody.'

'And only when she went into labour did you have any notion of the fact?'

'That's right, sir. I could see as she'd got a bit thick round the middle, sir, but I don't think as anybody thought anything of it, sir, what with the fashion for frocks with high waists and all.'

'So, in your opinion, she deliberately kept quiet about her condition?'

'She said she didn't want anybody to know.'

'And now she's killed the child, in a foolish effort to hide the fact of its birth. Hmm . . . From whom, I wonder?'

'I don't know, sir. Her folks, mebbe. They live local, sir.'

'Yes, I'm aware. A respectable family, I understand. And she seemed such a gentle sort of a young woman . . . Well raised. Who would have thought it, eh?' He effected to sigh profoundly. 'Very well, girl, thank you for letting me know. Naturally, I shall have to report this to the sheriff and the coroner. The law must inevitably and rightfully take its course. Has she said who the child's father is?'

'No, so. She hasn't said. But I think I know who, sir?'

'Then please enlighten me.'

'I'd rather not say, sir.'

'Then I entreat you to keep whoever you think it might be to yourself, girl. Damn it, girl, I demand that you keep this entire episode to yourself. It must remain secret. We don't want shame on our household to be broadcast far and wide. Do you understand?'

'Yes, sir.'

'Then get my daughters ready at once and take them down to my wife, so that they are removed from the nursery and the calamity that blights it. Can you lock the bedroom door meanwhile where the governess and dead child are, so that my daughters cannot get in and she cannot get out?'

'Yes, sir, I have the key.'

'Very good. Do it at once. And thank you.'

- - -

Isabel awoke shortly after nine o' clock that morning and rubbed her eyes. Her first instinct was to look at the child, and she screamed with horror when she saw her daughter lying lifeless, her throat cut, her blood soaked into the pillow on which she lay.

Then she saw the knife which had evidently been the instrument of the baby's murder.

She screamed again, made her way over to the door to seek help, and found it locked. She rattled the brass knob, then banged on the door insistently with her clenched fist.

'Somebody open the door,' she yelled. 'Somebody please open the door.'

But nobody was there. Rosie was not there; she had removed the children as instructed. Nobody opened the door.

For what seemed like an eternity, Isabel sobbed. She lay on her bed, crying into her pillow. How had this terrible thing happened? Why was her beautiful new-born baby daughter lying soaked in blood with her throat cut? Who had committed this appalling deed? In her utter confusion she stood up several times to look at the baby, just to make sure that what she had seen only minutes before was not just a trick of her bewildered imagination. When she had convinced herself that this tragedy was real and not a dream she tearfully lifted the child from its drawer and held it to her lovingly, smearing her own nightshift with blood, which also stained her hands and arms with its sticky, congealing redness.

Eventually, after interminable wretched hours, she heard footsteps, and the indiscernible mumble of men's voices. The key turned in the lock. Isabel stood up hoping that help was at hand, perhaps even an explanation and the naming of a culprit. Yet it was a strange man that stood in the doorway looking grim, with George Wilson, looking equally grim behind him.

'Good morning, miss,' the strange man said sombrely. 'I am the county coroner. What is your name?'

'Isabel Saxby, sir.'

'And you are governess to Mr Wilson's daughters?'

'Yes, sir.'

He turned to look at George Wilson and their eyes met. 'Miss Saxby, I understand that you have given birth to a child this day.'

'Yes, sir.'

'And that you have since murdered it.'

Isabel looked at the man in disbelief at the accusation, then at George Wilson, in a poignant plea for his help.

'No, you are wrong, sir,' she answered fervently, reeling from the unanticipated indictment. 'Why would I want to murder my own baby when I wanted it more than anything in the world?'

The coroner stepped towards the drawer where he had already seen the child lying. He raised its arm and it flopped lifeless back to its former position. He felt the tiny corpse.

'The body is cold,' he announced. 'It has been dead some time.' Then turning to Isabel, he said, 'At what time did you give birth?'

'Very early this morning,' she answered. 'I don't know what time it was.'

'Was there somebody here to help you?'

'Yes, sir. My nursery maid was here. She helped me through my labour. I could not have done it without her help.'

'So at what point did you kill the child?'

'I did not kill my child,' she protested, her eyes streaming with tears. 'Why would I do such a wicked thing?'

'But the fact that there is a knife at your bedside, and that you and the shift you are wearing are covered in the child's blood is sufficient incriminating evidence. It tells me that you are guilty of the crime.'

'But I didn't do it,' she screamed passionately. 'I wanted my baby. I am only covered in blood because I picked her up to hold her. But she was already dead, and I didn't kill her.'

The coroner turned to George Wilson, his expression grave. 'The evidence is plain to see, sir. I shall arrange for Miss Saxby to be removed to the Worcester City Gaol, where she will remain pending her trial.'

'Very well,' George replied. 'The law must take its course.'

'Worcester City Gaol?' Isabel queried. 'But I didn't do it. I keep telling you, it was not me that killed my baby. Why won't you believe me? Why do you want to send me to Worcester City Gaol?'

'Because you must go to trial for your crime, my dear,' the coroner replied coldly. 'Judge and jury will decide whether or not you are guilty.'

'But I want to see my mother first,' Isabel pleaded. 'Let me see my mother before you send me there.'

'I shall send for her mother if that's what she wishes,' George said to the coroner. 'In fairness, her family must know of the situation at once. Her father, I am aware, is a respected schoolmaster in Worcester. No doubt he will be horrified at what his daughter has done.'

- - -

A man was dispatched driving the Wilson's gig to fetch Susan Saxby, and she was duly delivered to Patchfield House, worried that Isabel was in some sort of trouble, yet unable to glean any information from the footman. At once, she was taken to George Wilson's study, where she encountered his grim face and the grimmer face of Mrs Wilson.

A chair had been placed in readiness in front of the desk, facing the master and mistress.

'Do sit down, Mrs Saxby,' George intoned calmly.

'Thank you,' Susan replied, and duly sat.

'I have sent for you because of a profoundly serious and very tragic incident concerning your daughter Isabel.'

'What has happened to her? Is she all right?'

'Very early this morning, Mrs Saxby, your daughter gave birth to a child, a girl.'

'Isabel gave birth to a child?' Susan queried, her face an icon of disbelief.

'Mrs Saxby. I would hardly have you brought to this house to tell you that your daughter had given birth to a child if that were not the case.'

'But I had no notion that she was with child and I only saw her yesterday. She's said nothing to me.'

'She's told nobody, it seems. Perhaps she was ashamed to tell you,' Mrs Wilson commented icily.

'Anyway, Mrs Saxby,' George went on, 'you may rest assured that a child was born this morning to your daughter.'

'So is my daughter and her child well?'

'I've seen your daughter and can report that she is recovering well. However . . .' he paused, then continued, 'the child was later found with its throat cut, and the instrument of the crime, a bloodstained kitchen knife was on your daughter's bedside table. Furthermore, her night attire was covered in blood—'

Susan gasped, interrupting George. 'Are you claiming that my daughter murdered the child she'd just borne?'

'The evidence is irrefutable, Mrs Saxby.'

'I cannot believe my daughter would do such an evil thing,' she exclaimed. 'She has not one iota of malice within her. Giving birth is one thing, but murdering your new-born child is another. There has to be some mistake, or even a conspiracy here.'

'I can assure you, Mrs Saxby, the evidence was there for all to see. There could be no mistaking the evidence. There is no conspiracy as you put it. The nursery maid who works with your daughter assisted with the birth and will testify to the fact. The child has since been taken away pending the inspection by the high sheriff. It will be buried in due course.'

'If my daughter has given birth to a child and it is dead and to be buried, then the responsibility for its burial should fall to her family, not the high sheriff or the parish, should it not, Mr Wilson? In which case, I would appreciate your assistance in facilitating the arrangement.'

'Of course, Mrs Saxby. I shall see to it that the child's body is consigned to you for burial at the appropriate time.'

'Thank you.'

The coroner has already arranged for your daughter to be conveyed to the City Gaol in Worcester, where she will await her trial. Before being removed thence, however, she has requested that she sees you. I have granted the wish, therefore you will be taken to her.'

'Is it known who the father of the child is?'

'Your daughter has divulged no such information.'

Susan raised her eyebrows. 'I certainly have my suspicions,' she said.

'Speculation is pointless, Mrs Saxby. If the girl will not reveal who the child's father is, only rumours will prosper. Unfounded rumours and gossip would undoubtedly be harmful to anybody wrongly cited.'

'My daughter will not withhold such information from me, Mr Wilson,' Susan declared. 'And once it has been confirmed, I shall expect fair and proper treatment of Isabel, by those concerned.'

'Provided, of course, that your daughter does not lie, and of that we shall never be sure. If she can murder her own child . . .'

'I can assure you my daughter would never murder her own baby, Mr Wilson, nor does she lie . . . sir.'

'But failing to confess that she was with child is in itself a form of lying, Mrs Saxby. She failed to confess to you – by your own admission – that she was with child, did she not?'

'I do not see it that way, sir,' she answered curtly. 'So may I see my daughter at once?'

George rang a hand bell and Abel Badger appeared.

'Badger, take Mrs Saxby to the governess in her bedroom. The wagon will be here soon to transport her to the gaol.'

Badger bowed, and held the door open for Susan to pass through. 'Follow me, please, Mrs Saxby.'

The key to the bedroom door was already in the lock. Badger turned it and opened the door without a word. The late afternoon sun was casting its rays on Isabel who was lying down, still sobbing. She was by this time cleaned up and dressed. Susan knelt down beside her and threw her arms about her. Once he saw that mother and daughter were reunited Badger headed back downstairs.

'What on earth have they done to you, Isabel?' Susan

cried, tears streaming down her anguished face.

'Oh, mother . . .' Isabel sobbed, holding on tightly to her mother. 'I'm so glad to see you. Have they told you about the baby?'

'Yes, my dear, they have.'

'Don't let them take me away. I've done nothing wrong. They say I killed my baby, but I did not do it. I swear I did not do it.'

'I know you didn't. But who did? And why?'

'I don't know, mother.'

'I have a shrewd suspicion that they are trying to hide something, my dear. But why did you not tell me you were with child? None of this would have happened.'

'I thought you would disown me, I thought you would reject me.'

'Reject you? Oh, Isabel . . . Of course we would not reject you. Why would we reject you at a time when you needed our support most? Oh, my child, what a silly girl you have been. You would have left this den of iniquity as soon as we knew, and you would have had your baby at home where you are loved and wanted, where your baby would be cherished.'

Isabel wept a fresh bout of tears. 'Oh, mother, I do see that I've been a silly girl . . . but please don't let them take me away,' she pleaded again. 'I didn't kill my baby, I swear. I wanted it. It was Robert's baby.'

'Yes . . .' Susan sighed with relief at the revelation. 'I imagined as much as soon as I was told you'd given birth. Now I suspect his father knows and is trying to hide the fact. He will deny it at all costs, to avoid a scandal, I presume – to avoid his name and reputation being besmirched. But does Robert know you were having his child?'

'No, mother. How could he? I haven't heard from him

since September when he left home to return to Cambridge. If he's tried to write to me they must have confiscated his letters. I'm sure he would have written. He loved me, I know he did.'

'Then why did he not send any letters to your home? He would surely have known we would pass them on.'

'I don't know, mother. Perhaps he did. But delivery of letters can be erratic, as you have said yourself many times, and if he received no replies to any letters he sent me here, he would have given up. He would have thought I didn't love him anymore.'

'Yes, maybe so,' Susan conceded.

Isabel wiped her eyes on the sleeve of her frock. 'When they take me away, will you and father still come to see me?'

'Of course we shall, presuming they will allow us to see you.'

'Oh, mother,' Isabel sighed. 'What will my father think of me?'

'The same as I do. He will not be judgmental. He knows you were in love. He adores you and will wish to support you. We shall both support you for as long as you need us.'

'Thank you, mother. But they tell me I shall have to be tried in a court of law. If they find me guilty then I shall be hanged.'

'My child, rest assured your father and I shall do all in our power to see that that does not happen. You are innocent of everything they claim you are guilty of.'

There was a knock at the door, and it opened unbidden. Abel Badger announced that a court constable and driver had arrived with transport to convey Miss Saxby to the City Gaol.

It was an effort for Isabel to walk, still weak as she was, and sore from giving birth, but Susan helped her down the stairs and out to the front portico steps of Patchfield House.

As word spread among the household, other servants had gathered morbidly to watch as the constable relieved Susan of her daughter and took Isabel's arm. He led her to an austere-looking black wagon that waited, with a single horse in harness, the driver perched on a high seat.

She was pushed inside it unceremoniously, the door slammed to and locked, only to be re-opened at Worcester City Gaol.

- - -

Chapter 19

Autumn 1839
Worcester Guildhall

A deluge of autumn rain was pelting the cobbles and bouncing off them like transparent butterflies. Rivulets running along the gutters on both sides of High Street were in spate, feeding puddles that were likewise restless with the downpour. The rain had kept many people away, but still a hardy crowd, mostly women, had gathered to see the arrival of the handsome circuit judge, Mr Justice Oliver Russell, arriving at Worcester's Guildhall with a troop of javelin men retained by the sheriff to escort him.

The elaborate Georgian building not only housed the court where the trial of Isabel Saxby was due to be held, but prison cells as well for others awaiting trial, sentencing and the gallows.

The renowned judge was accompanied by George Wilson Esquire and his wife, in whose Brougham they had travelled, and whose hospitality he had enjoyed the previous evening at Patchfield House. Judge Oliver Russell preferred the prestige and geniality of Patchfield, even though sizeable and comfortable serviced lodgings were at his disposal at the Guildhall.

Ushers met the judge, the Member of Parliament and his wife, holding umbrellas over each to protect them from the rain as they stepped down from the carriage. There, the judge and the Wilsons parted company; the judge to his lodgings to appraise himself of the day's work, the MP and spouse to the Golden Lion inn opposite, there to await the trial of their reckless former governess.

The High Sheriff of Worcestershire, Enoch Shadrak Bailiss, had in earlier days been a Whig Member of Parliament representing Worcester South. As such, he was a long-standing friend of George Wilson. In fulfilling his duties as sheriff, he had interviewed Isabel Saxby prior to her trial. At the Guildhall he presented his findings to Mr Justice Oliver Russell in readiness for this session of the Autumn Assizes. They too knew each other well from their time in parliament.

'There is no doubt that the girl killed her own child, Oliver,' the sheriff declared familiarly as they sat in the sitting room of his lodgings before the trial. 'Naturally, she protests her innocence, but then she would – nobody wants to go to the gallows. However, the evidence is beyond dispute I fear.' Enoch Shadrak Bailiss sucked on his pipe and exhaled a cloud of blue smoke; its aroma was not unpleasant. 'According to Arthur Daniels, our esteemed coroner,' he went on, 'the instrument of the child's death, a kitchen knife, the property of George Wilson, was at her bedside, and the defendant herself was smeared in blood. The father of the bastard is not known, but presumed to be some farm hand from one of the villages around Patchfield House, although in fairness this is hearsay. The defendant claims that George Wilson's elder son Robert is the father. This obviously represents an enormous problem for George, and a claim we must discount altogether and refute. Clearly, the girl was seeking recompense from the family, but such an admission could damage George's reputation and his standing in parliament at a time that is critical for him, and we would not want that, would we?'

'I am aware of all that, Enoch. I spent last evening with George.'

'Yes, well we all know that George is on the way up, tipped for high office, so anything reeking of a scandal in his domain, or about his family, would greatly upset his applecart, and could thereby radically affect us all – if you understand my meaning.'

'Indeed, that very situation has already been made clear to me, Enoch.' The judge sat back in his chair, his elbows on the chair's leather-bound arms, his fingers steepled in front of him.

'Therefore,' the High Sheriff continued, 'counsel for the prosecution has been specifically advised not to mention the defendant's wild allegation about paternity.'

'But the defendant might,' the judge remarked. 'I am anxious to know a little more about her. Her demeanour . . . Since she was a governess and by implication educated to some extent, I suspect she is not of the lower orders?'

'Quite so, Oliver. She had been employed as governess to George's two young daughters since July last year. She is still only seventeen years old and educated to a high degree as you rightly suggest. Her father is a well-thought-of schoolmaster at one of Worcester's prestigious schools – A highly respectable family. Therefore, I would not define her as of the lower orders.'

'Of course, she protests her innocence?'

'Vehemently, Oliver.'

'What about witnesses?'

'There is a footman-come-valet – one Abel Badger – and the nursery maid who worked with the defendant – one Rose Duckworth. She shared a bedroom with the defendant, and she assisted at the birth of the unfortunate child. According to her statement, she left the defendant sleeping and went to the servant's quarters for her breakfast. When she returned she found the child with its throat cut and the defendant asleep, but smeared in blood. The knife that was used to kill the child was at her bedside. The witness claims that as soon as she saw the situation she left the room and locked the door, then sought Abel Badger, who sent her directly to George to report the incident.'

'Yes, it all sounds straight forward, Enoch,' Mr Justice Oliver Russell decided. 'The whole issue is tantamount to a tragedy. A great pity . . . I see too many of these cases where young girls, mostly domestic servants, get into trouble. But nobody ever admits to being the seducer and fathering the child. It's no surprise that these girls are inclined to dispose of their unwanted babies, because they doubtless have no hope of rearing them. You would be surprised how many new-born end up at the bottom of wells, fouling the waters therein. But thank you, Enoch for your deposition. I have noted your remarks.'

Enoch Bailiss arose from his chair, shook the judge's hand and left. But as he left, an usher appeared, announcing that there was a woman demanding to see Mr Justice Oliver Russell.

'Who is she?' the judge asked impatiently. 'I am busy.'

'She wouldn't give her name, sir. But she reckons she knows you and says it's to do with one of the cases coming before your honour today.'

The judge sighed with exasperation. 'I am battling against all odds to prepare for this day's cases . . .' But he hesitated; the woman had intimated that she knew him. Also, there was a possibility that she might have some new evidence or anecdote that could be useful in whichever case concerned her. 'Very well, send her in, but tell her I can only spare her a couple of minutes.'

But the woman was already standing behind the usher. She barged forward and entered the room.

The judge glanced at her with frustration and irritation.

'You cannot come barging in here like this, woman,' he proclaimed impatiently. Then his eyes lit up, and his mouth opened wide. 'God in Heaven!' he exclaimed, standing to greet her. 'It cannot be . . .'

She was in her mid to late thirties now and bearing her years well. Being soaked from the rain did not mar her appearance as a fine-looking woman, decently dressed. His heart thumped as soon as he saw her, for he recognised her as somebody he could easily have made a fool of himself with years ago. He turned to the usher. 'Thank you, that will be all. I will see the lady.'

The usher left.

'It's been a long time, Mr Justice Oliver Russell,' she said smiling, deliberately using his formal title. 'I am so pleased that you remember me.'

'How could I ever forget you, Miss Tinkler?' he said with equal formality. 'And to what do I owe the unexpected privilege of seeing you again after so long?'

'I wish to talk to you about the trial of Isabel Saxby.'

- - -

Public interest in the trial was high, the tragedy that had triggered it having been reported in Berrow's Worcester Journal, along with much comment and speculation. The judge's professional standing and reputation as a ladies' man had heightened the interest. Thus what public seating was available within the courtroom at the Guildhall had been filled. However, the rear of the courtroom had no wall; it opened directly onto the vast entrance hall, where the interested and the morbidly inquisitive members of the public stood in a crush, craning their necks to witness the trial. The javelin men had taken their places, as had the officers and clerks; George Wilson and his wife sat in the gallery reserved for notables, which was constructed high in a side wall of the courtroom. There they waited apprehensively for the trial to begin.

The Clerk to the Court appeared and the courtroom fell silent as Mr Justice Oliver Russell duly emerged behind him from his lodgings. The usher rose to his feet and everybody else in court rose with him. They remained standing until the Judge nodded in acknowledgement and assumed his high seat. He was tall, his bearing was of an eminent man, distinguished, and he exuded presence. In a tier below him the Clerk to the Court had his head down having taken his seat. Next to him, other officers and counsellors were grouped, wearing serious expressions as they pored over their own papers. Petitioners of other cases due to come before the judge waited, along with their witnesses and other interested entities. Solemn silence reigned.

The Clerk to the Court summoned the jury, twelve just men and true, selected from the local gentry and, significantly, all known to George Wilson.

Once sworn in, the court was ready to receive the defendant of the first case of the day; that of Isabel Saxby, formerly governess at Patchfield House. A deathly hush fell over the court as she appeared in the dock, rising like an apparition up the steps from the cells below. She wore a plain blue day dress, her hair neatly tied up. Her youthful slenderness had returned, her face though pallid from being held in a dark, rat-infested dungeon long miserable months, was beautiful, like porcelain, and she exuded an air of dignity, composure, self-esteem, respect and perfect innocence.

The Clerk of the Court stood and read out the charge.

'Isabel Saxby, spinster late of the parish of Crowle in this county of Worcestershire, you are charged that on the thirteenth day of May in this year of our Lord eighteen thirty-nine, in the fourth year of the reign of our sovereign Queen Victoria, that being big with child on that same day in the house of your employer George Wilson Esquire, did give birth to a female child, which being born alive was deemed a bastard in accordance with the laws of the land. And that in that same place, by use of a kitchen knife, you did unmercifully cut the throat of the aforesaid child, as a result of which the said child instantly perished. Witnesses will be called before you to verify the charge.'

The first witness was Arthur Elijah Daniels, the coroner. He claimed that he was urgently called to the house of George Wilson on 13th May to examine events that had occurred there. He told the court that he was taken to the bedroom of the accused, Isabel Saxby, where he saw a new-born child lying on a pillow in the top drawer of a chest with its throat cut, having bled profusely.

'The accused,' he declared to the court, 'was sitting on her bed wearing a nightshift that was smeared in blood. A kitchen knife in the bedroom was also smeared with blood. Two days afterwards, I again visited the home of George Wilson Esquire, accompanied by the High Sheriff of Worcestershire and twelve jurymen who also examined the dead child to determine the cause of its death. Upon their oath did they state that the said Isabel Saxby, on the thirteenth day of May of the year of our Lord eighteen thirty-nine, did murder the child by cutting its throat with the said kitchen knife causing the death of the said child.'

Next to be called was Abel Badger. After the formalities of confirming who he was and his position in the Wilson household he was cross-examined by the prosecuting counsel.

'At what point, Mr Badger, were you made aware of the incident?'

'When the nursery maid, Rosie Duckworth, who shared

a bedroom with Miss Saxby, came to tell me what she'd discovered.'

'Please give your account to the court of what Miss Duckworth had discovered?'

'Having had her breakfast she got some milk from the kitchen for Mr Wilson's two daughters, then on returning to her bedroom what she shared with the governess, next to the nursery, she saw as the new-born child was lying in the top draw of the chest of drawers, where she herself had lain it after the birth, but it's throat had been cut while she was away, and it was dead. Not knowing what to do for the best, Miss Duckworth came to me for advice, and I told her she should report what she'd seen to Mr Wilson hisself.'

'But the accused was asleep at this time?'

'So Miss Duckworth thought,' Badger replied.

'Did you yourself see the child after it had been murdered?'

'No, sir. I only know what Miss Duckworth told me.'

'Thank you, Mr Badger . . . Your witness,' counsel for the prosecution said to counsel for the defence, one Cecil Boycott, whose services were being paid for by William Saxby.

'Mr Badger,' Cecil Boycott began, 'the nursery maid, Rose Duckworth, gave you an accurate account of what she had seen?'

'I believe so, sir.'

'So you only have her word to go on?'

'She had no reason to lie to me, sir, if that's what you're suggesting. She was shocked and surprised at what she found, sir, and very upset, especially as she'd attended the birth of the child.'

'And her seeking your advice, as to what action she should take, was your only connection with the incident?'

'Yes, sir.'

'Thank you, Mr Badger. That will be all.'

'Call Rose Duckworth,' the Clerk to the Court said.

Rosie Duckworth appeared on the witness stand, neatly dressed in her Sunday best, looking nervous and troubled.

The formalities over, the prosecution counsel said, 'Firstly, Miss Duckworth, tell the court everything you know about Miss Saxby, and your relationship with her.'

Rosie glanced uneasily at the defendant. 'Miss Saxby was employed last July as governess to Mr Wilson's daughters. We was never what you might call close friends, but we had to work together so we tried to get on. I noticed over the months as she was getting a bit of a belly on her, but I thought no more about it. As it turns out, though, she was a-carryin' a child, but she never said nothing to me, nor to anybody else that she was.'

'In your opinion, Miss Duckworth, did you believe that Miss Saxby wished to deliberately conceal the fact that she was with child?'

'Oh, yes, sir. Otherwise I'm sure as she would've said she was a-carrying.'

'Please tell the court what happened on the evening of the twelfth of May this year.'

'Well . . . Miss Saxby got back to Patchfield after visiting her folks in Crowle, like she did every Sunday. But she took to her bed as soon as she got back that evening, and was having birth pains. I said to her, "Do you think I'm stupid, Miss Saxby? I think as you're with child and about to drop it" I said. Anyway, she admitted it there and then, and she axed me if I would help her deliver the child. I told her I'd never done it before, but I said yes I'd try, 'cause I felt sorry for her.'

'So you delivered a healthy female child into the world.'

'By the grace of God, I did, sir.'

'Did Miss Saxby offer any indication to you as to what

she would do once she had the child?'

'Yes, sir, she said as she would leave next day, 'cause she didn't want anybody to know as she'd given birth. I told her she might not be well enough that soon, having just gone through labour.'

'So when Miss Saxby had been delivered of her child, what did you do?'

'I cleaned the child up and laid it in a drawer. Then I told her she must get some rest after what she'd gone through.'

'So she went to sleep? Is that correct?'

'Yes, sir . . . or so I thought. Thinking she was asleep, I went downstairs to the servants' quarters to have some breakfast and a mug of tea. I was tired and hungry, having been up all night with her, delivering her child.'

'And when you reached the servants' quarters did you tell anybody else what had happened that night?'

'No sir. It was clear Miss Saxby wanted nobody to know, and I respected that.'

'So please tell the court what you found once you returned to the bedroom you shared with Miss Saxby.'

Rosie glanced again at Isabel Saxby. 'I was shocked and saddened, 'cause I saw as Miss Saxby's child was lying in the drawer with its throat cut, and one of the knives from the kitchen was lying next to her, covered in blood.'

'So what did you do?'

'Right away I left to go and tell Mr Badger what I'd discovered, and ask what I should do about it.'

'And what did Mr Badger advise?'

'That I should go and tell Mr Wilson at once, so that's what I did.'

'Thank you, Miss Duckworth. Your witness, Mr Boycott.'

Counsel for the defence rose from his seat, adjusted his

spectacles and looked at his notes.

'Miss Duckworth . . . Why did you seek advice from the footman Abel Badger as to what you should do, and not the housekeeper or indeed the butler, who is head of the serving staff?'

'I don't know, sir. I was shocked and all of a fluster over what I'd seen. I didn't know what to do for the best, sir. But Mr Badger was there, sir, so I axed him.'

'I see. Did Miss Saxby at any time reveal the name of the father of her child?'

'No, sir. She never did.'

'Did you have any inkling as to who the father of the child might be?'

'No, sir, and maybe she didn't know herself.'

There was a murmur of disapproval from the public that the witness should infer the defendant was of a promiscuous nature.

'Please tell the court how much time elapsed after you left Miss Saxby resting and your return to your bedroom, when you found the baby lying dead with its throat cut.'

'I suppose it was about an hour, sir.'

'Plenty of time, I suggest for somebody to enter the room with a kitchen knife and murder the child?'

Rosie's face flushed red. 'I suppose so, sir, but who would want to do such a terrible thing?'

'I am asking the questions, Miss Duckworth. But since you raise it, perhaps you might answer it yourself. Who would want to do such a terrible thing?'

'Nobody I am aware of, sir. Nobody I know had reason to murder the child.'

'Let us turn to the kitchen knife, Miss Duckworth. Did you see the kitchen knife in the bedroom before you left it to go for your breakfast, or indeed at any time while Miss Saxby was in labour?'

'No, sir, I did not. I can only suppose as she must have hidden it.'

'Or . . . it is possible, is it not, that while Miss Saxby slept, the kitchen knife could have been brought in and used by anybody who wanted to enter the bedroom with the intention of killing the child?'

'I suppose it's possible, sir, but like I say, it's unlikely, as nobody even knew about the child.'

'Except Abel Badger, Miss Duckworth.' There was gasp from the public. 'He knew, because you had already told him of the birth yourself.'

'Yes, sir, Abel Badger knew.' She cast a quick glance at Badger who was looking at the floor uneasily, sensing all eyes on him. 'But he didn't do it, sir. It's obvious as it was Miss Saxby what did it, sir. She wasn't really asleep when I left her, and she did it herself while I was below stairs.'

'You seem quite certain of this.'

'I am, sir.'

'Thank you, Miss Duckworth, that is all.'

The Clerk stood up and announced that the defendant, Isabel Saxby was prepared to give evidence, to murmurs of surprise and approval from the public, so counsel for the prosecution duly commenced his questioning.

'Miss Saxby, you have heard the testimony of the witnesses in this case. It is damning evidence against you. May we hear your version of events, please?'

Isabel looked him steadily in the eye, and spoke calmly and clearly. 'It is true that Miss Duckworth helped me with the birth of my child, and that I asked her not to reveal to anybody that I had given birth. There was no need for anybody to know, because it was my firm intention to leave Patchfield House next day – with my baby – and make my own way in life – with my baby of course.'

'Why was it important for you to keep your pregnancy

a secret, Miss Saxby?'

'Because I wished to spare my mother and father the ignominy and shame of knowing that their eldest daughter had given birth to a bastard child. I had no wish to jeopardize my father's position at his school.'

'So you decided to kill the child and remove all traces of its existence.'

'No, sir, I did not. If I wished to remove all traces of its existence then why would I have fallen back to sleep if I had killed it, leaving the poor dead child for anybody to find and use as evidence against me?'

There was another collective gasp from the public as they realized the logic in Isabel's response.

'I will use the phrase of my learned friend while addressing the previous witness, Miss Saxby, and repeat that I ask the questions, not you. So . . . I put it to you that you feigned sleep, and while Miss Duckworth was away you used a kitchen knife which you had previously obtained and secreted, to murder your new-born child.'

'I did not obtain and secrete a kitchen knife, sir,' Isabel declared vehemently. 'Nor did I murder my own child. I wanted the child. The child meant everything to me.' Tears welled up in her eyes and she tried hard to maintain her composure. 'Somebody else murdered my baby.'

There was a murmur of sympathy from the public.

'But you have no notion of just who that somebody else might have been, do you, Miss Saxby? Nor do you have any evidence to support any such accusation.'

Isabel remained silent.

'Please answer the question, Miss Saxby. Do you have any evidence to support any such accusation?'

'No, sir.' There was a crack in her voice. 'I do not.'

'Because there was no other person involved,' counsel for the prosecution declared triumphantly. 'The evidence, along with the testimonies of the coroner, the High Sheriff and other independent witnesses, all state that your child was murdered by use of a kitchen knife, which was found at your bedside after the event, and that the night attire you were wearing was smeared in the child's blood. There can be no other verdict to this trial other than that you, Miss Saxby, are guilty of murder.' He collected his papers together and straightened them. 'Your witness, Mr Boycott.' He sat down, wearing a smug expression.

Boycott stood up again and pushed up his spectacles so that they sat firmly on the bridge of his nose. 'Miss Saxby,' he began again kindly, with compassion in his voice. 'Do you believe it possible that anybody could murder their own child whilst sleeping?'

'No, sir, I do not.'

'And you were most definitely asleep, were you not, by the time Miss Duckworth left you to seek her breakfast?'

'Yes, of course I was asleep. I had just given birth, and I was extremely tired, as any woman would be in the same circumstances.'

'But were you not overjoyed and excited about the birth of your child also?'

'Yes, I was overjoyed about the birth, and happy that my baby was born healthy, but the elation did not overwhelm my tiredness and prevent me from falling asleep.'

Boycott smiled. 'And the first you knew about the death of your baby was when you awoke sometime later and found – to your horror – that your baby, lying in the drawer, which thrived when born, was lying mortally wounded, its throat having been cut?'

'I cried with shock and horror when I saw her, the poor little mite. I was so distressed. My first thought was who could do such a thing. Then I picked her up, hoping that somehow she was still alive and that I might save her. But it was too late.' Isabel's eyes filled with tears and she wiped them away with the back of her hand. 'That is when my baby's blood soaked into my nightshift.' Tears continued to well up. 'Then, when I tried the door to seek help I found it was locked, so I could not get out. I was trapped, deliberately locked inside the bedroom.'

'Who do you think locked the door, Miss Saxby?'

'Whoever killed my baby, perhaps. Only Miss Duckworth had a key that I am aware of.'

There was another audible gasp from the public and a murmur of private discussions, fuelled by speculation over the defendant's allegation, provoking the Clerk to call for order.

'Did Miss Duckworth have any cause to want your child dead, Miss Saxby?' Boycott continued when order was restored. 'Especially as she was not averse to helping you in the delivery of your child?'

'At one point, she said that if she thought the child's father was Abel Badger, she would stifle it with a pillow.'

'Why would she say that, Miss Saxby?'

'Because she and Abel Badger were lovers, and she believed that he was interested in me.'

'Did you ever give her cause to believe you were interested in him?'

'No, sir, never. I have never been interested in him at all. But that did not stop him from trying to force himself on me a number of times, one of which she found out about.'

'So was Miss Duckworth jealous of you?'

'Yes, I believe she was.'

'And by her own admission, Miss Duckworth visited the kitchen after she left you with the aim of having her breakfast, during which time she could easily have appropriated a kitchen knife and hidden it within her clothing. Would you agree?'

'It's possible. It's even likely.' She avoided Rosie Duckworth's glare.

'Can you state with certainty that Abel Badger was not the father of your child.'

'I can indeed, sir. You see, Robert Wilson was the father of my baby. So why would I want to kill her? Robert loved me as I loved him, he wanted us to marry, but he was sent away, so I don't think he ever knew I was carrying his child.'

Isabel broke down at this while the public gallery erupted during this astonishing revelation, while George Wilson, in the notables' gallery, squirmed and shook his head vigorously. He looked steadily at the judge, a signal that such an accusation must be quelled.

But the judge's eyes were on Isabel. He sensed she was the victim of a conspiracy to hide the truth. He felt her pain. He felt sympathy for her. He admired her pluck as she gave evidence. He perceived that she was honest. She was as she had been described, and more; personable, dignified, forthright, educated, and not overwhelmed by the stiffness of the court, nor the allegations hurled against her. But his personal thoughts could not influence the sentence he had been motivated to deliver.

However, he was not convinced by the evidence, but the instrument or the will by which to investigate further what had really happened did not exist, and he was aware of this.

Counsels for the prosecution and for the defence each gave their summing up to the jurors, the former invoking them to bring in a guilty verdict, the latter claiming that all the evidence was circumstantial and could not be substantiated. Soon it was time for the judge to give his summing up and advise the jury.

'In these cases,' Mr Justice Oliver Russell pronounced, 'we must be absolutely certain that the evidence presented is accurate and unassailable. Certain aspects of the evidence I have heard today are troubling, inasmuch as I find it inconceivable that a woman who has murdered her new-born baby, whether conceived in or out of wedlock, would go back to sleep, leaving the evidence of the blatant crime of infanticide for others to discover, thus exposing herself to trial, and thereby the death sentence. This sheds doubt on the validity of the accusations made against the defendant. The evidence presented in this case is circumstantial. It is not conclusive. There was opportunity for another person or persons to introduce the kitchen knife to the bedroom and to use it to kill the child. If that was the case, that person is hardly likely to admit the offence in this court. This emphasises the need for more thorough investigations into such crimes, investigations which are seldom possible. However, we must also consider that nobody else knew of the birth of the child. Therefore, we must rely on the evidence produced to the court.'

Here, the judge realized that he was treading a very narrow and hazardous path. He wished to uphold his reputation for fairness and impartiality. Instinctively, he believed in the innocence of Isabel Saxby, that engaging young soul whose demeanour and performance in his court had brought a tear to his eye. Conversely, it must behove him to respect the position and the guidance of George Wilson, his friend, his sponsor, his future. As it had been explained to him in private, nothing must mar the forthcoming alliance between the Wilson family and the family and fortune of Wilson's good friend and colleague Sir Joseph Hulme. The verdict must not blacken the Wilson name, there must be no whiff of a scandal between his son Robert and the formerly employed governess. Therefore, he had to find a way of sparing the unfortunate defendant while satisfying the Wilsons. He was convinced that the witness Rose Duckworth was hiding information, that she was a part of a conspiracy to protect the Wilsons, and that the counsel for the prosecution was under instruction not to delve too deeply into her testimony, thus it had been hardly probing. Likewise, even the questioning of the counsel for the defence. Was influence being brought to bear on him also? Besides all that, there was something unhealthy about the relationship between Rose Duckworth and Abel Badger. At the next assize court he would strive to ensure that Rose Duckworth appeared, accused of this very infanticide over which he was now presiding, or at the very least, withholding evidence.

'So, gentlemen of the jury,' Mr Justice Oliver Russell intoned, 'I consign the future of the defendant into your hands. If you are not persuaded of her guilt, consider the months she has languished in a cold and dark prison cell already, awaiting trial, and declare her not guilty. If you are convinced of her guilt, then there is but one verdict. I ask you now to retire and consider your verdict, bearing in mind the guidance I have already imparted to you.'

As the jurymen left the court to consider their verdict the atmosphere in the courtroom became restless amid the hum of many conversations and bandied opinions. Rosie Duckworth and Abel Badger sat in silent contemplation side by side, each aware that their testimonies had not been convincing, and that their own futures might not yet have been determined.

- - -

After less than an hour, the jury returned.

'Have you reached a verdict?' the judge asked.

'We have reached a verdict, your honour,' the foreman confirmed.

'And what is your verdict?'

'We find the defendant guilty.'

There was uproar in the court, and Isabel looked

bewildered, fully expecting to be acquitted. Little did she know then of the potency and extent of George Wilson's influence. Her mother and father looked at each other in disbelief and mutual grief.

'Order!' the Clerk shouted. 'Order in court!'

It was time for the judge to sentence the defendant.

'Isabel Saxby,' he began, looking at her, and melting inwardly as her beautiful, sad eyes met with his. 'You have been found guilty of the crime of infanticide, as charged, which is the vilest form of murder. The charge against you is not an uncommon one. But there are circumstances that must direct my sentencing. I deem that the evidence against you is circumstantial and inconclusive, and I cannot in all conscience sentence you to be hanged by the neck at Red Hill until you are dead. Yet nor can I acquit you. By your own admission, you wished to keep the birth of your bastard child secret from all, which by implication means withholding the knowledge of its birth from all authority in this land. This in itself is a punishable crime. I therefore sentence you to seven years transportation to the prison colony of Van Diemen's Land. You will therefore be taken from this place to a prison, and held there awaiting the commissioning of a ship that will be charged to dispatch you thence, with others who have also fallen by the wayside.'

- - -

Chapter 20

New Year's Eve 1853
Port Stanley, Falkland Islands

The treeless landscape of the Falkland Islands appeared bleak in the extreme to Isabel and Ann as they ambled along a coastal path heading away from Port Stanley. They noticed a small squad of soldiers, marching some distance away in Stanley itself. Sheep dominated the landscape, grazing unconcernedly on the tussac grass which was native to the islands.

They walked some distance, Isabel opening up about the events of that fateful day in May 1839 when her child was born. They reached an outcrop of rock and decided to sit down and rest for a while. Some distance away along the coast a colony of penguins was evident.

'So, you were sent to Worcester gaol,' Ann said after hearing Isabel's account.

'It was a horrible experience,' Isabel commented. 'You cannot imagine. No words can describe it adequately.'

'How absolutely dreadful for you, though, Isabel, especially as you were innocent of the charges they made against you.'

'Ann, I don't think I could ever put into words my feelings at the time,' Isabel replied soulfully. 'It was the lowest point of my life. I had just given birth, I was weak, weary, sore and bleeding, and I just wanted to die. All this on top of the horror of finding my baby unaccountably murdered, as well as the heartbreak I still felt over losing Robert, whose help I was desperate for.' She plucked up a strand of tussac grass and held it between her gloved fingers, gazing at it fixedly. 'Until I met Robert, you see, I was just an ordinary young girl who lived a contented yet ordinary, and very conventional life. I was cocooned and cosseted and loved within my family. I was just sixteen and I never had any thoughts of meeting a boy, of falling in love, of eventually getting wed – such things seemed so far off – events that happened to other people. Besides, I had never been exposed to that sort of thinking, and living in a small village made it even more unlikely that I would meet somebody I might fall in love with. Suddenly discovering romance and passion with Robert changed my whole outlook on life, but in a flash. Yet because of my life before all that, I was so naïve and unworldly. In my naivety, never did it cross my mind that what we ended up doing would cause me to have a baby – such a thing could never happen to me – or so I thought – it only happened to bad girls.'

'But what was it like in gaol?' Ann asked.

'Oh, need you ask? It was horrid, appalling.'

'I can't imagine the horror, Isabel. Were you in the dungeon by yourself?'

'No. I shared a cell with other women.'

'And how long were you there?'

'It seemed like an eternity. I cried most of the time.'

'You poor thing – I imagine you would,' Ann remarked sympathetically.

'My first sight of daylight after I was sent there was when I was shifted to the Quarter Sessions to appear before the magistrates. I pleaded not guilty and hoped they would acquit me there and then, but it was not to be. Because of the seriousness of my alleged crime, and my not guilty plea,

I was taken back to the city gaol to await trial at the Autumn Assizes.'

'Did they allow you to have visitors?'

'Yes, thank goodness. My mother and father were allowed to visit me. My father visited me regularly, because his school was close to the gaol, you see. He came as often as he could, bless him. He was so heartening. He would bring me clean clothes, food, and ginger beer that my mother had made. Of course, he knew that I had not committed the crime, and he swore I would eventually be acquitted, which I found reassuring. It was obvious, he said, that somebody had come into the bedroom while I slept and killed my child, but proving who had done it would be difficult, he told me, especially if the truth were being deliberately concealed that Robert was my baby's father.'

'Do you have any idea who might have murdered the baby, Isabel?'

'At first, I thought it must have been Rosie, my nursery maid. But when I thought more about it I came to the conclusion that, if that's what she intended, she would have had a more convenient chance to kill the baby as soon as it was born, and pretending it was born dead. But she helped me through it, willingly enough . . . Anyway, it wasn't Rosie who did it. She might have been brash and lazy, but she was not evil to the extent that she would murder a new-born baby. All the evidence suggested that I had done it.'

Ann took Isabel's hand consolingly. 'Yes, it was all arranged to look as though you had done it,' she agreed.

Isabel sighed profoundly, tears misting her eyes.

'I'm amazed that Robert has not even mentioned all this to you, now that you have renewed your friendship after so long,' Ann remarked. 'For such a significant consequence of your affair with him, it seems an unforgivable oversight on his part.'

'I don't think it's an oversight, Ann, I believe he simply wishes to avoid talking about it. After all, I'm certain he was not aware that I was carrying his child, although he was certainly made aware later that I had had a child, and he must have known it was his.'

'So why are you still being so loyal to him? To my mind it's unforgivable that he should not have mentioned it, in whatever context he chose.'

'Oh, don't be so hard on him, Ann. Up to now I've had no wish to talk to him about it either. Maybe I should. Maybe I should get it out of the way.'

'Well, yes, I agree, because the whole episode has had such a huge impact on your life. I mean, how can you possibly forget something like that?'

'Well, I suppose he might have some conscience about it, because for years somebody has been transferring money into my bank account, and it just has to be him. He's in the business of banking after all. I'm loath to mention it though, because I would feel beholden to him if I did, and I have no wish to feel beholden, so I'm going to maintain my feigned ignorance.'

'I think you are right, Isabel. But your fiancé . . . Does he know about all this? I presume you have told him.'

'No, I haven't mentioned a word. I've been afraid to.'

'But don't you think you should?'

'Perhaps. But, Ann, I never plucked up the courage. Besides, if he knew, he would have ended our relationship, I'm certain. And I could not have endured that.'

'But what if he finds out?'

'I hope to God he never will.'

Ann shook her head and looked admonishingly at Isabel. 'You have a history of not declaring your troubles to those who would be most anxious to help and understand, and it has been to your disadvantage through life. Don't you see? When you return to Hobart Town and you're reunited with him I think you should reveal all. Tell him everything. If he truly loves you with all his heart he will understand and forgive you, especially as it all happened before he knew you.'

'I don't know, Ann.' Isabel shook her head. 'He's a very conventional man. He wouldn't see it as you see it. He has scruples.'

'Well, scruples or not, Isabel, it's a decision you'll make I daresay before you return home. I feel sure he would be most interested to hear of the wretchedness you have endured. It is enough to make the heart of any man bleed, scruples or no scruples. It must have been so harrowing for you.'

'Harrowing is hardly the word, Ann. The entire episode. You cannot imagine the ordeal of being locked up in a prison for months on end among some hardened criminals, not seeing daylight, suffering the stench, the rats. But the worst part was witnessing the degradation of others, especially other women.'

'What do you mean by degradation, Isabel?'

'Well, when you see a woman in her normal place, her home, or her work for instance, she behaves in ways that are in keeping with where she is and what she is doing. In prison they adopt different behaviour, in keeping with the prison world. Instead of maintaining their usual demeanour, so many allow themselves to abandon the civilised standards of normal living. They abandon their self-esteem, so as to match the activities and even depravity of life in prison where there are no standards of decency.'

'What do mean by depravity?'

'For example, I saw a young woman allow a gaoler to have his way with her just so he would give her more food.'

'You saw it happen?'

'Yes, I saw it all. Before the eyes of all who were there. She showed no shame.'

'What about the gaoler?'

'He just looked smug by the time he'd finished with her.'

'But did she get more food?'

'I don't know, but I suppose she did, if the man was as good as his word. As well as being the gaoler he also owned an inn, so he had plenty of access to food, and was not averse to selling it to prisoners if they had money to pay. If they had no money he took his payment in other ways.'

'You must have been relieved to get away from all that,' Ann said.

'That sort of thing goes on in prisons where there are women. They are taken advantage of relentlessly. I would rather have starved to death. Fortunately for me, my father used to bring me food and drink. Other inmates would sometimes try and steal it from me, so to thwart their efforts I began sharing what I could with the other women.'

'How long were you in that prison awaiting your trial? Ann asked.

'About six months. After my trial I was sent to Newgate prison to await a ship to take female convicts to Van Diemen's Land. I was lucky there, because I did not have to suffer it for more than a few weeks before a ship was ready. Some poor creatures had to wait more than a year in that dreadful place and suffer all its infamy.

'I was transferred to a government convict ship moored in the River Thames,' she went on. 'It was for women convicts only, and due to sail to Van Diemen's Land with about two hundred women on board, some of whom had children with them. There were some free settlers as well. We sailed on the tenth of December in 1839. To tell you the truth, it was like a breath of fresh air after prison. The captain and crew were well disciplined and treated us well.

We had a surgeon on board, and he had the welfare of the women at heart. We were even allowed on deck for fresh air. I remember only one incident when somebody broke the rules, and she was put in a box on the top deck and made to stay there for about six hours in the most uncomfortable position. From then on, all the women behaved well. The sad thing is, many of these women had done nothing seriously wrong. They were snatched away from their loved ones for the pettiest of crimes. It was heart-breaking for most of them to be torn from their families, sometimes from their own children. I found out later that many of them were treated appallingly on other ships, and I mean appallingly. This is what I learned from other women I've met since I've been in Van Diemen's Land. Some were beaten, flogged for the silliest reasons. The best-looking women were even taken as bed partners for the crew on some ships. It's no wonder so many arrived pregnant in Van Diemen's Land.'

'I trust you managed to avoid such a fate, Isabel.'

'My ship was not like that, fortunately. It was well run. We were divided into groups of anything between a dozen and fifteen women. I was chosen to lead one of the groups, because my record showed that I had been employed as a governess, and therefore had some education. Part of the work I was expected to do was to teach the illiterate ones to read and write, and teach them as much as I could about everything else. The most pleasing outcome was that all those women who were illiterate at the start of the voyage could read and write capably enough by the time we reached Hobart Town.'

'So that's how you came to be in Van Diemen's Land? It's quite a story, Isabel.'

'But there's more, Ann. You see, I already knew one of the woman convicts on board – Rosie Duckworth.'

'You mean the same Rosie Duckworth who was employed as your nursery maid? The one who assisted you in your labour?'

'Yes, the same Rosie Duckworth.'

'Rosie? So how did she come to be on a convict ship?'

'I asked her the same question, of course.'

'And?'

'She was brought before the magistrates at the next Quarter Sessions, because it was thought she had perjured herself at my trial. I know the judge at my trial was not happy with her testimony because he said the evidence against me was inconclusive, and at his instigation she was brought before the magistrates later, accused of perjury.'

'She was obviously found guilty?'

'Oh, yes. She was guilty all right. Once we had met up again she told me exactly what had happened after I had given birth to my baby and had gone to sleep . . .'

'Well?'

'Abel Badger killed my baby and deliberately left the knife he killed her with at my bedside. Rosie was covering for him at my trial, of course. She was obviously in his thrall, hoping to marry him, so she was anxious to protect him. To her credit, she apologised to me for her part in what happened. But what was done could never be undone, could it? She could never really make amends for what Abel Badger had done. Anyway, she confessed all to the court at the Quarter Sessions.'

'So presumably, Isabel, this Abel Badger character stood trial for the murder of your baby?'

'No, he didn't.'

'Why ever not?'

'Because, according to Rosie, as soon as he knew she was to appear before the Quarter Sessions, he disappeared. She said he had previously talked of them going to America to start a new life, and she believes that's where he went. He must have realized the truth would be revealed about his part in the crime, so he placed himself out of arms reach.'

'So he got away with it?'

'It would appear so – from that day to this, I imagine. And because he left Rosie in the lurch, she had no qualms about telling the court that it was he after all who murdered my baby.'

'But you were the person found guilty, Isabel. You should apply for a pardon.'

'Oh, I got a pardon – eventually. An absolute pardon.'

'Well, I should hope so too.'

'But I still had to serve my time for failing to report the birth of my daughter.'

'Oh, I see . . . But to get back to this Rosie woman . . . Did you have anything to do with her once you reached Van Diemen's Land?'

'No. She was sent to the Cascades Women's Factory, a place of correction. They organised the women into three different classes, and on no account were the classes allowed to communicate with each other. I was considered to be of good behaviour and reasonably educated – as reported by the surgeon on board the ship – so they said I was suitable to be sent into service with free settlers, when fitting situations could be found. Before long, I was given employment in a shop that sold fine ladies' accoutrements. Eventually, I earned my Certificate of Freedom, and with money that had poured into a bank account that had been anonymously set up for me, I was able to buy the business when the owner decided to return to England. Rosie, meanwhile, was employed in the making and mending of clothes in the Cascades, I believe, so I never managed to speak to her again.'

'You should write a book, recounting your experiences,

Isabel,' Ann suggested. 'I never heard such a story in my entire life. You really have seen so much.'

'And suffered so much, because of my love for Robert Wilson – and my own naivety.'

'But you got your reward by being pardoned.'

'Yes, but, Ann, the real reward has been living in Hobart Town. Had I not been accused of the murder of my child I would never have seen the lovely place. And it's been so good to me. I adore it.'

'Talking of adoration,' Ann said, 'Somebody who adores you very much is heading our way.'

Isabel turned and saw Robert approaching at some distance.

'Let's not give him any clue as to what we've been talking about.'

'But of course,' Ann agreed.

When he reached them, Isabel said, 'You tracked us down then.'

'It wasn't difficult.' His smile was warm on her. 'From the ship, I saw the direction in which you were heading. I believe Captain Cuthbertson is following,' he said, turning to Ann. 'I suspect he intends to steal you away from Isabel.'

'And I suspect you wish to steal Isabel away from me,' Ann answered astutely.

'Not so,' Robert replied with a smile for Ann. 'I am perfectly willing to tag along with two beautiful women, as long as that's acceptable to you both.'

Ann returned his smile politely. 'But I am not inclined to play gooseberry.'

'But you would not be playing gooseberry, Ann,' Isabel chided gently. 'Of course you wouldn't.'

'I trust you two have had much to talk about,' Robert remarked.

'Yes,' replied Ann. 'Isabel has been telling me about life

in Hobart Town and how much she loves it. Until now, it has been the last place on earth I would ever consider visiting, but from what she tells me I am evidently missing a great deal.'

'It's true,' Isabel said wistfully. 'It's so beautiful. The whole island is simply beautiful.' But Isabel felt she needed to change the subject. 'Robert,' she said, veering onto a topic she felt she could safely discuss with Ann at her side. 'I have never asked you about your sisters, Henrietta and Charlotte. Do they prosper?'

'Last time I saw them, yes, but you will appreciate it has been some months since. At the last count, however, Henrietta was engaged, and Charlotte had already married. She now lives in India, where her husband is an official of the East India Company.'

'It's good to know she's done well. I trust she's happy.'

In the distance, they discerned Captain Cuthbertson striding towards them. He waved.

'Here he comes,' Robert said. 'And missing his horse, I'll be bound. Why don't you go and meet him, Ann? I'm sure he would appreciate that.'

'Since I am aware that you wish to be alone with Isabel, I think I will,' Ann replied with a smile of understanding, and set off back in the direction they had come from to meet the captain.

When Ann was out of earshot, Isabel said, 'You do know she's a married lady, don't you? And yet you seem bent on throwing them together.'

'My reason for seemingly throwing them together is for purely selfish reasons, Isabel – because I want to talk to you privately.'

'Oh?'

'Because we have never broached the subject of the child you had . . . My child.'

'Strange that you should mention it now, Robert,' she answered wistfully. 'But what is there to discuss that's not documented history?'

'You must understand, Isabel, that I had no notion whatsoever after I left Patchfield House that you were with child.'

'I've always assumed as much.'

'Had I known, of course, things would have turned out rather differently.'

'Well, I would like to think so,' Isabel replied uncomfortably. 'But, since you did not know, you were in no position to intervene or influence the situation. I do understand, Robert . . .'

'Yet you went through hell because of it.' He looked at her with apologies in his eyes.

Isabel gave no response.

'It's the biggest regret of my life that I was not there for you at the time when you most needed me,' he went on. 'Had I been, I would have done something about it. In an ideal world we would have wed—'

'But we did not live then in an ideal world, Robert. What happened, happened, and cannot be changed. Our lives followed different courses afterwards, but we live happily enough.'

'Not I, Isabel . . . I have never stopped wanting you, nor will I ever. Not a day goes by when I do not recall the tenderness we shared, the pleasurable hours we spent together.'

'And not a day goes by when I do not recall the horrors I endured because of it. I had your child, and it was snatched away from me in its first precious hours of life. Nothing can ever erase those memories, or those deep, deep misgivings.'

'I would have died for you, you know.'

She smiled patiently. 'I suspect you would have died in vain, Robert. I am not the same person now that I was then. Life has hardened me to its harsh realities. I am no longer the naïve sixteen-year-old I was. But with my present life in Hobart Town I am more than content.'

'Nobody deserves to be content more than you do,' Robert stated.

'Thank you, I will accept that,' she responded. 'Because I could have been hanged for what your father and all his household claimed I had done. But my life was spared by a clever judge who saw through the flimsy evidence presented. Anyway, I'm getting hungry now. Let's make our way back to the ship.'

'Yes,' he said. 'We must get ready for the party later to let in the new year.'

~ ~ ~

Chapter 21

SS Great Britain

On the fourth morning of SS Great Britain's mooring at Port Stanley, Isabel swung her legs out of her bunk and put her bare feet to the floor. She stood on tiptoe and peered out of her deadlight. Port Stanley was slowly receding, and she felt the vibrations from the steam engine. They had at last set sail once again for England.

It was then she realized she did not feel well. She felt queasy, but it could hardly be seasickness, for the waters were calm, the ship was moving sedately, almost free of any rolling and dipping. She tried to recall what she had eaten the night before that might have upset her. Then she was overwhelmed by a wave of nausea. She needed to vomit, so she reached for her dressing-gown hanging on a peg on the door and put it on, then rushed to the water closets on the same deck, hoping one of them would be unoccupied. She burst in and retched immediately into the pan.

It tasted foul in her mouth. She spat out the residue of each bout between the spasms of compulsive heaving and tried to catch her breath. Her eyes were watering so she wiped them on her sleeves, and breathed deeply. Soon she felt better.

As she continued with her ablutions the thought inevitably struck her – was this a symptom that she could be carrying Barnaby's child? There had been a few mornings lately when she had not felt quite right, but the notion that she might be with child had never occurred to her; always she had assumed it was the rolling of the ship. When she failed to bleed at her anticipated time she had dismissed it as excitement over her imminent marriage, or concern about her ailing father and the rush and palaver of having to quickly arrange her passage to England. Now she realised she had missed another period of monthly bleeding that ought to have occurred before Christmas.

She wiped her mouth again, composed herself and hurried back to her cabin, encountering nobody on the way. She washed her hands in the bowl on her washstand and poured water into a glass, sat on her bunk, and drank. Whether she was with child or not, she had to dress and face the confined and ever inquisitive world within the ship. Today, she would be careful and heed what she ate; if she felt nauseous tomorrow morning and the morning after, it would almost certainly confirm her condition.

As she dressed, the irony struck her of the similar circumstances when last she was pregnant. The father of her child was absent, unaware that his offspring was growing in her belly. At once, she felt alone, but that was no reason to confess her condition to anybody, except perhaps to Ann. Nevertheless, when she arrived in England, would she have the nerve to confess to her mother that once again, after all these years, she was carrying a child but was still unmarried? Her mother would doubtless ask: had she not learned her lesson?

Her mother, though, need not know she was unmarried; she could tell the lie that she had married a most wonderful man before she left Van Diemen's Land. It was almost the truth and Isabel found some comfort in the ruse.

The next few mornings confirmed what she already

suspected. The ship sailed on through untroubled seas, calm and serene, so Isabel could not blame her retching on seasickness. There could be no doubt, she was with child. Her belly was getting harder, and her bosom was already perceptibly filling out. She had not told Ann of her condition; there was no need for her to know. By the time they reached Liverpool and said goodbye her pregnancy would still not be evident, and even though her belly would swell she would be able to conceal it with what she wore and how she wore it.

- - -

Three weeks later the SS Great Britain was crossing the equator and making good headway under sail and steam. For more than a week they had enjoyed calm seas and warm sunshine. Many of the passengers spent their days on the weather deck, captivated by pods of dolphins that looped in and out of the sea as they raced each other alongside the ship. They marvelled at the myriad flying fish that leapt from the warm waters and skimmed the waves at such speed.

After dinner in the evenings while the fine weather held, the Saloon class passengers held concerts on deck, in which Isabel and Ann performed. Others sang solos, and a group had practised some glees which they sang unaccompanied. Long since, the challenge of performing *Much Ado About Nothing* had been abandoned as impracticable.

The band of musicians, already assembled from the on-board talent, provided music for dancing. During one such balmy evening after a polka, Isabel sat down with Ann for a rest and to cool down a little. As they talked, laughing about certain incidents that had occurred as they compared their various partners, the band struck up with a waltz. At once, Robert Wilson was on his feet and approached Isabel with an outstretched hand.

'May I have the honour, Miss Saxby?' he requested with mock formality.

Isabel nodded with an exaggerated flutter of her long eyelashes, and stood up. He led her to the floor and they began their gentle swirls.

'I enjoyed hearing Ann sing and you play pianoforte,' he said. 'She has a fine singing voice.'

Isabel agreed. 'She does. She is an accomplished young lady in many ways. It's such a pity that her husband does not appreciate her.'

'Does he not?'

'Please don't mention that I told you, but she returned home one day to find him in bed with their maid.'

'Naughty boy,' Robert declared.

'But not an uncommon pastime,' she remarked wryly with a fleeting glance into his eyes. 'Things haven't been right between them since. It's why she accompanied her brothers to Australia in the first place when they decided to start a brewery there – to get away for a while. And who can blame her?'

He held her tightly around the waist, and smiled. 'If the maid was willing enough, though . . .'

'If the maid was willing enough, you cannot blame him? Is that what you mean?'

'Not if the maid threw herself at him, knowing her mistress was away from home.'

'Does that excuse him? Whatever happened to male fidelity?'

'Maybe he has no conscience.'

His face was so close to hers and she looked up and smiled into his eyes. 'You are holding me so close, Robert. People will talk.'

'Let them talk,' he replied nonchalantly. 'Are you worried about what people might think?'

Harking back to Ann's words, she said, 'Does it really matter on this ship? After all, in another five or six weeks we shall have disembarked, and nobody will even remember us.'

'So I have your permission to hold you tight? After all, I do enjoy feeling you so warm and so close to me. It reminds me of old times.'

'Except that times have changed,' she riposted.

'For you, perhaps, Isabel, times have changed. But not for me – at least where you are concerned. Some things remain constant.'

'But you know my situation, Robert.'

'And you know mine.' He paused and they concentrated on their dance steps for a few seconds. Eventually, he said sadly, 'I don't believe women can ever really understand men.'

'Perhaps they cannot,' she replied, 'any more than men can understand women.'

'Once, we seemed to have a perfect understanding of each other.'

'I think that was naivety, and we were both guilty of it,' she said.

At that moment, failing to concentrate on their dance steps in favour of their conversation, they faltered and had to pause before finding their feet again.

'Perhaps we were naïve at the time,' Robert conceded. 'Yet it all seemed sincere enough.'

'Of course it was sincere, but that does not mean we were not naïve. I at any rate was far too young to have been doing what we were doing.'

'You remember what we were doing then?'

Her eyes met his disarming smile. 'I don't need to be reminded of it,' she replied. 'Of course, I do. We were sweethearts – friends as well, but sweethearts don't wear for ever, any more than clothes do.'

'In our case I would like to think they do, Isabel.'

'When you are young, sweethearts should come and go, like the tides,' she said. 'Only when you have experience of a few sweethearts are you qualified to know who might be the most suitable for extended use . . . and even then I suppose it's all too easy to make a mistake.'

'Extended use,' he repeated with a smile. 'I like that. How eloquent you can be.'

The music finished and the two walked away from the dancefloor. A steward was walking in the opposite direction carrying an empty tray at his side.

'Would you bring me a bottle of champagne – the best – and two glasses, please?'

'Very good, sir.'

Together, he and Isabel strolled to the side of the ship, away from the throng. Robert leaned forward, his elbows on the handrail and looked out across the sea, which glistened by the light of the full moon.

'This is the sort of evening that dreams are made of,' he remarked.

Isabel made no comment.

'Don't you agree?' he urged.

'For some people, maybe.'

'Look at the stars,' he said. 'So brilliantly do they sparkle. Millions of them. And the moon. I don't believe I have ever seen it so bright.'

She looked at the moon and wondered whether Barnaby was also looking at the moon right then. If only they could communicate their thoughts, their love for each other, linked via the moon. Robert was talking, naming the various constellations in the sky, but she was not listening; she was thinking of Barnaby and the child growing in her belly. He would be so proud. She began calculating when she might expect its birth, and worked out that it would be sometime in July – she could be no more accurate than that. Which meant that by the time she returned to Hobart Town she would be sporting a big belly. What a surprise she would present to Barnaby when he saw her, for she decided she would keep it secret from him till her return.

The steward arrived bearing a bottle of champagne and two glasses on his tray.

'Please leave the tray,' Robert exhorted. 'I will do the honours.'

The steward duly left, and Robert placed the tray on one of the covered wooden frames that supported the companions, which was the term given to the constructions surrounding the lanterns that allowed daylight into the decks below. He sat down, opened the bottle of champagne, poured it into the two glasses. He handed her one and she thanked him.

He patted the lantern's frame beside him. 'Come sit by me.'

She sat beside him, and sipped the champagne, enjoying the tingling sensation on her nose.

'Here's to you, Isabel.' He raised his glass and drank. 'The love of my life.'

She felt her heart beating faster at his words. Once, a long time ago, he was the love of her life.

'And here's to you,' she responded with a smile.

'I am going to ask you something, Isabel,' he said, and she saw in the half-light that his expression was serious. 'I am going to ask you if you would deign to be my wife—'

She gazed into the glass of champagne, and watched the bubbles rise in their gentle ascent to the surface. Their eyes met and he caught her bemused, dismayed, sad expression.

'Please don't refuse me just yet, Isabel. Just let me say what I want to say.'

Her heart was beating fast, and she was feeling hot. But she held his gaze, waiting to hear what he had to say.

'I understand that you are engaged to another man now, but a woman can break off an engagement if she has sufficient reason or so wishes. I have much to offer, my darling, besides the love we shared which is rekindled in my heart, and which I am certain would soon be in yours. I am a wealthy man. You would want for nothing. I have two homes – Patchfield, with which you are acquainted, and Timberlake in Buckinghamshire, the home of my late wife. You could choose which one you would prefer to be mistress of.'

'It would certainly not be Patchfield,' she was too quick to point out.

'Then Timberlake,' he conceded, encouraged that she was about to accept him if she could make Timberlake her home. 'I can understand your reticence about Patchfield, although it is all changed, and none of the servants remain whom you knew.'

'But what about your mother?' she asked. 'Does she remain?'

'She does. It's her home.'

Isabel sipped more champagne.

'Timberlake is a fine house, Isabel. The estate is more than two thousand acres. There is a deer park, several tenanted farms, a huge formal garden, a full complement of very able and trustworthy servants. I come with other extras too, like carriages, a gig just for you, our first year or so of marriage travelling through Europe. Then there is my eternal love and my devout wish to replace the child you so cruelly lost before, the pain of which plagues me to this day. Please say you will be my wife, my darling, and I shall request Captain Matthews to marry us at your earliest convenience. What is your answer?'

Isabel took a sip of champagne, stalling for time so she could formulate her response. She placed the glass on the companion, took Robert's hand and stroked it gently.

'Dear Robert,' she began, and tears welled up in her eyes. 'It was a pretty speech, and I feel so flattered. Once, I loved you more than words could ever have expressed. Having got to know you again, I confess I am still fond of you . . . But not like before. You are still the same Robert – charming, considerate, gentle and kind – but life has changed you in the same way that it has changed me. We are not the same people we once were. And so I believe that were we ever to marry at this point in our lives, we would be heading for a marital disaster.'

'I don't see that, Isabel. I cannot agree with you.'

'So is this our first argument? Already we cannot see eye to eye.'

'I wouldn't call this an argument, my darling.'

She smiled, sadly. 'Robert, I am truly sorry, but I cannot accept your proposal of marriage, flattered as I am that you consider me worthy.'

'Because of this other man?'

'Of course. But it would be a monumental mistake for you . . .' She paused. 'You see, I am already carrying my fiancé's child.'

'Oh . . . I see,' he answered quietly, and looked into her eyes despondently. 'And do you love him as much as you loved me.'

She nodded and smiled. 'Yes, I do.'

'Then, Isabel, my darling, I wish you every happiness and contentment.'

They remained unspeaking for some little time, until Isabel spoke again.

'Perhaps . . .'

'Perhaps what?' He looked at her expectantly.

'Perhaps, if I had never met Barnaby, I might well have accepted your offer.'

'Perhaps,' he answered with a sigh, 'it would have been easier for me had you not told me so.'

'Perhaps I shouldn't have done.' She smiled affectionately.

'So twice I've missed you. Twice you've passed me by.'

'Therefore, I'm even more convinced that marriage between you and me was never meant to be. Fate has stepped in more than once and prevented it. I think we should both accept that. It is clearly ordained that we shall remain but fond memories to each other.'

- - -

Chapter 22

15 January 1854
Hobart Town, Van Diemen's Land

The Mount Nelson Signal Station was a three mile walk from Hobart Town, and one mid-summer Sunday morning it provided an escape from domesticity for Barnaby Micklejohn; he needed to be alone with his thoughts. The track to the summit traversed beautiful woodlands and took him high above sea level, affording panoramic views over the town and Bruny Island. Further to the east, he could see the Derwent river, blue, glittering in the sunshine as it flowed serenely past Bellerive and Opossum Bay and into Storm Bay. He was reminded poignantly of the day he and Isabel sailed upstream to that deserted sandy cove; it turned out to be a significant day in both their lives.

Flanking the river, lay an area of land under cultivation, dotted with cottages and gardens in bloom. Beyond that lay Hobart Town itself with its white houses, steepled and towered churches, and its abundance of trees. Ships, with their collective assortment of masts, lay basking in the soft and warm haze of Sullivan's Cove. Beyond the town the cultivated valley of the Derwent wound its way through inlets then, stretching toward some far-off hill, it was concealed for some distance by forested headlands, only to appear again further away, still meandering serenely.

Mount Wellington, meanwhile, towered majestically over all, its weathered face bathed in summer sunshine.

Also on the northern banks of the Derwent lay the Government domain, in whose park his daughter Miranda and Isabel's ward Polly would be skipping and frolicking, supervised by their governess. He had taken to Polly, despite what he regarded as her dubious ancestry; she was a bright little girl with a sunny disposition, and she adored Miranda. Miranda likewise adored Polly. They were like sisters, not so much in looks nor yet in their natures, but in the joy they shared one with the other. They never quarrelled, never fought, and Barnaby was content that these two little girls were so absorbed in each other. Isabel would be delighted to learn of their rapport, and that Polly was so happy. He would tell of it when he wrote.

Barnaby was slowly coming to terms with Isabel's absence. She had been gone some six weeks, and he was grieving for her. The grieving was becoming part of everyday life, and some days he withstood it better than others. Some days he tended to dwell on thoughts of her for longer than he should, and so made himself miserable. The lack of any letter was frustrating, but it was too soon yet to expect one; it might be four, five or even six months before he would receive word from her.

He was full of reflections, and feeling particularly downcast, despite the glorious vista he beheld in front of him. He wanted to be alone, he needed to be alone, to walk along the gentle slope to Mount Nelson under the canopy of woodland trees, and think of Isabel.

As he walked, his thoughts meandered over the precious moments they had shared. Memories flooded back ceaselessly. He recalled the very first time he met her when he had been invited to a house party given by mutual friends. Little did he think then that that utterly beautiful woman would eventually agree to become his wife. But she was by now hundreds, thousands of miles away – he had no means of telling how far. No longer could he talk to her, no longer could he touch her, take her hand, feel her sweet lips on his, or be touched by her warmth, her humour, her candour, or her love.

He recalled the exhilaration of that day sailing in his little boat up the Derwent, and how privileged he had felt to have shared it with her, for it contributed massively to what she called their 'progression'. It was a day he would never forget, and he hoped she wouldn't forget it either.

He asked himself why she had held back her love at first, but answered his own question when he recalled her words, and understood that she was concerned about what she would be giving up to become his wife. Of course it restrained her from making an early decision in his favour, but love won through in the end. So why hadn't they tried to spend more time together before she sailed for England? What wonderful, loving extra hours they could have shared. If only they could have brought forward their wedding and married before she left.

Now all they were sharing was a long, tedious and anxious wait before they could be together again. He recalled the joy and pride he felt when she at last agreed they should be married, and the plans they made organising everything. For the time being, however, she was gone, and the promise of such instant contentment had gone with her. How many more months must he wait until she returned to Hobart Town, and made his life complete again? He must try hard to be patient.

That afternoon he was due at Government House for a reception in honour of a visiting dignitary from England. It would take him an hour to get back home, so it was time to return thence to get ready.

- - -

He had reached Salamanca Place on his way home. People were out walking, relishing the sunshine in their Sunday best, hawkers were plying their trade, and the taverns were already enjoying brisk business. He could not help but notice that a woman was walking directly towards him, looking at him and making a beeline for him.

She was slender, thin-faced and dressed in ordinary clothes, but they were obviously well laundered and she looked presentable. In the fleeting moments that passed it was difficult to determine her age, but he estimated she was between thirty-five and forty years old. Although her face was vaguely familiar, he could not place her – not an unusual occurrence, since he often found it difficult to associate people with places or events.

However, she evidently recognised him, and she stopped to pass the time of day.

'Good day to you, sir,' she greeted, smiling as if he were an old friend.

'Good day, miss,' he responded amicably. 'Do I know you?'

'Well, I know who you are . . . You don't remember me, though, do you?' she added.

'Please remind me.'

'I was serving at the government house the day they held the celebration for the stopping of convicts coming here. Don't you remember? You was with Isabel Saxby, as I recall, and I remarked to you as how she'd done well for herself, and you said as how you was engaged to her.'

'I remember the occasion . . .' He paused, pondering as he recalled the moment and the brief anxiety it brought. 'One presumes then that you know Isabel.'

'Know her? I should say I know her. I worked with her at a place called Patchfield House back in the old country.

She was the governess for a while, and I was the nursery maid. Me name was Rosie Duckworth then. She might've mentioned me.'

'Not that I recall, Miss Duckworth.'

'Well, I ain't Miss Duckworth no more, as it happens. I'm wed now. I'm Rosie Flannagan. Married to an Irishman, I am. We both got our certificates of freedom some years ago. We're upstanding citizens now and doing all right. It's the best thing that ever happened to us both, being sent here.'

'Then good for you, Mrs Flannagan,' He smiled patiently. 'My compliments to Mr Flannagan too . . . But now I think about it, on that occasion I seem to recall you mentioning somebody called Gilbert Henderson in connection with Miss Saxby.'

Rosie Flannagan laughed. 'Gilbert Henderson ain't no person, sir. Gilbert Henderson is a ship. It was the convict ship what brought us here.'

'Convict ship? So what was Isabel doing on a convict ship? I presume she was a fare paying free passenger.'

Rosie laughed again. 'Lord, ain't she ever told you?'

'Told me what?' Barnaby asked earnestly.

'Told you about 'erself, about her life afore she came here.' Rosie was beginning to enjoy this encounter, for it was obvious to her already that this gentleman knew nothing about Isabel's past.

'I know she was a governess, in the employ of a George Wilson, the Member of Parliament.'

'Aye, that she was – for a short time. Until . . .' Rosie shrugged.

'Until what?'

'She ain't told you, has she?'

'All I know is that she said she was treated badly while she was there. So there's more?'

'You could say that, sir. Look, there's a bench over yonder, overlooking the quay. If we take a walk over there it'll take the weight off our feet and I can tell you more.'

Already his curiosity in Isabel's past was fervently aroused and urging him towards the bench with Rosie at his side. At the same time, apprehension seized him as to what he might be about to learn.

'I gotta get back to do me husband's dinner, so I daren't be too long, sir. How much d'you want to know.'

'Everything.'

His heart was beating fast, caused by the knowledge that he might learn something about the love of his life that perhaps he ought not to hear, or that she did not wish him to know. But Isabel had always been economical with stories about her life in England. So fateful curiosity urged him forward.

With no further words passing between them, they reached the bench and sat down.

'So tell me those things about Isabel that I am evidently unaware of.'

Rosie shuffled herself comfortable, and looked into his eyes. 'Well, sir, she was just sixteen when she came to Patchfield House, and a bit green, as you might say.'

'Green?' Barnaby repeated, puzzled. 'What does that mean in the context in which you have used the word?'

'It means naïve, gullible, foolish, innocent . . . *green*, sir. Oh, she was full of her airs and graces, but she hadn't got much idea about life. She fell in love with the master's son – Robert Wilson – and he with her, so I reckon. It was a big mistake though. Anyway, she had his bastard – I helped with the birth in the bedroom we shared – but it's a fact that Robert Wilson knew nothing about it. She wanted it kept quiet – about her giving birth – but it was my duty to report it to the master, else I would've been in trouble if I'd hidden the fact. So I told somebody I thought I could trust, and he took me to the master. After I'd reported it I went for me breakfast. When I got back to the bedroom we shared the new-born child was lying with its throat cut and the knife what had been used was lying beside her.'

Barnaby's heart thumped, his mouth was suddenly dry, and he felt uncomfortably hot. 'Are you saying that Miss Saxby gave birth to a child then killed it?'

'Well now, that's how it looked, sir, and that's how it was meant to look. The County Coroner and the Sheriff said she must've done it, so they said she was guilty.'

'My God!'

'Anyway, to cut a long story short, she was sent to gaol while she waited for her trial at the assizes. They found her guilty, sir. The judge should've sentenced her to be hanged, but he wasn't satisfied with the evidence, so he gave her seven years transportation instead. And that's how she came to Van Diemen's Land on the Gilbert Henderson, sir.'

'And this is the truth, Mrs Flannagan?'

'Why would I lie? I got no reason to lie. If you ask her she'll tell you as it's the truth.'

'But the claims you have made about Miss Saxby are not only profoundly serious, but also very troubling and distressing. So tell me, Mrs Flannagan, how you came to be on the same ship with Miss Saxby.'

'In a nutshell, sir, I knew exactly who killed Miss Saxby's baby, and it wasn't Miss Saxby.'

'Then I thank God for that,' he remarked.

'But I perjured meself at her trial,' Rosie continued, 'daft sod that I was, tryin' to protect the bastard what did do it. That's how I got seven years transportation as well.'

'So who did kill the child?'

'The fellow I told about the birth in the first place, who I thought I could trust, sir. He did it. But he disappeared off the face o' the earth as soon as I was arrested. I believe he scarpered to America afore they could arrest him.'

Barnaby sighed deeply. 'Mrs Flannagan, this is all news to me and extremely painful, as you might imagine. Miss Saxby is on her way to England right now to visit her parents. In the meantime I can check on what you have told me, of course. I can request to see government records of all convicts, and details of their crimes, even the ships they sailed on to Van Diemen's Land.'

'I'm sure you can, sir, and you should check it all to satisfy yourself as I ain't tellin' you no lies. Anyway, I must go now. You see, once I've got me husband's dinner, I'm off to work, serving at the reception at Government House this afternoon. So I daresay I'll see you there a bit later . . .'

- - -

After Rosie Flannagan had gone, Barnaby stayed, sitting on the bench overlooking the key, deep in thought. He failed to notice the gentle swaying of the ships' masts that lay berthed and at anchor, the soft lapping of the sea on the stone wall of the quay, the seagulls wheeling and shrieking overhead. What he had learned, if true, put a different complexion on his relationship with Isabel. He had been mindful that information about her life before Van Diemen's Land was unclear, but had considered it of little importance because of her demeanour. Nobody on God's earth seemed less like a criminal than Isabel Saxby. That same demeanour, her very nature, defied any argument that she could have been a convict sentenced to transportation for criminal offences. Yet Fate had intervened. Little wonder she was so knowledgeable about women convicts and the tribulations many had to suffer. Little wonder she employed former convicts so freely.

But she'd had a child at the tender age of seventeen – a bastard – doubtless conceived when little more than a child herself at sixteen, the bastard child of George Wilson's son. Always, when asked, she had been secretive about the men in her past. He remembered asking her once if she had had a torrid relationship with a man that she might be concealing, and she had replied that she would not tell him even if she had. Therefore, she did not want him to know.

Whether or not she had committed the murder of her child, she had broken the law and been sentenced to transportation. But just as significantly, she had given herself to another man, had had his child. Barnaby could not countenance the fact that she had not confessed it to him during their progression; she had wilfully withheld that information. Now it was obvious why; she was ashamed. It begged the question – how many other men had she given herself to?

Then the awful possibility struck him that if she were so promiscuous, how many other men had she lured into her lair in Bellerive? In hindsight, the invitation to spend a few days and nights there with her seemed so easily proffered, and proffered without guile or any semblance of propriety.

Had she taken him for a fool? Had he been so enchanted that he overlooked, or was blind to any flaws in her character? Why had he not delved more deeply into her past? Why had he not earlier consulted government records of free settlers and even convicts to glean more background on her? These thoughts and more troubled Barnaby acutely. Without delay, he must scour the records of female convicts transported to Van Diemen's Land, and either verify or disprove what Rosie Flannagan had maintained. Then he would decide what was to be done.

\- - -

Barnaby did not attend the reception at Government House that Sunday afternoon. For one thing, he had no wish to encounter Rosie Flannagan again. Instead, he spent the time at home, brooding, confused, and hoping with all his heart that Rosie's assertions were untrue, malicious lies. There was peace and quiet at home; the children had been shepherded to Sunday School, the governess and maids were taking their weekly sabbatical.

Alone, Barnaby wept.

The world seemed so cruel right then. Death had stolen his young wife and left its excruciating sting, which had been so hard to come to terms with. Now this. When he thought his future was settled, it was no longer; everything was upside-down again. And the cause of all this uncertainty was heading towards the other side of the world and was unreachable. It would be months before he saw Isabel again. It might be months before he even heard from her by letter.

Meanwhile, he must be guided by what any convict records revealed.

- - -

The Convict Department was where Barnaby headed after first putting in an appearance in his own office on Monday morning. He made his excuses to his staff; he would be gone a couple of hours. Then, after announcing himself in the Convict Department as a government officer he requested to see the convict record for one female, Isabel Saxby, transported on the Gilbert Henderson convict ship.

The clerk found and handed him a list of all the names of women convicts who sailed on that ship. Isabel Saxby was listed, with a note of her good behaviour whilst on board. So that part was true; she had been convicted and thus transported.

'There will be a record of her time in Van Diemen's Land,' the clerk said helpfully.

'I would like to see it, if I may,' Barnaby replied.

The clerk disappeared, then returned with a book. He

handed the book to Barnaby. 'Here, sir . . . Browse it at your leisure. You will find the name of the convict in question, and all details about her.'

Barnaby went to a table and sat down at a chair. He opened the book. Every page contained hand-written records of female convicts. Much was difficult to decipher; sections appertaining to different periods in a convict's progress were in different handwriting, some were untidy scrawls and hardly legible compared to those written in copperplate swirls by the more painstaking scribes.

He found the entry for Saxby, Isabel. It confirmed that she was formerly employed as governess in the household of George Wilson MP at Worcester. Her recorded crime was stated as infanticide of her bastard child and withholding notification of its birth. Her trial was held at Worcester Assizes on 24th November 1839, she was found guilty and was sentenced to seven years transportation. She arrived in Van Diemen's Land aboard the Gilbert Henderson on 24th April 1840. So that was no lie and he sighed despondently. Then Barnaby discerned from a section in poor handwriting that she had been pardoned, but evidently note of it was received too late, for the Gilbert Henderson had already departed for Van Diemen's Land with her aboard.

He was relieved that the pardon meant that she was not guilty of infanticide, but that did not alter the fact that she had given birth to a bastard child by the rogue son of George Wilson. This shone a different light on her morality. If, as now seemed highly likely, she was a woman of easy virtue, he needed to review their future relationship. He needed to think things through, weigh up the facts, and come to a decision as to exactly what he should do.

Also, he must try to find whatever information was available on Robert Wilson.

It was relatively easy. Government House possessed a recent copy of Burke's Peerage. Barnaby found a potted history of the life of Sir George Wilson, Bart, MP, his marriage to Florence Maude Webb, with information about his two sons and two daughters. On his death, Robert Wilson, the eldest son, inherited the title and became Sir Robert Wilson, the 2nd Baronet. He married Elizabeth Hulme, only daughter of Sir Joseph Hulme, and inherited the Timberlake estate on her death. He was a shareholder in the Union Bank of Australia and the Geelong and Melbourne Railway Company.

Investigation later revealed that the Geelong and Melbourne Railway Company had a total shareholding of eight hundred and sixty-five thousand pounds, an enormous sum.

That Australia connection at once set more alarm bells ringing. Being a major shareholder in either of those Australian enterprises would warrant attendance at meetings. So had he been a visitor recently to Australia?

Since acquiring this knowledge all sorts of possibilities troubled Barnaby as to whether this was in any way connected to Isabel. He must write to both companies requesting information on that particular shareholder, and if there had been any attendance at meetings. If he had been to Australia, he could feasibly have visited Van Diemen's Land – and if so, to what purpose? What if Isabel's sudden and unanticipated return to England had been instigated by contact with him? What if she had actually eloped with him?

Barnaby's imagination was running riot.

\- - -

Chapter 23

24 February 1854
England

Along with other passengers, Isabel leaned against the iron rail of *SS Great Britain's* weather deck as they came within clear sight of land, relishing the buffeting of the wind, the rain, and the salty smell of the sea. Sixty-two days after leaving Melbourne, *SS Great Britain* had arrived at Liverpool, and to mark her arrival fired a salute from its guns. Soon the ship was ploughing the broad estuary of the River Mersey, lined with docks, shipping, towering cranes and gantries. In the distance stood church towers and steeples, impressive commercial buildings, and tall chimneys volleying smoke into the steel-grey sky. She could discern the rolling hills of Lancashire beyond, rendered grey by the rain. When she was packing for the trip, Isabel was glad she had thought to include a warm coat and cape, recalling the cold and damp of English winters.

As the ship docked Robert Wilson appeared on the weather deck and stood beside Isabel.

'I shall be travelling on to Worcester, Isabel, so I thought perhaps we should make the journey together,' he suggested.

'You are going to Patchfield, and not to Timberlake?'

'Yes, I've decided it should be Patchfield. I consider it

my first duty back on these shores to visit my mother for a few days. I shall return to Timberlake at my leisure.'

'I'm sure your mother will be thrilled to see you, Robert.'

'Thrilled?' he laughed. 'I would not go so far as to say that. Thrilled suggests enthusiasm, which she lacks for anything. But she might be fairly pleased to see me after being so long away.'

'Well, as to your suggestion that we travel together, thank you. Yes, I had thought about it, and I see no reason why we shouldn't. After all, this railway malarkey everybody is so enthused about is all new to me. I'll be glad of your guiding me through its complexities.'

'It's hardly complex, Isabel, my dear. One buys a ticket to travel and one boards the train.'

'But which train?' she asked. 'How do you know which train to board? And does one train go all the way to Worcester – I mean, does Worcester even have a railway station?'

'We might be lucky, Isabel. When I left England, Worcester was due to have a new railway station at Shrub Hill as part of a new line that was opening up. I imagine it has been completed by now. At least, I hope so, as it will be most convenient for us. But to answer your question, you can get almost anywhere on the railways. Sometimes, you have to change trains at some point to get exactly where you want to be. For instance, when we leave Lime Street station here in Liverpool, we shall have to take the train that delivers us to Crewe. From Crewe we shall have to take another train that will take us to Wolverhampton, and then another from there to Worcester.'

'Well, it all sounds extremely complicated, Robert, but thank you for the explanation. Now, I must find Ann Carter. She's bound for the railway station too. Let's meet on the quay when we've disembarked, and you can take us.'

'It will be my pleasure,' he replied. 'I'll see you later.'

Isabel and Ann joined the throng of passengers assembling on the quay while the crew were depositing trunks and baggage. There was a scramble as people moved to claim theirs and be on their way, bidding final farewells to friends they had made on the long voyage. Robert reappeared, hailing one of the cabs that were lined up. He called Isabel and Ann to join him, then helped them inside before he and the driver lifted their trunks onto the roof.

When they arrived at Lime Street Station Isabel was in awe of its architectural grandeur. As she entered its portals she was astonished at the extent to which railways had developed in so short a time, almost into an art form; how they had become so rapidly embedded in peoples' lives, if the throngs occupying the platforms were any yardstick. She had seen nothing like it before and it seemed she had arrived back in an England at some hitherto unimaginable future time. It was a transport revolution.

Robert announced that the train they must take was due to leave in half an hour. He bore two first-class tickets for their journey, and informed Ann Carter that hers was the next London-bound train of the London and North Western Railway.

Then he moved to one side to speak to Ann privately. Isabel was unable to catch any of their conversation, but she saw Ann replying to whatever he was saying, then nod to him and look up into his eyes with smiling admiration.

All too soon it was time for them to part, with hugs and affectionate patting and promises to write to each other. Isabel and Robert boarded a railway carriage which they had to themselves. Before long the train began to move.

'It's so smooth,' Isabel remarked. 'But I can't hear a steam locomotive.'

'Because there isn't one,' Robert replied. 'At least not yet.'

'So what's going on?'

'Well,' he began, 'because this incline is too steep for a normal locomotive we are being hauled by a stationary engine situated a little way out of town at place called Edge Hill,' he explained. 'When we arrive there, in just a few minutes, they will hitch a locomotive to the front of our train and we shall be on our way.'

'It's astonishing, isn't it?' She enthused. 'So much progress in such a few years.'

'I know,' he said. 'Railways are the future – everywhere. And Britain leads the world. It's why I am investing in them, especially abroad.'

'Talking of investing money,' she said, believing this was an appropriate time to mention the generous amounts that were arriving in her bank account, and thankful for the cue, 'it's been extremely generous of you to send money to me all these years, and I am taking this opportunity of thanking you. So thank you, Robert.' She smiled enchantingly. 'But I also have to reprimand you. I have no wish to appear ungracious, believe me, but the truth is, I can manage perfectly well without it. I have a business that is profitable, and I am due to be married when I return home. Barnaby and I will be more than comfortably off, so please do not trouble yourself in future. In fact, I would appreciate it if you would allow me to pay the money back, or at least some of it.'

'I have not the faintest idea what you are talking about, Isabel,' Robert replied.

'Oh, come on, Robert, please don't be evasive. It was very noble of you to start it in the first place, but there's no point to it anymore. It's just a waste of money on your part.'

'Isabel, I really have no idea what you are talking about,' he reaffirmed. 'I have never sent you money if that's what you're inferring. Perhaps I should have done . . . Now you are making me feel guilty that yes, perhaps I should have done, after all the trials and tribulations you suffered on account of me. But I have never sent you money, nor has the Patchfield estate, and that is the gospel truth.'

'I don't believe you,' she said defiantly. 'You know very well you have, so why don't you own it? Who else would send me money?'

'Your own father?' he suggested.

'If my father had sent me money it would not have been anonymously. In any case, he could never afford the amounts I've been getting.'

Robert frowned, puzzled. 'So . . . if I am to understand you precisely, you have been receiving money regularly into a bank account in Hobart, from somebody in England, and that person wishes to remain anonymous?'

'Precisely. By way of a London Bank.'

'And you believe it's me?'

'Naturally, I believed it's you. Who else could it be? And am even more convinced it's you ever since you told me you are involved in banking.'

'On my heart, Isabel, I have never sent you money.'

'Honestly?'

'It's the absolute truth.'

'Do you swear it?'

'I swear it. On a thousand Bibles.'

'Well . . .' she sighed. 'Then I would dearly like to know who has.'

'Indeed, it's most generous of this mystery person, whoever it is. But I cannot claim the credit for it. If you ever discover the source, however, I would dearly like to know. I'm intrigued.'

'Well, if it's not you, maybe I'll never find out who it is.'

The train slowed to a halt.

'There – they'll be attaching that locomotive now. We

shall soon be on our way.'

'Yes,' she sighed. 'I shall soon be with my mother and father again, after so long.' She looked out of the window, but saw nothing; her mind was in Worcester. 'My two sisters are grown up now,' she mused. 'It's such a pity I've missed their growing up. I believe they have turned out to be fine young ladies.'

'Indeed, Isabel, if they are anything like you.'

They fell silent for a few minutes, when Isabel gazed absently again through the carriage window. Before long, a locomotive was attached and they felt the train shift forward to loud rasps of steam, and the clanks of shackles and buffers.

'I . . . er . . . wish to invite you to be my guest at Timberlake whilst you are in England,' Robert said.

'Oh, thank you.' The invitation came as a surprise, and at once Isabel was wary about accepting it.

'I have also invited Ann Carter,' he interjected. 'It would be an opportunity for you both to continue your friendship.'

Isabel said, 'Is that what your little *tête-à-tête* was about at Lime Street station?'

'Yes. I've told her she can stay as long as she likes. I suppose all will depend on the state she finds her marriage in once she's back home, don't you think?'

'I suppose so . . .' Isabel pondered a moment. 'Tell me, Robert, do you find her appealing? I've seen the way you look at her.'

'Well, Isabel, she is worth a second glance, you know. She is rather comely.'

'Oh, I agree, she's very comely, and very personable. But she's married . . .'

'For now, yes.'

'Oh, I see. You're hoping to turn her head.'

'I'm not sure that her head is turnable.'

'Oh, I think it is, Robert. I'm certain of it.'

'You're not jealous by any chance, are you, Isabel?'

'Of course I'm not jealous. But I have no desire to play gooseberry to you two, if that's what it might amount to.'

He laughed. 'Who says you would be playing gooseberry?'

'I do.'

'In any case, she might not be inclined to accept the invitation if she and her husband are reconciled. Nevertheless, if her marriage ends because of his infidelity, then I have told her she is welcome to come to Timberlake and spend time there to get away from any aggravation. It would no doubt be a relief for her. As I said, you are also more than welcome, of course you are.'

'Well I shall write to her, Robert, and glean the state of the poll from her reply. That will determine the issue.'

'Anyway,' he said, 'it's clear that you are not interested in a new liaison with me.'

'You know I cannot, Robert, even if I wanted to.'

'Of course, I understand since you are with child, and a fiancé forever present in the background.'

'But your circumstances, Robert, remain unchanged. You are the wealthy young widower with a vacancy for a new wife . . . or even a mistress . . .'

- - -

It was night time when the locomotive of the Oxford Worcester and Wolverhampton Railway hauled its carriages into the new Shrub Hill Station at Worcester. Once he and Isabel had alighted Robert hailed a hackney carriage and, their trunks loaded, they were ready to go.

'Crowle?' Robert queried.

'Didn't I tell you? My family don't live in Crowle anymore. They live in Friar Street now, in the city.'

He instructed the driver thus and the cab moved off.

'How long since they moved from Crowle?'

'In eighteen-fifty, soon after the last cholera outbreak. I don't know the house of course. As my father got older he found it too arduous to walk all the way from Crowle to his school and back every day.'

'Let us hope that your father is no worse than when your mother alerted you to his illness.'

'Well, I shall know soon enough.'

As they said their goodbyes, Robert reminded her about his invitation to visit him at Timberlake.

'Thank you,' she said, and gave him a peck on the cheek. 'I shall look forward to it.'

The driver clambered down from his perch and Robert alighted from the hackney carriage. He handed her down, lifted down her baggage and transferred it to the front door of the house.

Her eyes misting with tears, she turned and waved, illuminate by the glow of a streetlamp and the coach lanterns, and wiped her eyes with a kerchief. Meeting and befriending Robert Wilson again after all those years, which had highlighted the ardour they had once shared, had left its mark on her. Things might have worked out so differently . . . if . . . Life might have been so different . . . if . . . For such a small word, 'if' holds so much promise.

Having stood and watched the hackney carriage disappear into the darkness, she scanned Friar Street with its irregular black and white Tudor houses and their overhanging upper storeys. When she saw the forbidding walls of the City Gaol that shared a part of Friar Street she shuddered as she recalled the harrowing months she was forced to spend there. Whatever had possessed her parents to choose a house so close to the City Gaol, after all the horrid memories it was bound to invoke?

At last, she turned to the house. The glow of candlelight shone through a slit in the window drapes. Wondering what situation she was about to encounter, she tapped on the front door and waited, her heart pounding with expectation.

A young woman answered her knock and opened the door; a distinguished-looking young woman wearing a mantle and dress, and a striking bonnet, obviously dressed for the cold night. When she saw Isabel she bore no look of recognition, simply an expression that implied, who is this woman knocking at the door at this time of night? Then, her look changed to one of uncertainty.

'Daisy,' Isabel exclaimed eagerly. 'I would have known you anywhere. It's me, Isabel.'

'Ah! My goodness!' Daisy put her hands to her face in disbelief. 'Isabel . . . Oh, Isabel, come in out of the cold.' Isabel stepped onto the stone slabs of a Tudor hallway and felt the warmth of a homely ambience caress her. 'Mother!' Daisy called. 'Isabel is here! Mother!' Daisy and Isabel fell into a tight embrace meanwhile, that only years of absence from a loved one can engender. 'Nicholas – that's my husband by the way – and I were just about to go home,' she said, excited at the unanticipated return of her long-gone sister. 'We've been to see father, but of course we'll stay a while longer now that you have arrived. How was your journey? You look wonderful, Isabel. Are you tired?'

A door opened and mother appeared. Even by the light of the oil lamp Isabel could see that she had aged. She was drying her hands on a towel, which she flopped over her shoulder so that she could hug Isabel.

'Oh, Mother . . .' Isabel shut her eyes in this moving embrace. There was a lump in her throat, and she tried to force back tears that would not be stemmed.

Mother and daughter, unexpectedly but magically no

longer apart, tearfully held each other for some time, vainly trying to compensate for all the years they had not set eyes on each other; those long, long years when unfortunate events and the heartlessly indifferent law had conspired to keep them apart. Now all those destructive forces seemed distant and irrelevant.

When they released each other profuse tears were flooding both pairs of eyes.

'Oh, Isabel, I wish I had known you were coming,' was all Susan could think of to say.

'Well, I've got here quicker than a letter would, mother, so I didn't see the point in writing.' She looked at Daisy for support.

Nicholas was suddenly standing in the group.

'This is Nicholas,' Daisy said. 'Nicholas, this is my long-lost sister Isabel, come to visit us from Van Diemen's Land. Why don't you bring Isabel's trunk in?'

'You've had quite a journey,' he said as they shook hands. Then stepped outside for Isabel's trunk. 'Where should this go?' he asked, but received no response, for Isabel's appearance was naturally taking precedence.

'Let's not stand in this chilly hallway,' Susan suggested. 'Let's all go into the parlour. Kitty is in the parlour.' Then an excited call to Kitty. 'Kitty, our Isabel is here.'

They all trooped into the parlour, mother first. Kitty was already on her feet, smiling in anticipation of seeing the sister she had not seen for fifteen years. She, too, was a good-looking young woman, but dressed in day clothes, her hair a little awry from the day's activities. She reached out to Isabel and they embraced eagerly too, while a grey cat raised its head from a rug and looked nonchalantly at the newly arrived human into its domain.

'We didn't know whether you would come, Isabel, or even whether you had received mother's letter. It's such a long way to Van Diemen's Land. Letters take so long.'

'That, I do know,' Isabel responded happily. 'But yes, I'm here, at long last.'

'And tired, I imagine after your long journey.'

'Well it's taken more than two months to get here.'

'I don't know how you could withstand being at sea for so long,' Kitty remarked, as if they had never been apart. 'Was it awful?'

'Apart from one episode when we encountered a terrible storm, it was good,' Isabel replied. 'Anyway, how is father?'

'Poorly,' Susan, replied with suitably hushed tones. 'I don't think you would recognise him. He's a poor soul. He's gone to nothing. First, though, I'll brew some tea. I imagine you are tired and thirsty after your train journey.'

'No, no, let's have something stronger,' Kitty insisted. 'This is a time for a celebration now that our Isabel is home. And we've got such a lot to talk about. Come sit you down, our Isabel. Sit next to me on the settle.' The settle stood end-on to the inglenook fireplace, where a homely coal fire was burning, adding its dancing light to the candle-lit parlour.

'Are you hungry, Isabel? Susan enquired.

'I am. I haven't eaten since we changed trains at Crewe.'

'Well, there's food a-plenty. What would you like?'

'Oh, anything. Whatever is easiest for you.'

'I'll brew some tea anyway and when you have had something to eat you shall go up and see your father.'

'Will he be awake?'

Susan shrugged, a look of anguish on her face. 'He might be, but he sleeps most of the time.'

At least I've returned while he's still alive, Isabel thought to herself. *That's one dread eliminated.*

'And while you are with your father, I'll make a bed up for you.'

- - -

Isabel had a shock when she saw her father. He had shrivelled up, shrunk. His face was drawn, his nose looked pinched. His thin face bore a grey pallor, and she imagined he must be racked with pain. She sat on the chair at his bedside and watched him for a few minutes. Then, as if he sensed that somebody was there, he opened his rheumy eyes.

At first, he looked at Isabel with confusion, not recognising her, and she was disappointed that he might be delirious and fail to identify her anyway. She rose from the chair and helped him sit up and plumped up his pillows.

'It's Isabel,' she said quietly announcing herself. 'Your daughter, come all the way from Van Diemen's Land to be with you.'

'Isabel,' he croaked, his voice thin and weak, but his eyes brightening at the revelation. 'At last . . . I knew you'd come. I said to your mother.'

'You didn't know me at first though, did you? It's been so long.'

'I thought for a moment that I was dreaming, and you were your mother,' he whispered. 'You're so much like your mother was at your age – always a picture.'

'I'm sorry I've been away so long, Father,' she said. 'But life has been kind to me after all in Van Diemen's Land, and it's been so hard to leave it.'

'I'm glad for you, my dear. You deserve happiness and contentment after what you suffered. But you never married, did you?'

She shook her head. 'No, not yet, father. But I am due to be married when I return.'

That snippet of information seemed to pass him by. 'So how long shall you stay?' His eyes blinked lazily.

'For as long as you want me to,' she replied. 'I'll be here. My wedding can wait.'

She stroked his forehead gently. 'You're tired, father. Would you like me to leave you now? We can talk more tomorrow.'

'No, stay, Isabel. It's been so long . . . so long.'

She kissed him on the cheek. 'Of course I'll stay.'

'Bless you. Oh, you do remind me of your mother in her younger days.'

'I'm happy you think I'm like her.'

'This pain, though, Isabel . . . It's unbearable. I wouldn't wish it on anybody. There's some laudanum over there on the tallboy.'

She stood up, went to the tallboy and picked up the small fluted green bottle that held it. She uncorked it and put it to his dry lips, administering two drops.

'It helps relieve the pain,' he murmured.

'I know,' she answered consolingly.

He closed his tired eyes, and Isabel continued to sit with him, holding his hand. She thought he seemed at peace and she hoped that she had brought him some contentment just by being there. If so, it made the long journey from Van Diemen's Land worthwhile. As the minutes passed by to the rhythmic tick-tock of the clock standing on the mantlepiece over the fireplace, she felt his grip loosening. By the light of the oil lamp she watched him as he drifted into sleep. So much of his life had passed her by without her being aware of it; so too, half of her own life her father had missed. Seeing her develop into a woman had been denied him. How different their lives might have been, if only . . .

Eventually, she slipped her hand gently away from his and heaved a great sigh of sadness as she crept to the door. She opened it, turned around and leaned her head against the doorframe to take another look at her father, and recalled how he looked all those years ago.

Time and events had robbed them both of the joy they might otherwise have shared over the years, had robbed her of the wisdom he would most certainly have imparted, for he had always been an erudite and judicious man. To see him reduced to his present state was heart-breaking.

So she turned away, closed the door, and headed back down the stairs, to her mother and her sisters, where the atmosphere was more joyous because of her return to the fold.

'So tell us about Van Diemen's Land and what you have been doing all these years,' Daisy said. 'And why you have never married?'

- - -

Chapter 24

Worcester, England

Next day, Isabel wrote to Barnaby to reassure him of her love, to let him know that she had arrived safely and was looking forward to spending as much time as she could with her father, who was a poorly man. She told him also of the friendship she had developed with Ann Carter on board the *SS Great Britain*, and that she had been a delightful and entertaining companion throughout the voyage. Naturally, she felt it was not pertinent to make any mention, requiring explanation, of Robert Wilson.

The following day, after they had breakfasted and ensured that William Saxby was comfortable, Isabel said to her mother, 'I want to visit my baby's grave. Will you take me to it?'

'Of course, my dear. Kitty will stay and keep an eye on your father while we are gone.'

Before she knew it they were walking along Copenhagen Street to the undulating graveyard of St Andrew's church with its needle spire. Susan led her down a puddle-strewn pathway and they picked their way between the graves. Fronds of wet, limp grass brushed their skirts, but Isabel hardly noticed. She was about to visit for the first time the grave of her un-named daughter. Yet again, she was overwhelmed with unutterable sadness, for who knew what the unfortunate victim of George Wilson and Abel Badger might have become, had she been allowed to live.

At last they reached the tiny grave. Daffodils standing in a grave vase bowed their yellow heads in the breeze.

'We take it in turns to put flowers on the grave,' Susan explained quietly.

'Thank you so much, mother.' She looked earnestly into her mother's eyes. 'I'm so glad you do.'

Isabel read the inscription her mother and father had seen fit to have engraved into the headstone in her absence. It read: '*To the memory of Baby Saxby, who died tragically at the hand of scheming persons on 13th May 1839, but a few hours old.*

Isabel sat down on the adjacent cold grave and a spate of tears stung her eyes.

'I never had the chance to know her,' she wept. 'I hardly held her.'

'I know, my dear,' Susan consoled and put her arm around her.

'I remember her so well,' she blubbered. 'She was so beautiful, so helpless, so . . .' She broke down and sobbed, her handkerchief pressed against her mouth lest her crying be heard. Her eyes were streaming, her nose was running, she shivered with cold and felt utterly miserable as the abhorrent memories of that fateful day vividly returned.

After some minutes, she blew her nose as her crying subsided. Strangely, this brief communion, with the daughter she had never had the chance to know at all, elicited some comfort. This was the closest she had been to her child since she was dispatched so ignominiously to Worcester City Gaol years ago, and it was a profound moment. She would never forget the child, but would always live with the sadness of its unwarranted death.

The hard, cold stone of the grave was having a numbing effect on her hind quarters, so she stood up, shivering. 'Shall we go now, mother?' she suggested, wiping her eyes. 'I need to sit in front of a blazing fire now with a cup of hot tea.'

'So do I,' Susan agreed.

So their picked their way back between the graves, back onto the muddy path and Copenhagen Street, then home in Friar Street.

- - -

Over the next week Isabel spent as much time with her father as she could, sitting at his bedside day and night, talking to him when he was conscious and responsive. Much of the time though he was in a different world. The laudanum helped relief his pain but took him to an unimaginable fantasy world where she could not reach him. As the days passed she watched him descend further into a constant slumber which, on the seventh day of her stay, became an eternal one.

He passed peacefully away on the 3rd of March, a Friday.

The next day, Isabel wrote again to Barnaby, and this is part of her letter . . .

. . . You will understand, my dearest Barnaby, that it has been a Privilege to share my Father's last precious Hours with him, and I am satisfied that Together you and I made the right Decision that I should make the Voyage to England to see him. Postponing our Wedding was one of the most difficult Decisions I have ever had to make, and I know it was Emotional for you also, but it has proved to be the right decision after all. I would not have missed for anything spending the last few Days and Hours with that wonderful Man who had always given

unstinting Support and Encouragement to me, especially when I needed it most.

During those hours when she was not with her father, Isabel would enjoy endless reminiscences and discussions with her mother and with Kitty. Kitty, twenty years old by this time, had met a young man some twelvemonth earlier and was anticipating that he would propose marriage soon. They laughed girlishly as they speculated about how it might come about, when and where would they get married once he had proposed, and where she would like to live thereafter.

Despite those lighter moments, there was still William Saxby's funeral to cast its mantle of sadness over them. It was held on a blustery day at St Andrew's church, the sun bursting through occasionally to brighten the otherwise sombre interment that took place in the shade of its spire. Isabel was adamant that all three sisters should attend, and so support their mother. Nicholas in turn was there to comfort Daisy. Some members of staff of the school where William Saxby taught also attended, as well as long-standing friends.

When it was over, the family returned to their home in Friar Street, and a warm fire. They brewed tea and discussed the dear departed husband and father, recounting stories about him, many of which made them laugh, many that invoked admiration and respect. All poignantly reminded them how much they would miss him.

\- - -

Towards the end of March, Isabel and her mother Susan, found themselves alone one evening. They sat together on the settle in front of the inglenook fireplace while Susan was darning stockings by the light of an oil lamp and the flickering fire. Kitty was visiting the home of her suitor, a young man called Elias Willetts, and Isabel recognised it as an opportunity to have a heart-to-heart with her mother, to say things she could never say in front of her sisters. They talked about her life in Van Diemen's Land, and Susan asked the inevitable question of why she'd never married.

'Because up to now I was not so taken with any of the men I met,' Isabel replied honestly.

'All convicts, I suppose,' Susan suggested.

'No, mother. Not everybody is a convict. There are plenty of free settlers. In fact, we don't even mention the word convict, whether we're talking about them or to them – it can be too demeaning. When somebody has served their time they are entitled to settle down to a normal life, and most do. There are land grants available and there's work for everybody. There are fine schools, a hospital in Hobart, and several churches, as well as a cathedral.'

'It all sounds very pleasant, our Isabel.'

'And so it is, mother. It's also a beautiful place to live, with a lovely climate. You should think about leaving here and coming with me. If Kitty is going to be married and with Daisy already wed, you're going to be left on your own. We can find you a little cottage close to me and Barnaby.'

'Oh, I don't know, Isabel. It would be an upheaval.'

'But a sensible one, Mother.'

'In any case, I could never leave Kitty as long as she remains unmarried, and there's no certainty that she will marry. Nor would I ever see either Kitty or Daisy again, nor any children they might have in the future.'

'But you would see me often, and any children *I* might have.'

'So who is this Barnaby?' Susan queried, instigating a revelation that was already overdue. 'It's the first I've heard of a Barnaby. Who is he?'

'He's my . . .' She was about to say he was her husband, as she had planned to, to save face, but already she had declared that she was unmarried. 'He's my fiancé, mother.'

'Your fiancé? Are you planning to be married soon?'

'Just as soon as I get back to Hobart, mother. I've been meaning to tell you, but I wanted to tell you when I've got you alone. Barnaby and I were due to be married on the fourth of December, but that was the same day the ship *Great Britain* was due to sail to England, so we had to postpone our wedding at the last minute. As you can imagine, once I received your letter, plans to sail here were made in such a hurry, that I wasn't even sure I would make it to Melbourne on the mainland where the ship sailed from. It was either sail then, or wait for the next available ship. In which case, I would not have seen father before he passed away, as it would have been so much slower.'

'Well, I'm glad you made it, Isabel, although I'm sorry that you had to sacrifice your wedding. That must have been a big decision to make – to forego your wedding just so you could get a ship to bring you home.'

'It was heart-breaking – for both of us.'

'At least you'll marry when you return.'

'Well, that's the plan . . . And it had better come to fruition this time.'

'Oh?' said Susan. There was apprehension in her tone. 'Is there any reason why it should not?'

'No, but there's every reason why it should. You see, I'm already carrying Barnaby's child.'

'Ah, I thought so . . .'

'Can you tell?' Isabel enquired, startled at the revelation. 'Am I showing already?'

'You must know you are, Isabel.'

They fell silent for a few moments while Susan digested this information and all that it implied.

'Well?' Isabel prompted. 'Are you going to chastise me, for twice being pregnant, and still no husband to change my name and convert me into a respectable woman?'

'No, my dear.'

'Well, that's a relief.'

'Ever since you arrived,' Susan went on, 'I've thought you might be carrying a child. Your shape, you see – it's the same, I remember, as when you were carrying Robert Wilson's child. But I felt I should not mention it. I felt it was up to you to tell me first.'

'But this time, I shall marry the child's father. Then nobody will be able to call it a bastard.'

'Does this Barnaby know you are carrying his child, Isabel?'

'How could he?' Isabel replied. 'I don't think I conceived till November and I left for England at the beginning of December. I didn't even know myself that I was pregnant then.'

'Have you written to him to let him know?'

'No, I want it to be a surprise.'

'So how far gone are you?'

'Four, maybe five months. So I should have the baby sometime in July. I should be back in Hobart before it's born. If I know Barnaby, he'll be bewildered at first, and even a little conscience-stricken, but delighted all the same.'

'Tell me about him.'

When Isabel had told her that he was a widower with a young daughter, extolled all his virtues and denigrated his shortcomings, she said, 'You'll never guess who was on board the *Great Britain* with me . . .'

'Surprise me.'

'Robert Wilson.'

'You mean—'

'Yes, *him*. But he's *Sir* Robert Wilson now, you know. A

baronet. He inherited the title from his father.'

'Well, I heard his father had died. I hope he's rotting in hell.'

'His wife died as well. Robert's wife, I mean. He's a very wealthy bachelor again now – or rather a widower.'

'So what was he doing so far away in Australia?'

'He's something to do with banks nowadays, investments and all that. He holds stocks and shares in a new railway that's being built there.'

'Goodness me, Isabel. How did you feel seeing him again after all these years?'

'Shocked. Bewildered. I was quite offish with him at first, but by the end of the voyage we were friends. We could laugh again and talk openly about the past. I found I still liked him after all. He's still the same . . .' She paused while she pondered him. 'He's invited me to stay with him at the estate he inherited from his late wealthy wife.'

'Oh? And shall you go?'

'I don't think it would be such a good idea, Mother.'

'Well, he can't make you pregnant again, that's certain.'

The two women laughed at that, and it highlighted how they could easily and candidly converse, especially after being apart for so long. It also emphasised their now similar standings; Isabel was just an adolescent girl when she was transported, but she was a grown woman now, worldly wise and on a par with her mother.

'He told me that he'd never stopped loving me,' Isabel resumed. 'And he did ask me to marry him. He wanted me to give up all notions of marrying Barnaby and marry him on board the ship.'

'What a shame he was fifteen years too late.'

'I know.' They laughed again; they felt good and justified in laughing at those things that had been so distressing in the past. 'But I told him I was already carrying Barnaby's child, and that seemed to quell his ardour.'

'I suppose it would,' Susan agreed.

'He would still be a good catch for somebody, though. He's still the same pleasant character, polite and considerate. Wealthy, of course, but now more handsome than ever.'

'And a womaniser, I'll be bound,' Susan suggested disparagingly.

They fell silent again for a few moments while Isabel stirred the coals in the fire. A flurry of sparks flitted up the chimney and flames danced around the coals once more, lightening the room. The cat, duly disturbed from its prime position in front of the fire, jumped up onto Susan's lap.

'I was dreading telling you that I was pregnant again and still not wedded, you know, Mother. Even though it's getting obvious. I suppose that secretly you regard me as a woman of easy virtue.'

Susan shook her head emphatically. 'No, my dear Isabel. I could not be so hypocritical . . .'

'What do you mean – hypocritical?'

'I was in the same situation myself once . . .' Susan paused for Isabel's reaction.

'*You*?'

'Yes, me. I know what it's like to have a child out of wedlock and be alone in the world, Isabel, with nobody to support you, nobody you could turn to, least of all a husband.'

Isabel looked at her mother in astonishment. 'What on earth do you mean, mother?'

'Exactly what I say. I know what it's like to be carrying a child with the prospect of no husband, and therefore no father for your baby.'

'You mean you had a baby before you had me?' Isabel asked in disbelief.

'Not before you, Isabel. You . . . I had you . . . out of wedlock.'

Isabel stared at her mother in a state of shock and incredulity, unable to think of anything appropriate to say.

'I have always intended telling you,' Susan went on undaunted, 'but I never could, leastwise not while your father was alive.'

Isabel's heart was suddenly beating harder. 'Mother, I'm not sure what all this means. You'd better make it clear.'

'I realise it's going to hurt you, Isabel, but that's hardly my intention, believe me. I wouldn't hurt you for the world, but it will change the way you see me, I have little doubt. Yet I've always wanted you to know. You're a grown woman now – indeed, a woman of the world – so I know you will be strong enough and worldly enough to accept that I am but flesh and blood, and in my young days I went the way of the flesh, as they say.'

'Are you saying I'm a bastard, mother?'

'That is a horrible word, Isabel.'

'I agree it's a horrible word,' Isabel said, 'but if that's what I am, then that's what I am.'

Susan nodded, and Isabel saw how tears were welling up in her mother's eyes. Isabel was moved to tears herself, for this signalled a monumental moment for both. She realized it was just as hard for her mother to reveal this bolt from the blue as it was for herself to hear it.

'You see,' Susan continued, absently stroking the cat as it purred in her lap, 'the wonderful man you have always considered your father, is not your father.'

'Oh, my goodness, mother! . . .' She stood up, clearly agitated. 'I think it might have been better had you not told me. I have been perfectly content all my life believing he was my father, acknowledging him as my father, and loving him as my father. Not that I shall ever stop loving him – he was always a perfect father to me. He was a golden father.'

'Indeed he was, my dear, dear daughter.' Susan reached forward and took Isabel's hand and held it reassuringly. The cat, thus dislodged, returned to the rug in front of the fire. 'He always treated you as his own – no differently from your sisters who are his own flesh and blood. He never ever favoured one of you over another.'

Isabel squeezed her eyelids shut and a tear rolled down each cheek as she sat down again. 'So who is my real father? Do you want me to know?'

'Yes, I want you to know. It's important that you know. Your father – your real blood father – is Mr Justice Oliver Russell.'

Isabel gasped. 'Mercy! The judge who presided over my trial?'

'The same'

'Oh, my *God* . . .' She held her face in her hands.

'Years ago,' Susan continued, determined to explain, 'whenever he came to Worcester for the assizes, the streets would be filled with people. It was a time for celebration – more so then than now – and the spectacle of the young judge arriving with his javelin men brought out the crowds, especially the girls. The ladies loved him. Oliver Russell was such a handsome man. He would stay at his lodgings at the Guildhall in those days, and join in the celebrations during the evening, generally at the Golden Lion opposite. That's where I first met him. I was a serving wench in those days at the Golden Lion, and he took a shine to me. Likewise, I took a shine to him as well. I used to look forward to the assizes, because I knew he would always make a beeline for me and make a great fuss of me, and I loved him for it. Well, once when he came, we talked for ages and he asked me to go with him to his lodgings for a nightcap after the revelries. Why not? I asked myself. I was in love with him, and I'm certain he was taken with me too. I remember he told me all about his love of choral music. Anyway, I stayed there all night with him. I shared his bed with him. And the next night too.'

'And that's when you fell pregnant, I suppose,' Isabel deduced.

'Yes, that's when you were conceived.'

'Did he ever know you had had his child, Mother?'

'Not then. Nor for many years. Not until the day of your trial.'

'The day of my trial? How come?'

'That day I went to the Guildhall early with the intention of speaking to him before the trial. He was in his lodgings, working, and I managed to barge my way in – I was quite determined to see him. Of course, he remembered me as Susan Tinkler and once again made a great fuss of me. I told him then that Isabel Saxby, who was due to be tried for the murder of her own baby, was his own daughter.'

'My God! And what was his reaction?'

'He was shaken by the news.'

'I imagine he would have been. And he believed you? He believed I was his daughter?'

'Oh, yes, he believed me. Why shouldn't he? I had no reason to lie. It apparently did some good, because he found a way through all the legal procedures to prevent you from going to the gallows, even though the jury found you guilty, remember. He saved your life.'

'Good God! And later, I had a full pardon,' Isabel mused. 'So what happened after I was born?'

'I still lived with my mother, your grandmother Tinkler, although my father had already passed on by this time. She looked after you while I went to work in one of the glove factories. We needed the money, you see. Then one day – it was a Sunday – I was sunning myself on a bench in the Cathedral Close. You were about two years old and playing happily with a rag doll, and talking to it as if it were a real baby, when this man came up to me, and said what a beautiful little girl I had. I smiled up at him and thanked him for saying such a kind thing, and he sat beside me. We got talking and he told me he was a schoolmaster. We talked for ages and I thought what a lovely man. In no time I felt I could talk to him about anything, and I told him that although I had a child I was unmarried. I expected some show of scorn from him because of it, that he might get up and walk away, but there was none of that. Anyway, to cut a long story short, he asked if I would meet him again, and I said I would love to. From then on we met regularly – we began courting as they say – and eventually we were married. We rented that cottage in Crowle where nobody knew either of us. He was fifteen years older than me, and that was quite a difference in our ages. Then Daisy and Kitty came along in their turn.'

'I don't remember my grandmother Tinkler,' Isabel remarked. 'What happened to her?'

'She came to live with us – she had nobody else – but she passed away not long afterwards. She thought the world of you. I'm surprised you don't remember her.'

'Well, I was only a little girl, mother.'

\- - -

Chapter 25

Worcester

Due to her expanding belly, Isabel found it necessary to let out seams on her clothes while she, her mother and occasionally Kitty would knit as they sat in front of a blazing fire in the inglenook fireplace. Isabel's condition made it imperative to order new clothes to accommodate the unavoidable future expansion of her belly. She had told her sisters of her condition, and her plans to marry on her return to Hobart Town, which they accepted without condemnation, and even rejoiced at the wonderful news.

So they viewed trips to Worcester's shops as essential, and seized upon such opportunities with bubbling enthusiasm. Isabel decided she would buy some things for her baby, realizing that she might feasibly give birth on board the ship during its long voyage to Australia; it seemed sensible to be prepared for such an eventuality. Kitty, with a young woman's enthusiasm for such excursions, would accompany Isabel on these outings, as occasionally did Daisy. On one such expedition, Daisy let it be known that she too was carrying a child, so there was a combined interest in the acquisition of all things to do with babies. Daisy's revelation was also seen as a reasonable enough excuse for a double celebration. A newly opened chocolate house in High Street served the purpose admirably, providing delicious hot chocolate drinks, which they judged entirely suitable for their festivities.

The weeks progressed satisfactorily, except that Kitty's matrimonial expectations came to nothing; her beau failed to ask for her hand in marriage, but in a fervour of patriotism joined the army instead. The recently declared war in the Balkans heightened her fear that he would be sent to Gallipoli and be killed fighting the Russians, which left her distraught. She was too sensible a girl to allow anxiety to become a part of her love life, envisaging no romance and even less comfort in such a circumstance, so she ended the liaison. However, being a pretty girl and petite, it did not take her long to attract a new suitor, lifting her from her gloom and making her smile again. But she vowed that with this new beau she would take nothing for granted.

- - -

It was towards the end of April, just days before she was about to travel to Liverpool to board the *SS Great Britain*, that Isabel received a second letter from Barnaby. It read:

Wednesday 1st February 1854

My Dear Isabel,

I hope you are well, and that your Father's Illness is no worse. Polly misses you, and before I embark upon the thrust of this Letter, I must report that she is well and that she and Miranda are inseparable and joyous Companions.

You have been gone from me for nearly two Months now and it seems like an Eternity. I am thoroughly depressed with worry over You and find it exceedingly frustrating not having you near me to discuss some serious Concerns that have been brought to my Attention.

To get to the point; last Sunday, I took a Stroll to

the Mount Nelson Signal Station, to get away from the Domesticity of two little Girls, a Nanny and two Maids. I wished to be alone, to ponder you and Everything that you have come to mean to me without Distraction. As I returned Home I was accosted on Salamanca by a Woman who had previously seen You and me together at the Ball which was arranged for the Cessation of sending Convicts to Van Diemen's Land. You might recall the occasion, as it coincided with you suddenly feeling unwell, which I confess to considering strange at the time. She claimed that she knew You from your Days as a Governess. She gave her name as Rosie Flannagan, said she was a married Woman, but she was Rosie Duckworth when she knew You.

Mrs Flannagan and I had a most enlightening but also exceedingly disturbing Conversation, furnishing me with Details of how and why You came to be in Van Diemen's Land, about which You Yourself have signally failed to inform me. I learned to my absolute Horror that when you were little more than a Child at 16 Years old you had secret Love Affair with Robert Wilson (the elder Son of George Wilson MP, whom we once spoke about) and had his Child. As You can imagine I was very much distressed to hear this.

Mrs Flannagan then informed me that she Assisted with the Birth and that you were afterwards accused of murdering your Child, that You were found Guilty at the subsequent Trial, but escaped the Gallows because the Judge, in his Wisdom and fortunately for You, was not satisfied that the Evidence against you was convincing enough. Mrs Flannagan also reported that You were pardoned of the Crime, when it eventually came to Light that somebody else had killed the baby.

At first I was Sceptical about Everything the Woman told me. It all seemed far-fetched, so I made it my Business to find out whether there was a Convict Record for You. Lo and behold, one such exists, and it confirms what Mrs Flannagan told me.

But that is not all. Prompted by this newly aroused interest in knowing more about Robert Wilson I consulted a recent issue of Burke's Peerage we hold at Government House. It revealed some interesting Facts about him, not least that he had later Married one Elizabeth Hulme, although she had sadly passed away after Childbirth. Thus it appears that your Robert Wilson inherited the vast Timberlake Estate in Buckinghamshire. When his Father passed away he also inherited his Baronetcy and the Patchfield Estate in Worcestershire. It transpires that SIR Robert Wilson is now heavily investing in new Railway Projects in Australia, one of which is the Geelong and Melbourne Railway Company project. My enquiries in that direction have revealed that he recently attended Meetings of Shareholders, and was believed to have returned to England on board the SS Great Britain in December, the very Ship and the very Sailing that you embarked upon to visit your ailing Father.

This is all too distressing, because I fear it is not beyond the realms of Possibility that he might have made Contact with you before then. It would not be difficult to trace you as a former convict if you knew where to seek such Information, or possessed the Wherewithal to find out, as he must have. It plagues me that if that is the Case, you might have agreed to return to England with him to resume your former Attachment, while presenting me with the news of your Father's Illness as an excuse to facilitate your Elopement. Whether or not that is True, you must still have encountered him on board the Ship, so might still feasibly have resumed your past Liaison. If this is the case then you are Guilty of gross Infidelity, and your history, newly revealed to me, suggests you are not incapable of such Chicanery.

As a result of all this I have been beside Myself with Worry and Wondering whether I have made a complete Fool of myself. My Health is suffering as a Result. If my Suspicions are confirmed, whether they are wide of the mark or justified, I must consider myself released from our Engagement.

Apart from all the Foregoing, the Fact that You have deliberately withheld from me all Information about your history is something which I cannot excuse, as is the Fact of your giving Birth to a Bastard Child. Both are Blemishes on your Character and do not fit my Notion of an ideal Wife, nor indeed the Suitability to be Stepmother to my beloved Daughter.

I am slowly coming to Terms with what must inevitably be a Change to our Relationship, but pray believe me when I say it has not been easy. More accurately, it is unbearably Painful.

Of course, Polly will remain in my care pending your Return to this Island, always assuming it is your Intention to return, and I would be glad of your advice on this matter.

Yours very sincerely and with deep Regret,
Barnaby Micklejohn.

- - -

Isabel's dream of marriage to Barnaby Micklejohn, the father of her unborn child, thus suddenly disappeared. All her ideas for their future together lay in tatters. And all because of his apparently random encounter with that interfering busybody Rosie Duckworth. It was the worst of all worlds that Barnaby should hear of her past from the interfering busybody and not from herself. No doubt the interfering busybody would have embroidered her tale with looks of abject disapproval and skyward eye-rolling to emphasise her points that Isabel Saxby had been so infatuated with Robert Wilson that she was driven to defy convention and all considerations of morality, flouting respectability and self-esteem besides.

She tried to imagine Barnaby in some dusty office, going over convict records as he tried to procure confirmation of Rosie's words, but too distracted and alarmed to hark back to the truth, the undisputable truth of their love for each other, and the delectable moments they had shared, which for her overrode all of her other memories.

Oh, Barnaby, why are you so afflicted with conventionality? she said to herself. Why are you so stupid?

The truth, however, was dawning on her that she might never see him again, inducing painful memories of having been in this situation before, all those years ago. She felt a rising tide of panic and fear and looming calamity. Fifteen years had not rendered this similar situation any easier to endure. The pain she now felt was no different to the pain and anxiety of adolescent emotion which she felt as a sixteen-year-old girl. Yet still there was no antidote, except to see him, to be with him, and to explain as patiently and as sincerely as she could just how wrong he was.

And therein lay her hope: her explanation and her sincerity. But for now, feelings of desolation and hopelessness were overwhelming her. It hurt. By God, how it hurt. That he could even imagine she could be unfaithful to him, injured her pride beyond measure, after all the promises they had made to each other. As yet though, she had no remedy. She felt utterly helpless and frustrated due to the physical distance between them, having neither the ability to relieve her own pain, nor to assuage his. If only the good ship *SS Great Britain* had wings, so that it could fly to Hobart Town and deliver her – and their child growing in her belly – into his arms in hours instead of weeks.

The following morning she awoke early, troubled by an acute awareness of how much Barnaby must be suffering and her growing frustration at being unable to resolve the problem, for there was no respite in sleep. Isabel swung her legs out of bed and, leaving the creaking door of her bedroom ajar, to prevent the metallic clack of the latch waking her mother and her sister, crept bare foot across the uneven floorboards and made her way downstairs. She stood shivering, peering out of a mullioned windowpane that overlooked the back yard. Dawn was breaking. She raked the ashes out of the firegrate, shovelled them into an iron bucket ready to tip onto the midden outside, and laid a new fire using paper, kindling wood and coal.

Her thoughts, her pity, were especially for Barnaby, because his overworked imagination, his wild, irrational speculation, had led him to vastly wrong conclusions about her and Robert. Yet still the fact of her failing to confess that she had once given birth to Robert Wilson's child would remain an insurmountable problem, unless he could bring himself to accept that it was in the distant past, unchangeable and no longer relevant. If he could not accept that life had moved on and she was a different person now, then there was hope of neither marriage, nor a legitimate father for her unborn child. And yet . . . and yet . . . Could he be so dishonourable as to fail to acknowledge, once he knew, that he too had done what Robert Wilson had done before him, and had fathered her child? Would his innate sense of honour and responsibility override his instinctive orthodoxy?

The question was unanswerable.

She knelt before the firegrate, and with a match, lit the paper and watched as it ignited the kindling sticks. In the same way that the sticks of wood began to burn, so had her own partiality for Barnaby begun to glow. Her love for him was never a sudden thing, more a growing realization that she needed to be near him as often as she could, to feed off his warmth, his sincerity and his kind attention. Thus had been the course of their 'progression'. Always, there had been that appealing warmth that drew her closer, like the warmth now that induced her to huddle over the thriving flames while the cat, almost unnoticed, approached and brushed itself against the uncovered calves of her legs.

Being apart from Barnaby for so long was like a bereavement. She was feeling it more acutely than the grief of her father's death. It was all the more painful and tormenting because Barnaby had months ago admitted that he loved her heart and soul, but now his love had been tainted by what the interfering busybody had told him. What inner turmoil he must be suffering. Yet his torment could be no harder to bear than her own.

The sticks' flames were lapping round the coals now, so that red hot glimmers danced along their sharp edges, promising prolonged succour and ease. The fire of love within herself would likewise burn for a long, long time, for it was embedded in the less volatile foundation of admiration and respect which she had always harboured for Barnaby.

'What are you doing up so early?' a voice said quietly.

Isabel turned around and saw her mother standing at the door in her nightgown. 'I woke up early and couldn't get back to sleep,' she replied.

Susan ran her fingers through her bedraggled hair and yawned. 'Is it worrying you then, our Isabel, this letter of his?'

'What do you think?' she replied. 'The problem is that Barnaby would not have known when he wrote that letter that I am carrying his child. He would not even have received the letter I sent from the Falkland Islands, although I imagine he will have received it by now. I feel I should write back immediately, but what's the point? I know very well it would be a waste of time, because the *Great Britain* will arrive in Australia well before any letter that I might write today. I feel like writing, to draw out of my head the anxiety and the hurt I feel, but no, I must be my own messenger. So today I shall pack, ready for the journey to Liverpool and the ship.'

- - -

Accordingly, on the twenty-eighth of April, Isabel stepped up into the hansom cab that was to take her to Worcester's new Shrub Hill Station. From there she would proceed to Liverpool by way of Wolverhampton and Crewe by rail. She left to tearful goodbyes from her mother and sisters, who were destined never to set eyes on her again, nor she on them.

Rather than seek a hotel in Liverpool, because of late arrival that evening, she decided to break her journey at Crewe, and progress to Liverpool the next day, a Saturday, then secure her cabin aboard the ship. Her intention was to board immediately and make herself comfortable as soon as she had paid her passage.

The plan succeeded without a hitch, and Isabel settled herself into the same cabin she had occupied on the voyage out. Dinner on board that evening, and breakfast next day was proof enough that there was no Robert Wilson to divert her on this voyage. What passengers she did encounter, however, seemed convivial enough, though she entertained no hope of meeting another Ann Carter either.

On thirtieth of April and on schedule, the *SS Great Britain* departed Liverpool for Melbourne, steaming down the Mersey into the Irish Sea. Isabel went up to the weather deck and watched the English coastline slowly give way to that of North Wales. The April showers had relented and were making way for the kinder, warmer, sunnier weather of May. Despite the promise of an English springtime, when the trees would take on their brilliant green livery, she thanked her Maker that at last she was on her way home to her beloved Hobart Town, to Polly, to her shop, and not least to Barnaby, who desperately needed straightening out.

If reconciliation with Barnaby failed, she still had her shop, which provided a comfortable living. She would face down any scorn or condemnation she might receive because she had borne a child out of wedlock; although the conventions of life in Van Diemen's land were thankfully less rigid and more compassionate than they were in England. Furthermore, she had so far lived contentedly in Van Diemen's Land without a husband; indeed, she did not need a husband to support her financially, although it would certainly be better for her child to have had a father on hand.

Isabel soon realized that the Captain of the SS Great Britain on this voyage was different. It was no longer

Captain Matthews, but the man who had been First Mate. The new Captain, John Gray, a Shetlander, recognised Isabel from the voyage out from Melbourne, and went out of his way to speak to her and ensure she was comfortable, promising that she should dine at his table frequently. She replied that she would always be honoured to accept his invitation. From her point of view, because different people were invited to dine with the captain, the opportunity to befriend other passengers was increased.

However, circumstances changed unexpectedly, denying any opportunity for the time being to make new shipboard companions; after just one day into the voyage Captain Gray let it be known to all that regrettably, the *SS Great Britain* must put back to Liverpool. The problem was a mechanical one, he explained. The shaft which was connected to the propeller that drove the ship forward had welded under friction to the sleeve that housed it. There was no alternative but to replace it back in Liverpool. Hence they were unable to continue their voyage.

'Will it take long?' Isabel asked the captain, frustrated that there should be any such delay.

'Too long for my liking,' Captain Gray replied in his appealing Shetland accent which was strange to Isabel. 'The thing will have to be stripped out and a new shaft refitted. It could take weeks, I fear. It might well be six weeks before we're ready to sail again.'

'But that will take us well into June,' she said, despair heightening. 'So what should we passengers do in the meantime?'

'Well,' said Captain Gray, scratching his head under his cap, 'Maybe go home, till Gibbs Bright – the company that owns the ship – let you know the date of the rescheduled sailing. I imagine they'll place a notice in *The Times* newspaper announcing the new departure date. So throughout May – and into June if it stretches out that far – keep your eye on it. You'll have plenty of notice.'

'So in the meantime, we buy *The Times* every day?'

'I suspect any such notice given will be repeated daily nearer the time but, aye, that would be your best option,' Captain Gray answered deferentially. 'I can only apologise for the gross inconvenience to you, Miss Saxby, and to everybody else.'

It was then that Isabel decided that she had fortuitously been offered the chance to do the thing she dearly wanted to do earlier, had she possessed the nerve and the time to do it. This excellent opportunity was not to be wasted.

- - -

Chapter 26

England

When the *SS Great Britain* returned to Liverpool, Isabel made the train journey back to Worcester and the tender mercies of her mother and Kitty. Both were still grieving over the loss of William Saxby, husband to one and father to the other, and she hoped her reappearance would help relieve it. Her unanticipated arrival in Friar Street inevitably surprised them both.

From a downstairs window, Kitty saw the hansom draw up, and was amazed to see Isabel alight from it. She rushed to open the front door, in a flurry of curiosity and surprise.

'Well, our Isabel' she greeted breathlessly. 'This is unexpected. Wait till mother sees you back here. So, have you changed your mind about returning to Van Diemen's Land after all?'

'No, I haven't,' she said, taking off her mantle and bonnet as she entered the hallway, while the driver of the hansom cab lugged her baggage into the house. 'The ship had to turn around and return to Liverpool because of a problem to do with the steam engine.' She paid the cab driver and closed the door.

Susan appeared. 'Isabel,' she exclaimed when she saw her daughter. 'How come you're back? Have you changed your mind about living in Van Diemen's Land and getting wed? Did you think it for the best?'

'No, I haven't changed my mind, Mother,' she replied, and explained the circumstances of her return to Worcester.

'Those steam engines,' Susan declared scornfully. 'I rue the day. What was wrong with the ship continuing under sail? You said it could when you were here before.'

'I don't know, mother. I'm not the captain.'

'Well, it will be lovely to have you here while they get it mended,' Susan affirmed. 'We should make the most of it. Let us have a mug of tea. Are you hungry after your train journey?'

'A mug of tea would be lovely, mother, but I shall eat when you eat.'

'So how long will you have to wait for the ship to be fixed?' Kitty asked.

'Nobody is quite sure. Maybe six weeks the captain said. They'll post notices in The Times newspaper when a new sailing date has been arranged.'

'But what a nuisance for you,' Susan declared. 'Especially as you are so anxious to get back and see your Barnaby.'

'I know . . . I'd better write to him today. If I'm going to be here for another six weeks, a letter should reach him before I do. Also, I've had a thought as to what I might do in the meantime.'

'What's that?' her mother asked.

'I think I shall visit Robert Wilson at his Timberlake Estate. I shall write to my friend Ann Carter as well, to see if she can join me. You never know with her, what with her marital complications.'

'Safety in numbers?'

'Not that, mother. But she and I got on so well. And a few days with her at Robert's estate will be like another holiday, with servants running around all over the place, at our beck and call.'

'Perhaps Kitty could join you?' Susan suggested.

'That's an excellent idea, Mother. Would you like to, Kitty?'

'I'd love to, Isabel, but I've really got nothing special to wear for such a grand house with servants bowing and scraping all over the place. Indeed, the servants might have better dresses than I do.'

'If that's your only fear we'll go to the shops,' Isabel suggested. 'We can soon remedy that.'

At the first opportunity to be alone once she had resettled in Friar Street, Isabel wrote to Barnaby. It read:

My Dearest Darling Barnaby,
You poor, poor boy. What on earth has induced you to think all those awful things about me? I am truly angry with you for imagining that I could be as fickle and as reckless as you suggest. But I feel sorry for you too, for putting yourself through those horrid agonies of doubt. How could you doubt me after all we have meant to each other? Indeed, I encountered Robert Wilson on board the ship, but it was as much a surprise for him to see me, as it was for me to see him. We came to treat each other as old friends throughout the voyage, but you may rest assured that I kept him at arms' length because I had no romantic interest in him whatsoever.

Meanwhile, the ship Great Britain *sailed first for Melbourne on 30*th *April but had to turn back because of a problem with the steam engine, and cannot recommence the voyage for a few more weeks, so I am compelled to stay in England longer than I intended. Naturally, I can hardly wait to see you and am extremely frustrated because of it.*

As regards the other issue you wrote about in your

letter, namely my giving birth to a child when I was only 17 years old, and all the anguish that went with it, I shall talk to you about when I see you. If you happen upon Mrs Rosie Flannagan again in the meantime, who considered it her Obligation to reveal all this before I did, do pass on my compliments for her Marriage to the unfortunate Mr Flannagan.

What happens to you and me in the future after what you said in your letter is your decision, dearest Barnaby, but I want you to know and to understand absolutely that I love you dearly, and only you. Nothing has changed. How could it indeed? My hopes and dreams of a Future with you, and our two delightful girls have not changed either.

My love, always,
Isabel

Isabel also wrote to Ann Carter, and received a reply by return. Yes, she would love to meet her again on a visit to Timberlake, and proposed a date in the middle of May. Isabel, in turn, wrote to Robert Wilson, referring him to his open invitation, suggesting that she, her unmarried sister Kitty, and Ann Carter visit him at Timberlake on the date suggested by Ann. She received a reply within four days, confirming the arrangement.

So Isabel and Kitty set off on their journey by train. They took a second-class compartment, which they had to themselves. Kitty was intensely curious about Robert Wilson, and Isabel's relationship with him. The girl was aware of all that had happened, from family talk over the years, but she wanted to hear her sister's side of the story.

'So did you love him dearly?' Kitty asked as the train rumbled and huffed through rolling hills and greening countryside.

'Yes, I did,' Isabel replied candidly. 'He was the world to me?'

'But you don't love him now, do you?'

'I'm not in love with him anymore, Kitty. That was years ago. But it doesn't mean that I don't like him. He's a very personable man and good company.'

'I find it hard to imagine why your love for him had already dried up and withered by the time he reappeared years later, when you were so much in love before.'

'Because the passing years and events change us, and change the way we look at things,' Isabel replied. 'You see, I suffered so much because of my love for him. I admit that I consented to everything we did, and had his child as a result. Then I blamed him for not getting me out of the situation I found myself in. So my love turned to resentment, because I believed he could have saved me, when he did not. Encountering him again so unexpectedly within the confines of the ship, compelled us to spend weeks on end at sea, when it would be difficult to avoid each other. So we got to know each other again. At first, I was indifferent to him because I still blamed him, but the more we talked the more I came to realize that he was not to blame for not helping me. His family, particularly his father, kept him from me by sending him away until I was out of the way. Once I knew that, I began to see him in a different light. He was older, more mature, yet still the same pleasant, considerate man I originally thought him to be. I like him, Kitty. I like him very much now. But I am not in love with him. There is a difference, you see – a vast difference – between liking somebody and being in love with them.'

'But what if he asked you to marry him?'

'He already did. But I turned him down. I told him I was carrying Barnaby's child.'

'But if you hadn't been carrying Barnaby's child, Isabel, would you have married him then?'

Isabel laughed. 'It would have depended. If I had never met and fallen in love with Barnaby, yes, I might well have accepted him. What woman wouldn't? But I had met and fallen in love with Barnaby, and I still consider myself promised to Barnaby, even though he might have different thoughts on the matter now. So the question of marrying Robert is no longer relevant. In any case, I don't think it would work.'

'So you still have some feelings for Robert, though?'

'Different feelings, Kitty. He's a friend now, and I quite like his friendship.'

'But if he's a baronet, and owner of all that property and wealth, he must be anxious to marry again and have a son who can inherit everything.'

'I daresay such things have crossed his mind,' Isabel concurred. 'But he'll have no difficulty in finding an ideal woman to fill the vacancy, I can assure you.'

'What if he took a shine to me, Isabel?' Kitty mused.

'It would be sensible for you also to take a shine to him.'

'Would you mind if he did?'

'Of course not. But he's a good deal older than you, Kitty. There's quite an age gap.'

'But our father was fifteen years older than our mother, wasn't he? And I see no difficulty with that. It worked for them.'

- - -

The Timberlake estate was situated near the village of Shabbington in Buckinghamshire. The house replaced the earlier version which was destroyed by fire in the reign of James the Second. This later pile, a vast and sprawling edifice of Palladianism, stood in the centre of an undulating park. It looked across formal gardens, a lake, orchards, the more modest houses of the tenanted farms, and meadows and hedgerows for as far as the eye could see.

From Oxford, Isabel and Kitty took a hansom cab to Timberlake, and after what seemed like a markedly long journey capped by an infinitely long driveway, it pulled up before the pillared mansion, its façade reminiscent of the portico and steps of Patchfield House. But Timberlake was far grander. At once two servants and a footman flew out to greet her and Kitty, quickly followed by Robert. Once introduced to Kitty he embraced them both and ordered the footman to take the two Miss Saxbys' bags to their allotted bedrooms.

'You've grown somewhat, Miss Saxby,' Robert said admiringly, addressing Kitty. 'You are quite the elegant young woman now, so much like your sister. Last time we met, I recall, you were just a little girl. We played pall mall together, remember?'

Kitty, blushing, replied, 'Indeed we did, sir. I remember it very well. But please call me Kitty.'

He smiled warmly. 'Kitty it is then. And I'm Robert. None of this *sir* nonsense. Agreed?'

'If you say so,' she said, blushing even more intensely.

'It's lovely to see you again, Robert,' Isabel said with an enchanting smile. 'Has Ann arrived yet?'

'Not yet. I suspect she'll arrive from a different direction. You came via Oxford?'

'Yes, on the new railway line. Work was still going on in places.'

'You must be tired, Isabel. You too, Kitty. Let's go inside and I'll order you some refreshment. Then you can both rest.'

'Thank you, Robert. It was a tedious journey.'

'I trust you are keeping well, Isabel,' he said, glancing at the bump on her belly.

'Very well, thank you.'

'I was so sorry to hear of the death of your father.'

'Thank you. I'm just happy I was able to spend time with him before he passed away. I could easily have missed him. So I'm glad I made the journey to England.'

- - -

Ann Carter arrived late that same afternoon. It was a touching reunion for Isabel. While Ann took command of the bedroom allotted to her, Isabel joined her to take advantage of the opportunity before dinner to bring each other up to date with their respective love lives.

'Your sister is a very pretty girl,' Ann commented as she hung a day dress in the wardrobe. 'Exquisite looks obviously run in the family.'

'She *is* a pretty girl,' Isabel agreed, sitting herself on the bed. 'Not that being pretty is always such a blessing. I think sometimes it can be a curse.'

'Yes, I suppose it depends what sort of male characters prettiness attracts,' said Ann, turning to her travel bag. 'Unless a girl is clever with it, of course. In which case it can be a blessing. After all, a clever girl can always outwit a clever man, especially if being pretty is in her armoury. If she uses her brains she will be able to attract the right sort of suitor.'

'Well, she seems bright enough, Ann. I believe she will do well for herself. So tell me . . . how is your husband?'

'Contrite,' replied Ann perkily. 'Delightfully contrite.'

'So he deeply regrets his shenanigans with your maid?'

'I think he regrets being found out,' she replied matter-of-factly, this time shaking the creases out of an evening dress. 'Whether he regrets his shenanigans is another matter. I presume he enjoyed the encounter– possibly many – so what's the point in him regretting it, or them.'

'But you are reconciled?' Isabel asked.

'Hardly. We still live in the same house, but I do as I want, and not what he wants, if what he wants doesn't suit me. D'you think this dress will be suitable for dinner this evening?'

'Without doubt. You wore it on the ship, I remember.'

'I know. Which means Robert will already have seen it.'

'Oh, I doubt if he'll remember,' Isabel said. 'Men don't. Anyway, you were saying how contrite your husband is.'

'Yes, I was about to say, it's amazing how his contrition has given me the upper hand.'

'Hence, you were able to leave him at home and visit Timberlake of your own accord?'

'Precisely.' She smiled with satisfaction. 'So what about you, Isabel. I see you are somewhat rounder than last time we met. You must be six months gone at least.'

'More like seven. But I'm keeping well. I had hoped to be back in Hobart when my baby was born, but that looks unlikely now that my voyage home has been delayed.'

'Your Barnaby will be disappointed that he will have missed the great event.'

'I would like to think so, but I really don't think he will be interested,' Isabel responded sadly and with a shrug.

'Oh?'

'Yes . . . I received a letter from him . . .' She burst into tears.

Ann sat beside Isabel on the bed and threw her arms about her and gave her a hug. 'Do you want to get it off your chest?'

'Yes. I'd like to know what you think. You see, he got to know about my past . . .'

\- - -

Dinner that evening was convivial, conversation was light and witty. Kitty sensed she was in another world, and was somewhat overawed by it, especially at the way servants seemed to be eternally hovering, waiting for you to stop eating so they could take your plate away and replace it with another. An aspect that also surprised her was the way conversation never seemed to be inhibited, even while servants were in the room and could hear every word. And yet Kitty did not feel out of her depth; she contributed to the conversation unhesitatingly, and was the centre of attention for much of the time.

After dinner, they all sat in the elegant drawing room, lined with paintings of the Hulme family's ancestors. To Kitty, each of the ladies in every painting looked the same, wearing the same soulless, vacant expression, the same long noses, and she privately wondered whether the artists who did the work were earning their fees under false pretences.

Eventually Ann decided that she must retire to bed; it had been an arduous day travelling from Guildford.

'Why don't you go up too, Kitty?' Isabel suggested. 'I would like a word in private with Robert.'

'Yes, of course,' Kitty replied, and withdrew.

When both women had left the drawing room, Robert said, 'You wanted a word in private, Isabel? How can I be of help?'

'You must know Oliver Russell, the judge,' Isabel began. 'Indeed, whether he is still alive.'

'You mean *Sir* Oliver Russell. He was knighted some years ago. And yes, he is still alive. Very much so.'

'I'd like to meet him, Robert. I imagine you know where he lives.'

'Oh? Indeed I do. What's it worth?' he teased.

'It's worth a great deal to me. Please, Robert, if you know where he lives, tell me. It's important that I visit him.'

'I can arrange that for you, Isabel. He lives in Long Crendon, a stone's throw from here.'

Isabel's eyes lit up. 'Could you, really?'

'For you, yes, of course. I'll send a footman over with a note tomorrow, asking when it might be convenient for him to receive you. He's retired now, so he's at home most of the time I believe.'

'Would you do that, please?'

'I said I would.'

'Oh, thank you Robert. You have no idea what that means to me. But please don't mention my name in the note you send.'

'Hmm . . . Intriguing. Very well, I won't, if that's what you wish. I'll just say that an utterly charming and beautiful young woman, who wishes to remain anonymous, is anxious to make his acquaintance. Shall you take your sister with you?'

'No, I must go alone.'

'Excellent. Then I shall take great pleasure in showing Kitty around the estate while you are gone.'

'As long as it's a fine day for it, I imagine she will enjoy that, Robert.'

'She reminds me very much of you when we first met, you know.'

Isabel noted a dangerous warmth in his eyes.

'Yes, I rather thought she might.'

- - -

Chapter 27

Long Crendon, England

Two days later, Isabel was alone inside the Timberlake brougham on her way to Long Crendon to meet the man she had only ever known as Mr Justice Oliver Russell. His reputation had once invoked the fear of God into her, and yet he had ultimately stirred her trust. Until a mere few weeks ago she had never had any inkling whatsoever that William Saxby was not her father. There had never been any reason to doubt it. Her mother's surprise revelation that he was not had shaken her, saddened and disappointed her, for she loved and revered him dearly. That her real father was none other than Mr Justice Oliver Russell had come as an even greater shock, albeit less of a disappointment for reasons unaccountable to Isabel. Since hearing that unexpected truth, she had come to realize that she not only owed him a debt of gratitude, but was disposed to become at least acquainted with him.

The coachman halted the brougham outside a magnificent half-timbered house with leaded windows, some mullioned, and a thatched roof. Its red brick walls were uneven, bulging slightly as its timber frame had warped with age, but it looked enchanting. Its foregarden was alight with the colourful blossoms of spring flowers, which waved tentatively in the gentle breeze.

The groom opened the carriage door and handed her down.

'Thank you, Nesbit. I have no idea how long I shall be.'

He bowed graciously. 'We are at your service, ma'am.' He rushed ahead and opened the front gate for her, stepping aside for her to pass.

With her heart beating fast, Isabel walked slowly to the front door, and tugged on a bell-pull, wondering what on earth she was going to say to the judge. But she would think of something, for this visit was important to her, and would be her only opportunity to see the man and get to know him a little. She was anxious too, that her high presumptions of him would not be dashed by any judicial pomposity or disdain for her.

A maid opened the door, a mature woman, whose age Isabel estimated at about fifty.

'I've called to see Mr Justice Russell,' Isabel announced. 'I believe he is expecting me.'

The maid stepped aside readily, apparently aware that the judge was expecting a visitor. She looked Isabel up and down, glancing briefly at her belly and no doubt drawing correct conclusions about her condition. 'Please step inside, ma'am. May I take your cape? It's quite warm in the parlour.'

'Thank you.' Isabel doffed her cape.

'And your bonnet, ma'am?'

'Yes, my bonnet, thank you.' Isabel took off her gloves, wondering whether the maid was looking for a wedding ring on her bare left hand. She undid the ribbons of her bonnet and took it off, then handed them all to the maid.

'The judge is in the parlour, ma'am.'

'I trust he is well?'

'Oh, yes, ma'am, he's quite well,'

While the maid took charge of Isabel's accoutrements, she glanced around the lobby in which she found herself. On its quarried floor a grandfather clock stood against one wall, its slow tick-tock steadily measuring time. A dresser adorned with papers, paperweights, a candlestick and other trinkets occupied another wall, and under the curving staircase was a hatstand from which hung two walking sticks and a scarf.

'I'll take you to the judge now, ma'am.'

She followed the maid through an unlit passage before arriving at another door. Once inside the room, she announced, 'Your visitor, sir.'

'Ah, thank you, Agnes.' Mr Justice Oliver Russell stood up to greet this young woman whom he knew not, and studied her face, adjusting his spectacles the better to see her. 'Good day to you, my dear. It's not often that I get requests from young women to see me these days,' he said. 'To what do I owe the pleasure?'

For a few moments, Isabel was tongue-tied, not knowing how to begin. This man before her, the great judge, was her father, and he was holding out his hand in a gesture of hospitality, naturally unaware of their kinship. He was an old man now; his face manifested more lines than she remembered, but it was the same face that had gazed at her with such empathy across the courtroom in Worcester's Guildhall all those years ago. How could she forget that face, patrician, distinguished, dignified? His hair was white, but he had a full head of it.

'Please sit down,' he said kindly, and gestured her to a high-backed chair facing his in front of a roaring log fire in yet another inglenook fireplace.

'Thank you,' Isabel uttered at last, and sat down.

The room was oak-panelled, lit by a single leaded window, on the ledge of which was an earthenware vase packed with spring flowers. The sun's rays beaming through the window illuminated a Turkish rug set before the hearth of the inglenook fireplace.

'You requested to see me, young lady,' the judge prompted. 'I presume you have a name?'

'My name is Isabel Saxby,' she proclaimed, regaining her confidence. 'You might remember me.'

'Isabel Saxby . . .' He reflected on the name for a few moments, his eyes closed, as if in disbelief at hearing it. When he reopened them he said, 'Isabel Saxby? Of course I remember you. I often think of you, my dear. How could I ever forget? That horrid business at Patchfield House.'

'As you say, sir, that horrid business.'

They both seemed stumped for words then, which created a noticeable silence. For the judge it was the first time in his life he had been dumbstruck, struggling for appropriate words.

Isabel took the initiative. 'I really don't know what to say to you, sir,' she remarked candidly, 'and yet there is so much I want to say – so much that I need to say.'

He smiled benignly. 'Then say whatever is on your mind.'

'Then let me begin by thanking you for the way you conducted my trial, for the kind consideration you afforded me when I was at the lowest ebb of my life. Besides which,' she added emboldened, 'and no less importantly, I understand that you are my father.'

There, it was out.

The old judge leaned forward in his chair and there was an expression of unbounded joy and even humour in his eyes, to Isabel's delight and relief. 'Exactly what I was just thinking,' he declared joyously. 'So your mother told you, did she?' He smiled contentedly as he reached out and held her hand. 'How is she?'

'She's well, thank you.'

'I am so glad to hear it . . . And no less happy that she told you I'm your father. Isabel Saxby . . . Well, well . . . My own daughter . . . My word . . .' His eyes became glassy with tears of emotion, which moved Isabel to tears also. 'At last I get to make your acquaintance.' He let go of her hand and grabbed a handbell from a small table at his side and rang it. 'You have travelled over from Timberlake, I understand. You will be in need of some refreshment.'

'You are very kind. Thank you.'

The maid appeared, summoned by the bell.

'Agnes – Miss Saxby and I would like some tea.' Then to Miss Saxby, 'Is tea to your liking, my dear?'

'Tea would be lovely.'

When Agnes had left the room, he said, 'If you are at Timberlake, one must assume that you have renewed your friendship with young Sir Robert Wilson?'

'Yes, indeed,' Isabel replied. 'We encountered each other again quite recently aboard the *SS Great Britain* on its passage from Melbourne in Australia to Liverpool – to our mutual surprise, I must confess. I came to England to see my father, you see – sorry, my adopted father, William Saxby – because he was extremely ill. Unfortunately, he passed away in March.'

'I am sorry to hear that,' the judge said. 'But your mother is well, you say.'

'She is in good health and bearing his loss well.'

'An enchanting woman . . .' He sighed at memory of her. 'And a widow now . . . Well, well, well . . . I only knew her in her younger days. She was a delightful girl. You must pass on my fondest wishes.'

'I will. Of course I will. She'll be happy to receive them. It was after my father died that she revealed that you are my real father. As you might expect, the news came as an enormous shock to me.'

He emitted a little chuckle. 'I imagine it would, and one that must be difficult to come to terms with, no doubt, after so many years believing otherwise. So are you due to return to Australia, Miss Saxby, or are you here to stay?'

'Oh, please call me Isabel, since I am your daughter.'

'Very well, Isabel. Likewise, you must find a suitable appellation for me in view of our new-found blood relationship.' He smiled warmly.

'Indeed, I shall. But to answer your question first, I am due to return to Van Diemen's Land in just a few weeks.'

'So soon?'

'I must. Before I do, though – ever since my mother told me who I really am, I have felt compelled to meet you and take the opportunity to thank you for the consideration and fairness you showed me at my trial.'

'Oh, that trial . . .' He raised his eyebrows and frowned. 'It's the most memorable I ever presided over . . .' He paused. 'The Wilsons . . . You were set up, you know. Did you know?'

'Set up? What do you mean?'

'George Wilson, may his soul rot in hell, had your baby murdered and made to look as if you had committed infanticide.'

'He *authorised* it?' she queried.

'There's no doubt of it. I was a guest at Patchfield House for the assizes, and he made clear to me exactly what the verdict must be. He was aware that his son Robert was the father of your child, and he'd already contrived to get him out of the way. He desperately wanted you out of the way also. You see, he and Sir Joseph Hulme had agreed a marriage between Robert and Sir Joseph's only daughter, whose name eludes me.'

'It was Elizabeth. But I knew all that,' she said.

'The one certain way, George Wilson said, was to have had the child eliminated and ensure its mother was sent to the gallows for infanticide. That was his way of telling me that I must ensure a guilty verdict at your trial. Of course, it was a veiled threat.'

'Could he do that? After all, you were a judge.'

'Under normal circumstances no, of course not, but he was extremely influential and above the law, and he was in a position to jeopardize my career unless I complied with his wishes. Sending you to the gallows was his way of shutting you up so you could not interfere with the deal he'd made.'

'I always suspected there was something like that at stake,' she remarked.

'Well, it was an advantageous arrangement he'd made for all parties. Sir Joseph would benefit from a lucrative directorship with the fur trading company in Canada that was largely under George's control, as well as a gift of land there, in return for George being nominated for a baronetcy and a seat in the Cabinet of William Lamb's – that's Lord Melbourne's – Whig government. I learned about this plan from Sir Joseph himself. I knew Sir Joseph well. He was very influential in the Whig party. Additionally, young Robert would ultimately inherit his estate via marriage to his daughter, as indeed he has done.

'But back to your dear mother . . . She suddenly appeared in my lodgings in Worcester, you know, and pointed out that I would be trying my own daughter for murder. Did she tell you that?'

Isabel smiled and nodded.

'That revelation put rather a different emphasis on things,' he continued. 'I was suddenly in a cleft stick. How could I sentence my own daughter to death, especially if she were not guilty of the crime with which she was charged? The fact is, I should have stood down and postponed the trial, to be presided over later by a different judge, but to what end? You would have been found guilty and hanged.

So I carried on, aware that nobody but your mother knew of our kinship.

'It did not take me long to see a flaw in the prosecution's evidence, so I was justified in not passing the death sentence upon you even though the jury, not unexpectedly, found you guilty. This flaw enabled me to ensure that the main witnesses be brought to court again. The fact that you had conveniently – as it turned out – failed to report the birth of your child – due to limiting circumstances and through no fault of your own, I admit – afforded me authority to change your sentencing to transportation, thus sparing your life at a stroke, but also satisfying George Wilson's wish to get rid of you. I apologise whole-heartedly for dislodging you from the bosom of your family, Isabel, but at the time it was expedient for both of us.'

'Please don't apologize. You see, Hobart Town has been wonderful to me. Now it's my home. Nor would I change it.'

'Yes, I gathered that you had settled down there. I believe you have done well for yourself?'

'Yes, I have, but how have you gathered that I had settled well in Van Diemen's Land?'

'I have ways and means.'

'Does that mean you know more about me than I thought you did?' she asked.

'I have known you are my daughter since the day of your trial. Do you not consider it natural that I should be interested enough to find out how you were faring from time to time?'

'So did you know I was coming to England?'

'Of course not, my dear. How could I? News does not travel as quickly as that."

Agnes entered carrying a tray on which were placed a tea pot, cups, saucers, cakes, gingerbread and all the paraphernalia required for tea.

'Would you like me to pour, sir?' Agnes asked.

'If you would be so kind, Agnes,' the judge replied graciously. 'Agnes has been with me for some years now,' he said to Isabel.

'I have indeed,' Agnes remarked proudly, arranging the cups and saucers. 'Some twenty years.'

'Indispensable, she is.'

'Thank you, sir.'

There was a break in the conversation until Agnes had served the tea and left the room.

'Since my dear wife passed away Agnes has been a godsend,' he commented.

'I was going to ask whether you had a wife,' Isabel said.

'I used to. She sadly passed away some nine years ago.'

'Is that a painting of her on the wall over there?'

The judge turned to look. 'Yes, that's Lavinia.'

'Do you have children?' she asked, wondering if she was now to be told of half-sisters or half-brothers.

'Sadly, no.' The judge sighed. 'Lavinia and I were never blessed with children. So when I learned that I had fathered a daughter with your mother I was quite overcome. It was all news to me. It was a thrilling revelation, Isabel, yet simultaneously it was the biggest regret of my life. For just as soon as I had learned of your existence circumstances obliged me to get rid of you. You will never know how it tore me apart. Here was a daughter – a child that had eluded me in marriage – a beautiful young girl to boot, who was desperate for my help and whose future was in my hands. My heart went out to you. No doubt you perceived it. I recall vividly that you were like an angel in that witness box – so self-assured, so calm and so obviously innocent of the crime with which you were charged.'

'Do you mind if I call you papa?' Isabel asked earnestly, suddenly changing the direction of the conversation.

'Papa? Oh, indeed yes, please do,' he exclaimed and squeezed her hand. 'I like it, I like it very much. You know, Isabel,' he continued, 'I knew that at some point you would seek me out. I don't know how I knew, or even why, but it always seemed to me that I would know you before my days were over. It was always a matter of being patient. And here you are. At last. And you are so like your mother. So like your mother . . .'

'Everybody says so,' she commented, her eyes moist with tears.

'Please help yourself to a gingerbread, Isabel. Agnes makes them and they are delicious.'

'I will, thank you.' She took one and put it on a small plate which she held on her lap, then took a bite.

'If you will allow me to make an observation, Isabel,' the judge said.

'Mmm. Please do.'

'It appears to me that you are carrying a child. If I am wrong, I apologise.'

'No need, papa. You are not wrong.'

'Then I trust you are wed this time?' The gentle banter of familiarity was in his smile and she laughed, for he was in no position to criticise or condemn her due to his own affair with her mother.

'No, I'm not wed,' she answered unhesitatingly, and without shame, 'but I intend to be on my return home.'

'Not to young Sir Robert Wilson, then?'

'No, certainly not to Sir Robert. Why? Would you have any objection if it were?'

'My dear, you are a free spirit and at liberty to secure your own husbands and thus your own destiny, but I would not recommend it, nor advise it.'

'Why?' she asked, fired by curiosity at this surprising admission.

The judge reached for his cup of tea and took a sip. 'Merely that Sir Robert seems to have cultivated a taste for fathering children wherever he goes.'

'Is that true?' Isabel was astonished to hear it, but at once decided that she ought not to be.

'The man is a popinjay. I was repeatedly called upon by his father to deal with claims for paternity against Robert. There was one such young woman in Cambridge whose father demanded satisfaction. Another in Italy, where Robert spent some time between his Cambridge days and his marriage to the Hulme girl. In that instance the girl with whom he had fathered a child was from an aristocratic Italian family from Rome, I recall. Another similar suit was from an angry and very wealthy father in Venice. George Wilson never contested any of them – he simply paid up but made it clear there would be no further payments. One supposes that young Sir Robert concludes his own arrangements nowadays.'

'I didn't know,' Isabel said lamely, wondering if there was now some poor unfortunate in Australia who had succumbed to his charms more recently.

'Of course, you would not be aware of these things, Isabel. So, let me sum up by declaring that Robert Wilson would not be the ideal husband for you, or anybody else for that matter, and certainly not a husband I would choose for a daughter of mine.'

'I'm glad you have enlightened me,' she remarked, thinking about Kitty, who was highly likely with Robert at that moment, being shown around the Timberlake estate, and probably wildly imagining herself as the lady thereof. Kitty with her big blue eyes and long eyelashes, romantic and impressionable, must be told this before she fell under his spell. 'But, as I said, papa, I was never about to marry Sir Robert. I intend to marry somebody else back home on my return – a fine man – a widower.'

'Then I hope you make it there before your baby is born,' said the judge.

'I confess to having doubts,' she admitted. 'But as long as there is a surgeon on board . . . But perhaps you will get to know all about it from your spies.'

'Oh, I have no spies,' he said. 'Nothing quite as secretive.'

'Then how do you get to know about me?' she asked.

'Through the right channels I could get a report of your convict details sent to me, but I only ever did that once to ascertain when you were due to receive your Certificate of Freedom. I was naturally anxious to know about my only daughter, you see, and it was gratifying to learn that all through, you were noted for good behaviour and setting an example to other women. I also know that you bought the costumier business in which you were once employed.'

'How?' she asked. 'How did you know that?' And then it dawned on her, like a flash of lightning, and she laughed. It was at once so obvious. 'It's you!' she exclaimed. 'It's you who's been sending money every year to my banking account in Hobart. It has to be you.'

'It was the least I could do,' he explained with a smile and a shrug. 'How else could I help the only daughter I ever had, whose future I had jeopardised in the first place by sending her to the other side of the world. I needed to help you, Isabel. I felt it my duty to help you, and I thought it was the best and most useful way for you.'

'Oh, papa,' she breathed. She stood up, went to him and bent down to kiss him on the cheek. 'If only I'd known, but it was all done anonymously.'

'Because it was neither desirable nor necessary for you to know who your beneficiary was.'

'But I wanted to know, papa, if only to say thank you, but I could not find out. Anyway, I don't wish to sound ungracious or ungrateful, but will you please allow me to ask you to cease sending me money from now on? I have a thriving business, you see, and am well able to stand on my own two feet.'

'As witnessed by the elegant and capable young woman I see before me, of whom I have every reason to be proud. Very well, my dear Isabel. But I see another way of redeeming myself.'

'Do you feel that you still need to?'

'I do. By means of your mother . . . Your dear mother . . . She is a widow now. How does she fare? I mean, what are her private means? I owe her a great debt of honour for bearing my beautiful daughter.'

'She relies on a small pension provided by the school where my father used to teach.'

'Then she will need financial assistance. Does she have an account at a bank?'

'I don't think so, but I can help her arrange one.'

'Then please do, Isabel, and let me know which bank. I shall see to it that she is comfortable in her dotage.'

'You are exceedingly kind, my own dear papa. I cannot thank you enough.' Her eyes were glazed with tears of admiration for this wonderful man.

He took her hand again. 'Your taking the trouble to visit me here to today is thanks enough.'

'It's been my absolute pleasure,' Isabel said inadequately, and sighed. 'But I must leave you now, papa.'

'Will you come again tomorrow?'

She shook her head. 'I intend to return to Worcester tomorrow. But I shall write to you – regularly. From Hobart Town too.'

'I know you will. But I would deem it a monumental favour if will you do one more thing for me, Isabel. Would you?'

'Of course, if it's within my ability.'

'There is some new-fangled process called photography, by which you can have your portrait done. Will you please have your portrait done and send it to me?'

'Of course. I've heard of it, this photography process, and I believe there's a shop in Worcester where I can get it done.'

'Excellent. Thank you. Otherwise I shall forget what you look like, and that would be a catastrophe.'

- - -

After a tearful goodbye, Isabel returned to the waiting brougham which took her back to Timberlake. There she found Kitty amusing herself at a pianoforte with Ann Carter standing beside her.

'I'm sorry I've been so long away,' Isabel said.

'That's all right,' said Kitty. 'I've been playing, and Ann has been singing. She has such a lovely voice.'

'Kitty plays well,' remarked Ann. 'Better than you, Isabel, if I'm truthful.'

'Well, that's not difficult to achieve, I suspect,' Isabel replied with a laugh. 'Anyway, how was your tour of the Timberlake estate?'

'It's huge,' Kitty enthused. Robert showed us round in his gig. It was a bit of a squash with three of us in it, but we managed, didn't we, Ann?'

'Well, you are both so lovely and slender, I would not have thought it difficult. So where is Robert now. I must tell him that we are leaving tomorrow.'

'So soon? Kitty protested.

'That's a pity,' Ann remarked sincerely. 'Why must you leave so soon?'

'There are one or two important things I must arrange before I leave England, and time is of the essence. I'm sorry Ann, but at least you'll have Robert to entertain you.'

'But who will chaperone us?' Ann enquired, feigning an impression of propriety, but only for Kitty's benefit.

'Do you need a chaperone, Ann?'

'Indeed. Perhaps I should leave tomorrow as well.'

'I would not have thought it necessary,' Isabel assured her. 'I'm sure Robert will be the perfect gentleman, and delighted for you to stay a little longer. I know he was so looking forward to your visit.'

'Was he really?'

'Most definitely.'

'In that case, I might. Nevertheless, I shall be sorry to see you both leave so soon.'

\- - -

Robert and Ann accompanied Isabel and Kitty to the Great Western Railway's Oxford station in his brougham. They said their goodbyes with promises to write to each other regularly.

When they finally boarded the train, Kitty asked the question that had been plaguing her. 'Isabel, why did we have to leave Robert and Timberlake so soon? I thought we would be staying longer. I was so enjoying myself, being treated like a lady.'

'I imagine you were, but it was in our best interests,' Isabel answered.

'I don't see how,' Kitty pouted.

'Then I'll explain. Yesterday, I called on Mr Justice Oliver Russell, the man who conducted my trial in eighteen-thirty-nine. I wanted to thank him for being so lenient with me and all that. Of course, Robert came up in conversation, and I learnt that he has been fathering babies all over Europe, especially in Italy. The judge said he has cultivated a taste for it, which I thought was a novel way of putting it.'

'Oh,' said Kitty.

'Well, I saw the way you looked at him, but more significantly I saw the way he looked at you, as if you were a target for his next exploit. That's why we left.'

'Oh,' Kitty said again glumly. 'So am I not allowed to choose whom I wish to flirt with?'

'You can flirt with anybody you wish to, but not Robert Wilson.'

'Are you sure you're not jealous?'

'I am certainly not jealous, Kitty. Besides, you have a beau already who seems to think the world of you, and he seems such a very suitable, well-mannered young man. He'll do for you.'

'Well, as long as I have *your* approval,' Kitty stated huffily.

'There's another reason, Kitty.'

'Which is?'

'Robert has his eyes set on Ann.'

'But she's married already.'

'I know she is, but don't believe for a moment that he considers that an impediment. And nor does she.'

'Goodness, Isabel,' Kitty exclaimed. 'Exactly what sort of people have you been engaging with?'

'It's opened my eyes, Kitty.'

- - -

Chapter 28

A notice in *The Times* newspaper declared that the steamship *Great Britain* would depart Liverpool, bound for Melbourne in Australia, on Tuesday the thirteenth of June. An accompanying news article explained the reason for the ship's return to Liverpool after its earlier aborted departure in April.

Having read the notice Isabel decided she would leave Worcester on the Sunday, allowing herself plenty of time to make the journey to Liverpool. Susan, Daisy and Kitty insisted that this time they would accompany her to Liverpool where they would spend the night. Once they had seen her safely on board the ship, they would return to Worcester.

'You are big with your child,' Susan reminded her, 'so we shall be there to look after you should anything untoward happen.'

Isabel could not argue with the logic of this precaution, so was delighted to go along with it. The extra company of her family on the train journey would be a welcome bonus.

After her visit to Long Crendon Isabel had complied with Sir Oliver Russell's request for a photograph. In order to make a family event of it, she persuaded her mother and two sisters to join her, since she believed it would be a good idea to have photographs of them all to take home with her. So they all trooped to Worcester's pioneering photographic emporium and, after the initial giggling and banter associated with the novel experience of keeping perfectly still while posing, became fascinated by the mystical new process. Isabel ordered two albumen prints of herself, one for her mother, and one for the judge, and four prints of the family group. All to be framed. One of the framed prints – that of just herself – she sent, secretly and carefully wrapped, with a long accompanying letter to her new-found father.

The judge and his increased relevance to Isabel was kept secret from Kitty, and indeed Daisy, as was Isabel's opening of a bank account for her mother. Susan had no desire for her two younger daughters to know that in her youth she had borne Isabel illegitimately, fathered by the judge – at least not yet. For the time being, this was to remain a skeleton in her cupboard.

'So how shall you explain to them your visit to the judge's house when he invites you?' Isabel astutely asked her mother when they were alone one evening just before she left.

'*If* he invites me,' Susan corrected. '*If* he does, and I accept, then I shall have to consider either telling them the truth or making up some cock and bull story. But he hasn't asked me yet.'

'But he will, Mother. Once he feels an acceptable period has passed since father's death, he will. Count on it. And who knows what might come of it? He's written to you already in affectionate terms, hasn't he?'

'He's written, thanks to you, but I would say more in friendly terms than affectionate.'

'Well, it's early days, Mother. I imagine he's just testing the water, so to speak.'

'Anyway, I have replied.'

'In affectionate terms?'

Susan smiled patiently. 'In friendly terms.'

Amused at her mother's response, Isabel laughed.

'However, I'm not sure it's right for me to accept money from him,' Susan continued.

'Why on earth not? If he wishes to ease his conscience by doing so, then let him. He means well and he can afford it. He's a good man, Mother, and he wishes you well. He feels obliged, because he couldn't help you before when you needed help. Enjoy the journey, don't fight it just for the sake of convention, and let's see what happens.'

'Nothing will *happen*, as you put it.'

'Of course, you'll keep me informed when it does, won't you?' Isabel suggested with a wry smile. 'I shall write to him anyway, so if you won't tell me, he will.'

'You!' Susan said, chuckling with mild but amused exasperation. 'You and your modern ideas.'

'Well, you can't live in the past all your life, mother,' Isabel insisted. 'There's a future before you just waiting to happen. You've been a good wife to father, but sadly he's gone now. You've been a good mother to us girls, but I left home a long time ago. Now Daisy's gone, and I reckon Kitty will be wed soon enough. It's time for you to think about yourself now, and what would be best for you. Besides, I want you to be happy and comfortable as you get older. I don't want to be worrying on the other side of the world about whether you have enough money to live on. Nor do you need to be lonely in your dotage. So you have my blessing if—'

'I shall miss you, Isabel,' Susan interrupted, her eyes misting. 'I just wish you would make England your home again, and let me stop worrying about you.'

'I know, mother, but I couldn't even if I wanted to,' Isabel sighed, also pushing back tears. 'You know why.'

- - -

Before leaving Worcester, Isabel thought about her long-lost, unnamed daughter. Accordingly, she bought flowers and took them to St Andrew's graveyard where, accompanied by Kitty, she laid them on the tiny grave; it would be the last time in her life that she would have such an opportunity. Kitty watched with tearful eyes, and promised that the family would forever decorate the grave in remembrance.

Isabel still had money to spend on suitable presents for Polly, Miranda and Barnaby, as well as small gifts for her maid and her two shop assistants. So on the same outing she bought beautifully dressed German-made bisque dolls for the two little girls, while Barnaby was to receive a handsome pocket watch.

- - -

As she approached the docks Isabel sniffed the tang of the sea, and it struck her how much she had missed it while she'd been in Worcester. Liverpool was clearly a sailors' town if the number of ships lining the quays and docks was any yardstick. Akin to Hobart, the sailors would come ashore, frequent the inns, get drunk, fight, occupy the prostitutes and seduce any amenable young women. Isabel was reminded of her late friend Catherine, seduced by some transitory matelot who originated from somewhere that only God was aware of, and gave birth to Polly in consequence.

Susan, Daisy and Kitty boarded the *SS Great Britain* with Isabel, before saying goodbye. They were astonished by the size of the ship and impressed with the facilities. Isabel showed them around the Saloon Class areas, including the dining saloon, the ladies' boudoir, her cabin with its bunk beds, wash basin and chair, and even introduced them to Captain Gray. He made a great fuss of them, promising that Isabel would be well-looked-after. He took them to the galley where meals were prepared and cooked, and even showed them the massive steam engine that powered the ship. He was also at pains to explain what had caused the delayed departure in April.

'We have a hundred and thirty-eight crew and three hundred and forty-nine passengers on this voyage,' he said proudly, 'mostly emigrants, a good many hoping to make their fortunes in the gold rush, I daresay. Most of 'em are in third class and steerage. They'll be a boisterous lot, I suppose, but we'll keep 'em under control. Everybody will be in good hands on this ship.'

Reassured by what they had seen and heard, the Saxby women left Isabel after about an hour so that they would be home before dark. Their goodbyes were emotional, accompanied by abundant tears and promises to write as often as possible.

The *SS Great Britain* duly sailed next day as rescheduled. Isabel stood alone in the throng that had assembled on the weather deck to watch the departure. She was sad at leaving her mother and sisters, and disappointed that there had been no further opportunity to spend more time with her new-found father. Through her tears, the sight of land gradually faded from sight as they reached the open sea.

As the voyage progressed, Isabel was reluctant to become involved in the on-board activities devised by other passengers, because of her condition, so mostly kept herself to herself. She read a great deal to pass the time and spent longer in her cabin than she did on the outward voyage. She made a point of seeing the surgeon to advise him of her condition and the extreme likelihood that she would give birth during the voyage. After enquiring about her general health, he promised to be on hand.

During the long hours, days and weeks at sea, Isabel pondered a great deal about her return home, and what to expect when she arrived back there. So much had happened in the meantime. Although it had been a massively difficult decision whether she would make the journey to England in the first place, she would not have changed a thing. Every minute had been worth the sacrifice. She was thankful that she had seen and spent time with the man she had always believed to be her father during his last days. Never would she have been able to repay him for the kindness and patience with which he had always treated her as a young girl. Indeed, his support and encouragement at the time of her trial had been considerable. To make the epic journey to see him was the least she could do. The fact that William Saxby, whose name she had been blessed with, was not her real father continued to be a niggling source of disappointment, and would remain so. Yet her real father, Oliver Russell, was no disappointment at all; she was extraordinarily pleased about it. She was convinced that ultimately, he and her mother would at least consider embarking on a permanent relationship in their advancing years. Theirs had been a love affair, albeit an illicit one, and Isabel herself was none other than their lovechild. Nothing would give her greater satisfaction than to hear that they had married.

As to Barnaby, she thought about him a great deal too, and was becoming more philosophical about him. Due to the excitement of meeting and getting to know her real father a little, as well as the activities with her family in Worcester, Barnaby had been taking a smaller share of her thoughts of late, despite his worrying letter. As the *Great Britain* conveyed her nearer to home he began to dominate her thoughts again. She could only put down his wild imaginings to the heartache and anxiety which she was aware he would endure without her. Robert Wilson she had adequately explained away in her reply to him, but the fact of her having Robert's child in her teen years would take some excusing from Barnaby's point of view. Whether Barnaby could ultimately bring himself to accept it, was the stinging question and she had no idea as to its answer. This was her biggest worry, but she believed the single line of defence she possessed – her unborn child – might work in her favour . . . She was anxious to get back to Hobart Town as quickly as possible, to confront his frustrating conventionality and banish his demons.

Almost six weeks into the voyage Isabel gave birth to a healthy boy in her cabin. During her labour she was attended by the ship's surgeon and a stewardess experienced in midwifery, and the birth was duly recorded in the ship's log. The baby was to be called Oliver William. Many passengers took a great interest in news of the event and, discovering that the woman was Miss, as opposed to Mrs Saxby, began a ship-wide collection for her which raised a generous fifty-eight pounds. Thereafter, Isabel was regarded as a celebrity, but as a pariah by the more straight-laced passengers.

Even in the unusual circumstance of giving birth onboard ship, and with limited help, Isabel took to motherhood easily. It all came naturally. She felt everything that a mother should feel for her new-born and, when she fed Oliver William, she savoured a gratifying ache inside her breast, and a feeling of satisfaction as he sucked readily. She lived in a haze of daydreams, with just one thought persisting; how would Barnaby react to his new son?

The days at sea seemed to pass more quickly, and Isabel's happiness was increased as her anxiety over Barnaby lessened. Her whole life was being transformed. Oliver William generated feelings and emotions she'd never experienced before. As she looked into the child's clear blue eyes she felt the utmost love and contentment. She began thinking of Barnaby and his demons less, though she loved him no less. Her love for her child was different: she recognized it as obsessive, protective, caring, and utterly selfless. The thought crossed her mind that when she gave birth to Robert Wilson's child, she had been robbed of these sublime maternal ecstasies.

At first she worried ceaselessly that her baby was breathing while he slept. She would bend over his crib and listen closely for the sweet whispers of his breathing, though it was sometimes difficult to hear due to the inherent noises of the ship and the throb of its engine. During the night he only had to sigh or snuffle, and Isabel would rouse instinctively, ready to do whatever she felt necessary to make him comfortable.

- - -

The voyage continued without incidents. The oceans behaved, remaining relatively calm, all outside influences having little or no effect on the ship, its crew or its passengers. However, unforeseen situations on board were unexpectedly a threat to everybody; the surgeon diagnosed smallpox in two passengers. In a desperate effort to prevent the spread of the disease throughout the ship, the two patients were quarantined. They died of the disease and were buried at sea.

So, although the *Great Britain* arrived at Melbourne on 18th August, after 66 days at sea, the mandatory declaration to the port authorities that there had been cases of smallpox on board during the voyage, meant that the ship and the ship's entire company must be held in quarantine, away from the port for some weeks.

This further delay was the source of more frustration for passengers, and especially for Isabel. Her first thoughts were whether the surgeon might have infected her and her baby – particularly her baby. It was an anxious time, and the further delay in getting back to Barnaby was simply further aggravation. She felt she should write at once to Barnaby, since a letter from Melbourne would reach him in a matter of days, so she asked whether a personal letter from the ship would be allowed. The request was denied; the entire ship was in quarantine, she was informed; there must be no contact with the outside world either in person, or by exported items that might have been touched by infected passengers.

Whilst the rest of the passengers in Saloon Class made merry, and continued with their glees, their plays, their poetry readings, their petty concerts, and religious services of a Sunday, Isabel found the enforced quarantine tedious as well as frustrating. Oliver William naturally occupied her, but she was anxious now to see Polly, and not least Barnaby to learn where she and Oliver William stood in his life. Occasionally, she would take the fresh air with her baby on the weather deck when Melbourne's mercurial weather permitted. Frequently, other passengers would intercept her to take fawning looks at the baby and enquire how she was coping with a new-born on board.

After three weeks, to everybody's relief, the *Great Britain* was released from quarantine. On the seventh of September, a Thursday, a jubilant Captain Gray wished to indulge the passengers. He ordered that the ship's cannon be fired, and skyrockets set off to celebrate their evening arrival into port at Sandridge. The euphoric gesture, prompted by almost three months confinement aboard the ship since leaving Liverpool, unfortunately created a great deal of disquiet among Melbourne's citizens. The Russians were invading, they believed, since the British were at war with them in the Crimea. In response, a mob duly advanced on the port wielding sticks, guns and any other item that would serve as a weapon, to repel the imagined invaders. A small cavalry force drummed up by the military also galloped toward the port.

Meanwhile there was an abundance of activity and crowding as the passengers prepared for disembarkation and organized their baggage. Isabel realized that the hotels would be besieged by disembarking passengers, and with a baby to care for, decided to request permission to remain on board till next day, which was compassionately granted.

When she left on the following morning she enjoyed plenty of help with the transfer from ship to the quay, and assistance in gleaning information about the sailings of the *Tasmania* to Hobart Town. It was then she learned that the cannon-firings and skyrockets escapade had not delighted Melbourne's officialdom, and editorials in the Melbourne Argus roundly condemned it. When she read about it she smiled.

\- - -

Chapter 29

Hobart Town, Van Diemen's Land

The *Tasmania* steamed into Hobart Town's quay on the afternoon of Monday the twelfth of September. Isabel emerged on deck, holding Oliver William, and breathed in the crisp, clear air breezing in from the Southern Ocean. Mount Wellington rising out of the earth like some great benign monster, looked huge and meek, yet majestic while still wearing its crown of snow.

'We're home at last,' she cooed softly to the child, his blue eyes wide as he gurgled contentedly.

The sun broke out from behind a white cloud, and seemed to smile its welcome. Isabel smiled back, filled with the joy of it all. She had come home. She hoped she would never have to leave again.

Already, a group of passengers had disembarked and were lingering on the quay shielding mounds of baggage like watchdogs. Once her own baggage was deposited there Isabel tipped the steward and looked around, vainly curious as to whether Barnaby might have appeared to welcome her back. After all, he might have been able to glean information about the *Great Britain* arriving at Melbourne, especially if news of the fiasco of the gun firing and fireworks had reached Hobart Town. He could have checked the comings and goings of the *Tasmania*. But if he had, either he'd decided to ignore it – and her – or he'd had no notion that the ship had returned to Australia, for there was no sign of Barnaby. In any case, she had not relished the thought of a fraught reunion on the quay in full view of everybody; maybe he shared the view.

She was keen to get home, and several hansoms were lining up in readiness for a fare, so she beckoned the driver of the next cab. He loaded up her baggage and she gave him the address on Napoleon Street.

The horse toiled on bravely while Isabel's eyes were greedy for every remembered detail. Not a stone had changed while she had been away, and she loved every inanimate object for its solid dependability. Spring was breaking, the trees were verdant, some flowers were in bloom. For her it was a second spring, for she had already seen magnolia trees blossoming in England.

The cab drew up outside her house and with relief she saw its familiar form, its hipped roof, its white window frames with drapes still closed beyond the panes, and her front door which seemed to extend its welcome home. Then there was the glorious view beyond the house.

'At last I'm home,' she said to herself, and tears filled her eyes.

The driver clambered down from his perch. He unloaded Isabel's baggage then handed her down while she was holding the baby. With her free hand she opened her reticule, found her kerchief and dried her eyes.

'I'm a little overwhelmed at coming home at last,' she told the driver unnecessarily as she found some coins and paid him, including a handsome tip.

'Thank you kindly, ma'am,' he said.

'I've been away so long, you see,' she explained while she searched for the key to the house.

He nodded his understanding with a smile, then considerately lugged her trunk and bags to the front door. Perhaps he felt sorry for her, she thought, on her own and carrying a baby. Whatever it was that inspired him to help her, she thanked him.

She opened the front door and went inside. The house was cold. There was nobody to greet her; no Polly, no Sarah. She laid Oliver William down carefully on the seat of an armchair and made sure he was warm and comfortable. Her first job was to light fires to warm the house. When they were burning she donned her cape and bonnet again, picked up Oliver William, and set off to buy food. She had no thought then of visiting her shop – her shop must wait until tomorrow. It occurred to her that while she was among the shops she must also buy a crib for Oliver William to sleep in, and a baby carriage in which to transport him. She located suitable items in Elizabeth Street, and the new crib was delivered by cart that afternoon. Meanwhile, Oliver William enjoyed being pushed back and forth in his new wicker baby carriage.

Isabel was relieved simply to be back home. As she stood looking out of her bedroom window, having made ready the crib for its precious, tiny occupant, she began to realize how much she had missed Van Diemen's Land, how much she had missed the salty smell of seaweed at the quay, the beautifully clean, smut-free air, the unequalled panorama of the Derwent estuary as it flowed into Sullivan's Cove. Even if Barnaby rejected her she could still enjoy all that – with Oliver William of course. Her life, her future was changing, and it would change either with or without Barnaby. Whichever way Fate decreed, she felt she would make herself content, with no regrets.

So that night, she went to bed almost at peace with her lot, with the new crib and its precious tiny occupant at her bedside. She was happy, and for now she wanted to be alone with her baby and wallow in her joy at being home.

The problem of Barnaby had yet to be resolved, however.

- - -

Next morning, when she had raked out the ashes of last night's fires, she laid fresh ones, and lit them. Oliver William roused tetchily when she lifted him from his crib, and rubbed his eyes with his tiny fist. She fed him, and when she was happy that he was satisfied she treated herself to breakfast. That done, it was time to go out, so she wrapped him up warmly, and donned her cape and bonnet. With Oliver William ensconced in his baby carriage, she pushed him to her shop on the corner of Murray Street and Liverpool Street. To her boundless gratification, it looked the same as when she left it.

She lifted the baby from his carriage and held him in her arms, leaving the carriage on the pavement. As she opened the shop door the bell tinkled routinely, signalling her entrance, as did the sound of her dainty heels on the hard floor as she stepped inside. The familiar musty, smell of cotton and wool prevailed, and it struck her how she had missed that too. Her two assistants, Rhoda and Maisie glanced simultaneously at the arrival of a customer, then caught each other's eye as they realized just who had entered. They rushed forward together, grinning in instant pleasure at seeing the woman who was both employer and friend, after being so long away.

'How are you two?' Isabel asked, her eyes sparkling in anticipation of their greeting.

'You're back at last, ma'am,' Rhoda declared. 'When did you get back?'

'Yesterday.'

'And who is this little person in your arms?'

Isabel looked down at the baby fondly and proudly. 'This is my son, Oliver William. Isn't he beautiful?'

The two young women stepped forward the better to see the child. To their oohs and aahs, Maisie gently pulled down the edge of the blanket in which he was wrapped, for a better sight of him.

'Oh, he *is* beautiful,' Maisie exclaimed. 'But we had no idea—'

'Neither did I when I left for England,' Isabel said nonchalantly, laughing at her own lack of prudence.

Maisie glanced in wide-eyed astonishment at Rhoda, and Rhoda's equally astonished look suggested that they had hitherto considered Isabel morally incapable of indulging in intimacies that caused the conception of babies before marriage.

'But you didn't get wed, did you?' Maisie said.

'No, Maisie, I didn't.'

'But you will, I suppose? Soon.'

Isabel shrugged. 'We shall see,' she answered economically. 'Anyway, I see I still have a business. Has everything gone well? Have you maintained decent stock levels? Have you banked the takings regularly?'

'Oh, yes, Miss Saxby. Everything is in order,' Maisie affirmed. 'We've been terribly busy while you've been away, and Mr Micklejohn popped in from time to time, just to make sure all was well.'

'Oh, and how does he seem?'

'The same as ever,' Rhoda replied. 'Polite, pleasant and quite jovial.'

'Jovial? He had no right to be jovial.'

They all laughed.

'Haven't you seen him yet?'

'I hope to see him later,' Isabel answered. 'I shall call on him this evening and introduce him to his new son.'

'Doesn't he know yet that he has a son?' Maisie asked incredulously.

Isabel gave an impish smile. 'It will be a complete surprise to him.'

'I suppose we won't see so much of you in the shop then, now you have a baby to care for,' Rhoda suggested.

'Well, not too much at first, Rhoda, but that depends.' She was aware that it hinged on whether she and Barnaby married, and also whether the governess might be prepared to act as nanny to the baby.

'So how was England?' Maisie enquired.

And Isabel gave them a brief run-down, explaining that her father had passed away while she was there, and snippets about her sisters.

As they spoke the bell of the door tinkled again and a new customer entered, whereupon Isabel took the opportunity to retire to the back room to gain a perception of business while she had been away, while poring cursorily over bills and other correspondence.

\- - -

A little after half-past seven that same evening Isabel made her way nervously to Barnaby's house, pushing Oliver William in his baby carriage. The child was sleeping soundly, his belly having been sated. Barnaby would be home from his work, and she reckoned the Micklejohn household would already have dined. She was anticipating an emotional, fraught encounter.

The evening was crisp with a cooling breeze but cold. Having passed all the familiar landmarks she arrived at the front door of his house, and tapped tentatively on it with the brass knocker. Her heart was already beating faster.

Within a few moments she heard the mechanical sound of the doorknob being turned. The door opened, and a familiar face peered around it. It was Sarah, her own maid.

'Good evening, Sarah,' she greeted with a warm but nervous smile.

'Oh, ma'am, tis you, indeed!' Sarah put her hands to her face momentarily in disbelief and joy at seeing Isabel again. 'You're back from your travels, so you are. And is that a baby in the baby carriage, ma'am?'

'Yes, it's a baby, Sarah. I've come to see you all to introduce him to you. Is Mr Micklejohn at home?'

'You'd better come in, ma'am.' Sarah's expression was one of bewilderment at what it all meant.

She helped Isabel raise the carriage up the steps. Once inside she left it in the hallway, lifted the child out and held him.

'The baby's itching to meet his father,' she remarked, to make it clear that the child was not fathered by somebody else.

Sarah seemed in a fluster. 'Oh, I'm sure Mr Micklejohn will be keen to meet his son, did you say, ma'am?'

'Yes, it's a boy.'

'And what's his name, ma'am?'

'Oliver William.'

'Well, Mr Micklejohn will be delighted, to be sure. But he's out at present, ma'am. The Royal Society, I believe.'

'Of course, it's Tuesday.' Her sigh was a mixture of disappointment and yet relief at being spared the ordeal a little longer. 'I should have remembered.'

'Would you like to wait for him, ma'am? Polly and Miranda are not yet in bed. Would you like to see them?'

'But of course I would, Sarah. Anyway, how have you been? Have you settled in here while I've been away? Has everything been to your liking?'

'Oh, yes, ma'am. It's been very pleasant here, and the girls are such a delight. But I'm sure glad to see you back, that I am. Anyhow, how was England and your father?'

'My father sadly passed away shortly after I arrived, Sarah, but at least I saw him. At least I had a few days with him, so it was worth the trip, and it was lovely to see my family.'

'Oh, that's wonderful,' Sarah replied with sincerity. 'Anyway, come and see the girls. They'll be cock-a-hoop that you're back home.'

She followed Sarah into the parlour. Polly and Miranda were sitting together at a table. Polly was scrawling letters and Miranda was drawing, each with a blacklead pencil. An attractive young woman was sitting in an armchair, sewing, and in her trepidation Isabel feared the worst.

'Girls, look who's come to see you,' Sarah announced.

They looked up from their work and Polly leapt down off her chair with a shriek of delight and ran to Isabel, flinging her arms around her hips, enveloping herself in Isabel's skirts in the process. Isabel, in turn, reached down and stroked the child's loose hair.

'Oh, Polly, you've grown so much,' she cooed.

The young woman in the armchair put down her sewing and approached Isabel with a friendly smile.

'Polly is very generous with her affection, don't you think?' the young woman commented.

'She is, and I'm so glad of it,' Isabel replied.

'I'm Candida Simpson. I'm the girls' nanny – or governess, whichever you prefer.'

'I wondered if you were. How do you do?'

'I'm well, thank you. The girls call me Candy. You must be Miss Saxby. I'm delighted to meet you. I've heard so much about you.'

'Thank you,' Isabel replied, comforted by the revelation.

'Would you like me to hold your baby while you give Polly a proper hug? She's been so looking forward to your coming home.'

'Bless you, yes, Miss Simpson.' Isabel carefully handed the baby over, and Miss Simpson returned to her seat with Oliver William nestled in her arms. Isabel turned to Polly, stooped to the child's level, and embraced her. Tears flowed. 'I've missed you, Polly,' she breathed. 'Have you been a good girl while I've been away?'

'She's been as good as gold,' Candida Simpson called over. 'She's not been a minute's trouble.'

'I'm so glad.' She held Polly at arms' length and took a good look at her. 'Yes, you've grown, haven't you? And you're so pretty. I've brought you and Miranda presents from England, but you shall have them tomorrow.'

Meanwhile, Miranda slipped from her chair and stood beside Polly, swinging her shoulders gently, her hands together in front of her, as she waited to be greeted and fussed.

Polly grinned girlishly, but with some apparent shyness. 'When did the baby come, mama?' she asked.

'When I was on board the ship on the way home.'

'Is it a boy or a girl?'

'A boy. I think we have enough girls for now,' she announced flippantly.

'What's his name?'

'Oliver William.'

Polly turned to Miranda. 'I have a new baby brother,'

'Well, he's my new baby brother too,' Miranda claimed, not to be outdone.

Isabel smiled and held an arm out for Miranda, and Miranda submitted to Isabel's embrace, for Barnaby's daughter should never feel as if she were being left out or disregarded. Hence, she hugged the two of them simultaneously. It was a thoroughly emotional moment, and these two children reminded her poignantly of the two little girls, Charlotte and Henrietta, to whom she was governess all those years ago, and not least her own sisters when they were children. More tears misted her eyes.

Sarah meanwhile had been standing watching passively as the reunion unfolded. She interrupted them, saying, 'Let me take your cape and bonnet, ma'am, and I'll make some tea while you wait for Mr Micklejohn to come home.'

'Thank you, Sarah,' Isabel replied. 'What a lovely idea. But I won't wait here for him. I'll have tea though, thank you, then I'll go to the Royal Society's meeting house and wait for him there. He'll be so surprised to see me.'

'That he will,' Candida remarked. 'But shall you want to take the baby along, Miss Saxby? Why don't you leave him with us until you get back?'

Isabel pondered the offer a moment. 'Would you really mind, Miss Simpson?'

'It would be a pleasure. I'm sure he won't be any trouble. He seems to be quite settled.'

'That's truly kind. Thank you so much.'

So for the next half hour Polly and Miranda gave their undivided attention to Oliver William, who was comfortable with Candida. While Isabel regaled them with stories of life on board the *Great Britain* and how they survived the awful storm and took shelter at the Falkland Islands, they all drank tea together. She told them about the wonderful railways in England that enabled everybody to travel quickly to almost all parts of the country.

Eventually, she looked at the clock ticking steadily in its wooden case on the mantelpiece and said she ought to leave in order to meet Mr Micklejohn. Accordingly, she donned her mantle and bonnet, kissed the little girls goodnight and hoped that the baby would be no trouble while she was out, for it was the first time she had been without him since his birth.

- - -

As she waited outside the Royal Society's meeting house, Isabel was reminded of the first time they met there, on the night that Barnaby made clear his feelings for her. What a change in her life that meeting had initiated, and yet life so far had not been transformed in the idyllic way they had planned. So much had happened since to thwart their schemes. It was Shakespeare who claimed that the *course of true love never did run smooth*, and it seemed manifestly so in their case. Nor yet had Barnaby's anxieties been resolved and smoothed over, so uneasy times existed that they must yet encounter and resolve.

Eventually, the front door of the Royal Society's meeting house opened. The lantern from inside threw shadows forward of men leaving the meeting, amid the guffaws of male banter. She stood aside to let the first few of them pass. Some saw her and raised their hats, wishing her good evening as they passed by. Eventually, in the dimness she discerned Barnaby in conversation with another man as they ambled along the path to the street. Her heart was beating fast, and she began trembling, suddenly feeling hot.

'Goodnight, John,' she heard him say. He turned to say something more to his departing colleague, and so walked straight past her without seeing her.

'Barnaby?' she called out.

He stopped in his tracks, and turned.

'Isabel?' he queried, incredulous.

'Yes, it's me. Did you not see me?'

'My godfathers! No, I didn't see you, Isabel. Forgive me. How long have . . . I mean, how long have you been back?'

'I arrived back home yesterday,' she answered.

'I had no idea.'

'Well, why would you have?' She was excusing him, and recognised that her lack of self-confidence before him had prompted her to, a lack she had never experienced before with him. The feeling was alien to her nature. 'So here I am, come to meet you from the Royal Society,' she said brightly. 'Rather like that meeting we had more than a year ago.'

'I remember it well,' he said. 'How did you know I would be here?'

'Because I called at your home. I have seen the girls already, and met their governess – she seems a jolly decent young woman. I saw Sarah as well, of course.'

'I see,' he replied.

No arms flung about her to welcome her back, no kisses, no affectionate words, not even a smile was forthcoming that she could discern.

'The girls seem well, and how they have grown in the nine months I've been away! They are like sisters, aren't they?' she suggested, hinting that they should remain so if their guardians were joined in matrimony. 'They seem very content with each other.'

'Yes, I believe they are.'

'And the girls in the shop tell me you have called in to see them from time to time.' She realized she was finding it necessary to force conversation.

'Once a week or thereabouts,' he answered brusquely. 'They seem to know what they are doing. I didn't find it necessary to interfere.'

'Well, thank you for keeping an eye on them. I appreciate it.'

'I said I would.'

Isabel sighed. 'Barnaby, you seem very offhand?'

'Do I?'

'Yes, you do. I hoped you might be glad to see me, but you have your funereal face on, I discern. I can only assume you're not pleased to see me,' she commented. 'I am disappointed at your detachment. At least you could try to be amenable. You seem so aloof, so indifferent to me.'

'Do I?' he answered again.

'Yes, you do. Don't you even have a smile for me?'

'Would you see me smile in this darkness? The truth is, Isabel, I wasn't expecting to see you. It's such a surprise, that's all. Let's face it, you've been away so long. Nine months as you said. At one point I believed that I would never see you again.'

'Yet here I am, Barnaby . . . Have you any notion why?'

He gave no response.

'Well, are we going to stand here all night talking about how long I've been away?' she prompted. 'Or should we take another moonlit walk in the park and watch the Derwent twinkling in the moonlight?'

'Very well, if you are not going to be too chilled.'

'That's very considerate of you. You said the same thing the first time we walked in the park together that first evening,' she answered chirpily, encouraged. 'I'm warm enough, thank you. I think a winter in England has hardened me.'

'Then let's take a walk. We have much to talk about.'

So they turned and headed towards the park. She linked her arm through his experimentally, and he seemed content to accept it.

'So how was England?' he asked as they ambled along unhurriedly.

'Everywhere was greening up beautifully when I left,' she replied cheerfully. 'Spring was in the air. I had my first experience of the railways, too.' She paused, and turned to look at his face in the moonlight. He was looking straight ahead, but she was unable to discern his expression. 'I was impressed with what they've done with the railways. It's a different country to the one I left behind all those years ago.'

'They were building railways well before I left England.'

'Yes, I suppose they must have been. Anyway, I want you to know that in so many ways my trip was worthwhile in the end,' she added, being forthright in her endeavour to force a discussion on the touchy subjects they needed to discuss.

'I'm glad for you,' he answered, but his tone was still cold, he sounded disinterested.

Her heart was sinking at his lack of amenable responses, at his remoteness. 'Frankly, Barnaby, you don't seem that interested.'

'Do you think so, indeed, Isabel? Well, why might that be, I wonder?'

'Why don't you tell me?'

'Very well. Do you think it might have something to do with the fact that your erstwhile lover Sir Robert Wilson was on board the ship with you?'

'I see,' she said resignedly, sighing deeply, deflated. She unlinked her arm from his. 'Well, Barnaby, I received your silly letter suggesting all sorts of wild indiscretions on my part. God knows what you were thinking. I was never so upset in all my life. How could you possibly think so little of me after all we've meant to each other? And why would you wish to make yourself miserable with such self-inflicted stupidity? What drove you to imagine such nonsense?'

'Your past history drove me,' he answered bluntly.

'Did you not get my letter explaining about Robert?'

'Yes, I got your letter. But how do I know that what you said is true?'

'Because I would never lie to you, Barnaby. So I'll tell you again, to your face. I had no idea Robert Wilson was going to be aboard that ship. How *could* I? Yes, of course we talked once we had met again, and why wouldn't we? We even dined together on a few occasions, but that does not imply there was any more to it than that.' She paused for breath and sighed with frustration. 'We renewed our friendship, yes, but that's all it was – friendship. We did not become lovers again, as you wildly insinuated. Why would we indeed? I am a different person now to the girl of sixteen I once was. This time, I had no interest in him in that regard. Anyway, I was promised to you, which meant everything.'

'I would dearly like to believe that, Isabel.'

'Whether you believe it or not is entirely up to you, Barnaby. Nevertheless, it is the gospel truth. But if you cannot, or will not believe it, then there is no hope for us. The trust will have disappeared like a puff of smoke. So I shall walk away from you this instant.' Her own stoniness saddened her, but her feminine defiance was dictating her route through this emotional maze as she looked sternly at him. Obviously, the events of her youth had wounded his sensitivity, and she wished more than anything to give it balm, but his intransigence was not only breaking her heart, but it was annoying her. 'I will not be accused of something I am not guilty of, Barnaby.'

'Ah . . . Which very conveniently leads us to another point, does it not? Your trial, and your hiding from me the fact that you were transported as a convict.'

'For a crime I did not commit,' she protested. 'And for which I received a pardon.'

'Oh, yes, your convict record confirms all that,' he said cynically, 'but it in turn revealed the fact of your giving birth to a bastard child when you were just seventeen years old – a child by no less a personage than your beloved Robert Wilson. That's just something else you failed to tell me about. How can I reconcile that fact with the woman I fell in love with?'

'Well, believe it or not, Barnaby, I am still the same

woman you fell in love with. I have not changed since last time you saw me. And for your information, I am still just as much in love with you as I was when I left, even though you are doing your utmost to stifle it with your priggishness and obstinance. Just because I did not feel up to revealing my past does not change me or what I feel for you. I failed to tell you because I believed my past would create a barrier between us, and I did not want to create any barriers. We were happy, Barnaby, you and me, were we not?'

'Yes,' he agreed. 'We were.'

'So why would I upset that happiness? Why can you not accept that what was in the past remains in the past, and cannot be undone? It's finished, it's history. I am not that young, naïve girl I was then. Yet you are obviously content to ruin everything we had, just because you are so bound up in petty conventionalities and what society might think. Although, by now I would have thought you must surely have noticed that society here in Van Diemen's Land looks at such things with rather more compassion and tolerance than it does in England.'

'So you have said all along, Isabel. But you must understand that I have been through hell these past few months. I was so happy with you, as you know – I was so content, so looking forward to our future together, but despite your declaration of love, I am a man of principle and standards . . . Please try and understand that.'

She stopped walking. 'I see,' she said flatly. 'Then you shall have all the time in the world to contemplate your principles and standards. I'm leaving you now. Please don't follow me. I can make my own way home.'

'No, Isabel, I insist on escorting you home.'

'Certainly not, Barnaby. Such gallantry is a sham – despite your being a man of principle and standards,' she added cynically. 'In the circumstances I don't want your chivalry. Find a bench, why don't you, and ponder what we have just said to each other. It's either goodnight or goodbye. It's your choice, Barnaby.'

She turned round and left him floundering.

- - -

Isabel made her way alone in the darkness to Macquarie Street and Barnaby's home to collect Oliver William. From time to time she glanced behind her to ascertain whether he was following, but she was unable to determine it in the darkness.

She was aware, however, that it seemed all over between them. As she had feared, he would never accept what had transpired in her life before he knew her. It struck her that it was just as well that they never married in the first place, because if she had confessed about her past once they had been wed, that would have almost certainly ended the marriage anyway.

The dream was over.

Life would go on as it had before she met him – with the exception, of course, that she now had his child, a child he was as yet unaware of – for the time had not been right to tell him about Oliver William. When he did eventually know – if she ever deigned to tell him – he would probably deny the child was his anyway and point the finger at Robert Wilson. She shed no more tears; she had virtually reconciled herself already to the likelihood of his rejection. Nevertheless, she was sad; sad that Barnaby was so old-fashioned in his views, so set in his ways, so conventional, so unbending, so unforgiving, so blind, so unadjusted to the ways of Van Diemen's Land.

She arrived at his house and rapped the door knocker. Again, Sarah answered it and let her in.

'Did you see him, ma'am?' she enquired.

'Only briefly,' Isabel replied. 'I had to leave him. Is Miss

Simpson still in the parlour?'

'Yes, please go through, ma'am.'

'Before I do, Sarah, I want you and Polly to come back home tomorrow. I'll send a cab round to collect you and all your things. Would mid-day give you time to get yourselves ready?'

'Oh, yes, ma'am, mid-day will be fine. I look forward to being at home with you again and back to normal.'

'Good. I shall leave word with Miss Simpson of this arrangement.'

Isabel entered the parlour, and saw that Candida Simpson was still holding Oliver William as she sat in the armchair in front of the log fire, which seemed to be burning itself out.

'I hope he's been no trouble, Miss Simpson.'

'I've not heard a thing from him,' the governess replied warmly. 'He seems a very placid child.'

'He is,' Isabel agreed. 'Thank you so much for looking after him for me. But your arms must be aching if you've been holding him all this time.'

'Oh, hardly at all, Miss Saxby.'

'Anyway, I'll relieve you of him now and I'll take him home. Tomorrow at about mid-day I shall send a cab to collect Polly and Sarah, to take them home.'

\- - -

Chapter 30

Hobart Town

Isabel did not sleep well that night. Her conversation with Barnaby kept flowing through her restless mind like a river in full spate. Over and over, her words and his repeated themselves relentlessly in her head. She thought of things she could have said instead of what she had said, and wondered whether she had been too impulsive, too defiant, too aggressive, too impatient with him. Yes, she had pretended to be hard, at the same time torturing herself, and her heart was bleeding profusely in consequence.

During the night, she kept a lamp burning in case Oliver William cried out and needed attention, which in turn rendered sleep harder to achieve, yet only once did she have to get up to attend to him. When daylight appeared through the narrow slit between the curtains, she arose. The child was still asleep, so she left him, made up the fires, including those in Polly's and Sarah's rooms, and turned down their beds to air them in readiness for their return later. She made herself a breakfast of eggs and cold ham with yesterday's bread, and followed it with two successive mugs of hot tea. She took a duster and a tin of carnuba wax and polished the furniture, because Sarah would have enough to do when she and Polly returned. After she had cleaned the windows and wiped every dusty surface, Oliver

William woke up crankily, so the rest of her time she spent with him, determined to elicit smiles. He was seven weeks old, growing, and coming along well.

With mounting eagerness, she awaited the time when she must take Oliver William to the quay to find a hansom cab that would collect Polly and Sarah and their baggage from Barnaby's home. As the time approached, she looked out onto her garden and realised that in her absence it had degenerated and was in dire need of attention; she must hire a gardener to straighten it out, tidy it up and re-stock it in time for summer. She found herself saying as much to her child, nestled in her arms.

She heard a knock on her front door. Perhaps it was Sarah and Polly despatched by Barnaby. She answered it.

'Barnaby!' she uttered, surprised to see him, and instantly her heart began to thump.

'Isabel. Thank God you are here.'

He had a bewildered look about him. In the daylight he looked pale, he had bags under his eyes, he looked amazingly older, and her heart went out to him. He gazed at the child in her arms. Tenderness, curiosity and anxiety were evident in his expression.

'Candida and the girls told me you have a baby – a boy. I have to know, Isabel – is he mine?'

'Of course he's yours,' she replied gently, reassuringly.

'Why did you not tell me?' There was a look of such sadness in his expression, of infinite regret and resentment, suggesting her silence about the child had been deliberate.

'You'd better come in,' she said. 'But I'm due to go out to find a cab to collect Polly and Sarah.'

'In due course,' he replied dismissively as she stepped aside to let him in.

She led him into her sitting room with its delightful view.

'Do sit down,' she said. 'Would you like a cup of tea?'

'Not now, Isabel, thank you,' he replied. 'I want to talk to you first. I want to apologize – profusely. Last night, you rather caught me unawares. I was hardly expecting you to turn up after the Royal Society's meeting. You must understand that I'd been harbouring grievances about you for weeks on end.' He looked into her eyes, and she could see he was deeply troubled. 'Stupidly, I know – I see that now. Unfortunately, I could not curb my tongue, and all those grievances had to be aired. I am truly sorry, Isabel. I was wrong. I do most humbly apologize. Then, when I finally got back home, Candy was waiting up for me, and she commented what a lovely placid child you have. "What child?" I asked . . . I was astonished. Isabel, I have not slept a wink all night. That you have had a child is a complete surprise to me. Why did you not tell me? Why do you persist in withholding things from me?'

'Because . . .' she began, pausing a moment to choose the right words and phrases. 'You made it clear, Barnaby, that you could not reconcile my past with your own rigid principles of what was acceptable and proper in a wife. Well, I understand that perfectly. So, because it seemed I am of no further interest to you, then neither is my child. Hence, I saw no need for you even to be aware of him. As I have told you before, I have an independent streak in me. You know well enough that I'm able to look after myself, so I can more than adequately look after my son. Nor would I ever ask you for any recompense for being his father.'

'Then the child will always be regarded as a bastard.'

'The word carries no stigma with me, Barnaby. Let me tell you why. Let me tell you another part of my history that your delving into my past could never have revealed, because it's something I knew nothing about myself until I was in England.'

'Is it something you wish me to know about?' he asked.

'Yes, I do, because it completes the circle. You see, after my father died, my mother decided that I should be made aware of who I really was. She told me that the man I always regarded as my father – that lovely man William Saxby – was not my father after all. You cannot imagine how much that surprised and upset me. So, it turns out I was a bastard child too – and that's yet another reason for you to reject me. My mother, you see, fell pregnant with me when she was twenty years old, out of wedlock.'

'My God!' he uttered, his voice low. He was clearly agitated.

'Some years later she met and married William Saxby, and they had two daughters together, my half-sisters, Kitty and Daisy. And good old William Saxby gave me his name.'

'But did your mother tell you who your real father was?'

'Oh, yes. Yes, she did. It was none other than the judge who presided over my trial – Mr Justice Oliver Russell, no less. He and my mother fell in love it seems when he was a circuit judge, but he was already married . . . and yet he had no children by his wife.'

'Did he know you were his daughter?'

'Not until the day of my trial. My mother made it her business to inform him of the fact on the day. She visited him just before the trial, to let him know whom he might be sending to the gallows.'

'Then that would explain a lot about the verdict and the sentencing,' he said.

'It might,' she conceded. 'Anyway, once I got over the shock, I plucked up the courage to visit him. Oh, Barnaby, he is such a lovely man, and because I liked him so much it overshadowed the sadness and disappointment of learning that William Saxby was not my real father. Hence the baby's name – Oliver William – after them both.'

'Very appropriate,' he remarked.

'Did I ever tell you that some kind soul was sending me money regularly from England?'

'I don't believe you did. Something else you failed to tell me.'

'Well, anyway, it was him all along – Judge Oliver Russell. He acknowledged my existence. So you see, Barnaby, the fact that both me and my son are bastards does not bother me in the least.'

They sat facing each other, and conversation stalled for a few seconds. Isabel gazed out of the window, at the spring sunshine glistening on the sea, then at Barnaby, waiting for him to make some comment.

At last he remarked, 'Isabel, I have been grossly unfair with you.'

'Unfair?' she queried, wishing for clarification of what he considered unfair.

'Yes, unfair. I have thought the worst of you, and yet you are the epitome of virtue when it comes to fairness. You are a more righteous person than I could ever hope to be. Oh, I can understand well enough why you kept your past from me, but as you rightly pointed out to me last night, what has happened in the past cannot be changed, although we can and do change from the persons we use to be. I must accept that you fell in love with Robert Wilson when you were very young, and you were free to do so, of course. That you had his child—'

'I had his child because I was in love with him, and not because I was promiscuous,' she protested, interrupting him. 'Yes, I was young, and very naïve.'

'I do understand that,' he answered patiently, and Isabel saw that today he was being far more rational and reasonable than the previous evening. 'I am coming to terms with that. Apart from it all, the fact of your own illegitimacy becoming known to me is not another reason to reject you, as you suggest. Rather it is yet another reason for us to continue where we left off last December . . . if you'll still have me.'

'Do I perceive guilt on your part, Barnaby?' Isabel asked pointedly. 'Because if you feel guilty simply because you fathered my child, then I must refuse you. Likewise if you are suggesting that we marry because you feel sorry for me,'

'On the contrary, Isabel. I do not feel sorry for you. You are one of life's survivors and will always cope. You will always battle through and win. And I know full well that you would look after my son. But apart from being utterly and completely in love with you, I wish to be the father of my son too, in every way possible, to help him to every advantage in life.'

'So why this change of heart?' she asked. 'Last night you made it clear enough that you did not want me. But now that you know you have a son by me . . .'

He shook his head and looked into her eyes earnestly. 'Isabel, I've had no change of heart. My heart harbours the same intense feelings for you as it has all along. It was my head which needed to change. I have misjudged you, I've imagined all sorts of tomfoolery of which I know, deep in my heart, you are incapable. I have been too unyielding in my views, I have berated you for failing to tell me about your past, when I myself have withheld information about my past, for exactly the same reason that you have – in case you rejected me. I simply cannot continue with my iniquitous hypocrisy.'

'Oh,' she said, astonished at this sudden confession. 'What have you failed to tell me about yourself, Barnaby.'

'The mere fact that I was born a bastard too.'

'Oh,' she said. 'Then we are on level ground.'

'How succinctly you express it. The fact is, Isabel, my

mother gave birth to me when she was seventeen years old, having been seduced by the eldest son of a household where she was in service,' he explained. 'She received nothing from that family for her trouble except a dismissal notice. For years she lived in penury, reared me in penury – until she met and fell in love with a decent man who saw no stigma in her having had a child out of wedlock. He became a father to me, like William Saxby became a father to you. They went on to have children of their own – my half-brothers and -sisters, like your mother and William Saxby. My stepfather went on to do well for himself – for all of us – and paid for my education. Hence the reason I was able to get work in law and in the civil service.'

Isabel listened with avid interest and tears in her eyes, tears that rolled down her cheeks, to fall and be soaked up by the baby's shawl.

'Therefore, I want my own son to be brought up with the same care, security and love that a loving father can offer. Please, Isabel, do not refuse me that privilege. Will you be my wife, as we intended all along? Who knows, we might have more Oliver Williams in the future.'

'Are you sure?' she asked, softening. 'Are you quite sure you love me enough?'

'More than mere words can tell. You must know it, Isabel.'

'Then I will,' she answered simply, and her smile illustrated her relief and thankfulness. She was content to accept him with all his imperfections. She got up from her chair, leaned over and kissed him. 'Now, Barnaby Micklejohn, why don't you hold your son for a while and get to know him a little?'

'Of course I will, and gladly. Thank you.'

She handed him the baby and he accepted his son with a smile.

'You see, he has your eyes,' she remarked.

'And your beautiful mouth.' Barnaby smiled as his son gazed up at him with his enquiring blue eyes. 'It must have been hard giving birth aboard ship, though,' he suggested. 'Who was on hand to supervise it?'

'The ship's surgeon and a stewardess. They were wonderful. It's not so unusual for babies to be born at sea, you know. Some famous people have been born at sea.'

'Then our son might well have an auspicious future if precedence is anything to go by.'

\- - -

Isabel Saxby became Mrs Barnaby Micklejohn on the afternoon of Sunday 19th November 1854 in a ceremony at St David's cathedral. The number of guests was small; just a few friends; Rhoda and Maisie from her shop, Sarah, her maid, Candida Simpson who was happy to look after Oliver William, and the other servant from Barnaby's household. Polly and Miranda were in their element as bridesmaids and fulfilled their roles with unrestrained enthusiasm.

Over the next few days, the family moved into Isabel's house on Napoleon Street, and settled in. The intention was to find another, larger house eventually, but there was no rush, and life moved on contentedly and cheerfully.

When Oliver William was a little over two years old, the devoted couple had another child, a girl, whom they called Susan Rebecca, after their own respective mothers.

\- - -

Three years had elapsed since their marriage when Oliver William heard the postman put letters through the letterbox. He toddled off to pick them up and handed them to his mother. One was postmarked Oxford, addressed to her, its envelope was written in a woman's hand. She opened it, unfolded the letter and read.

My dearest Friend Isabel,

It is grand to know that You and Barnaby are well and enjoying Married Life, and that your Son and new baby Daughter are faring well. However, since the Post takes so long to reach each other from the other side of the World, you might well have had another Child by the Time this reaches You. If so I hope you are All prospering.

My own Life has taken a turn for the Better, and I am anxious that You should know about it, even though You are so far away. You see, Isabel, I think of You often, and in many Ways I wish we lived in closer Proximity to one another so that we could meet frequently and talk like we used to aboard the good ship Great Britain. But back to my own Life; I am now a divorced lady due to my infidelity, and my ex-husband's family have disowned me – they say I am a fallen woman – but what do they know? I am as far from fallen as it is possible to get.

Consequently, Robert and I became free to Marry at last, which we did in June on a beautiful Summer's Day, so I now rejoice in the Title Lady Wilson. Can you imagine? Me? Lady Wilson. Of course, I get to wear that Coronet occasionally that we talked about! At the time of writing this short Letter our beautiful Daughter Isabel is now seventeen Months old and the Apple of her Father's Eye. You will glean from that, that she was conceived out of wedlock, which I unashamedly admit, and was the reason for my ex-husband divorcing me!

Life at Timberlake is a Joy, and I have never felt so Happy and Content. I know that you will not begrudge me my Happiness nor my Situation, and I realize that if it had not been for You introducing us in the first place Robert and I might never have spoken to each other aboard the Ship, let alone become Close. I do hope and believe I have your blessing.

I am sorry that this is such a short letter, Isabel, but the duties of a Lady as well as a mother mean I have much to occupy me! Please write to me soon, dearest Isabel. A long Letter will do very well, and I promise to write a long Letter back.

Affectionately Yours,

Ann

PS. Robert sends his fondest Regards.

The End

About the Author

Nancy Carson was born and bred in the Black Country, that part of the English West Midlands that lies between the eastern fringes of Wolverhampton and the western edges of Birmingham. Dudley was her home town, and though she has travelled widely she still lives no more than 6 miles from her birthplace.

Throughout her life she has been a 'people-watcher' and believes this has given her a clear insight into human interactions – male and female – especially when it comes to relationships. So, her stories spring from the broad canvas of human nature. The characters that populate them have often been inspired from life, as have the situations she sometimes places them in. Many have been embellished, some not.

Nancy Carson is the author of several published novels, with plans for more.

Other titles by Nancy Carson

Trilogy:

The Dressmaker's Daughter
The Factory Girl
Rags to Riches

Stand Alone Novels:

A Family Affair
Daisy's Betrayal
Poppy's Dilemma
The Railway Girl
Missing You

Duology:

A Country Girl
A Fallen Woman

Short story:

The Girl from the Opera House

Printed in Great Britain
by Amazon

39337058R00249